# NO OTHER OPTION

# NO OTHER OPTION

## MARCUS WYNNE

A TOM DOHERTY ASSOCIATES BOOK
NEW YORK

NO OTHER OPTION

Copyright © 2001 by Marcus Wynne

This book is printed on acid-free paper.

Design by Heidi Eriksen

A Forge Book
Published by Tom Doherty Associates, LLC
175 Fifth Avenue
New York, NY 10010

www.tor.com

Forge® is a registered trademark of Tom Doherty Associates, LLC.

ISBN 0-312-87795-1

First Edition: September 2001

Printed in the United States of America

0  9  8  7  6  5  4  3  2  1

For Caprice, first, last, and always

# ACKNOWLEDGMENTS

No one writes a novel alone. And no one publishes a novel without the help of many people. I want to thank those people here. In the literary world, I want to thank my agents Ethan Ellenberg and Michael Psaltis; my editor at Forge, Brian Callaghan, and the other members of the Tor/Forge team: Linda Quinton, Karen Lovell, Seth Lerner, Bob Gleason, Kathy Fogarty, Jennifer Marcus, and the grand old man, Tom Doherty.

In years of military and government service, I was privileged to work with some of the finest operators in the world, some of whom are my brothers in all senses of the word: Federal Air Marshals Scott "T-Bone" Ralston and Francis Xavier "Butch" St. Germaine watched my back in more than forty countries. MSgt. John "Rhino" Onofrey and MSgt. Jim "Moonbuzzard" O'Neal, both of U.S. Army Special Forces, and First Sgt. John "Johnny B" Bolen of the 82d Airborne were all cofounders with me of the North Korean Hunting Society. There are many others who can't be named from other jobs and other places, but I want them to know I think of them.

I was lucky to have the tutelage of some fine instructors and senior war dogs when I was coming up: Dennis Martin of CQB Services, Liverpool, England; Ed "Eduardo" Lovette, Special Forces and Central Intelligence Agency; CSM Forrest K. Foreman, DELTA, JSA, Special Forces; First Sgt. Michael "Iron Mike" Dacszyn, Free Polish Airborne Brigade, OSS, Special Forces, 173d Airborne, 82d Airborne Division; First Sgt. Jim Nobles and First Sgt. Bobby G. Taylor, 82d Airborne Division; Donald Gene "The Love Machine" Tyson, Navy SEAL, BUD/S instructor, Federal Air Marshal. Special thanks to Buffy, the Great Spauldino, Dante Morrell, and Lofty, for reasons they know all about.

Special thanks to Dr. Al Holland of NASA for his close reading and psychological expertise.

My good friends who supported me in many ways: Rick Diamond, Colonel David Dean, Rick Faye, and all the rest of you.

Thanks to Karl Sokol of Chestnut Mountain Sports, 2317-1 Whipple Hollow Road, West Rutland, VT 05777, for smithing the finest fighting High-Powers around.

And as always, thanks to my wonderful wife, Caprice, who put up with my madness long after any sensible woman would have shipped me off. She took up my slack and watched my back while giving the best close readings. Thanks, honey. I couldn't do any of it without you.

**ACKNOWLEDGMENTS**

Virtually every covert intelligence organization and elite counterterrorist unit has one or two anecdotal stories about ex-operators who have "gone bad" or "over to the other side." However, hard information is hard to come by and guarded like "the family jewels," lest it become public and bring discredit on the whole unit. There are even one or two unverifiable stories floating around the community about units sending their own men out to kill those who have gone off the reservation before they can do too much harm.

—NEIL LIVINGSTONE,
*The Cult of Counterterrorism*

# PART 1

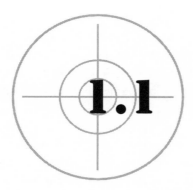

Jonny Maxwell fled north through the Kansas night, his hands steady on the wheel of his second stolen car, following the undulant ribbon of I-35 over the gentle hills and past the dark farmhouses settled among the even rows of corn. Only the lone headlights of an infrequent passing car broke the midnight darkness.

He shook a cigarette from the Marlboro hard pack the car's owner had left on the dashboard. He noticed how his fingertips trembled, and he willed them still. Only when the tremor subsided did he light his cigarette.

Jonny's reflection shone on the inner curve of the windshield, the long hard lines of his face lit by the dim-green dashboard lights and the cigarette lighter's red coil. He was pleased with how little exultation or fear he saw on his face.

This wasn't like Beirut or Bosnia or Syria or Guatemala or any of the other dirty little hellholes he'd fought in. There'd been others with him then—men he'd thought of as his brothers—ready to call down the high-tech wrath of the Stealth bombers and their precision munitions, or to pull on their balaclavas and take up their weapons to come to his aid.

Or to avenge him if he fell.

But he'd fallen alone this time, and there was to be no help for him.

The chemicals of fatigue and stress flowed through him like drugs and, for a moment, the reflection of his face blurred before his eyes. He skinned his lips back in a fierce grimace and exhaled sharply, twice, through his nostrils to clear his head. He needed a break.

Up ahead, where the road seemed to rise into the night sky, a brightly lit roadside rest stop gleamed between the highway and the dark cornfields. Jonny turned the Cavalier into the parking area and idled slowly forward while he looked the rest stop over. On the far side of the concrete shelter over the rest rooms and vending machines was a parking area for the big interstate trucks. Three semitrailers, their lights off, were parked there. On the passenger car side of the stop there were only two cars besides Jonny's. Parked well away from the lights was a beat up Camry, a man slouched in the tipped-back seat, his head lolling against the window in the abandon of deep sleep. In front of the rest rooms was a black Toyota 4Runner. The driver, smoking a cigarette, sat on the hood and stared up at the night sky.

Jonny pulled in next to the 4Runner and shut off his engine. Jonny got out, stretched, and nodded to the other driver.

He was a college kid, early twenties, blade thin in black Levi's and a black T-shirt, with a scraggly goatee that barely concealed his weak chin. He nodded back to Jonny and said, "Look at this sky, will you? It's beautiful out here."

Jonny regarded him in silence for a moment, long enough to make the boy shift and pluck at the knee of his pants, then looked up at the stars.

"That it is," Jonny said.

He went into the rest room and urinated for a long time. He lingered over the sink and thoroughly washed his hands. When he came back out, the college kid was still there, staring up at the sky. The parking lot was still except for the steady click of cicadas. The boy looked at him and nodded again, avoiding Jonny's steady gaze.

Jonny moved close and pointed at the 4Runner's license plates. "You from Minnesota?"

"I go to school there, St. Thomas. In St. Paul."

"I know the area. Nice place. You grow up around there?"

"No, my family's in Cedar Rapids."

"Didn't want to go to the U of I in Iowa City?"

The boy rushed to laugh. "No. Too close to home."

"Yeah, I remember thinking the same thing."

"You go to U of I?"

**MARCUS WYNNE**

"No." Jonny smiled and looked around the parking lot. The Camry driver was still lolled back asleep in his seat, the car half-obscured by shadows. There was no sound or movement from the trucker's side of the rest stop. "I went to UCLA."

"How'd you like Los Angeles?"

"Never been."

"I thought you said . . ."

"It was the Tegucigalpa campus of UCLA. In Honduras. You know what that means, UCLA? Unilaterally Controlled Latin Assets."

Jonny interrupted the boy's puzzled look when he pointed at the 4Runner's side panel. "Somebody really keyed your door here. Messed your paint job all up."

"What?" The boy slid off the hood and stepped between the two cars. "Where?"

Jonny pointed low on the rear passenger door. "Right there."

"I don't see anything . . ."

When the boy bent low to examine the side panel, Jonny clamped the boy's head, one hand over his mouth and the other at the back of his head. He snapped the boy's head back and then sharply over, twisting the struggling student around faceup. The  boy's legs buckled and the whole weight of his body centered at the base of his neck when Jonny levered the thin neck into the crook of his arm. Jonny jerked sharply upward, once, and heard the dull wet pop of the neck breaking. He turned the limp head and extended it twice to ensure the neck was broken and the spinal cord hyperextended. The boy flopped, twitched, and was done. The black jeans darkened with urine as the bladder let go. Jonny eased the body down between the two cars. He looked over the roof of the 4Runner and slowly scanned the rest stop. The sleeping man in the Camry still slept. There was no one out on the trucker's side and no one in the rest rooms.

He opened the 4Runner's rear door and wedged the limp body into the backseat. There was a faded green cotton sleeping bag wadded on the floor, and he pulled it over the body up to the neck, as though the boy were sleeping. Jonny pursed his lips, then reached out and palmed shut the boy's eyes. Then he got into the driver's seat, turned the keys hanging in the ignition, and drove slowly out of the rest stop.

**NO OTHER OPTION**

The wind howled in and the roar of the jet engines grew even louder as the rear ramp of the C-141 jet transport lowered, opening the interior of the aircraft to the freezing cold night sky. Thirty thousand feet below, the Arizona desert spread out like a rumpled sheet rucked high in the west to make the Santa Rosa Mountains; the lights of Phoenix to the north and Tucson to the south gleamed like flashlights from beneath a ragged blanket; the sprawling and well-lit airfield at Marana looked like a glowing postage stamp.

Dale Miller shuffled toward the ramp with the five members of his team. All of them wore heavy padded overalls and helmets with goggles beneath, their faces hidden by the oxygen masks linked to the bail-out bottles secured alongside their parachute pack trays. Their individual weapons were secured along their sides. Dale's breath was loud in his ears, magnified by the oxygen mask, even over the aircraft noise and static from his helmet-mounted radio system. He looked at the Air Force jumpmaster, whose tilted head indicated he was listening to instructions from the cockpit on his helmet intercom. Dale flexed his knees and rode the plane as though it were a surfboard, stomping his foot in impatience and gripping a teammate's shoulder.

"What's the holdup?" he said into his throat mike.

"Air Force," Jim Dewberry, his teammate, said. "They got to break in a cherry on our time."

One of the other jumpers looked over at Dale and shrugged in disgust.

The jumpmaster was shouting so loudly the jumpers could hear him over all the other noise, "Say again! Say again!"

Dale said, "No. We waited long enough. Let's go." He pushed at his teammates. The jumpmaster reached out as though to grab him and Dale slapped his hand away. He checked his goggles and shuffled out onto the ramp, which flexed beneath him like a diving board. His knees bent to absorb the motion. He felt for the plane's rhythm, and when the ramp came up beneath the soles of his boots, he sprang with it, tumbling like a leaf in the rushing slipstream behind the jet aircraft. The other jumpers brushed past the protesting jumpmaster and followed him out into the dark.

Dale fell through the dark sky. He spread himself wide like a frog in midleap and let his increasing speed turn him. Banking his arms slightly and cupping his hands, he adjusted his fall and lined up on the edge of the Marana airfield so far below.

Far off on the horizon was the early glimmer of dawn.

The altimeter and stopwatch on his chest board counted off the numbers and the time: altitude steadily decreasing, elapsed time increasing. The rushing air plucked at his jumpsuit and mask. The rush of adrenaline had peaked and evened in his gut. His blood pounded in his ear. He grinned and brought his arms in  close to his sides to increase his speed and flew like an arrow at the ground. A few moments later he checked his altitude and flared back into a stabilizing position, arms and legs spread wide, and then deployed his rectangular parachute. He reached for the control toggles, checked his canopy, and then looked to see the rest of the jumpers lining up on him. They were neatly stacked, trailing above and behind him, the dark parachutes almost invisible against the night sky. The only sound the hiss and flutter of their chutes, Dale's team spiraled down behind him toward the drop zone below.

Dale loved this part of the jump. After the heady rush of the fall, this sense of flight, with only the sound of his parachute cutting neatly through the air and the sight of the ground turning beneath him, gave him a sense of peace he rarely felt anywhere else. He tugged one toggle to turn the chute across the wind. In the east long fingers of light reached across the desert. The Marana airfield and the planes parked there, tiny toys from his altitude, grew larger. As he turned toward the edge of the drop zone, where a medical vehicle and an Air Force HUMV were parked, he saw a single figure standing alone, staring up at the descending parachutes.

Ray Dalton watched his team descend on the drop zone. One after another, in neat order, they flared their rectangular chutes to slow their descent and turned into the wind. They landed upright and running, quickly shedding their parachute harnesses and deploying their weapons. He felt a little swell of pride, carefully concealed, as he watched his handpicked men—drawn from the finest elite military units and the best graduates of the Central Intelligence Agency's Special Operations Program—move briskly and efficiently through the end of their parachute exercise.

He rubbed his hip, where a steel and ceramic replacement joint had been implanted after a jump much like this one had gone wrong. He'd been a colonel in the Special Forces then. He still carried himself as though he wore a uniform, though these days he shoehorned his tall and angular frame into the tweedy horse-country look favored by the CIA's upper management. His sartorial blending was one of the few concessions he made to internal politics. Many of the new breed of intelligence managers, Ivy League yuppies and political appointees for the most part, were put off by the air of quiet competence and potential violence that Ray cultivated. He liked it that they were afraid of him. He liked it that they had to put up with him.

Who else did they have who could bring these hidden warriors to heel?

There were only twelve men in the unit code named DOMINANCE RAIN. DOMINANCE RAIN was closely modeled on the Israeli *kidon*, or bayonet units: teams of state-sponsored and -trained assassins who systematically killed those whom the Israeli government decided were significant threats to Israel and Israeli citizens. The *kidon* targeted terrorists and their support structure anywhere the new breed of transnational terrorist set up operations. And the disappearances and deaths of the terrorist main players served notice that there was nowhere outside the reach of the long arm of Israeli justice.

The U.S. President liked that idea. After an airline hijacking in which a young U.S. serviceman was beaten to death, the President signed the special executive order authorizing the creation of DOMINANCE RAIN. He pulled out all the stops and let slip the leash on his finest dogs of war to take the fight to the terrorists and other targets of national interest on the new battlefield of transnational low intensity conflict.

The resulting collaboration between the Department of Defense's Special Operations Command and the Central Intelligence Agency's Special Activities Staff was one of the best special operations teams in the world. It was too bad, Ray thought, that more people—other than the president and a tiny handful of his advisors, and a few senior DOD and CIA officials—didn't know just how good his boys were.

The men of DOMINANCE RAIN wouldn't attract attention in a crowd. They had the relaxed confidence of men who'd been tested many times and never found wanting. They came from Delta, Special Forces groups, Ranger battalions, Navy SEAL teams, Marine Force Recon, even a handful with no prior military experience who stood out during the Agency's Paramilitary Officer Course. They all shared extraordinary technical skills in shooting and the black arts of weaponry, hand-to-hand combat, explosives, driving, lock picking, and other esoteric skills; a working knowledge of at least two or three languages, and extensive undercover operational experience.

Their psychological profiles stymied the best psychologists and psychiatrists in the world. One described them all as innovative, unconventional thinkers who combined utter ruthlessness with an innate ability to thrive under stress.

Dale Miller and his teammates were some of the best special operators in the world. And they answered only to Ray Dalton.

Ray waved away the approaching young Air Force lieutenant in charge of the Combat Control Team.

"Sir, we can't allow those kinds of safety violations . . . ," the lieutenant began again.

"I'll deal with it, Lieutenant. Thank you."

The lieutenant hesitated, then backed away. "Sir. Yes, sir."

Ray watched Dale laughing with the other men as they gathered up their parachutes. He remembered Dale as a twenty-six-year-old staff sergeant in the Delta Selection Course, when Ray had been Delta's Operations Officer. At thirty-one, Dale was stocky and prone to swagger, but he'd matured and deepened since Ray had poached him for the special project that became DOMINANCE RAIN. His wife, who kept an appraising eye on all Ray's charges, said that Dale had gotten darker. And in a way, that made sense. It went hand in hand with the job.

He waved the young operator over. "Dale!"

Dale jogged over as the other men razzed him.

"Bad dog, Dale! Bad dog!" one yelled.

Dale was still flushed from the jump. "Hey, boss . . . ," he said. He tugged at his nose and grinned at the ground.

"You pissed off the Air Force," Ray said.

"Yeah."

"Don't do it again."

"Roger that."

"Walk with me," Ray said. He pulled out a thin Honduran cigar. "Want one?"

"Thanks, boss." Dale took the cigar and leaned it into the flame from the battered Zippo lighter with the Special Forces crest that Ray held out. "What's up? I saw the Gulfstream. We got a job on?"

Ray drew hard on his cigar and wreathed his head in smoke. A breeze came and blew the smoke away. He walked a little farther, away from the parachute rigging shed where the other men gathered with their bundled parachutes. Beyond the Gulfstream jet parked on the tarmac nearby, there were two old DC-3s. On the far taxiway a green Evergreen Air 747 cargo plane was parked. All the way across the facility, far across the runways, the dim lights of the Federal Law Enforcement Training Center's Marana facility gleamed in the early light.

Ray examined the burning end of his cigar. "Jonny Maxwell escaped from Leavenworth last night," he said. "He was being transported for an off-site medical examination. One guard is missing. The other was found in the trunk of the transport vehicle. Dead. In the parking ramp at St. Louis International Airport."

He watched with interest how Dale stiffened and lost his swagger. The color rose and then fell in the young man's face. His cigar dangled forgotten in his hand.

"Jonny broke out," Dale said.

"The U.S. Marshal's Service has responsibility for federal fugitives. They're putting together a special Fugitive Investigative Strike Team to go after Jonny. The Outfit wants us to have an observer aboard to advise the Marshal team. You're it."

"Why me? You know how this is going to look," Dale said.

**MARCUS WYNNE**

"Has to be you. Who else knows him better? That's what you said at the trial, right?"

Dale flushed and looked away. "I was under oath . . ."

"Doesn't matter now. You're the best man for this mission. We need somebody inside to make sure things are taken care of. You're going in as an SF advisor who knows Maxwell. Help them with profiling and so on. Advise them on how he'll think, tactics, all that."

"I don't know what to think about this."

Ray spat a shred of tobacco to the ground. "You don't have that luxury." He paused. "How do you feel about him? Now?"

Dale stared at his cigar, the ash gone cold. He flicked the dead coal off the end with his fingertip.

"I asked you a question." Ray concealed his interest in the way Dale's head snapped up and his cold midwestern blue eyes burned into his boss's face.

"He was my teammate and my friend," Dale said. "He went bad. He was a criminal who got what he deserved. I helped put him away. It was the right thing to do."

"Yes. You helped put him away. And it *was* the right thing to do. Not everyone thought that way though, did they?"

"No sir, some people did not."

Ray was a master at reading the tide of human emotion and he knew just when to cut across it.

"He was your friend, Dale. I know that. He was my friend, too. I know how you feel and I know how you felt. This is the best thing you can do to help Jonny. Help them find him, talk him in. Jonny was way out of bounds before. But he's really gone off the reservation this time. He's killed at least one, more likely two, correctional officers. He's playing for keeps and this is for sure: it's going to get ugly if he decides to fight it out. You've got to prevent that. You know him better than anyone else ever did. Find him for me. Work with these people. Bring him in."

"Let me see your lighter."

Ray handed Dale his lighter and watched the young operator busy himself with his cigar. The red glow lit his drawn face and a thin cloud of blue smoke hid his mouth.

"What if he can't be found?" Dale said.

"Then you'll be TDY for a long time. As of now, there is no higher priority. There are issues . . . OPSEC issues. If he's gone this

**NO OTHER OPTION**

far, there's no telling what he might do. There's a lot of people in this world who'd love to know what Jonny Maxwell carries around in his head."

"He'd never go over to some tango operation. He'd never do that . . ."

"You don't know that," Ray said. "It could happen."

Ray studied the earnest and pained young face and remembered another young man's face, a proud Nicaraguan-American who'd worked for him. The Sandman was a warrior and a patriot with a great love for his native Nicaragua. He'd gone off the reservation, gone his own way to help his people the best way he knew how. But when his methods became extreme, and threatened to draw unwanted attention to the covert actions in Nicaragua, hunters came for him—men from his past, men who knew him and knew how he fought.

His brothers in arms. Who hunted and killed him.

Ray had circled the killing ground in an Intelligence Support Activity Beechcraft King Air light aircraft, listening to the staccato gunfire of the bitter battle in the jungle below and the harsh commands and labored breathing of men on the radio. He'd taught himself how to turn off the tide of disgust and sadness he felt when he heard the Sandman's voice on the secure radio frequency calling his name when the ISA assault team overran the Sandman's patrol.

He'd had practice since then with that reflexive quashing of emotion, and he called on it now as he said what needed to be said.

"I didn't want to believe that Jonny worked for me in forty countries, saved hundreds of American lives, sat at my dinner table with my wife and three daughters, and was raping women all the time. I didn't want to believe that he'd end up in prison. I don't want to accept that he'd kill American civilians to break out.

"But we don't have the luxury of thinking like that. He has to be found. The National Command Authority has a finding out. Jonny's name is in it."

Dale turned his back to Ray and faced the rising sun. Ray squinted at the young soldier's back and waited for him to speak.

"What if I find him and he won't come in?" Dale said.

Ray nodded. He dropped his smoldering cigar and ground it into the dirt beneath his tasseled loafer.

"Then you'll have to take him out, Dale."

**MARCUS WYNNE**

**1.3**

"I want a piece of this asshole," said Detective Nina Capushek of the Minneapolis Police Department's Sex Crime Unit. She glared out the passenger side window of the unmarked squad car as it sped through downtown Minneapolis. "I want him to get one little hair out of line with me."

Detective Herb Dunn looked over at his partner and said, "We're going to collar him just fine."

"It's because she fought him," Nina said in a tone Herb knew well. "She had defense wounds. A seven-year-old girl with defense wounds. And MacDouglas knew the family, knew the girl, he worked for the lawn service on that neighborhood route. It was him, Herb. I got that feeling. I know it. It was him and I'm taking him out."

Herb took a deep breath that strained his big belly against the seat belt. "You're going to have to grow a thicker skin if you're going to last, Nina."

Nina's green eyes narrowed as she looked over at him. Her full lips were drawn tight into a thin line. She was silent for a long minute.

"Do as you say, not as you do, is that it, Herb?"

He shrugged, discomfited as always by her cool and appraising gaze, and concentrated on his driving. After twenty-one years on the job, he thought he had every nuance and turn of the complex relationship between two cops in a squad car thought out. But then God

had to mock his vanity by seeing that he got partnered with this drop
dead gorgeous thirty-year-old ex-Fed who coupled some of the best
street cop instincts and moves he'd ever seen with an almost psychic
intuition about people. Nina just knew things about people, and her
insights into dirtbag minds—and into his—kept him off balance in
a way he didn't allow himself to think of as threatening.

She broke the silence with a laugh, shaking her head like a
doting aunt at a well-loved but incorrigible nephew. She patted
Herb's belly straining the buttons of his frayed white oxford shirt
under a worn and greasy polyester tie.

"Is this what you mean by growing a thick skin?"

"Have some respect for your elders, young lady, or I'll turn you
over my knee."

"Quit teasing me, old man. You know I like that. Will you cuff
me first?"

"Jesus, Nina!"

Herb's ears burned and he couldn't help it. He thought he'd be
used to it by now. Nina was young enough to be his daughter, if he
and Mary had had any kids, but her mouth was as bad as any crusty
cop on the beat. She leaned back in her seat, still laughing. Herb
liked the sound of her laughter; she sounded so young and carefree.
The worry and care and endless compassion for the victims and their
families she saw every day were aging her. She channeled her fierce
rage into a ruthless and obsessive hunt for the offenders. She was
one of the best investigators he'd seen in twenty-one years of law
enforcement. And she was the best partner he'd ever had. It didn't
hurt that she was gorgeous and fun to be around. The main thing
was, whether they were wrestling with a suspect in an alley or canvassing neighborhoods for witnesses, she was right there beside him,
measure for measure.

Herb eased the unmarked squad through the back alleys off
Thirty-first Street into the back parking lot of the run-down Uptown
apartment building. He eyeballed the lot, then backed the car into a
slot marked RESERVED FOR MANAGER ONLY. Nina bounded out of
the car, patting her right hip where her Sig-Sauer P-228 9mm rested
in the Bianchi Paddle Holster Herb had bought her for her thirtieth
birthday. Herb squeezed his left arm in and felt the comforting
weight of his four-inch Smith & Wesson Model 625 .45 ACP revolver.
Three thick moon-clips rode on the other side of his shoulder holster

and tucked in his left hip pocket was a Smith 642 hideout .38 snub. He got kidded about his heavy weapons, as the offenders they hunted were rarely violent when apprehended; most sexual predators saved their violence for the weak, helpless, or unarmed. Robbed of surprise, size, or weapons, most sex offenders were pathetic waste. Some career criminals who majored in robbery or burglary and minored in rape might fight, but most just went along. But Herb had worked the street too long to ever underestimate the danger of the human scum they dealt with.

Nina went up the concrete stairs to the boarded-up security door at the back of the building. The lock had been jimmied and pried open so many times that it slid right out of the ragged doorsill when she tugged it open. Two men, one Hispanic, the other black, stood just inside, passing a smoldering crack pipe between them.

"What is this?" the Hispanic said.

Nina plucked the hot pipe from his fingers, dropped it, and crushed it underfoot. "Police," she said. "Get gone."

"We gone, we gone," the black man said, taking his friend by the sleeve. "Ten-four, we gone."

"Move," Herb said. The men walked away quickly, looking back over their shoulders.

Nina drew her pistol and started up the stairs, two at a time. Herb caught himself grinning at the sight of her muscular ass in her close-fitting blue slacks. He snapped his head around at the sound of the door behind them opening.

"Out of here!" he hissed at the Hispanic man peeking through the door. The man disappeared in a hurry.

Nina paused on the landing above, listening. Herb came up behind her and murmured, "We're good." He positioned himself in front of her and led the way down the narrow hallway, noting the apartment numbers on each door. The cheap wallpaper peeled away from the wall and molding. The doors were poorly stained hollow core laminate, with tarnished pseudo-brass doorknobs. There were a variety of locks; apparently the landlord allowed tenants to install their own. The two detectives stopped outside Apartment 216. Nina listened at the door. The television inside was turned up loud. She nodded to Herb, who stepped past her and pressed himself against the wall on one side of the door. Nina stood to the other side, reached out, and tapped sharply on the door.

**NO OTHER OPTION**

"Hey, Dan!" she called. "You there?"

There was the shift and scrape of a chair on a linoleum floor and then the heavy pad of bare feet to the door.

"Who is it?" The voice was sour.

"Me," Nina said, swinging her head out where he could see the flash of her long hair and little else through the peephole.

"Who's me?"

"C'mon, Dan. Open the door," Nina said in a whiny voice.

The lock turned and Dan MacDouglas peered out through the partially open door. His face was unshaven and lined with lack of sleep; there was a fresh scrape down one cheek. He saw Nina and Herb, and in the surprisingly fast reaction of a cornered animal, tried to slam the door shut. Herb hit the door hard and bulled it open with his shoulder, stumbling as the resistance suddenly vanished. MacDouglas ran down his narrow entryway through the front room toward the back bedroom. Nina grabbed Herb's arm to steady him, then squeezed by him and raced after MacDouglas.

"Nina! Dammit!" Herb said.

Nina shouted, "MacDouglas, stop! Police!" She eased round the cover of the bedroom door, exposing only a sliver of her and the muzzle of her weapon locked out in front of her. MacDouglas was throwing magazines and photographs out the window. At the sight of her, he snatched up a long hunting knife from the floor beside his bed.

"You want some of me, bitch? You want some, bring it on." MacDouglas hunched his weight forward and swiped the air with his knife.

Herb entered behind Nina and brought his revolver up to challenge MacDouglas when Nina's first shot rang out. She fired again and again, so rapidly that the brass cases seemed to hang in the air, one of them clinging to Herb's collar, hot and burning on the soft flesh there. In the slowdown of time that comes with life-threatening action, Herb saw the fabric of MacDouglas's T-shirt flutter and begin to spot with red. But what he would never forget was Nina's face, the grim wide-eyed green glare of the hunter with her prey in her sights, and under that the unmistakable satisfaction as she put seven 9mm 124 grain Hydra-Shoks into the heart and upper torso of Dan MacDouglas.

**MARCUS WYNNE**

Jedediah Isiah Loveless—Jed to his friends—was a chaser and proud of it. Not skirts, though he'd done a fair bit of that in his time. He was a man-chaser, one of the best, a flat-faced, narrow-eyed, sunburned, and knotty-muscled five feet eight inches of former Force Recon Marine. He'd spent a few years after Vietnam as a cop in Texas before an old Marine buddy lured him into the U.S. Marshals Service. Jed came just in time to ride the Marshals' roller-coaster fortune, from their near rock-bottom days as seedy prisoner escorts to the heady days after their capture of the escaped spy Christopher Boyce led to their expanded mandate as the premier federal manhunters.

He'd been summoned, in the middle of the night, to the Target Acquisition Center in Arlington, Virginia, for a briefing on one Jonathan Harding Maxwell, formerly of the Fort Leavenworth military penitentiary. He made the calls and pulled together just the right team for this operation, which was how he came to be out here at Washington's Reagan National Airport to meet one Master Sergeant Dale Miller, the Army's handpicked liaison for this Fugitive Investigation Strike Team.

Jed had a good position, his back to the wall, where he could see people deplaning off the flight from Phoenix. One of the men coming down the jetway had the look Jed recognized: a concealed wariness, a casual look that scanned the crowd, close, then far, back and forth, lingering on hands and eyes, waistbands, shoulders and ankles—all the places where the giveaway tells and body language of an armed man—or woman—register.

Jed grinned when he saw the young man make him. The soldier was neatly dressed in khakis and a chambray work shirt under a brown leather pilot's jacket. He didn't stick out in the crowd. He looked like any other traveler, a little more athletic maybe, but not too out of the ordinary.

Jed liked what he saw. He had a fondness for the shooters who, if the truth be known, were a band of surrogate sons to him, the father of daughters. Years of seasoning and experience had taught him to read men, to know the strengths and weaknesses they wore like skill-identifier badges. This one had seen the elephant. Might even have French kissed him once or twice. He was a good age, early thirties, still young and strong but with enough seasoning to be near his peak. Jed didn't think any gunfighter reached his peak till after he'd been on the job for at least seven to ten years, with some serious up close and personal confrontation time, and that generally took well into a man's middle thirties. It took that long for the illusions and bullshit to begin to sort out in a man's life, and for the true nature of his character to rise like the inner surface of a stone rises after years of running water pass over its face. Time, trouble, and how they handled it was what determined a shooter's life—and his face.

He pushed off the wall and held out his hand. "Dale Miller, right?"

The soldier had a good grip. "That's right, Mr. Loveless."

Jed grinned. Score one for the young gun. "Mr. Loveless was my daddy, Dale. Call me Jed, all my friends do." He gestured at the small blue-green Cordura duffel in Dale's left hand. "That all your gear?"

"Travel light, freeze at night. You know the drill."

"Hooyah, I surely do," Jed said. "You eat? They feed you up on all that good airplane food?"

"All the peanuts and pretzels a growing boy could want."

Jed laughed. "I got a car out front." He led the way through the crowded concourse. He noticed how Dale kept his bag in his left hand and stayed slightly behind and to the right of Jed. "What kind of shooter you packing there, son?"

Dale grinned. "Browning High-Power."

**MARCUS WYNNE**

"Who makes your leather?"

"Greg Kramer. Wear a lot of Sparks, too."

"Young, good-looking, and he's got good taste in gun leather. I bet you get more ass than a toilet seat."

Dale leaned back in his chair and appraised the other members of the Fugitive Investigative Strike Team. The men were seated, grouped by affiliation, around a circular table in a windowless conference room buried deep inside the Marshals Service Headquarters in Arlington.

Two of Jed Loveless's handpicked marshals from the Special Projects Unit sat across from Dale: Edgar Harris, a wiry, edgy former city cop from Cincinnati, who ignored Dale's outstretched hand; and Tommy La Roux, a thick-boned Cajun with an unruly mop of black hair who shook Dale's hand firmly and said, "Dale, good to meet you."

Jed sat at the head of the table, facing the door. He tapped his pen impatiently against the yellow legal pad on the table in front of him. At the opposite end of the table was a reed-thin FBI agent who'd introduced himself as Ted Nakamura from Behavioral Sciences. Nakamura looked more Indian than Japanese, and fidgeted while polishing his thick glasses on a handkerchief.

Once everyone was settled, Harris said, "What do we need a psych profile and a spook for?"

"Dale's not a spook," Jed said.

Harris ignored Dale and spoke only to Jed. "He's not a cop. What's the military doing here?"

"Maxwell isn't your run-of-the-mill fugitive felon, Edgar," Jed said. He tapped his pen hard against the table. "We might need a little extra insight into the methods of his madness."

Tommy La Roux laughed with the deep-bellied ease of a man who laughed often. "Edgar don't like nobody but police, Dale. He's got a nasty, suspicious mind because he spends too much time chasing shitbags. Don't mind him. We're glad you're here."

"Speak for yourself," Harris said.

"I'm glad to have a couple of experts around," La Roux said. He looked first at Dale, then down the table at Nakamura. "Maybe you guys could explain to this old country boy how Maxwell got through all that good psychological-type screening you put him

**NO OTHER OPTION**

through. I haven't read all the file, and"—he paused and looked speculatively at Dale—"there's some big gaps in his record. Sure seems like he was looked at close, though. Shouldn't there have been some, what do you call, behavioral indicators?"

La Roux was a lot sharper than he wanted people to know, Dale thought. He met La Roux's quizzical look, then turned to Nakamura, who pushed his glasses up on his long nose, smudging the lens with a sweaty forefinger.

Nakamura cleared his throat, looked at Jed and then at Dale. "A little, um, background might be in order. I've reviewed the military psychologist's records on Maxwell . . . um, anything you want to add, just jump in, Sergeant Miller, feel free . . ."

Dale crossed his arms. "You go ahead. I'll fill in later." He gave no sign that he noticed the look that Harris gave La Roux and Jed.

Nakamura blinked as though something were in his eye. "What, um, Delta Force does, what they do with their testing, is select in for certain behavioral traits, and then select out for undesirable combinations of those traits . . ."

"I'd think that raping women and murdering cops would be an undesirable combination," Harris said. He sighed when Jed glared at him, and began to doodle furiously on his notepad.

30

Nakamura continued. "From our perspective, that's true. But some of those behaviors grew out of traits, attributes, that are, um, highly prized in military special operations personnel. Like any behavior or attribute, they can be . . . less than desirable . . . depending on the circumstances. Maxwell was a highly capable and experienced special operations soldier. He'd shown that in numerous classified— even to us—operations, dangerous operations, all over the world. Indicators? After the fact we can find plenty. The truth is, though, that he was selected to do exactly everything that he's done with the exception of rape."

"I'm going to want you to come back to that first part," Jed said. "But I don't understand the rapes. This guy was a hell of a soldier, the best of the best—in the Army anyway." He winked at Dale, who allowed himself a small smile at the attempt. Harris snorted and didn't look up from his doodling. "He was no stranger to discipline and honor. What the hell happened to him?"

Nakamura bobbed his head rapidly. "That's an interesting question. Sexual aggressiveness, up to and including sexual assault, is a phenomenon associated with any group of men involved in high risk operations or contact sports. Football players, wrestlers, boxers, soldiers, police officers, race car drivers . . . the aggressiveness needed to succeed in those fields goes hand in hand with a high sex drive. What prevents most men from crossing the line from aggressive sexuality to sexual assault are situational constraints and internal moral structure. Maxwell had been raping for a long time and managed to keep himself from getting caught." He glanced quickly at Dale. "And not ever letting his teammates know. He . . ."

"I'm sure this is real interesting for somebody," Harris said. "What I want to know is where this guy is going and what he's going to do next. In my humble opinion as a mere cop, that's what profiles are for. I don't give a shit what kind of interesting psych case he is. I want him behind bars and on trial for the murder of those officers. Period." He shot a challenging stare at Dale. "I don't give a shit what kind of Rambo hero he was supposed to be. He's a dirtbag rapist and cop killer."

"Edgar," Jed said.

Harris closed his mouth and drummed his fingers hard on the tabletop. He shrugged, dropped his head, and began to elaborate on his notepad drawing. From where Dale sat, it looked as though he were drawing a pistol.

"Go on, Ted. Then we'll hear what Dale has to add," Jed said. "Just give us the quick sketch. You said he did everything he was selected to do. What do you mean by that?"

Nakamura wiped one hand on his wrinkled gray trouser leg. "His ability to compartmentalize. The rapes were executed with all the planning and skill that a highly trained commando could bring to it. Yet he was able to keep that out of his work. He didn't see any conflict between the jobs he did for his country and the jobs he did . . . for himself. That's one. The initiative and ruthlessness to seize on an escape opportunity and do what needed to be done to make sure he got away clean. Focus on his mission. That's another."

"What mission?" Jed said.

"Getting away. His method shows planning and forethought and knowledge of police operations. His physical showed high liver enzymes, which can be related to alcohol abuse, liver failure, any number of medical conditions. I've got someone checking to see if it can be artificially induced. The prison hospital has no facility for the kind of detailed workup you need to determine the cause. Two guards escorted him off the prison to a hospital in St. Louis. And the trail, so far, stops with the prison sedan in the long-term parking lot at St. Louis International with one guard dead in the trunk. His neck was broken." Nakamura looked as though he were pleading with Dale to say something. "Maxwell is some kind of hand-to-hand combat expert, I believe."

"He had lots of training in close quarters battle," Dale conceded. "Breaking necks is easy if you take someone unaware."

La Roux scratched the back of his neck. "Remind me not to sit in front of you."

Harris cleared his throat and shook his head from side to side. He drew in large letters beneath his elaborate pistol: BULLSHIT.

Dale took a deep breath through his nose and out through his mouth, and willed his hands to relax. Nakamura took off his glasses and rubbed at the smudged lenses with a tissue he took from his pants pocket. "It may be that Maxwell wasn't actually planning an escape at all. He may have seized the chance when it presented itself, precisely as he's been trained to do and as his personality predisposes him to do. He may be running on autopilot, doing escape and evasion in a hostile environment with nowhere to escape to. He has no place to go, no one to turn to, nothing to go back to, no family, no friends, nothing outside of the military community that has ostracized him since his trial. We need to understand what kind of isolation he's feeling right now. He's someone to whom the sense of belonging to something larger than himself was paramount. Drummed out of his unit in disgrace for a shameful series of crimes, the humiliation of being imprisoned with men he could only look down on . . ."

"He's no better than any of them," Harris said.

"He'd think he is, though," Nakamura said, riding over Harris's words. "That's one of the clearest indicators in his profile. He thinks he's different from everyone else. He's very intelligent, IQ of 135 . . . and after reading the report from the Delta psychologist"—another long look at Dale—"I believe he had some understanding of psychological testing. Delta uses their psychometric test instruments differently than clinical psychologists do. They select for men who are capable of working completely alone, under inhuman pressure, but who at the same time are capable of working as a team member and drawing on sophisticated interpersonal skills while undercover. Max-

**MARCUS WYNNE**

well's profile indicates that he thought he should be ashamed of some aspects of his personal behavior. Now we can see what those were. The original interpretation was that Maxwell was in some way compensating for a poor self image resulting from childhood emotional and physical abuse. The unit psychologist's call was that he was sure the adaptations Maxwell made were, in the context of military special operations mission requirements, useful . . . no matter their questionable effect on his mental health."

"You've lost me," Jed said.

Nakamura put his glasses back on and peered around the table. "Many of the characteristics and behaviors desirable in a special operator are attributes that would be considered unhealthy elsewhere. Obsessive attention to detail, focus that eliminates any considerations outside of the mission, extreme physical aggressiveness, the ability to lie congruently, a lack of emotional dependency that borders on sociopathy—there's a very fine line here. You see the same thing in police profiles, for that matter: aggressiveness, fascination with authority, capability for violence, love of the rush."

"They've got you pegged," La Roux said to Harris.

"Fuck you," Harris said.

"Back on track," Jed said. "So where does this take us?"

"We know what direction he's *probably* going to develop in. The main organizing structure, the framework of his life, was built around his identity as a Delta soldier. He was a superb technical operator. You could consider his skill his religion. His job was a monastic structure he built to live in. He built a structure of extraordinary skill to compensate for, to deny, the injured inner self crippled by the abuse he most likely suffered as a child. He needed that structure and it was taken away from him. Or rather, more interestingly, he set himself up so it would be taken away from him. It's as though he wanted to be caught—look at how it finally happened: he leaves a custom-made glove available only to Delta operators and pilots from the Nightstalker helicopter unit in a victim's home. This from a man who was able to work undercover in the most hostile terrorist environments in the world and never get caught.

"Now he has no structure. He didn't build one in prison. And he needs one, one where he can excel, where he can exercise his skills, achieve control and self-gratification. He needs a structure that mirrors back his careful construct of himself, the construct that sus-

**NO OTHER OPTION**

tains his ongoing rationalization. That rationalization justifies, to him, his actions."

Nakamura leaned forward and gripped the table edge.

"I think Maxwell is heading down the track, building up speed, to an intersection not too far away. He's either going to leave the country, find himself a military position as a mercenary or an advisor in Africa or Latin America, or he's going to stay right here in the States and become the very best criminal he can be. It all depends on how circumstances unfold for him over the next few weeks. It's going to be one of those two tracks."

Dale unfolded his arms and sat forward, adjusting his holstered High-Power as he did. "How do you get to that conclusion, Agent Nakamura?"

Nakamura seemed grateful for the question. "If he stays here, he can't go backward. He can't go back to the structure he had before. That means he has to build one. Where can he do that? He's not the sort of man who could adopt a quiet civilian life and stay in the background, work in a grocery store or a gas station. He needs to exercise his skills, to prove his excellence, and the best venues for that are the criminal or mercenary realms."

Harris set down his pen and nodded. Dale saw that his interest was piqued.

"That's useful. What about his structure in prison?" Harris said. "Who was he celling with?"

"At the time of his escape, no one," Nakamura said. "His previous cellmate was another Army master sergeant, John Murphy, who was doing twenty for trafficking in stolen military weapons. He was supplying M-16s, M-60s, grenades, even light antitank weapons to white supremacist groups and outlaw motorcycle gangs across the Pacific Northwest. Murphy was transferred from the cell to the prison infirmary two months ago, after he was diagnosed with liver cancer. He died three weeks ago."

"That's interesting," Jed said. "Maybe that's where Maxwell got the idea about the liver enzymes. How close were they?"

"We don't know," Nakamura said. "The guards say Maxwell kept to himself. Other than Murphy, just idle conversation with a few other prisoners. We're talking to them. No known problems, but one of the guards mentioned that Maxwell was a suspect in the beating of a black prisoner who was found in the showers. He's still in

**MARCUS WYNNE**

the hospital, been in a coma for two weeks with a cerebral hematoma."

"Somebody kicked his ass fierce," La Roux said.

Nakamura nodded. "Maxwell was suspected, but he denied it and there was no proof. Nobody saw anything."

Nakamura took a deep breath and fell silent. He paged slowly through his notes.

La Roux looked over at Jed, then at Dale. "Well, partner, you worked with this guy, is that right? What is it that you guys did together?"

Dale sat very still, his face blank. His index finger tapped twice, then once. *Chest, chest, head. Knocks them down and keeps them dead.* "I can't discuss specifics . . ." he began.

"We're all on the same side here, Dale," Jed said.

". . . but I can say that Jonny Maxwell was the senior NCO in my troop when I came on with Delta. We worked a lot of operations together, we were in Bosnia, the Gulf, a lot of places together. We had a close working relationship, just like you guys get when you work with somebody for a long time in hard places," he said.

Harris curled his lip. "He was a friend of yours, wasn't he?"

"Yes he was," Dale said. His finger tapped, then stopped. "For a long time, I considered him a friend."

"You testified against him at the trial though," Harris said. "Said you'd been suspicious of his behavior, saw signs of, what did you call it"—he leafed through the case file in front of him—"aberrant behavior. Is that right?"

"Yes," Dale said.

"Did you challenge him on it before you testified against your partner?" Harris said. "What's up with that? You guys were friends?"

Dale avoided their eyes and looked at the wall above Jed's head. "I thought I knew Jonny Maxwell. As much as he let anybody know him . . . What's he going to do? I think Nakamura is on track. I don't know if Jonny planned his escape. If I had to bet, I'd say no. I think he just seized the opportunity, the same way he would if he were a prisoner of war. He's out, he's hunted, and he knows the game. He's trained to know how you think. He's had lots of practice in the real world, staying ahead of local security forces, which is how he's going to think of you. He knows what you're going to do, what moves you're going to make, and what order you'll make them in. The one thing you can count on is that he won't do anything you'd expect your average fugitive to do. Right now, he's going to take it twenty minutes at a time. Strictly survival stuff. He's got to get a vehicle—if he hasn't found a way onto an aircraft—get a safe house, get money and documentation. He's got tasks to do, to create a temporary refuge to further refine his escape and evasion plan. And he'll make that as foolproof as he can."

"What's he planning to do?" La Roux said.

"What Nakamura said, I think. Either leave the country, go merc, or stay here and go major league bad guy."

"You think this guy is so tough," Harris said. "We've taken down tough guys before, Miller. Some of you commando types, too. Remember that guy Vasquez, Tommy?"

"Enrique Vasquez," La Roux said. "Oh, yeah. He was a hard old boy. He was Vietnam something."

"He was some kind of Vietnam-era CIA slash Special Forces slash fucking Phoenix Project ninja assassin," Harris said. "He was working as an enforcer for the Outlaws biker gang. Killed a state trooper in Oklahoma, a local sheriff in Texas, and a whole shit pot of people the Outlaws were pissed at. We ran him down. He gave us a good chase, but we ran him down."

"Old Edgar had to get face-to-face with Enrique," La Roux said. "You put what, three rounds of double-ought in his chest?"

Harris laughed. He never looked away from Dale's face. "Put a hole in him big enough to pass a six-pack through."

"I believe you did just that," La Roux said.

"We tracked him, bagged him, and tagged him. Everybody thought he was a tough guy, too."

Dale met Harris's challenging gaze with a level, neutral face. He looked at Jed and La Roux, who watched for his reaction. Nakamura stared blankly into space.

Dale nodded slowly. "I realize you're good at what you do. I respect that. But I don't think you get it. Let me tell you something about Jonny Maxwell. During the Gulf War, when Kuwait was occupied, the Iraqi Republican Guard and several divisions were in and around Kuwait City. They looted the city, raped and pillaged, crushed the little resistance movement that was starting up.

"The security around Kuwait City was as close to seamless as the Iraqis could come up with—and it was pretty good. Patrols day and night, electronic surveillance to prevent air penetration, ground sensors on the roads to augment the roadblocks, minefields on the foot approaches.

"Jonny Maxwell went into Kuwait City by himself. Not once, not twice, but on five separate occasions, he went in alone to do close target reconnaissance, mark air targets and landing zones, and to coordinate what was left of the resistance. He was captured once, by a patrol. He only had a pistol. He killed all six members of the patrol before they could turn him over to a prisoner processing team. Then he continued and completed his mission. And he went back again after that. When the Iraqis had thousands of men, some of them highly trained, searching for him.

"He eluded military patrols, dogs, police units, and special military hunter-killer teams. Alone, on foot, armed with a pistol and without any backup.

"Don't fool yourself into thinking that he's just another criminal with some military history. He was as good as it gets in a hard world."

Harris sat back in his chair and crossed his arms. La Roux nodded, impressed, and looked at Jed, who made notes on his legal pad.

"What's he like to do?" Jed said.

"He likes to be by himself. He likes to shoot. He likes to hunt. He owned a Harley, he likes to ride. He likes to rape women. That's it," Dale said.

"Does he like to fight?" Jed said.

Dale took his time answering. "In the sense of picking a fight in a bar for fun, no. He wouldn't start one like that, but he'd finish it if someone brought it to him. But if it's a mission . . . once the balloon goes up, once he's in contact and the fight is on, there's nobody better. He's never more alive than when he's in the middle of the fight. That's how he made his name. It's all he's lived for, all he's trained for, all he's ever thought about. Being in the moment, in the fight. Running the game. That's what he's about. If we hunt him, if we corner him, we'd better be ready to go all the way and then some. Because that's the only way he knows how to go."

According to his driver's license, Chad Bergh was twenty-two years old and resided at 1742 Seventh Street in St. Paul, Minnesota. Now he lay beneath three feet of loamy dirt in a field, his grave bordered by tall rows of corn, just off a gravel utility road not far from an isolated off-ramp.

In the idling 4Runner, Jonny replaced the license and poked through the rest of Chad Bergh's wallet: American Express and Gold Visa cards; a social security card; a St. Thomas University student ID and library card; thirty-two dollars in assorted bills; a family photo of Chad with mom, dad, and two sisters, one not bad-looking, and an ugly dog. A yellow Post-it note with several four-digit numbers and the word "gandalf" written on it. PIN numbers for the credit cards and a password, he guessed.

You could tell so much about someone by looking in their wallet. The kid's whole life was in there.

Too bad for him.

Jonny threw the wallet into the glove box and wiped his hands on his pant leg. His Levi's were too short in the leg and too loose in the gut; the Cavalier's driver had been short and fat. He'd wept silently when he stripped off his clothes and handed them to Jonny. It reminded him of the Iraqi salesman he'd killed on the highway outside of Baghdad during the Storm. The Iraqi had the same resigned but defiant look when he realized how it was going to end.

Jonny drove away with his lights off. The gravel crunched beneath the slow rolling wheels of the 4Runner. When he hit the paved road that returned to the highway he turned on the lights and accelerated down the ramp. On the empty highway the headlights bored into the dark. The speedometer was at ninety before he noticed he was speeding.

He eased off the gas. He felt as though he were short of breath, as though something were pressing on his chest, and he forced himself to breathe deeply and slowly, forcing the oxygenated blood deep into his tissue, washing out the adrenaline and the . . . what? He saw the boy's face, the surprise and the fear and the sad resignation he'd seen so many times before. In one of the African hunting books he enjoyed, there was a story about a white hunter who was mauled by a lion. The hunter described how a peaceful sense of lassitude came over him when the lion's jaws clamped down on him, how he hadn't felt any pain, only a sense of pressure . . . the pain came only after his friends rescued him and the full extent of his injuries became apparent.

It must have been like that for the boy. He was sure of it.

Jonny put those thoughts away on the shelf in his head where he kept such things. He'd learned how to do that a long time ago. He'd been ten, and Gene Tovares, a neighbor sympathetic to the quiet boy from the loud house, had taken him on his first hunt into the rugged northern California foothills. Jonny sat in a tree stand and waited for the dogs to run the deer past him. He felt a deep churning in his stomach when the adrenaline rose up as his deer appeared, and he learned to ride that wave down in the same moment, as hunters have done for thousands of years. The Winchester Model 94 .30-.30 rifle thumped back into his shoulder socket and the buckhorn sight tracked up and then down again. The lever was cool in his small hand as he ratcheted it down, then up, reloading automatically without ever having been taught how. The deer rose up onto its hind legs, its front hooves thrashing the air as though it were boxing an invisible opponent. It staggered forward a few steps and then collapsed into the grass, shuddered, and grew still in a spreading pool of blood.

Time stood still with the scent of gunpowder. He felt a strangely familiar satisfaction. He paid no attention to the praise of the other hunters, big bluff hardworking men with the smell of coffee, sweat, whiskey, and raw blood around them. It was as though

**NO OTHER OPTION**

there were two parts to him, and one part had woken for the first time—a part that rose and turned, sniffing for the rich scent of blood that filled him with warmth and sudden unexpected strength, put timbre and fiber into his voice, and put the pathetic misery of his other life in a small dim shadow down in the corner of the brilliant picture laid out before him.

His first man had been the same.

Later, on the road, his plan began to take shape. Minneapolis would be good. It was close enough to Milwaukee and far enough away to keep law enforcement from connecting him to his stash—if they even had an inkling about it, which he doubted. They would have no way of knowing, but it was important not to underestimate the opposition. All operators kept one or more stashes of money, documents, and weapons for those times when you might get caught short on a job . . . or had something going that was better left outside the regular requisition channels.

More than a few of the boys had screwed themselves out of their pensions that way. There had been mass reassignments, demotions, and prison sentences handed out after the Department of Defense Investigative Service tore apart the voucher and budgetary practices of the special ops paramilitary teams. It was only human that there would be abuses—credit cards with no limits that you never had to pay, multiple identities, briefcases full of freshly minted hundred-dollar bills, expensive cars, lavish safe houses maintained for cover . . . heady stuff to senior enlisted men who were lucky to be pulling down two grand a month after taxes. Some of them got greedy and got caught. Or got screwed by their bosses.

Or their friends.

He put that thought away. The early morning light swelled in the sky. The gleaming skyline of Minneapolis grew in the distance.

Jonny checked into an anonymous Super 8 Motel near the Minneapolis–St. Paul International Airport. From the room, he dialed the toll-free number on the back of the Visa card, and at the prompting of the mechanical voice that answered, entered in the card number and the last four digits of Chad Bergh's social security number. The metallic voice said there was a balance of $137.42 on a credit line of $9750.

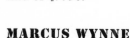

**MARCUS WYNNE**

Operating funds were the first priority. After hiding himself beneath sunglasses, a thick watch cap, and a super-sized plastic coffee mug he held to his face, Jonny worked his way through four different ATM cash machines in the suburbs around Minneapolis. The local machines would only allow a $500 cash advance against a daily ceiling of $2000. He figured he had twenty-four hours before the automated theft and misuse software would flag the pattern of large cash advances. But that should be enough time.

The next stop was a computer superstore, where he purchased an Apple G-3 Powerbook and had the RAM maxed out while he waited.

"Nice machine," the checkout clerk said as he put the computer box back into Jonny's shopping cart.

"They're supposed to be," Jonny said. "I'll need it for school."

"Going back?"

"Grad school."

"Better you than me. I had enough. Thanks for shopping Computer World."

"Thank you."

He concealed the computer box beneath the sleeping bag in the back of the 4Runner, then drove up I-35W to Lake Street and into the Uptown District at the intersection of Hennepin and Lake. The  streets were lined with large and small shops, trendy restaurants, bars, and coffee shops. He parked in the public ramp behind the Calhoun Square shopping center.

Inside the enclosed mall he went into the Gap and purchased several pairs of black Levi's, half a dozen black and half a dozen white T-shirts, and several denim shirts in black and blue. From a vendor's cart in the atrium, he bought a pair of Ray•Ban Wayfarers. He bought a low-cut pair of black Doc Martens work shoes in a store called Hobnailed and Naught. The young woman waiting on him had her lips, nose, ears and tongue pierced with gleaming silver beads.

"Present for someone?" she said as she put the shoebox into a shopping bag.

"Me," Jonny said. "My friends tell me I need to get with the times."

She looked at his ill-fitting Levi's, baggy flannel shirt, and the Wayfarers hiding his eyes. "They may be right."

**NO OTHER OPTION**

"Whatever." Jonny was glad for his hidden eyes. *What you don't know won't kill you.*

On the way back to the Super 8, he stopped at a Target and bought toiletries, underwear, socks, and a home barber's set. Back in his room, he laid out clothes on the bed, then took the barber's set out of its plastic sleeve and went into the bathroom. He studied himself in the mirror. Three days of beard stubble covered his face. His medium-length brown hair had thinned out and receded from his forehead. He cut his hair as short as he could with the barber's scissors, then ran the electric clippers over his head till only a close stubble remained. With a safety razor, he shaved his head completely bald and removed all of his facial hair except for a slightly crooked goatee. The bald look smoothed out his features and took at least five years off his thirty-six.

He showered off the stray hairs, then dressed in new patterned boxers, a black T-shirt, black Levi's, a thick black leather belt, white socks, and the black Doc Martens. He didn't recognize himself when he looked in the mirror, nor would anyone else who'd known him. Prison had trimmed him down to 175 pounds of stringy muscle and bone. The Jonny everyone else knew was closer to 190, with medium long hair, and favored T-shirts, flannel work shirts, blue jeans, and cowboy boots. Now he looked like a hip coffee barista in his late twenties, as far from the image of Jonny Maxwell, former commando and escaped convict, as he could be.

The Ray•Bans were the final touch.

"I'm a hip dude," Jonny said, studying himself in the mirror. He needed to work on the smile. It was too edgy. He let himself slouch a little. Yeah, this would work. He'd fit right into the Twin Cities large student community, with its transient population and cheap lodging. And taut-bodied young women.

He'd think about that later.

He unboxed the computer and ran a diagnostic on the internal modem and communications program. Everything checked out as it should. He preferred the Apples to the IBMs they'd been issued in DOMINANCE RAIN. He liked uncomplicated machines that did what they were told and gave him no problems.

After a final run through the ATMs tomorrow, Chad Bergh's card would be done. He'd have to move fast to set up the next phase.

**MARCUS WYNNE**

He picked up the phone, entered *67 to block the Caller ID, then dialed Chad's home phone number and got his answering machine. He entered the remote access number from the Post-it note in Chad's wallet. There were three messages, two from friends looking for Chad, one from Citibank, just like clockwork, telling him to call and verify a number of recent transactions that didn't meet his usual profile. The card would most likely be frozen tomorrow, but if he went right after midnight he could hit all the ATMs and get another $2000 out.

Now it was time to work.

Jonny plugged the computer modem into the phone jack and entered a toll-free 800 number into the communications program. The modem buzzed and beeped as numbers played across the screen. A splash screen came up: RESTRICTED ACCESS. AUTHORIZED USERS ONLY. THIS SITE IS MONITORED AND UNAUTHORIZED ATTEMPTS AT ACCESS WILL BE PROSECUTED.

At the password prompt, Jonny entered "War666Dog." The verification prompt came up and he reentered the alternate SYSOP password he'd inserted into the program years before and hit RETURN. A directory of files rolled up.

"Bingo," Jonny said softly. "Welcome to the jungle."

He typed rapidly, his shoulders twitching as though he were playing an elaborate pinball machine, the cursor bouncing from screen to screen: CREDIT CARDS, CREDIT REPORTS, DRIVER'S LICENSES, PERSONAL REFERENCES, BACKGROUND HISTORY. Long dormant identities, created years before as part of the DOMINANCE RAIN start-up, were hidden away in this corner of the unit's dedicated mainframe.

Jonny spun his legend, to deceive and ensnare, like a spider spins a web. First the bare threads that held the whole together: background, friends and family; credit references and credit cards. All the addresses and past employment and credit references were laboriously backstopped by the hardworking clerks in the CIA's Special Support Unit, who made sure that the little stops and checks that people use when they characterize someone were all there.

The substance of life is woven from lies, he thought. It's so easy to reinvent yourself, to airbrush out the bad, to highlight the good, to create a new life for yourself and for your new acquaintances.

**NO OTHER OPTION**

How many times do people do that, gloss over jobs they'd rather forget, relationships left in smoking ruin? Or build up and expand something into something else that bore no resemblance to the truth?

It was something special operators did. The ability to do it well was the stamp of the true professional. And the back doors into the corporate and government mainframes the contract hackers had so cunningly fashioned gave the operator elite the tools they needed to take the game to its technological pinnacle.

But it took a certain kind of genius to use the tools well, and Jonny was a genius and a grand master at the game, both on and off the playing field. He'd learned how to play as a boy, glossing over the aftermath of his father's rampages and his mother's helpless bleating that kept him up at night, and left him with dark bags under his eyes, nodding off in the back of the classroom.

Mrs. Morton, the kindest of his three fourth-grade teachers, said, "Why are you so tired all the time?"

"I was up late reading," he'd say, his mouth crinkled in the pseudo-smile he practiced every night, a big grin to hide the flat dark stones his eyes were becoming. Deep down in the reptile brain, part of him remembered how easily she accepted that small lie, and he'd learned then that women would so often accept the lie rather than face the frightening burden of the truth.

He paused at the keyboard and listened for a moment. There was only the distant sound of closing doors and the far-off hum of traffic. He looked into the mirror behind the desk. Deep lines ran down his cheekbones to the corner of his mouth, lines that pulled like marionette wires to expose his large canine teeth when he smiled. His eyes were dark brown, hidden as though beneath colored contacts, so often masking his true feelings, the eyes of a child of rage looking out with dumb fury at the world. It wasn't Fortune's face. But maybe it was the face he'd earned. He rarely allowed himself to think about that. He believed in keeping his mind on the task in front of him at all times. Right now, that was the creation of his legend, backstopping his credit and job references, and integrating those fabricated transactions into the sea of data that flowed around the world, through the back doors the government had created for him and his brother assassins in DOMINANCE RAIN.

**MARCUS WYNNE**

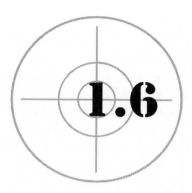

The front room of Nina's condominium overlooked Lake Harriet in the quiet Linden Hills neighborhood of southwest Minneapolis. It was late afternoon, and the paved paths around the lake were filled with people walking, biking, or Rollerblading. Nina was dressed comfortably in hiking shorts and a baggy T-shirt, her long legs curled beneath her in the heavy green overstuffed armchair she'd inherited from her father. "The Big Green Monster" she'd named it as a child, when her father had held her on his lap, the two of them cozy in the cushy depths of the chair. After he died, she brought the armchair home and tucked it into the sunny window nook that looked out over the lake. Sometimes, when she dozed off in the chair, she felt her father's arms wrapped tight around her.

She liked to sit and look out at the water and the people. While she didn't like crowds, she liked to people watch. She told herself it was to keep her observation skills sharp. The comfortable front room, like the rest of her home and her desk at work, was neat, tidy, and organized. Pictures of friends and family dominated the decor. Plain oak bookcases were filled with framed photos and ceramic figures, as was the false mantle above the gas-operated fireplace.

She looked at the silent phone, then stood and stretched like a cat, the long muscles of her legs and arms tingling. The phone rang. She smiled at her precognition and rubbed the tense muscles in the small of her back.

"Hello?"

"Hey, girlfriend," Herb said. He sounded nasal and slightly wheezy. "You're not doing naughty things to yourself are you?"

"No. I wore out the batteries in Mr. Happy. Pick me up a couple, will ya? Double As?"

"You'll just have to go manual till I get by the store," he said, laughing. "Jesus, what I wouldn't give to hear you at Confession."

"Your heart couldn't take it, old man. How are you?"

"I'm good, Nina. Can't get a damn thing done around here, though. Need my partner back. How about you? You need anything? Besides batteries?"

"I'm good to go. I wish they'd get me back on the job. I don't need this."

"Take the time, it's free."

"Whatever." Nina paused. "The shrink came by the other day. Didn't stay long."

"What'd he have to say?"

He's too casual, Nina thought. She shook her head slowly and grinned at the floor, appreciating his barely concealed concern. "Well, he *was* a little worried about me sleeping with my pistol in my mouth . . ."

"Fuck you!"

". . . and I told him I had this unresolved oral fixation 'cause I was never breast-fed . . ."

"Nina . . ."

". . . and I was wondering if that was related to post-shooting syndrome?"

There was a long silence.

"Nina, none of that is funny," Herb said. "This is your job . . ."

"Lighten up, Herbie. I know about my job. I'm the one out here, not you. The only thing bugging me is my caseload's gathering dust while I'm sitting here on my ass."

Herb sighed. His wheeze was even more pronounced.

"Speaking of fat asses," Nina said. "When was the last time you ran farther than the toilet? Your wheeze is getting worse."

"Ah, it's these allergies. Summertime pollen, all that." Herb sounded contrite. "Speaking of asses, hurry up and get through this shooting board bullshit and get yours back here. I'm tired of looking at Malone's."

**MARCUS WYNNE**

"You better watch yourself, old man. I get jealous," Nina said, laughing. "Just remember who saved your tired old ass."

"You," Herb said. His voice turned flat and serious. "You did."

Later, Nina walked slowly around Lake Harriet. Normally she'd be running two laps around the lake, but today she lacked the energy for a run. She strolled along, hands jammed in her pockets, a blue fanny pack at her waist hiding a Sig-Sauer P-230 stoked with Corbon +Ps, her badge and ID, a cell phone and her pager. She ignored the appreciative looks the passing men gave her. They were mostly sun-tanned and healthy yuppies, biking, blading, or running, calling out "Left! Passing on your left!" as they zoomed by.

She stopped near the band shell, then walked out on the pier to watch the sailboats tacking back and forth on the far side of the lake. The ring of anchor chains and the creaking pier sounded loud in her ears. A lone gull squawked overhead. For a moment she felt disoriented, as though she were looking through the wrong end of a telescope that zoomed the whole world down into a dime-sized vision of Dan MacDouglas falling backward, the shock and surprise on his face as the last firings of his brain registered that he was, quite suddenly, dead.

Killing a suspect in the line of duty was a frequent topic of discussion at both the Federal Law Enforcement Training Center when she'd gone through as a rookie criminal investigator for Treasury, and the Minneapolis Police Academy, where she'd gone through after she quit the Feds and returned to Minneapolis to look after her father. She didn't participate in the macho bluster that the men took comfort in. Some of the other women bought into that, out of some mistaken sense that they had to talk and act like one of the guys in order to be a cop. Then, as now, Nina went her own way in all things, in her carefully preserved private life as well as on the job. She'd made up her mind a long time ago that her life, her partner's life, and the lives of innocents were worth more than any violent dirtbag. She'd made peace with herself about killing a long time before she had to.

That didn't necessarily make it easier, though she was surprised at just how little it affected her. After all the lectures and talks about post-traumatic stress, she'd expected something more. She didn't feel sad, she didn't feel mad, she didn't feel depressed. After the initial rush of adrenaline, she only felt ... satisfied. Satisfied that she and Herb weren't hurt. Satisfied that her training had served her well in the test. And satisfied that she'd killed that sick, evil son of a bitch. She'd never be able to say that out loud, except maybe to Herb. He'd been both surprised and dismayed by what he saw on her face during the shooting. But he was her partner.

She smiled down at the reflection of herself in the green water beneath the pier: a tall, athletic young woman who might be a stockbroker, an accountant, a business executive—or a blooded street cop. Nina liked that about herself; she liked to surprise people. It preserved the distance she liked to keep. She especially relished how often male cops underestimated her because of her looks. More than one had been surprised by her performance, and many of the other women officers looked to her for an example. She liked that, too. Nina believed in mentorship. It was how things got done, how people got ahead. She'd had good mentors in her life.

Uncle Ray was one, her dad's tough and wiry younger brother, an ATF agent who avoided the FBI agents who hung with his brother, a street agent who was proud of his undercover work breaking up arms smuggling rings in the outlaw biker gangs. His stories had taught her the difference between a cop and an agent, and had been one influence in her decision to quit the Feds. He'd eaten his gun one bad night, when something out of his past came up in him, not long after she'd found out about Dad's cancer.

Nina turned and walked away from the reflections in the water and the memories they raised. Her quick footfalls sounded hollow on the old planking of the pier. Ripples of water flowed out from the pilings like whispers in an empty room.

She walked along the lake, then cut across the trolley tracks and up the hill into the two-block-square shopping area that anchored the Linden Hills neighborhood at the intersection of Forty-fourth Street and Upton. She waved to Steve the butcher when she passed the meat shop, peeked in at the children playing in the front window of the toy store, and stopped at Sebastian Joe's Ice Cream Café for a coffee. The tree-shaded courtyard hadn't filled up yet, so she was able to find a table near the street to sit with her paper and French Roast. She became restless after a few minutes; she often did when she thought of Ray. She took her coffee and paper and walked down Forty-fourth Street toward her condo. Halfway down the block, in front of the old brownstone building across the street from where Old Joe, the Italian immigrant retired from General Mills, kept his lush garden, a sign said ONE BEDROOM APARTMENT FOR RENT.

Won't take long for that to go, Nina thought. Apartments didn't last long around here.

Curled in the Green Monster, Nina sipped her coffee and turned the newspaper pages with increasing violence. For once the *Star & Tribune* had dealt evenhandedly with a police shooting, even though the reporter dwelt more on the perceived issues of a woman working sex crimes instead of the issues of a cop taking out a dirtbag in a justifiable shooting. She threw the paper on the floor.

She knew what she needed and where she could get it.

She pulled a light flannel shirt over her T-shirt and went out the door. She got into her four-year-old Jeep Cherokee and drove around the Chain of Lakes the back way into downtown, past the Walker sculpture garden and Loring Park onto Hennepin, then over into the northeast to Torrone's Bar and Grill. She went straight through the back door marked EMPLOYEES ONLY into the bar and slid onto her favorite stool beside the waitress station.

Years as a construction worker and amateur bodybuilder had given Joe Torrone—the sixty-year-old owner, bartender, and occasional bouncer—a powerful frame that even at sixty was still knotted with intimidating muscle. He turned his pit-bull head stiffly and grinned at his favorite customer.

"Yep, the most beautiful girl in the world, and she has to walk into my bar," he said in a Bogart imitation bizarrely skewed by his thick northern Minnesota accent.

"We'll always have Paris, Joe," Nina said. She loved this old man who reminded her so much of her father. She leaned on the bar and scooted her stool closer, twining her legs around the stool braces as she did when she was a little girl sitting with her father in this same bar.

"It's good to see ya, baby girl," Joe growled. He looked down to hide his pleasure. "Been too long. Ya been to Confession?"

"Why?" Nina said. She was surprised by the chill in her voice. "Should I have been?"

**NO OTHER OPTION**

Joe froze. A bar towel dangled forgotten in his shovel-sized hands. "What am I saying, I wasn't thinking. Jeez, Nina, I'm sorry," he said. "That's not what I meant, that thing what happened . . . me and my big mouth. Empty head. Jeez, Nina, I'm sorry, I didn't even want to say nothing."

"Just get me a drink, will you, Joe?" Nina said. She forced a laugh. "Can't a girl just get a drink around here?"

Joe looked at her for a long moment, then ducked his head and hurried to mix her a dark Ron Rico and diet Coke on the rocks. "Yeah sure, you betcha. On the house for the most beautiful woman in it."

"You're doing better, sweet mouth man."

Nina savored the sweetness of the strong rum and Coke while she looked around. Torrone's was a blue-collar workingman's bar. Her father and his FBI cronies would meet here after work or raids. He often brought her in to have a Coke and one of Joe's homemade bratwurst at lunchtime. They'd watched ball games here, threw popcorn at the TV when the Twins screwed up, carried on and had lots of laughs. It was Joe Torrone who organized the food and drink for her father's wake, and big Joe had been a pallbearer at both Uncle Ray's and her father's funerals. After she moved back from DC, she began to frequent the bar again. Torrone's had passed the torch as the prime cop bar, so she rarely ran into anyone she knew on the job. Joe kept the riffraff out, so she didn't have to worry about running into "professional acquaintances."

She came for the occasional drink, to watch the games with Joe, and for an infrequent uncomplicated date if she found somebody she liked. Most of the men she dated dropped out after a while. If they didn't know already, they learned not to gossip about her in Torrone's. Joe was known to slap men off barstools for off-color remarks to or about ladies—and as he would tell anyone who cared to listen, Nina was first and foremost in his circle of esteemed ladies.

There were a few other men and women in the bar who waved or nodded in recognition at Nina. A couple of tables were occupied by old retirees from General Mills, Pillsbury, or Honeywell, old-timers from the mills who came in to play dominoes and reminisce endlessly over cheap pitchers of beer and the good, simple food that came out of the small back kitchen. Standing at the end of the bar was one loner, a young guy in his late twenties, in rough work clothes, his shoulder-length hair unbound around a pale, thin face. He caught Nina's eye and smiled, shyly.

Nina liked the shy look. "Who's that guy, Joe?"

Joe pursed his lips. "Works up the street at the machine shop."

Nina studied Joe before she spoke. "You know I love you best and most, Joe. But you're not my daddy."

"What do you see in these guys, Nina?"

"Just what I want to, Joe," Nina said. "Just what I want to."

She picked up her drink and moved down the bar to sit beside the young machinist.

**NO OTHER OPTION**

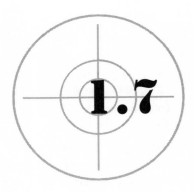

"What are you thinking about?" Jed said, drumming his fingers on the wheel of his unmarked Crown Victoria. He goosed the gas, then braked, inching along in the Beltway's bumper-to-bumper afternoon traffic.

Dale shrugged and stared out the side window at the other cars alongside. Two lanes over, a young blond girl in a battered Honda Accord dug first clockwise, then counterclockwise in her ear with a ring-festooned finger, bobbing her head to loud Snoop Doggy Dogg.

"Tell me about it," Jed said. "Anything's better than rush hour radio."

"You hunt?" Dale said.

Jed grinned, keeping his eyes on the Camry in front of him. "Is the Pope Catholic? You?"

"Not really. I was thinking of the first time I went."

"Your daddy take you?"

"No," Dale said. "Jonny did."

They were out in California, in the mountains near the old Hunter-Leggett Army Base south of Fort Ord, abandoned after the demobilization of the Seventh Light Infantry Division. They were using the old facilities to train and refresh on their small-unit patrol and immediate action drills. The team stood down for the day; the other operators headed for the showers and fresh grilled steaks after.

"Let's take a ride," Jonny said.

Dale thought it was a quick run for beer. Instead, they drove over the green rolling hills into the Santa Cruz Mountains, around the base of Mount Umunuhm, topped with the abandoned structure of a distant early warning radar from the fifties and sixties, and through the small town of New Almaden, a former mercury mining town where the raw red dirt that hid silver mercury was ripped from the mountain sides with gigantic water sluices. It was a rough town. Small houses were separated by yards fenced off with twisted wire strung between rusty steel pickets. Among the houses were double-wide trailers fronted by rough poured concrete steps, where sullen, tired women sat and stared at the men, dressed in worn Lee jeans and ripped heavy flannel shirts, who worked on the cars blocked up in the yards. The central downtown district was only three blocks long. Two stop signs and you were through it, and onto the narrow roads twisting like a broken-backed snake through the dense scrub oak, manzanita, and juniper pine that matted the red dirt hills like three-day-old beard.

"I grew up around here," Jonny said, breaking the long silence. He pulled the rental car off the narrow two-lane blacktop into a pullout where a dirt fire trail branched away from the main road.  The pullout was littered with crushed twelve-pack boxes for Miller Genuine Draft, condoms and wrappers, a lone pink sock. Jonny shut off the engine and got out. He opened the trunk and took out the M-4 carbines they'd been training with and locked a fully loaded thirty-round magazine into each one.

"Let's go," he said.

Dale took the rifle. "What are we doing?"

"Hunting."

"This is illegal. We can't hunt with these."

"Up here, nobody cares," Jonny said. "The only cop around here I used to hunt with when I was a kid. He knows who and how I am. We won't have any problems. C'mon. Let's go."

Jonny set off down the fire trail, his carbine carried casually in one hand, stepping long and quiet on the packed dirt. Dale looked at the car, then the empty two-lane country road. He scratched his nose, then followed slowly behind Jonny. It pissed him off, how Jonny didn't even look back but knew that Dale was coming. The woods seemed full of silence as they left the road behind. Behind him the engine ticked as it cooled. The warmth of the summer sun filtered down between the trees. A slight breeze cooled his skin.

Jonny knelt beside the trail where the soil was turned up. "Looky here," he said. He took a small twig and poked at some large knotted feces, still fresh, in the middle of a torn up patch plowed by many small hooves. "Pigs, about six or seven of them." He looked down into the small canyon beneath the fire trail and picked out a narrow footpath. "Probably bedded down right now."

"Pigs?" Dale said.

"Feral pigs. Crossbreeds between the old Russian boars the Spanish brought over here to hunt back in the old Conquistador days and regular domestic pigs that got loose. They adapted real well to this climate and terrain. They're the perfect pest. Around here they're nuisance game, trash game. There's no limit and no season—you can kill as many as you want. All day, all night. These fuckers will make you fight, too."

"What are we doing here?"

"The old boars . . . they're smart. They'll hunt you if you piss them off, believe it." Jonny nodded in satisfaction. His eyes were bright. "We'll come back, closer to dark."

It was like he wasn't really here, Dale thought. He could be talking to himself. He started when Jonny said, "Yeah."

"Yeah, what?" Dale said.

"No worries, bro," Jonny said. He stood and worked one knee slowly, back and forth. "I'll show you what to do. We'll do just fine, you and me. Just like we always do."

"What are we doing? Firing up pork chops? What is all this?"

"Doing our business. You'll see. I'll show you."

They drove back to New Almaden and had a beer and a greasy hamburger in a worn-down bar, a ramshackle old storefront with the glass partly boarded up and a haphazard collection of rickety booths and chipped wooden tables surrounded by vinyl-backed chairs. The two of them ate in silence. Jonny ignored one older man who nodded to him when he came into the bar. After they ate, they got back in the car and drove to the tiny market three blocks down. Jonny drove around back, then rummaged in the garbage bins until he found a half case of wilted lettuce, gone brown and soft.

"This'll do," he said, putting the box in the trunk.

**MARCUS WYNNE**

They drove back to the pullout. The sun was low in the sky, casting long shadows beneath the trees. Dale followed Jonny back down the fire trail. He was always following Jonny somewhere. Always in his shadow. Jonny strode ahead, his M-4 in one hand, the waxed cardboard lettuce case in the other. He paused, knelt, then followed the narrow, barely perceptible game path down the hillside into the small canyon below the fire trail. He went halfway up the far side of the canyon, busting brush, then entered into an open area surrounded by several tall old oaks with thick heavy branches.

Jonny threw the rotten lettuce into the grassy open area, tearing the heads apart and spreading the rotten bits near the trail. He gestured for Dale to follow him. Jonny stopped beside an old oak tree, its trunk scarred and gnarled. He bent and cupped his hands together to make a stirrup for Dale to climb up.

"Get up," Jonny said.

"What are we . . ."

"Get up."

Dale stepped up and grabbed the lower branches. Someone had nailed old pieces of two by four as a crude ladder to get halfway up the tree where a rough platform of plywood and two by four beams made a precarious seat. Dale settled himself cautiously, his M-4 sling looped around his neck, a spare magazine in his field jacket pocket.

Jonny climbed nimbly up into a tree directly across from Dale. From their vantage points, they could see up and down the length of the little canyon, and overlooked the open area strewn with rotten lettuce. Dale saw that they had great fields of fire, interlocking together across the open kill zone.

They waited in silence. Darkness fell. The long shadows grew together and knitted themselves into a shroud of darker grays and blacks. Dale's eyes adjusted and he began to pick out details as his peripheral vision came into play in the gloom. He watched Jonny watching their kill zone. Jonny had a gift for stillness that was unusual in a door kicker. Most assaulters had an aggressiveness and a need for action, the need for speed, unlike the snipers who could lie still, scope welded to their eyes for hours, days if necessary. Jonny had a loner's streak unusual in the more gregarious assaulters and more common among the snipers. Some of the other operators muttered about Jonny being high and mighty, but none of them disputed his ability.

**NO OTHER OPTION**

And once Ray Dalton had plucked the best from the best for his secretive special project, Dale found himself working closely with the legendary Jonny Maxwell. For the youngest operator to make the grade for Delta, to be handpicked for the most tightly compartmented special project in the U.S. arsenal and thrust into a close partnership with one of the top operators in the world was heady stuff. Or so he'd thought in the beginning. Beirut, Bosnia, Iraq, Kuwait, Guatemala . . . he'd been and done. Made his bones. At Jonny's side. Or as his shadow.

He still didn't know what to make of Jonny. They were friends, yeah, brothers in a way that made sense only if you didn't speak of it. But he'd never gotten far beneath the shell of competency and aggressive leadership that Jonny kept up. No one had. It wasn't just being private—many operators were private people who enjoyed their downtime. But Jonny never seemed to fully join in with the laughter and the easy camaraderie of the brotherhood he was such a respected member of. Despite what some of the others said, Dale didn't think it was because Jonny thought he was better than everybody else. That he was better was self-evident. No, it was as though he were hesitant about joining in, hesitant about dropping his guard—even with men he trusted his life to, and who in turn trusted their lives to him.

Dale was stirred by slow movement beneath him. He felt the adrenaline well up inside him. The first pig entered the clearing, moving slowly, its absurdly small legs and hooves daintily stepping, pausing at the edge of the clearing and then forward to the grass to snort and root at the rotten lettuce. Two more followed. One was quite large, with pale tusks that gleamed in the dim light.

He was surprised by how silently they moved. Like shadows. The only sound they made was the clack and gnash of their tusks and teeth as they rooted up the sod. There were at least three more, lingering in the shadows at the edge of the clearing. He looked up to see Jonny regarding him from his tree stand. Jonny was wearing his Walkman headset strung around his neck. He had a strange smile on his face as he looked at Dale.

Jonny raised his hand, palm out, the hand signal for attention. He pointed two fingers at the pigs rooting below, then brought his M-4 to his shoulder and braced his legs against the tree branches supporting his stand. Dale watched him track the muzzle slowly from one pig to the next, taking his time with target selection. Jonny looked up at Dale and gestured for him to raise his rifle. It was a strange and new sensation for Dale; he had never hunted before. In all honesty, he hadn't yet killed anything other than some rabbits and chickens during the survival training in the Operator's Course. He raised his rifle and noticed that the glowing tritium dot on his front sight was trembling with his heartbeat. The sudden whiplash snap of a round going off surprised him. There was a steady cadence of single shots. Jonny was systematically putting one round as quickly as possible into each of the pigs.

The pig Dale had been aiming at leaped straight up and whirled around in midair, gnashing its teeth. He fired once, twice, three times. At least one of his shots threw up dirt beneath the pig, but others hit it. It staggered a few steps and fell.

Dale's ears rang from the hammer of gunshots. The new smell of burnt gunpowder and hot metal overrode the stench of rot that hung foglike in the clearing. The dead pigs were huddled, still black shapes on the grass below. Jonny climbed down from his stand, and Dale carefully climbed down and joined him.

Jonny covered the still forms with his weapon as though they might still pose some threat. Dale knelt beside one dead pig, curious about the effect the 5.56mm full metal jacket rounds had. The small bullet had entered just behind the shoulder, tumbled and ripped great gouts of flesh and bone out. The destruction was all out of proportion to the size of the bullet.

"Impressive," Dale said. He'd never seen for himself what the M-193 rounds they carried did to flesh. The operators shunned the newer SS-109 round, which didn't tumble and break up and inflict damage the way the older round did.

"This is what it's like," Jonny said. "Dead pork. Easy. You'll know about that soon enough. We'll be into the shit soon, all of us. That's what we do for good old Ray. You'll be lighting them up and bam, then it's all over. Just the smell and a lot of dead pork." He nudged one pig with his boot. "The killer ape likes the smell."

"What are you talking about?"

"Killer apes, Dale. You, me, all the boys. We're the best of all the killer apes. One long line of monkey-fucking ancestors stretching

**NO OTHER OPTION**

back to one big bull ape with a club in his hand, putting it upside his opponent's head, dragging the women back to the cave . . . that's why we do what we do."

Dale tugged at first one ear, then the other, as though he could pull out the tinny sound that lingered there. "What's killing pigs got to do with it?"

"We're predators," Jonny said. His eyes narrowed as he went on. "Most people try to fool themselves. Say it's not a nice thing to be. We're all children of killer apes. That's what's underneath the nicey-nice mask we put out for the world. Deep down in the brain, someplace down there in all the folds, there's this part that loves this. This is what we were made to do." He kicked one of the pig carcasses. "This isn't sport. This is our task. Ridding the world of pests. These aren't for eating. These are for killing."

"I thought you ate what you killed. I thought you were a sportsman."

"There's hunting, and then there's hunting. I like the one kind, the stalk, the careful planning, the satisfaction of the kill. Those you earn. And then there's this . . . it's different. No better or no worse. It's our job. Right here, this is our job. Do it efficiently. This is how you need to train for it. You live the life, you walk the talk, you got to have the lessons soaking in all the time. Everything we do is training for the hunter, for the aware man. We live on that level. That's why we were picked. That's why we're the ones who'll be doing what needs to be done."

Dale tensed as though against an imminent blow. "This is training to you?"

Jonny pulled his lips back in a grimace that showed his canines. "I just told you. You think I talk to anybody like this? I want you to see this, to know this. This is part of my training for you. Do you see the difference between what we just did and the ambush drills we just spent a week practicing? You need to feel it, have the emotions, know what it's like outside of training. No earplugs, no blanks, no rinky-dink-leg-grunt wannabes who fall down when we go bang. This is the real thing. This . . . is . . . it."

Dale stepped back. "The real thing is when we have a mission and a green light. I listen to you, man, and I try to understand. Why don't you just tell me things instead of running me around like I'm a dumbass?"

"Because some things you don't get by talking about it," Jonny said. "Some things you just need to do. Jesus, how hard is this to get?"

"Whatever," Dale said. "I'm through here. Are we going?"

Jonny looked down and shook his head from side to side. He slid his headset up over his ears and touched the START button of his cassette player. "Yep."

"Then let's go." Dale began to turn away, then said, "What are you listening to?"

"Bitch music."

"That was some of the principal evidence against him at the trial," Dale said. He stared out the side window at the withered trees beside the freeway. "He tape-recorded some of the attacks, the . . . rapes. He kept them in a little cassette box. All of us saw them at one time or another. He was always taping different music off CDs, stuff like that. We all had Walkmans or Discmans to take on planes with us or kill time with in hotels. We had covert radio gear designed to fit inside the Sony bodies, we used those a lot."

Jed inched the car along at exactly seven miles an hour. "You ever go hunting again?"

"I went with Jonny and a couple of the guys out to Montana, later. Right after the Storm. That was different. I liked the walking, up in the hills. It's beautiful country. I didn't get anything, but I didn't try real hard."

Jed glanced over at Dale. "Something change for you after you got some combat time?"

Dale turned away from the window and looked at Jed with surprise. "I don't like to kill unless I have to. I didn't want to think something had rubbed off on me from Jonny."

Jed shrugged. "I still like my hunting. After I got back from Vietnam there was a short while where it seemed as though I'd lost all pleasure in it. But I got over it. There's something pure about a good hunt. When I was a boy in South Carolina, my daddy used to take me out. Those were some of the best days of my life, those days out in the woods with him."

"I like being outside. I like the woodcraft. I just never really felt the need to kill anything. Nothing against it . . . just wasn't something I enjoyed."

**NO OTHER OPTION**

"Different strokes for different folks. I like to eat venison, all sorts of game. I kill to eat and I eat what I kill." Jed rolled down the window and spat, narrowly missing the bumper of the BMW beside them. The BMW driver, a frazzled-looking woman, gave him a dirty look. "That kind of thinking, that Jonny Maxwell kind of thinking, that's something dark and nasty. It dirties what is clean and good. It's the rationalization of a sick mind. I saw a lot of that in Vietnam. There were some guys who got to be like your buddy Maxwell. They thrived on it. It drove them." He shook his head in sharp negation. "No. You let those snakes in your head and they'll take you over. Don't get yourself all confused trying to sort it all out. It's not that hard, what we do. What we do is what we do. Thinking about it too much slows you down when you can't afford that. If you have to think about it too much, then it's time to get out."

"You ever think about getting out?"

"Fair question," Jed said. He nodded. "I thought about it for a while when I got back. I bummed around, thought about buying me a fishing boat, do something different like that. Jo Anne, she's my bride, she was the one who pointed out that I wasn't happy unless I was being of service. Of use. That's what got me back on track. That's the difference between guys like you and me and guys like Maxwell. We serve others. We think about other people. Maxwell, all he ever thought of was himself."

"He's not that easy to peg," Dale said. "There's more to him than I ever knew and I worked with him and trusted my back to him for seven years. I never really knew anything about him and I counted him as a friend. And he counted me as one. Maybe his only one. He looked out for me. Other people, too. He helped me out, showed me the ropes, covered me when we first got into the shit over in . . . overseas." He paused. "He thought about other people. Not many, but some."

There was an edge in Jed's voice. "Did you say that at his trial, too?"

Dale turned away and looked out the window. "Maybe someday you'll find yourself in the same position. We'll see what you say." He paused. "Yeah. I said that, too."

"If you think that, maybe you shouldn't be here. You need to get your head past this if you're going to be a help instead of a hindrance. I won't have any unspoken agendas, you understand me?

**MARCUS WYNNE**

You want to help your friend, help us find him and bring him back in without any more people losing their lives," Jed said. His tone was harsh, cutting through the fog Dale felt.

"I know what I have to do, Jed. And I'll do it. Don't worry about me."

"I won't worry because I'll be watching you. You make that kind of mistake and you're gone. *Comprende?*"

"I'm the only chance you've got of finding him. And I will."

"We'll see, won't we?"

**NO OTHER OPTION**

**1.8**

Jonny Maxwell and Jeff Winger, a rental property agent, stood behind a converted brownstone on West Forty-fourth Street, three doors down from the Sebastian Joe's coffee shop in the Linden Hills neighborhood of southwest Minneapolis. Less than a hundred yards from where they stood, the bike and jogging paths ringing Lake Harriet were crowded with people.

"I'm Billy Martin," Jonny said. He shook the rental agent's hand firmly. "Nice to meet you, Jeff."

"Hi, Billy. Glad you could make it." Jeff Winger was tall and cadaverous, with a breathy voice. "You work for Northwest, you said?"

"I'm a flight attendant. Used to be in customer service, though I guess I still am, in a way."

"You must travel to a lot of places."

"Yeah, I've got good seniority."

"Well, let's take a look."

Jeff led Jonny through the back security door into a small hallway. There was a numbered door on either side, Five to the left, Six to the right. The rental agent opened the door to Apartment Five with a key selected from a large ring. It only took a moment for Jonny to walk through the small living room, kitchen, bathroom, and one bedroom.

"I guess I'm paying for location, huh?" Jonny said.

"You *are* in a great location. But you knew that already. Apartments just don't stay vacant down here. We never advertise, just put the sign up front and whammo—we fill the place." Jeff rattled his keys for emphasis.

"That's why I called as soon as I saw the sign. This is a great neighborhood. At least I remember it that way." Jonny turned slowly in the front room. One window looked out on the alley, the other on the small garden and lawn directly behind the building. "What's this building like? The people?"

"Nice people . . . couple of graphic designers upstairs, an environmental consultant and his wife, couple of college boys above you . . . they're quiet, though. Small building, but people pretty much mind their own business here. Everybody gets along. We don't put up with troublemakers."

"You won't have any trouble with me," Jonny said. He touched the tip of his tongue to his upper lip. "I just like to know, since I travel so much . . . it's still pretty safe around here, no break-ins or burglaries or anything? Since I'm on the ground floor . . ."

"There's never been a burglary in this building," Jeff said. "Even with all the foot traffic on this street during the summer, we don't get any problems. It's a nice, quiet, upscale neighborhood."

"I guess so, if you're getting $625 a month for a ground-level one-bedroom."

"That's just a little below median for this neighborhood, and that's only because the building is a little older . . ."

Billy Martin's rental application showed that he'd been a Detroit-based employee of Northwest Airlines for the last five years. The company's employment office, after checking their computer where Jonny had deftly inserted the new record, would verify if asked that Billy had just been reassigned to Minneapolis. Jonny left $1000 cash as a rental deposit, which left a big hole in his limited funds. He'd have to deal with that now. That meant a trip to Milwaukee, six hours east, to dig into one of the stashes he'd scattered across the country for emergencies. This wasn't the sort of emergency he'd anticipated, but his advance preparations and the contacts he'd developed would serve him well.

He drove to the airport, the few things he'd accumulated—computer, clothes, and toiletries—hidden beneath a blanket in the 4Runner. He went to the Remote Parking Lot and cruised slowly as though looking for a spot. Of the several 4Runners parked there, two

**NO OTHER OPTION**

were black like Chad Bergh's. One was spotted with dirt and had been parked for a while. Jonny found a spot nearby and took a screwdriver from the glove box. Then he caught the shuttle bus to the main terminal. He wandered through the terminal, browsed in a bookstore, and bought a *Combat Handguns* magazine.

"Could I have a bag for this?" he asked the girl clerk waiting on him.

"Yes, sir. Here you are," she said, handing him a flat plastic bag.

From a pay phone near the bookstore, he called Chad Bergh's answering machine. There was a message from Citibank and one from a girl named Molly who said she'd missed Chad in class. The ATM machine beside the pay phone advanced Chad Bergh's card another $500 in cash. Then Jonny sat in the Burger King, ate a sandwich and sipped coffee while he watched the sun go down over the runways. Once it was fully dark, he caught the remote parking shuttle back to the parking lot. He walked through the parking lot, the bookstore bag swinging in his hand. He stopped by one of the 4Runners he'd spotted earlier, then knelt quickly and unscrewed the plates and dropped them into the plastic bag. Glancing occasionally at the guard shack near the exit, he repeated the operation several times, replacing some of the plates with those he'd taken from other 4Runners while keeping others. He went back to his car and drove out of the lot, paying in cash. Jonny followed the airport perimeter road to Interstate 495, then to the intersection of I-94, where he headed east, across the gentle rolling hills of Wisconsin, toward the lights of Milwaukee.

Darrin "Snake" Pissolt overlapped the barstool creaking under his 260 pounds. His huge arms flexed like hairy, sunburned hams as he sipped from a bottle of Leinenkugel's beer lost in his fist. The sleeveless denim vest he wore was blackened and stiff with grease, punctuated with ceramic Nazi and biker pins and military decorations. The back of the vest bore the colors of Satan's Outlaws, one of the few outlaw biker clubs that had the organization and ruthlessness of the Hell's Angels.

"I don't know you, dude," Snake said. "I don't think I want to, and I *know* you don't want to get to know me."

Jonny smiled from beneath his mirrored wraparound sunglasses and three days of stubble. His young hipster look had disappeared under several days of fresh beard, a ragged muscle tank top, dirty Levi's, a greasy baseball cap, and thick-soled combat boots. He sipped slowly at his beer and looked around Max's Lounge. Two other Satan's Outlaws, deep in conversation, sat at a corner table. A few other bikers, wannabes or loners, sat evenly spaced at the bar, giving each other plenty of room. Two hard-looking peroxide blondes, who'd logged too much time on the back of a scooter, sat at the end of the bar and smoked cigarettes.

"No, you don't know me," Jonny said. "I know something about you, though. LRRP, 173d Airborne. Ia Drang. You worked for Iron Mike Daczyn. He was the only man you were ever afraid of. You got a partner name of Doyle Norton doing life in Leavenworth. He told me you were the meanest motherfucker that ever lived, and there was no one else he'd want to watch his back in a hot LZ. He said you'd do anything for a brother, and that he was the closest brother you'd ever have."

Snake turned on his stool and looked down on Jonny. "He'll always be my brother. Who the fuck are you?"

"I'm a pilgrim, bro. A loner looking for a little help from the Brotherhood."

Snake called to the bartender, a hunched man with the watchful eyes of an ex-con. "Yo, Terry! I need the key."

The bartender nodded and reached under the bar and brought up a wooden dowel with a key tied to it with a piece of frayed string. He slid the dowel down the bar into Snake's hand. Snake stood up, all six feet five inches of him, and moved with the ponderous grace of a big man across the gritty floor.

"C'mon," he said to Jonny over his shoulder.

Jonny followed the big biker to the back of the bar, where Snake used the key to enter a stockroom. He led Jonny around the stacked cases and kegs of beer to another, smaller room in the back. A soiled mattress lay on the floor. A grimy sofa was pressed into the corner; a table with one chair and a telephone resting on the chair were against the back wall.

"Sit," Snake said. He sprawled out along the sofa, and lit a long thin stogie he plucked from inside his vest. "Want a smoke?"

"Yeah," Jonny said.

Snake tossed him a cellophane-wrapped cigar and a lighter. The lighter was an old Zippo, the chipped and worn crest of the 173d Airborne Brigade soldered on its side. Jonny flicked the lighter to life, puffed the cigar into a good flame, then tossed the lighter back.

"History," Jonny said.

Snake nodded. "There it is. We're going to talk now. You first."

"Heard from Norton lately?"

"I might have."

"He mention a problem he had inside with the niggers?"

Snake leaned forward and rested his elbows on his knees. His eyes were sunk like gun barrels into creased sockets. "You the one he mentioned helped him out on that?"

"I might be... if you'd heard from him."

"You might be a cop don't know he's dead yet," Snake said, blowing smoke rings at the yellow stained ceiling.

"Would Doyle tell a cop about what Iron Mike did to your mustache?"

Snake touched his upper lip, then grinned. "Not even if they held an iron to his balls," he said. "You're bringing a world of shit to my door, bro. I'll do what I can. Once. For Doyle and what you did for him. After that, I don't ever want to see you again. Understand?"

"Sure," Jonny said.

"What do you need?"

"A gun. And somebody to run a little errand for me. Pick up a package I got someplace. Somebody trustworthy and low profile."

"What kind of package?"

"Nothing hot. Stuff I need. There won't be anybody watching it. Nobody but me knows where it is. But it don't hurt to be careful in my circumstances."

Snake laughed. "No shit? In your circumstances? Fucking A right, your circumstances. That's all you need?"

"Pretty much."

"Gun's no problem. You got any preferences?"

"High capacity 9mm or a .45."

"I got a Glock 19, a .357 Smith Model 19, and a Beretta 92F. Any one of them, two reloads, box of ammo, a grand even."

"I got $500 now. I can give you the rest when I get my package."

"Let's see your money."

Jonny pulled out a small roll of bills, peeled off five one-hundred dollar bills and held them up. "Let's see your shooter."

Snake slid his hand down in between the cushions of the sofa and produced a Smith & Wesson Model 19 revolver with a two-and-a-half-inch barrel. The copper and lead noses of the hollow points gleamed from the cylinder as Snake pointed the revolver at Jonny.

"Bang, bang," Snake said. "You're dead."

Jonny took his wraparounds off and, smiling slightly, gazed steadily at Snake. "Where's the Glock?" he said.

"When I get the rest of the money. I'll rent you this .357 and two speed-loaders for $500. That'll be your deposit on the Glock."

Jonny shrugged. The test wasn't worth blowing the whole deal over. He took the revolver from Snake, popped the cylinder, and examined the fresh Federal hollow points. Snake handed him two Safariland speed-loaders bristling with hollow points and a soft padded case for the revolver.

"Girl I know," Snake said, settling back expansively into his sofa. "She'll do for the package pickup. Little hooker, works in a strip club downtown. Known her for a long time. Cost you another $500."

"When can we set that up?"

"Couple of hours. She'll be working. We can go by and check out the show. Nice tits." Snake yawned. "Anything else you're going to need?"

Jonny tucked the revolver into his waistband and pulled his tank top over it. He tucked the speed-loaders into his right-hand pocket.

"Yeah," he said. "I need something."

"What's that?"

After Jonny told him, Snake was silent. He stared at Jonny. Then he burst out laughing.

Sherry Stivers licked her glossy red lips and pushed out her impressive breasts, the best that money could buy, at the young black man behind the counter of the Acme Storage Facility in downtown Milwaukee.

"Well, my boyfriend?" she said. "He wants me to pick up some things for him? I just don't want to be messing around in any dirty old stuff, you know? Would you be a sweetheart and let me into this unit?"

Ollie Davis couldn't look away from her breasts. "Sure, I'll be doing that for you. No need for no woman to be getting herself dirty messing round in all those old boxes. Sure, I'll do that for you."

He took the slip of paper she handed him and looked up the locker number. "Nobody been calling on this for some time," he said. "It's down here, you come with me."

Ollie went down an aisle lined on both side with padlocked wire cages, each as tall as a man and about half that across, with heavy wooden and wire doors.

"You got his key, right?" he said, stopping in front of locker 47-B.

"Sure do," Sherry said.

She handed Ollie a lone brass key on an old key ring. It fit the big Master padlock holding the hasp in place. Inside the big locker were several large packing boxes, double sealed with tape; a rusty old bicycle, the Schwinn Classic; a couple of open boxes filled with old magazines and newspapers; and on top of a stack of boxes farthest  from the door was one box set off from the others by the faded and curling red ribbon wrapped around it.

"That's it, there," she said. "The one with the ribbon."

Ollie took it down, dusted it off with a bandanna he pulled from his rear pocket. "There you go, pretty lady. Don't feel like too much is in it."

"Oh, thank you! It's just some old legal papers and stuff that he needs."

"It's got a little more weight than that to it. You want to open it up and be sure?"

"No, you know how you men are. He'll want to do that himself, I'm sure. Thanks! You're a doll!"

Sherry walked away briskly, the brass brads on the pockets of her tight Levi's winking at Ollie as he followed her, shaking his head and grinning in wonder, out into the front office. Sherry went out through the front office, down a flight of stairs, and back out onto the street. She started down the block, but Jonny intercepted her only a few steps from the door.

"Hey, Sherry," he said.

**MARCUS WYNNE**

"Hey, dude!" the stripper said. "I got your box here. Let's go find Snake."

"I'll take it, Sherry. I got my car over here," he said, pointing at the 4Runner. "We'll ride over to Snake."

"Whatever." Sherry handed Jonny the package. He handed her $500, then tucked an extra $100 bill into her tight pants pocket.

"For your trouble," he said.

"No trouble at all, cowboy." She took Jonny's arm and walked him across the street to the 4Runner. Jonny opened the passenger door and held her elbow as she got in, waiting until she was settled to gently shut the door.

"You're such a gentleman!" she said.

Jonny smiled at her, his eyes invisible behind his mirrored sunglasses. He drove down the street and around the corner to where Snake sat parked on his bike. He slowed to a stop and let Sherry out.

"Tell Snake I'll hook up with him a little later," he said, studying her body.

Sherry grinned at him. "Whatever. I do okay?"

"You did great, honey."

"Nobody's called me honey in a long time," Sherry said. She licked her lips and arched her back. "You need anything else, you got my number, okay?"

"Sure. Maybe I'll see you at Snake's place later?"

She smirked. "Yeah, I'll be there. He always gets romantic, when I bring him some money."

"How about you?" Jonny asked. "You get romantic, somebody brings you some money?"

"Oh, yeah. I'm real romantic."

Jonny laughed. "We'll see. Later on. Tell Snake I'll see him later."

"Okay, bye-bye!" Sherry ran across the street to Snake, the thin sheaf of bills sticking out between her fingers as she waved good-bye to Jonny.

Jonny drove away from downtown toward the airport. There was a small park there, on the perimeter of the airport, where people sat in their cars or on the small lawn or at the picnic tables to eat their lunches and watch the airplanes boom by overhead. People came and went, and paid little attention to anything except the airplanes

**NO OTHER OPTION**

and their lunches. Jonny backed into a parking spot where he could see both the entrance and the exit of the lot.

He tore open the triple taped and sealed package for a quick inventory. Inside a double-bagged plastic sandwich bag were three complete sets of identification: driver's licenses, passports, social security cards, and credit cards. The licenses and passports all had his picture, but each one had subtle differences: glasses and blond hair in one, mustache and receding hair in another, gray hair and a beard in the last. He could work with them. There was a manila folder taped shut and wrapped in thick rubber bands. He tore it open and fanned through the $10,000 in $50, $20, and $10 bills. An Emerson CQC-7 titanium folding fighting knife. Two handguns: a customized Karl Sokol Counterterrorist Special 9mm Browning High-Power, the one-inch stub of barrel protruding from the frame threaded for a suppressor, and a Smith & Wesson 642 stainless steel .38 snub revolver. An AWC suppressor and six spare magazines for the High-Power. A shoulder holster, inside-the-pants holster, and a belt scabbard for the Browning and an inside-the-pants holster and ankle holster for the .38. Boxes of Corbon's 115 grain 9mm+P+ for the High-Power and two boxes of Glaser Safety Slugs; Federal 158 grain +P .38 for the revolver and one box of Glasers.

Jonny smiled. He looked around to make sure no one was watching him. He hefted the High-Power. He liked the feel of the pistol in his hand. When he'd been flush with money, he'd had Karl Sokol build him five pistols, each exactly the same as this one. They all had the same grips, were sighted to the exact point of aim, and shot exactly alike. One was stashed in a mail forwarding facility in Seattle; another in a storage unit in Los Angeles, another in a safety deposit box in New York. One had been taken from him when five police SWAT teams had descended on him when he was arrested in Georgetown. His nostrils flared at the memory of a SWAT cop snatching his High-Power away:

"You don't deserve a pistol like this, shitbag!" the cop said.

Jonny would never forget that cop's face. He hoped they met again someday. He closed the box up for later. The .357 hidden under his shirt dug into the skin behind his right hip as he got out of the 4Runner. He went around to the back and opened the hatch, and slid the box beneath the carpet into the spare wheelwell where he'd made space. There was also a small gym bag stuffed in there. The top gaped open to expose a roll of lightweight sashcord, a white pillowcase, a roll of duct tape, and a new, unopened box of Trojan Lubricated Condoms.

**NO OTHER OPTION**

"We'll be talking to you soon, Jed. Take it easy. Later, Dale," Tommy La Roux's tinny voice came from the speaker phone in the middle of the conference-room table.

"All right, boys. We'll talk tomorrow," Jed said to the air. He pushed the OFF button, lifted the handset, and then set it down again. "Maybe we'll have something then."

His voice was raspy and tired. He rolled his neck to get the kinks out and looked at Dale. "Any great ideas?"

Dale shrugged. He pointed with his chin at the draft press release for the *America's Most Wanted* television show. "There's always that."

"It may come to that."

Dale stirred the stacks of paper on the conference table with his finger. There were lead sheets, case files, reports of interviews stacked inches high in disorderly piles all across the table. One report from the Kansas Highway Patrol detailed the discovery of a Cavalier stolen from the St. Louis International Airport in a roadside rest area. The body of the owner was in the trunk. The other guard was still missing and assumed dead and dumped somewhere. Despite the best efforts of federal, state, and local law enforcement, it seemed as though Jonny Maxwell had dropped off the face of the earth.

Jed pushed a yellow legal pad with his notes from the teleconference with La Roux and Harris, who were in Leavenworth interviewing prisoners and guards, into the closest stack. "Whole lot of nothing, there. Plenty of snitches with nothing concrete, looking to trade some good time for bullshit."

Dale raised his eyebrows and said nothing. He looked up at the door when the cute blond secretary—Debbie?—assigned to the task force came in with a long, curling fax.

"Master Sergeant Miller?" she said. "This came in on the secure fax for you. From someplace in Virginia." She smiled brightly. "I thought it was important . . ."

Dale favored her with a slow smile. "Thanks, Debbie. For bringing it so quick."

"Oh, you're welcome."

Dale took the fax and watched her take her time leaving the room.

"I'm going to have to keep my eye on you," Jed said.

Dale grinned as he skimmed through the fax. His smile faded and he sat up straight, folded the fax over and began to read through it again. "Jed, I've got something here."

"What you got, Chico?" Jed said. He rubbed his eyes as though he could push the tired away.

"A hit," Dale said. "Certified Jonny Maxwell hit."

Jed's feet hit the floor hard as he stood and came around the table. "Let me see that."

"Hold on. It wouldn't make sense to you."

"What is it?"

"I had CIA run a check on all the backstopped identities Jonny ever used. Nobody ever turns them *all* in . . . you never know when you might get put onto an operation at short notice. You need some documentation that you know is working instead of something cobbled together at the last minute. There's been activity on a Visa account issued to one of his covers. It's been inactive for several years, renewed, but inactive."

"Let me see that damn thing." Jed took the fax and flipped through it. "Milwaukee . . . cash advance and a rental car. Son of a bitch! This is in the last twenty-four hours."

Dale took a pen from his pocket and pointed to a series of numbers on a chart at the bottom of the fax page. "That's the ATM identifier and bank code. Can your people pull the videotapes from the ATM, and send somebody to the car rental without being overt about it?"

**NO OTHER OPTION**

"We know what we're doing, son."

Dale saw that Jed was too tired to bother hiding his sarcasm. "I didn't say you didn't know what you were doing, Jed. You want to know what Jonny's thinking, right?"

Jed took a deep breath and cracked his knuckles. "Okay. Sorry. What's the angle?"

"He's too smart to take this risk without calculating it. This might be a test to see if that card is flagged. Jonny might be using this for two reasons. One, he needs to and it's the only thing he's got. He must have had it stashed somewhere. Two, he wants to see if anybody's onto this identity. If your guys get spotted, and he'll have some way of watching his back trail at the car rental or the bank, then he'll know that you know about this identity. And that will tell him that I'm involved . . . or somebody like me. And that will make it a different ball game."

"Why?"

"The info about his operational identity wouldn't be available to you without our direct involvement. This kind of stuff, it's compartmented. Nobody knows it who doesn't need to, and law enforcement doesn't need to know."

"There's some difference of opinion on that."

"I know, I know," Dale said. "But he'll know then that it's guys like me. He'll think differently, change his game, if he knows it's one of us. He's looking for a law enforcement response, not another operator."

Jed stared at Dale with red-glazed eyes. "That makes sense. So what do you recommend?"

"Get somebody into the car rental without being obvious about it, see if you can find the clerk that was on duty. Same thing with the ATM videotapes. Bury the inquiries in some other kind of inquiry. Jonny will have some way of watching, some procedure, a paid-off clerk or something like that, to let him know if people come around asking questions."

Jed picked up the phone, punched in a number, and gave terse instructions to the person on the other end. He hung up and said, "What else?"

Dale stared at the wall and crossed his arms. His index finger tapped twice, then once. "Milwaukee . . . that would make sense. We've done a lot in the Upper Midwest."

**MARCUS WYNNE**

"What were you doing up there? Winter warfare training?"

"Some of that. We ran operations against the nuclear missile and bomber bases to assess their security—and ran operations surveilling the bad guys watching us test the security. It's a soft route in and out of the country, the whole Upper Midwest. Head north into Canada anywhere along the midwestern border, it's real easy if you've got halfway decent ID. Then over to Toronto or Montreal and you can pick up an international flight anywhere you want to go."

"Think that's what he's going to do?" Jed said.

"That's my guess, if he's that close to the border. He's going to need more money."

"How do you know?"

"He's using the credit card, right?" Dale said. "Maybe it's a test, but he's exposed himself twice for a rental car and a cash advance. Those are operational expenses. He could have been across the border and gone. If he hasn't jumped yet, it means . . . it probably means he's working on getting money together. Have there been any recent reports of any unusual armed robberies, big cash takeoffs, anything like that in the Milwaukee area?"

Jed scribbled more notes on his legal pad. "I'll get onto that right quick. What else, Dale?"

"Something big and quick. I don't know if he'd do a bank or an armored car right off . . ."

"He'd do that? By himself?"

"If he had to. He'd want something big with cash, but low-key in terms of exposure. Like a gem wholesaler with lots of stones and cash around, or a major drug dealer sitting on cash . . . anybody who might have lots of cash around, but not be as hard a target as a bank or armored car."

"Would he find some help up there?"

"I don't know, Jed."

"Let's get some bodies on this," Jed said. He turned to the phone. As he punched in numbers he said, "Then we're getting on a plane to Milwaukee and sniff the ground for ourselves."

Tommy La Roux held out a greasy bucket of KFC Extra Crispy. "Want some chicken? Couple of legs left."

"No thanks," Dale said. "I'm watching my figure."

Tommy shrugged and continued down the aisle of the U.S. Marshals Service B-727—the Con-Air Special. Dale and Jed sat across the aisle from each other. Tommy and his partner sat several rows behind them. An assault squad from the U.S. Marshals' elite tactical unit, the Special Operations Group, huddled in a convivial cluster at the rear of the aircraft, joking among themselves. They all wore black coveralls with the SOG patch and a U.S. Marshal cloth badge sewn on the breast, and their booted feet were kicked up on the black Cordura duffel bags that held their assault gear and weapons.

Dale hooked his thumb back toward the assault team. "These guys know what they're doing?"

Jed looked irritated. "They've got a hell of a lot more trigger time than any military unit I know of. They do all our high-risk apprehensions and serve warrants and work special operations like this. They do a lot of training. They got to get through a hell of a selection course before they make SOG and once they do, we keep them busy out in the real world."

"What I mean is do they understand who they're going to take down?"

"The team leader does," Jed said, pointing out a tall, Pancho Villa mustachioed marshal leading the horseplay. "I gave him a brief."

"If it goes, I want to be in on the operational brief."

"Of course."

From behind, Edgar watched and listened to Dale with interest. "I don't think the Delta man wants to do the deed, Tommy my boy."

La Roux stripped the last of the meat from the chicken leg he worked in his mouth. "Who wants to bust a buddy? Shitbag or not?" He rummaged in the bucket for another piece of chicken. "Don't matter no how. This is our show from start to go. He's just here to applaud our sterling professionalism and to gape in wonder at our incredible investigative skills."

"Would you bust me?"

"For what?" La Roux said around a mouthful of chicken.

"Anything, you know, if I broke out of prison, whatever."

"What would you be in for?"

"What does that matter?"

"It matters." La Roux threw the well-gnawed chicken bone at

**MARCUS WYNNE**

his partner. "Well, it does. Yeah, I'd bust you. Bust you in a Cajun minute. Slap the cuffs on you and your girlfriend too—if you had one besides Rosey Palm."

"I wouldn't bust you, Tommy. I'd do you like Robert Duvall did Jimmy Caan in *The Killer Elite*. I'd shoot you in one elbow and the other knee." Edgar thought for a moment. "No, I'd probably just shoot you in the balls. Not in the dick, just in the balls."

La Roux, chicken grease gleaming on his chin, considered his partner. "You, my friend, are one silly sick motherfucker."

"And you two couldn't have a conversation if they took away the word fuck," yelled one of the SOG marshals.

La Roux held up his hand and extended his middle finger without looking back. "Back in the cage, Mad Dog. We got no raw meat or little girls for you."

Jed looked back down the aisle and grinned at the raucous laughter. "America's finest federal law enforcement," he said with the exasperated pleasure of a Little League coach or a proud father. "You see what I got to put up with?"

"I know what you mean," Dale said. He wondered how many of these men were going to die.

**1.10**

Jonny slouched down in the driver's seat of the Cavalier. The rental car tilted to one side with the weight of Snake Pissolt in the passenger seat. Without his colors on and wearing a heavy denim shirt, clean Levi's, and a hard hat, Snake looked like an oversized construction worker on his way to the job site.

"Something tells me you done this kind of thing before, bro," Snake said. He lit a stogie and held the lighter out for Jonny, who leaned his own cigar into the flame.

"You been in the big house. You can learn a lot of things there," Jonny said.

"Not like this."

They were parked on a one-way street two blocks from the service entrance of the main Milwaukee branch of First Bank. Equipped with binoculars and a stopwatch, they clocked the departures of the ATM Service Fast-Cars—armored vehicles that serviced the proprietary ATMs of the largest bank operation in Wisconsin.

"How we doing?" Jonny said.

"We got the times," Snake said, looking down at the clipboard on his lap. A generic bill of lading listed various items: the fake SKU numbers represented the license plate numbers of the different Fast-Cars; the price next to the stock numbers indicated the time of departure from the secured area.

"Then let's go," Jonny said. He started the Cavalier and pulled away from the curb. "What's the story on this Lee Harvey?"

"Wannabe. Young punk. Did some time in Stillwater, over in Minnesota, for GTA. He's related to Sherry's cousin or something."

"Is that going to be a problem?"

"With Sherry? Hell, no. If she figures it out, she won't care. She can't stand him. Moans about how he's always staring at her tits and how sick it is since they're related."

"What about our tools?"

"You're really into this secret squirrel shit, huh? Yeah, I got all the 'tools.' Got all the fucking explosives, too."

"Where'd you get those?"

"Stole it off a job site up north a couple of months ago. Commercial dynamite, det cord, blasting caps, water gel, chemical fuses, all kinds of good shit. Wrapped some of that chemical fuse around a snitch's neck and stuck a blasting cap up his ass." Snake shook his head in mock sorrow. "What a mess that made."

"Who was he?"

"Snitch working for ATF, those sorry bastards."

"They work you pretty hard?"

"Yeah. We got it cleaned up out here, mostly. The Twin Cities Chapter, though . . . we got some work to do out there. I'll probably be heading that way when we get done with our little gig." Snake shifted in his seat.

"You like that kind of work?"

"You one of them deep thinkers or what? Don't worry about what the fuck I like or don't like."

"I'll worry about what I think I need to worry about," Jonny said. "Like this Lee Harvey. Is he going to do it or do we have to worry about him?"

"He'll be all right, dude. He ain't got to *do* anything except sit there and wait for us to show up, make sure the car is gassed up and ready to go. He don't know nothing beyond that." Snake laughed nastily. "He sure don't need to."

Snake and Jonny were dressed for rock and roll. Both wore Carhart mechanic's overalls, with web belts and drop holsters on their thighs for their chosen sidearms: Snake had a battered old Army .45 and Jonny his High-Power, with spare magazines on the opposite thigh. Each had an M-16, courtesy of the Michigan National Guard and the Outlaws' excellent cross-country arms-running operation. Snake had swapped out the standard stocks for the new collapsible M-4 stocks, which made for easy handling inside the Cavalier. Tactical slings held the weapons across their neck and strong side shoulder. Each man wore around his neck, offset to the weak side shoulder, an olive drab bandoleer. In each bandoleer pocket was a twenty-round magazine. The M-16s had a Redi-Mag locked in place, which held two thirty-round magazines side by side in the magazine well. Thin black balaclavas were rolled up on their heads and Oakley shooting goggles, like ski goggles, hung around their necks.

"Countdown," Jonny said. He allowed his adrenaline to kick up a notch.

Snake rocked in his seat. "Let's get some."

The Cavalier rolled up a hundred yards behind the Fast-Car as it pulled to the curb in front of the side entrance to the Warren Mall. The back door of the armored car swung open and the rider debussed, two heavy bags in his hands, to meet his escort at the right rear of the vehicle. The driver remained inside, the engine idling.

"Stand by," Jonny said softly, pulling his balaclava down and his goggles up. Snake did the same.

Jonny pulled the Cavalier forward to a halt behind the armored car, in the blind zone of the side mirrors, as the two security guards turned to enter the mall. He and Snake rolled out fast, M-16s shouldered, collapsible stocks locked out. They charged the two guards. The escort guard turned and looked over his shoulder, which gave him just enough time to shout "What!" before Jonny shouted "Get down! Get down!"

The guard carrying the money bags dropped them and spun, his hand dropping to his holstered revolver. Snake double-tapped the trigger on single shot and put two rounds into the boy's chest. The concealed body armor didn't slow the high velocity rifle rounds, which knocked the guard off his feet and into the revolving side entrance door. The escort officer fumbled for his revolver, his face blank with the shock of realizing that he was already dead. Jonny shot him in the face. A skull fragment flew off the back of the guard's skull so hard that it starred the plate glass behind him. Jonny spun to cover back toward the Fast-Car. The driver gaped at him from the passenger side window.

"Bags!" Jonny snapped.

**MARCUS WYNNE**

Snake quick-scanned the scene. A few cars, slowed to watch; several shoppers already fleeing away from the door inside the mall; two women frozen in fear ten feet away. "Get down!" he shouted. The women dropped instantly. Snake let the rifle drop out of his hands; the tactical sling he wore let him sling it to one side and free both his hands to seize the sacks. He scrambled back toward the Cavalier, Jonny drag-stepping beside him, his rifle shouldered and tracking back and forth through all 360 degrees of the kill zone. Snake reached the Cavalier's passenger door and threw the sacks into the rear seat, then reshouldered his rifle and shouted to Jonny, "Move!"

Jonny crossed between the armored car and the Cavalier, collapsed his rifle stock and let it hang across his chest as he swung behind the driver's wheel. "Clear!" he shouted.

Snake collapsed the rifle stock as he slid in and slammed the door, the muzzle tracking right, out the window, as he shifted his grip. "Go! Go!" he shouted.

Jonny threw the car into gear and accelerated backward from the Fast-Car. He hit the horn as he backed up. A woman in a Ford Explorer behind him slammed on her brakes, narrowly avoiding a collision. Jonny backed past her, then turned the wheels out and sped away through the lot. A Warren Mall security pickup truck suddenly pulled out in front of them.

"Oh, you fucking idiot," Jonny cursed as he stomped the brake pedal.

"You want some? You got some, motherfucker!" Snake snarled. He leaned out the window and pulled the trigger in rapid single shots, punching holes in the truck door and blowing out the windows in glittering arcs of glass. The young black security guard threw his hands up and fell sideways, screaming, in the truck's cab. It was only a minor obstacle, but the delay he caused was to prove critical.

Milwaukee Police Department Officer Dave Demos was coming out of the mall's main front entrance after his coffee break. A Greek family ran a gyro shop in the mall that served great coffee, and he made it a point to stop in once a day and chat with the family. The unmistakable crack of rifle fire stopped him dead in his tracks, then sent him in a sprint to his squad car, the radio, and the 12-gauge shotgun there. He started the car and hit the radio mike with one hand even as he drove, quickly but cautiously, through the parking lot in the direction of the gunfire, when he saw the Cavalier and Snake lighting up the mall security truck.

Demos was no stranger to gunfire. His first tour in Vietnam had taken care of that, and almost twenty-odd years on Milwaukee's streets had shown him his share of armed encounters. But the cold-blooded execution of the mall security guard—a young kid by the name of Rodney Strong, not unknown to Demos—that set him off. Somebody was going to die today. Demos ran his squad at a fast intercept angle, calling off the plate number on the Cavalier as he got closer, then dropped the mike and put both hands on the wheel as he struck the rear of the Cavalier a glancing blow designed to push it forward into the mall security truck. Demos unlimbered his shotgun as he went out the door and behind the engine block and wheelwell of the left front tire, racking the slide of the Remington Police 870. His first round of 00 buck went into the right rear of the windshield, down low, to shatter and knock out the glass so that he might have a clear shot at the occupants—and in the meantime mess them up a little and let them know that he was out here and that he was pissed.

Jonny heard the cachunk of the slide over the din and ring of gunfire and breaking glass. He was familiar with the shotgun; it was one of his favorite weapons for close quarters work. He'd been tunneled in on the mall security guard and hadn't seen the police cruiser blindside them. But he could see it now.

Snake screamed and thrashed in the passenger seat. Several of the buckshot pellets had struck him and lodged in the bullet-resistant vest under his Carharts, high on his upper back.

Jonny dropped the transmission into park and swung out his door. He popped up from behind his car and squeezed off two rifle shots at the exposed head of the policeman, who ducked. Jonny thumbed the selector to full-auto and sprayed the hood, engine block, windshield, and door of the police cruiser with shots to cover his advance. The cop—Jonny gave him credit, he had balls—held the shotgun up and fired in his direction, exposing only his hands for a moment. Jonny advanced, still firing, around the police car. The cop got off one last shot in Jonny's direction before Jonny stepped all the way around the cruiser and fired at the cop desperately racking the slide on his shotgun. The shotgun's wooden butt shattered and sev-

82

eral rifle rounds slammed into the officer, knocking him back. The bolt locked back on the M-16 and without hesitation Jonny dropped the slung weapon and drew his High-Power and fired at the officer until he was still. He quick-scanned the area, heard the sirens far off and growing, and speed-loaded the High-Power. He ran back to the Cavalier, switching the Redi-Mag on his rifle as he went, jumped behind the wheel, and drove out of the parking lot, leaving death and ruin in his wake.

Behind him, in a pool of blood, Officer Dave Demos struggled for consciousness.

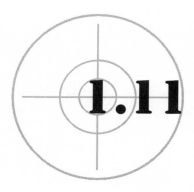

**1.11**

"What a bloodbath," Jed swore. He stood, with Dale and the other marshals, in the Warren Mall parking lot, which had become a sea of flashing lights from police cruisers, ambulances, and fire trucks. Milwaukee Police officers held back the press crews and the crowd of onlookers.

Jed turned to Dale with anger. "Still feeling reluctant?"

"I never was," Dale said.

Jed addressed himself to Edgar Harris and Tommy La Roux. "So what's the final tally?"

"Both armored car escorts, dead on scene, most definitely DOS. Mall security guard, DOS," Tommy said. "Thirty-two-year-old mother of three, critical. Stray round got her, another one went right between the two kids in the backseat. Milwaukee cop Demos, critical, all shot up but wearing a good vest. Lost part of his jaw and one ear, probably the sight in at least one, maybe both eyes, partial paralysis from rounds lodged near his spine, so on and so forth. Ballsy cop, he went down fighting and then some. Witnesses figure he might have got the passenger side shooter. They said the guy that came out of the car was just like something out of a Rambo movie. Just came on and kept coming . . . ran the rifle dry and switched to his pistol just like that, lit that cop up."

Dale ignored Tommy and stared out at the yellow-taped crime scene around the wrecked police car and mall security truck.

"Ain't no doubt it's our boy," Edgar said. "The Cavalier tags check out. And they found this." He showed a plastic evidence bag with a pistol magazine, a few rounds still in it, to Dale. "You recognize this?"

Dale took the evidence bag and looked at the pistol magazine. It was a Browning High-Power magazine, the floor plate etched with "Chestnut Mountain Works" and the number 3.

"Didn't you say he carried some custom High-Power?" Edgar asked. "That's a High-Power mag from Karl Sokol's shop."

"That's what it is," Dale said.

Edgar took the bag out of Dale's hands. "Yeah, that's what it is, all right."

A huge black man in a crisp Milwaukee Police Department uniform approached the marshals and said, "Jed, what you got on this son of a bitch?"

"Boys, this is Willie Mac, AKA Lieutenant William MacFarland, Milwaukee Police Department," Jed said.

MacFarland shook hands all around and studied Dale with interest as he listened carefully to Jed's precise rundown on Jonny Maxwell. "So, this is one serious bad guy we're fixing to tangle with here," he said. "I'm going to get this out on the air and get our tactical team briefed."

"I got some good boys with me here, Willie Mac," Jed said. He nodded toward the two Chevy Suburbans where the SOG assault team stood by. "But we will surely be grateful for any help you might offer."

"Might offer my ass, Marshal," Willie Mac said. "This son of a bitch shot the hell out of one of my officers. This is my meat on the table today, son."

Jed led the big lieutenant away from the others. "Let's take a walk, Willie Mac."

"Well, that's going to take some sorting," Tommy said. "You got any ideas, Dale? What's he likely to do now?"

"This was a total goat fuck," Dale said. "Sloppy, high profile, poor extraction."

"Goat fuck for all these people, maybe," Tommy said. "Your pal got away with the goodies though, didn't he? And it was just pure luck that Milwaukee cop was here. The witnesses figure it didn't take the two of them more than two minutes max to take out those guards, grab the cash, and go. Our would-be hero security guard

**NO OTHER OPTION**

rams into them, but he's got no gun, so he dies in place, and then Demos rolls in and lights them up. Even with all that, they're out of here at least three to five minutes before the first unit responding to Demos's call gets on scene. Three, maybe four or five murders if those other folks don't make it, a shoot-out, a robbery, and a get-away in under eight minutes. Not too shabby for a goat fuck, if you ask me."

"We used to use these kinds of scenarios for training, Tommy," Dale said.

"You'd rob armored cars?" Edgar burst out.

"We'd *plan* to rob armored cars, banks, and other hardened facilities," Dale said. "It forces you to think through the problems in a real-world, real-time environment. We'd do the surveillance and the work-up, walk through the placement, even dry-run it. For training."

"The more I find out about you guys the less I think of you," Edgar said.

Dale ignored him. "Even with only two shooters, this was sloppy. It wasn't necessary to kill those guards. He would have surveyed the lot and made that police car, known where the mall security truck was. It's not like you could miss those if you were looking for them. And leaving behind one of his private magazines . . . that's beyond careless, beyond stupid."

Edgar squared up to Dale. "Maybe he's not as shit hot as you or anybody else thought. Maybe he's just a careless crazy violent freak who slipped through your high and mighty fingers and he's making you look bad. I don't think you got a thing to say to me or anybody else about this guy, so why don't you just shut up and get of our way while we do what we do best—put assholes like your buddy Maxwell behind bars."

"You don't know what you're dealing with," Dale said.

"Nither do you, fool," Harris said. He turned his back and stalked away.

**MARCUS WYNNE**

Officers Frank "Franco" Thompson and Eugene Murphy had been cops for a long time, so when they spotted the maroon Cavalier with the shot out back window behind the abandoned warehouse, they called it in immediately, before they got out of their car. They advanced carefully, Franco covering his partner with the shotgun, Murphy with his Beretta 92F and a twenty-round magazine in place. Murphy cautiously peeked into the car.

"Nobody here," he said.

"What about the trunk?" Franco called.

"Wait one," Murphy said. He opened the door and reached onto the driver's seat. "You're not going to believe this."

Franco advanced and pressed on the trunk to make sure it was latched shut, then joined his partner. "What you got?" he asked.

"The lame-o left his wallet!"

"You got to be kidding."

"Check it out," Murphy said. "Snake Pissolt, I'll be damned. We know this cocksucker."

"Better call it in and we'll secure the rest of this for the crime scene boys."

"Oh, yeah. This will make us some points." Murphy went back to the squad and got on the radio. "Dispatch, this is Squad 269, we found some ID in the vehicle..." He went on to give a detailed description of Snake Pissolt and his address from the Wisconsin driver's license.

Franco went around the vehicle carefully, not touching anything, noting the crumpled metal, the bloodstains on the passenger seat, the expended .223 casings on the floor mats. He shook his head at Snake's stupidity. He knew Snake; he'd been one of six officers who once fought the huge biker to a standstill taking him into custody after a bar fight downtown. Smart enough to pull something like this armored car heist and stupid enough to leave his wallet behind. What a mope. Franco didn't see any keys in the ignition or on the floorboard. He went back to the driver's side door, still open, reached in, and popped the trunk release. The trunk opened a few inches. Franco stepped to the side, still cautious, and used the muzzle of his shotgun to open the trunk.

The military spring activator pin, designed to be used with a trip wire like the one inside the trunk lid, pulled easily out of the detonator, giving Franco just enough time to see the wire running from the trunk lid into the lumpy plastic bag wedged against the spare tire. In that place with no time inside his head, Franco put it together, spun on his heel, and took two long steps away from the car before the six sticks of dynamite went off and lifted him from his feet and threw him through the windshield of his squad, where his body smashed the radio microphone into his partner's mouth.

Jed and his task force studied the smoking ruin of the Cavalier and the squad car. The Suburbans with the SOG assaulters were parked a short distance away; the men talking with the other responding officers while the forensics team continued to pick through the wreckage.

"The way he had the device wedged in front of the spare tire, that directed the blast out," Jed said. "Those boys are lucky. Some serious contusions, the one that went through the windshield got his head laid open to the bone and his partner lost all his teeth on one side and broke his jaw, but all in all they're going to be okay."

"Some okay," Edgar said. "Nothing about this is going to be okay till we got this guy tagged and bagged."

"We got him now, buddy," Jed said, exultation in his voice. "We got him now." He checked the fresh surveillance photograph, taken from a State Patrol helicopter, of Snake's Milwaukee residence. "We got people in place, we're ready to rock and roll. His truck's there, his bike's there. As soon as the city is set, we're going to roll

**MARCUS WYNNE**

in and block it off, evacuate the houses on all sides and take these pricks off the boards."

"I think you ought to hit his place right now. Fast and hard," Dale said.

"Hey, for once, something we agree on!" Edgar said.

Tommy looked at him and shook his head negatively. He drew his Government Model .45, press checked it for the reassuring sight of the shiny brass case in the chamber, then slid it back into the concealment holster beneath his leather jacket.

"Too many civilians around to be taking these guys down if we get a fight, Dale," Jed said reasonably. "This isn't one of your military operations. We don't do collateral damage here. We've got to get those people out of there before we tackle these boys."

"That just gives him more time to prepare," Dale said. "What if they figure out they left the wallet in the car? They've had time enough to set up a living hell for your entry team. They've shown they've got explosives, they know how to use them, they're prepared to fight, they've got automatic weapons . . . hell, this *should* be a military operation, since they've had time to harden that place."

"What're they going to get out of that?" Jed said impatiently. "They're on a cul-de-sac, we got air coverage, we'll have every cop for two counties, we got the SOG making the entry and covering it with our snipers. They got no place to go. We can afford to wait it out if we have to. We'll talk his ass out. He might expend a lot of ammo, it won't do him any good. We won't have any more civilians in the line of fire."

"He'll see it going down," Dale said. "You send people door to door taking people out, he'll see that. He'll make your surveillance and your spotters. He'll have thought about this already. He's getting ready for this fight!"

"Let's just go get him and get all this dancing over with," Edgar said, his voice rich with disgust. "I'm sick and tired of all this talk, talk, talk. So far this guy has busted moves all around us, busted up three cops, killed at least three people and got a bunch more on the critical list. It's time to get the deed done and punch his ticket."

"When you're running the show, you can make that call, Harris," Jed said. "Till then, you march when I say march, you got that?"

Edgar stormed off to the parked Suburbans and joined the SOG in sorting out their tactical gear. Tommy shook his head sor-

**NO OTHER OPTION**

rowfully and followed his partner, draped his arm around Edgar's shoulders and tried to lead him away. Edgar shook his arm off and began an angry harangue, inaudible from where Jed and Dale stood.

"Goddam, this has got everybody stirred up," Jed said. "Dale, I appreciate your input. But this is a law enforcement issue. We've got civilians to take care of. This isn't an option. No collateral damage . . . we're the good guys, remember? I been there too. So let's get our wagons circled for this briefing. You bring up what you just told me, but let our boys figure out their own solutions. They're good at it, you'll see."

"They'd better be," Dale said. "They're going to need to be."

## 1.13

"Mouse" Baker had a long narrow face, oversized ears, a pointed nose, and a thin mustache. The deep smile lines in his face that just saved him from too ratlike a look were deceptive, for Mouse, like Snake Pissolt, was one of the Satan's Outlaws top internal security enforcers, a stone-cold contract killer who'd murdered the wives and children of men who crossed the Outlaws. His weakness for little girls contributed to the numerous counts of rape, statutory and otherwise, that filled out the ten pages of his criminal history. His latest girlfriend, sixteen-year-old professional runaway Darcy Darnell, clung close behind him on the painfully restored classic Harley Panhead that roared down the cul-de-sac to Snake's house. Mouse steered the Panhead up onto Snake's ragged front lawn and shut the bike down. Darcy, nearly bursting out of her halter top and cutoff jeans, climbed off and stood waiting beside the bike till Mouse dismounted.

Mouse swatted her on the ass and said, "C'mon, baby. Let's go see my brother." He stomped up on the porch and banged on the door. "Snake! You home, dude? Open up!" He peered through the window, then looked around the side of the house at the truck and chopped Harley parked under the open carport. He tried the unlocked front door, then led Darcy into the house. "Snake! You home?"

"There's nobody here," Darcy said.

Mouse walked through the house. "Must be at the store or

something. That's weird." He grinned at Darcy and pushed her in the direction of the bedroom. "Just you and me, baby. Get naked."

"What if somebody comes back?"

"We're brothers. We share everything." He pushed her into the bedroom and shut the door. As he took off his pants, he looked over at the Mossberg 590 shotgun leaning in the corner. Good old Snake. Once a grunt, always a grunt.


Mouse's arrival was duly noted by the troopers in the State Patrol helicopter flying overwatch, and relayed to the Mobile Command Post set up by the Milwaukee PD and the U.S. Marshals.

Jed snapped orders around Dale as though he weren't there. "Let's get it done. Get the civilians out of there now!"

Things happened. Barricades went up, drawn quickly from trucks that rolled smoothly into position. Plainclothes officers went door to door and escorted residents through the side yards where uniformed patrolmen herded them to safety. SOG snipers, toting their Remington Police 700 accurized bolt rifles, climbed onto rooftops or positioned themselves back from open upper windows, criss-crossing 16362 Hilow Road in a field of interlocking fire from deadly accurate weapons in the hands of men most willing to use them. A UH1-B helicopter, on loan from the Wisconsin Air National Guard, appeared in the sky and circled synchronously with the State Patrol's Bell Ranger, keeping the whole operation under their eyes. Milwaukee City PD, with assistance from the Milwaukee County Sheriff's Department, set up cars and posted uniforms on the outer perimeter. The Milwaukee City SWAT team shrugged into their black overalls and prepared to enter and secure the inner perimeter. After a heated discussion—and a call from the U.S. attorney—Lieutenant Willie Mac MacFarland reluctantly conceded to the SOG assaulters the right to make the entry. And after much shouting, Jed refused Dale the right to make that entry with them.

"For Christ's sake, Dale. You're a professional. How would you take it if some guy, no matter what his credentials were, showed up on something like this and demanded that you let him enter with you? No way, soldier. You're sitting this out, right here with me," Jed said. The lines of strain were deep on his face. He turned his back on Dale to listen to the radios set up in long racks inside of the command and control van set up by Milwaukee PD.

Dale went out into the light and away from the ozone and stale coffee smell of the C&C van. He ignored the crowd of police officers and the growing crowd of civilians gathering behind the barricades and stood by himself, breathing deeply. He felt someone come up behind him and looked up to see Tommy La Roux.

"Smoke?" Tommy said, holding out a crumpled pack of Camel shorts.

Dale took one. "Next best thing to a cigar, these things."

"Kill ya just as quick," Tommy said. He lit both their cigarettes with a match pulled from a crumpled matchbook. "This must be pretty tough for you."

Dale shrugged, and wouldn't look at Tommy.

"I can't imagine what this must be like for you," Tommy said. "You guys were tight, worked together, played together."

"I'm not going to nut out on you, Tommy. Don't worry about me."

"Whatever."

They smoked in silence. The clouds of smoke gathered for a moment, then a breeze swirled the blue smoke away.

"How ugly is it going to get?" Tommy asked.

"Ugly," Dale said without hesitation. "He's had time to get ready. People are going to die today."

Tommy dropped his cigarette and ground it into the asphalt. "It's your buddy's turn today."

Mouse's partners rode him hard about his taste for young chicken. He made no excuses. One of the best things about them, besides their tight bodies, was that they didn't have enough experience to tell a good fuck from a bad one. He rolled off of Darcy, who lay there blinking and sweaty, and reached for his Marlboros on the nightstand. He took out two cigarettes, lit them, and tucked one into Darcy's mouth before she started yammering on about whatever shit sixteen-year-olds yammered about. Mouse lay back, content with himself, and blew smoke rings at the ceiling. Where the fuck was Snake? It was strange that he'd left both his bike and his truck here. He sure wouldn't walk anyplace. Maybe some broad was giving him a ride. Mouse snorted at the thought.

The sound of a helicopter circling kept coming and going through the screen of the open window. It reminded him of all

**NO OTHER OPTION**

Snake's stories about the Nam. Mouse had been too young for that, but it sounded like a hell of a time. Bad eyesight and flat feet kept him out of the military, and besides, he wouldn't put up with some fucking drill sergeant yelling his shit in his face. Make him eat that big round hat, crazy motherfuckers. He grinned and shook his head.

"What are you thinking about, Mouse?" Darcy asked.

"Why do you always ask that?" Mouse said tolerantly. "You always ask me that."

"I just want to know what you're thinking. I want to know if there's something I can do for you."

"Oh, yeah," Mouse said, sticking his finger in her mouth. "There's something you can do for me."

"Mouse!"

"I gotta piss." Mouse rolled out of the bed and checked himself in the mirror. His pale white skin was wreathed in elaborate tattoos; his jailhouse tats were woven into the more expensive and artistic skin art he bought for himself. Despite his otherwise lean frame, he had the solid foundation of a beer belly developing. He scratched himself as he went down the hallway to the toilet. The bathroom window was broken, patched with a piece of cardboard that flapped back and forth where the tape had peeled away. As he urinated, he reached up with his free hand, annoyed with the flapping, and pulled the cardboard off and threw it on the floor.

Sound carries on still air. The sharp crackle and hiss and terse sounds of a police radio are unmistakable to those with experience of them, and Mouse had no shortage of experience with the police. He put his face to the broken window and peeked out and saw cops, loaded down with the black combat shit that meant SWAT, moving into position around the house. He turned and ran back to the bedroom, pushing Darcy aside as he stepped into his greasy Levi's, buttoning them quickly over his bare skin, abandoning his boxers on the floor. Mouse stepped into his big engineer boots and threw on his colors. He grabbed up the Mossberg shotgun Snake kept propped in the corner and began tearing through the dresser drawers looking for extra shells.

"What's going on? What's going on?" Darcy said. She tugged at his arm and he slapped her aside.

"You listen to me! Get dressed and get under the bed, now! Don't say another word. Just do it!" he snarled at her.

**MARCUS WYNNE**

Darcy whimpered as she pulled on her scanty clothing. Mouse shoved her onto the floor and prodded her under the bed.

"Just stay there. I mean it," he said.

He found a box of 00 buck in the second dresser drawer under a stack of skin magazines. Mouse had no specific idea why the cops might be busting in, but there were plenty of reasons why they'd get a fight, whether it was Snake or Mouse or both of them they were looking for. He had no intention of doing any more hard time and whether it was for murder, rape, or arms trafficking, that's what he was looking at if they took him. He checked the loads in the Mossberg and slid three more rounds into the extended magazine, which gave him eight in the mag and one in the chamber, two spares in his pocket. That would probably get him to his bike and, depending on how many cops were in place, get him the fuck out of here. He thumbed the safety off and with the shotgun at port arms peeked out the front window. There were cops across the street hiding behind a low hedge. He could see their uniforms in the gaps between the shrubs. The biker, tense with adrenaline, stepped quietly through the front room and into the kitchen, where he peeked out the side door into the covered carport where Snake's bike and truck were parked. The truck keys were hanging from a nail beside the door. Mouse took them in his left hand, hung the ring from one finger, and put his sweaty hand back on the shotgun slide. He eased open the door.

Pressed up against the low wooden wall that fenced in the carport, SOG Marshal Hank Le Beau, a New Orleans Cajun, sweated in his Nomex coveralls and whispered into his throat mike, "In position." He slowly rolled his head out around the corner of the low wall.

The SOG team had decided to use the covered approach and make primary entry through the side kitchen door. That avenue of approach provided usable cover for both approach and retreat, if that became necessary, as opposed to the exposed approach to the front door, covered by the Milwaukee SWATs. Between Le Beau's position behind the low wall were the Harley and Dodge Ram pickup. Then the door. Le Beau's team would move around the truck and stack beside the house wall, then hit the door hard. It didn't look heavy or reinforced, but to be sure, Le Beau and his partner carried a concrete-filled steel ram.

**NO OTHER OPTION**

Le Beau's heart rate skyrocketed when the kitchen door slowly opened. He saw the shotgun and the silhouette of the man behind it. It was hard to see more clearly, as the carport and the door were in shadow, partially obscured by the vehicles. Sweat steamed up Le Beau's shooting goggles as he squinted from the sunny fence into the dark.

"Armed suspect," he hissed into his throat mike. "Armed suspect at the door!"

To Mouse's hyperalert ears, the low mumble and hiss from just a few steps away was all it took. He threw the shotgun to his shoulder and fired over the pickup truck into the wooden wall. The 00 buck blew a hole the size of a big grapefruit in the thin slats and tore into the side of the third man in the stack, knocking him down. Involuntarily, his hands tightened and the convulsive grip on his MP-5 submachine gun triggered a three-round burst into the side lawn as he fell. Behind him, his partner, armed with a HK-53 .223 assault rifle, unwound from his crouch and stepped over his fallen partner to protect him and fired six rapid shots at the figure in the door. Two shots glanced off the truck, the lightweight 40-grain Federal Blitz hollow points disintegrating, two more buried themselves in the wood doorsill, one whipped by Mouse's ear, nicking him as he ducked back, and one flew untouched through the kitchen, into the front room, and out the front window, which disintegrated into a shower of glass. Across the street, rookie SWAT member D. J. Johnson felt something strike his face. Whether it was glass, a bullet fragment, or bird shit, he'd never know. He screamed out, "They're shooting at us!" and clapped his hand to his face. His partner immediately began to fire his AR-15 rifle into the broken window and every other officer on the line began to do the same. Bullets began to shred the front room; glass shattered; the air grew thick with white dust as the Sheetrock disintegrated under the buckshot, 9mm and .223 rounds tearing into the front of the house.

Mouse screamed as he racked the shotgun and charged out the side door, racking the gun again and again as he fired at the SOG team. The entry officers, front and rear of their downed partner, went into an immediate action drill to evacuate the wounded man; the others opened up. Mouse and the marshals were seven yards apart; the only cover between them was the pickup truck, which grew more perforated and shattered with each second. Mouse stumbled across the fallen Harley motorcycle and leaned across the hood of the pickup, setting off a cannonball of flame each time he fired the shotgun. Le Beau quartered around the rear of the truck, where he had a clean shot, and put a short burst of 9mm into Mouse's head from six feet away, dropping him straight down and cross-legged beside the truck. The rounds pouring into the house from the front confused Le Beau; he couldn't tell who was shooting at whom, so he fell back with his team, covering their retreat to their covered stack point in the next yard.

"Cease fire, cease fire, goddammit!" Willie Mac's bellow sounded up and down the line of police officers. The big lieutenant hunkered down and went down the line, checking on his men. "Where did the fire come from? Who shot first?"

"They shot from the house, Lieutenant," one cop said. "Scratched D.J."

"D.J.! Are you all right?" MacFarland said.

"He's okay, Loo. Just a little nick," D.J.'s partner answered.

There was a sudden silence over the battleground. Sirens grew in the distance. The crackle and hiss of the radio grew loud with command and control demanding explanations and situation reports.

"Does anybody know what's going on?" someone muttered.

"Stand by," Jed said into the radio handset.

On the other end, the reassembled SOG assault team hunkered down in their covered position. Their wounded partner had been swept away to an ambulance, ammo had been redistributed, breathing controlled. They were ready to go—again.

"Snipers have a clear view into the front room and most of the kitchen, now that we've shot the front of the house out," Jed said. "No movement, nothing, inside. Just that dead mope in the carport and that isn't Snake Pissolt." He turned to the lead hostage negotiator, a world-weary and cynical-looking detective named Carter. "Go get on the horn and see what you can do."

Carter unfolded his lanky frame out of the metal folding chair in the C&C van. "If there's anybody left in there to talk to," he said. Dale followed him out. Carter walked slowly through the side yards to the Milwaukee PD perimeter. He raised the bullhorn and said,

"Occupants of 16362 Hilow Road! Come out with your hands raised! This is the U.S. Marshals Service and the Milwaukee City Police Department!"

Carter lowered the bullhorn and looked at Dale, raising one eyebrow in a "Whadda ya expect?" look. There was a moment of silence. Carter raised the bullhorn again when Dale took his arm and said, "Look."

Darcy Darnell stood trembling on the front door, her hands raised, the front of her pants wet. "Please don't shoot me! Please don't shoot me!"

Four SOG members swept her up, one on each arm, the other two covering. They carried her off through the side yards to where a medic waited. The marshals searched her roughly, and while the medic checked her for injuries, asked her who else was in the house.

"Nobody," Darcy said, weeping and near hysteria. "Nobody's in the house. He just left me there, Mouse just left me there!"

A dynamic entry by the SOG, preceded by flashbang distraction grenades, confirmed her report.

"All clear," the team leader said on the radio. "Only one suspect and he's DOS."

"Well then," Jed Loveless said, throwing down the radio handset. "Just where the hell are these guys?"

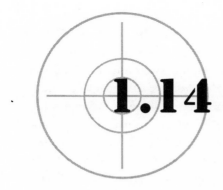

"Sherry, where the fuck is my wallet?" Snake bellowed. "Did you take it, bitch?"

Sherry answered quickly. "No, I didn't, I'm sure it's around here someplace, Snake. We'll find it, baby."

"Get your ass to looking, then. Lee Harvey! Get me that god-dam Jack Daniel's."

The lanky wannabe biker, who'd been huddled and quiet in the corner, hurried off to the kitchen to rummage through the groceries he'd brought in. Jonny watched him go in amusement. He was in the front room of Snake's family cabin, north of Milwaukee and just outside a small town called Horicon. They'd dumped the Cavalier less than three miles from the mall, where Jonny had spent a few precious minutes preparing some surprises for the officers sure to find the car. In the meantime, Snake and the nervous Lee Harvey transferred the money bags to the trunk of Sherry Stivers's late-model Honda Accord. They stashed the rifles, coveralls, and other gear into locked duffel bags that went into the trunk as well. The pistols stayed out and handy. They drove away as sedately as they could with Snake constantly thumping the seat and shouting at Lee "Slow the fuck down, fool! We don't want anybody to notice us. You get our asses in a jam and you're the first one to fucking die, you understand me?" And so it went on the easy drive north to Horicon, where Sherry had stocked the isolated cabin after letting her boss know that she needed a few days off.

Jonny walked slowly around the front room. There were old framed lace doilies on the wall. One said "Most of all, let love guide your life." Another said "Home Sweet Home." The wooden frames were caked with greasy dirt from years of neglect. The furniture had once been nice. Now the couches were pocked with cigarette burns and the cushions stained from an assortment of fluids. It smelt of dank decay and old cigarette smoke. Even through the years of neglect and abuse by Snake and his biker pals, you could see that this cabin had once been the pride and joy of a working class family, who'd taken care and made it homey. Now it was just a few steps away from being a rat's nest. Of course, in a way, it already was.

Sherry, seriously flustered, came back from the bedroom. She hurried from one place to another in the front room, kneeling to look under the couch, and running her hands over the cracked bookshelves heavy with biker and tattoo magazines.

Jonny smiled. "Find it?"

She shook her head furiously, not looking at Snake, who was occupied with his Jack Daniel's bottle. "I can't find it anywhere!"

"Probably left it at the Milwaukee house," he said. "I wouldn't worry about it."

"*You* don't need to worry about it, slick," Snake said. "That's her problem. Come have a drink with me, bro. We kicked some serious ass today."

He held the bottle out to Jonny. Jonny took the bottle, held it to his lips, and tilted it back. He only allowed a taste to pass between his lips. The sweet burn of the sour mash was good, but he needed to keep his head clear. Besides, booze wasn't his favorite form of release. He looked at Sherry, on her hands and knees looking through the magazines on the bottom shelves of the bookcase.

Snake caught his eye. "You want some of that, bro? Knock yourself out. It's some good pussy."

"Maybe later," Jonny said. He looked at Lee Harvey. "You all right there, Lee?"

"Yeah, man, I'm cool, rock solid," Lee said, glad to be recognized. "That was some righteous action today. Was on all the radio. Ought to be on TV by now . . ."

"Fucking TV don't work," Snake said. He laughed. "Maybe we'll go buy one. Get us a big screen!"

"Where's my bag at, Sherry? The canvas one?" Jonny asked.

**MARCUS WYNNE**

"In the bedroom, on the floor, next to the bed," Sherry said, still searching.

"Don't bother looking for that wallet, Sherry. It's not here," Jonny said. He went into the bedroom for a moment.

"How do you know?" Snake said. He tilted the bottle up and took a long pull. The booze kindled a warm flame in his belly, easing the pain in his shoulder and upper back. Jonny had given him two extra-strength Percodans from his medical kit after treating the lacerations and bruising the buckshot pellets had left, despite the body armor. The whiskey interacted with the painkillers, giving Snake a smooth, mellow, and relaxed buzz, slowing him way down. "How do you know?" he said again, less belligerently. He turned and looked at the bedroom door, where his last thought was how Jonny, standing there with his pistol leveled at Snake's head, looked just like an advertisement from a gun magazine for one of those high-speed shooting schools.

"You don't have to kill me. Really, you don't. I'll leave town, I'll go someplace else, someplace far away. I'll never say anything to anybody, please, Jonny!" Sherry pleaded from the bedroom, where she was spread-eagle on the bed, tied down with new white sashcord to the four corner posts of the cheap wooden bedframe. "I'll do whatever you want, I'll fuck you any way you want, you don't have to kill me!"

Jonny turned his head from where he was bent over Snake's body and said, "If you're not quiet, I'm going to gag you. You won't like that. Or maybe I'll just cut your tongue out. You'd like that even less."

"Okay, okay," she said. Tears streamed down her face. "I'll do what you say, I'll forget your name, whatever, please . . ."

Jonny walked back into the bedroom, peeling a long strip of duct tape from the roll he was working with and plastered it across Sherry's mouth. He squeezed her right breast, once, hard, then went back to the task of wrapping Snake's big form up in a plastic painter's dropcloth. Snake's face was slack with death and surprise. The sub-sonic 147-grain Hydra-Shok had entered right on the bridge of his nose and violently expanded in the aqueous tissue of his brain. The resulting hydrostatic shock had distorted his features. One eye was blown completely out of its socket, the other protruded, barely held

**NO OTHER OPTION**

in by the muscles in the orbital ridge. The forehead bulged. Even robbed of some velocity by the AWC suppressor on his High-Power, the round did its job. The noise of the action cycling, and the pop of gas as the slide retracted, was minimal as he'd swung the weapon onto Lee Harvey and put a round through his ear and into his brain, which dropped him midstride to the door. Jonny was quite pleased with the ammo's performance. Federal had surely ironed out the bugs, and even out of a pistol instead of a submachine gun, it performed the task it was designed for quite well: punching through skulls at close range for silent elimination. Sherry had been easy. One powerful sidearm blow to the nerve plexus on the side of her neck had stunned her; tying her up took only moments for someone of Jonny's experience.

All in all, not too bad for being out of practice.

Jonny taped the last fold of plastic in place and wiped the sweat from his eyes. People just didn't realize how hard it was to handle a dead body, especially someone Snake's size. The phrase "dead weight" came from someplace, didn't it? Jonny grinned at the thought. He looked at what he'd set up. He'd put the kitchen table in the front room and set Lee's body, propped in a chair, at the table. Snake's body was beside the front door, wrapped like garbage set to go out. The device he'd been working on came out of his bag and went on the table in front of Lee Harvey.

Jonny went into the kitchen pantry and came back with the two-gallon propane canister Sherry had picked up for him at the store. He hummed quietly to himself while he worked on the device he was assembling at the table, setting the dual firing trains, checking the circuits, cutting fuse, and checking the dynamite sticks. The sound of Sherry straining to breathe through her nose from the bedroom grew louder. Jonny grimaced, annoyed at the interruption, and went into the bedroom. Sherry's eyes were bulging from the difficulty of forcing breath through her nose, which was clotted with mucus. The tape across her mouth bulged and flattened as she struggled to breathe. Jonny took a Kleenex from the box he'd set beside the bed and wiped her nose delicately.

"Better?" he asked her.

She nodded her head yes, her eyes filling with tears. Jonny reached down and adjusted his penis, bulging uncomfortably against his jeans. Time enough for that, later.

**MARCUS WYNNE**

He went back into the front room and continued working for some time. Finally satisfied, he went outside to the enclosed garage, looking around carefully to make sure no one was passing by on the road at the end of the driveway. The nearest house was over a quarter of a mile down the road. He cut a length from the garden hose, dried and curling in the neglected lawn, then siphoned several gallons of gas from Sherry's car and topped off the tank on Lee Harvey's motorcycle, and put the rest into a variety of containers. He brought them inside the house and left them in the kitchen for now. Then he spent a fair amount of time working on Lee Harvey's body, getting the position just right, placing the special items he'd decided to sacrifice appropriately. Finally, he was done.

Time for a little well-earned R&R.

He stood over Sherry, then placed his hand on her chest and felt the racing rhythm of her heart. He took his knife out and punched a small hole in the center of the tape, over her mouth, between her lips, and the sound of her raspy breathing filled his ears. He took the clean white pillowcase and put it over her head, then knotted it snugly, but not too tight, around her throat. She struggled against the ropes and he pressed her back onto the bed firmly.

"Easy, baby, easy," he soothed.

Slowly, taking his time, he cut her clothes away, careful not to mark her skin with the razor-sharp serrations of the fighting knife. She had wet herself and he wrinkled his nose at the acrid smell of urine. He hated it when they did that. He took the damp washcloth he'd set beside the bed and cleaned her up. Jonny reached for the box of condoms that he'd set beside the bed, but stopped when he remembered that it didn't really matter this time.

"Well, I'm fresh out of ideas," Jed said. The last light of the day drew shadows across the faces of his tired task force and the looming Lieutenant Willie Mac. "What about you all?"

"Our gang unit is working up Pissolt. They'll fax it over as soon they have it all," Willie Mac said. The big black man spat on the ground. Across the street, the department shooting teams were going over the houses, marking off shooting positions, expended cases, and bullet holes. "The guys will be out here for hours. Let's go over to the van, check the fax, see if anything else has come up. We've got people canvassing the neighborhood where the car got dumped. Forensics is working what they can out of the car." He led them toward the command and control van, then stopped short. "Oh, fuck," he said. "If it's not one thing it's another."

"What's . . ." Jed stopped when he saw what Willie Mac was cursing about. Five TV vans were parked beside the C&C van and a small horde of reporters pressed up against the temporary barricades. Dale looked up and saw the telephoto lenses mounted on the booms protruding from the top of the TV vans. They were all directed at them.

"C'mon, Loveless," Willie Mac said. There was no mercy in his voice. "You're going to ride this train all the way with me. The rest of you get lost. Jed, that's my Public Affairs Officer over there and guess what? You and me, we're going on national TV."

"Great." Jed spat. He followed Willie Mac. Dale and the others hurried into the C&C van, pushing aside the cameras and micro-phones thrust at them.

Edgar slammed the door shut behind them and kicked a fold-ing chair the length of the van. "Son of a bitch!"

"See how he is?" La Roux said to the SOG team leader. "Lack of pussy makes him stupid."

"Fuck you, Tommy," Edgar said. He threw himself into a fold-ing chair, crossed his arms across his chest, and glared at Dale, who returned the look.

"What?" Edgar snapped. "What is your problem?"

"Cool yourself off, Harris," Dale said. "I'm sick of your temper tantrums."

La Roux caught Edgar as he lunged out of the chair at Dale. He pushed his partner back down into the chair and said, "Dale, you and Mad Dog take a walk while I talk with my partner."

"Fine with me," Dale said. He slammed the door open and almost hit one of the local SWAT cops coming in.

The SOG team leader followed him. "Shit. I'd give my left nut for a cold one right about now."

Dale ignored him and walked faster.

"Whoa, dude, hold up. We don't want to march off too far. Something's going to break soon." The marshal had a conciliatory tone to his voice. "Don't hold it against Edgar. He's an emotional boy under all that. He's got blue nut of the adrenal gland, is all."

"Got a bad fucking attitude, too."

"Well, there's that," the marshal allowed. "He's just frustrated. He's one of the best chasers we've got and this guy is giving him more grief than he's used to." He looked around at the horde of cops, the crowd of locals pressing the barriers, the press crews, and the helicopters circling overhead. "Some three-ring circus, huh? You ever seen any shit like this? I expect Geraldo Rivera to pop up soon, or maybe Jerry fucking Springer. You think? Cross-dressing SWAT cops or gay bikers on acid or something?"

Dale had to laugh. "Why do they call you Mad Dog?"

"Well, there's a story to that," the marshal said, grinning.

"I imagine so."

"How long you been with Delta?"

"Nine years."

"You know Jim O'Neal, or John Onofrey, or Terry Hall?"

**NO OTHER OPTION**

"Sure. Good guys."

"I ran into them down at Clint Smith's shooting school, right after he set up Thunder Ranch. Solid guys. Don't say much, but then none of you guys do, even to an old Green Beanie like me."

"Who were you with?"

"First Group, then Seventh. I was in the door-kicking company there. Thought about going out for Delta, but it was time to move on, you know what I mean? This is a good gig we got here in SOG. Lots of action, good guys, work hard, party hard. Plus we get to swagger around in these cool threads and talk shit."

"I started out in Seventh."

"Yeah, I heard."

"Checked me out?"

"Wouldn't you?"

"Yeah."

"I heard you were solid. You work in some kind of spook operation nobody will talk about, down there in Special Projects. For Ray Dalton, who I know all too well and who still owes me whiskey from the time I saved him from a heinous ass-whipping in Itaewon, Seoul, Korea," Mad Dog said. "And Ray, last I heard, was sheep dipped for the Christians In Action."

Dale studied the marshal more thoroughly. The walrus mustache, genial demeanor, and the good old boy act did little to hide the sharp intelligence behind the pale blue eyes.

"You seem pretty well informed, Mad Dog," Dale said. "What other things do you hear?"

"More than a little about this old boy Jonny Maxwell and you. Kind of cold, the powers that be sending a man's old partner out to whack him, don't you think?"

"That's an interesting spin."

"Yeah. Interesting. That's one way of putting it, I suppose. You see why Edgar might be a little put off by you? On one hand, the man's partner coming along . . . he might not be putting forth his best effort, you know? On the other hand, what kind of cold son of a bitch would sign on to kill his ex-partner? Either way, it don't reflect real favorable on you." Mad Dog twirled the end of his mustache. "You hear talk in the community about what you guys get up to. Makes me wonder what you're about. Here. Now." He paused. "Want to fill me in?"

**MARCUS WYNNE**

Dale saw all the levels of meaning in Mad Dog's face. Sympathy for another SF operator. Cold and dispassionate manipulation to draw out what he might need to know. Curiosity. And a carefully hidden hint of disgust.

"You ever make a mistake in judgment?" Dale said. "Misjudge somebody, think somebody was a friend when they weren't? Ever been betrayed by somebody you trusted?"

"Of course."

"Think about what you would and wouldn't do, then. Before you run all the sympathetic good guy shit on me. Think it through. I'm here to do my job, just like you. Find him, talk to him if he gives me the chance. Tell you what you need to know to take him if he won't. That's my job. I don't like it, didn't want to do it. But I took it on and I'll see it through. I won't like it and I'll have to teach myself how to live with it. But I'll damn well do it."

Mad Dog smoothed the ends of his mustache. "I don't envy you."

Dale shrugged and turned away. One of the Milwaukee cops waved at them from the C&C van.

"Hey! La Roux wants you two in here!" the cop yelled.

Inside the van, La Roux was huddled with a Milwaukee SWAT over a fresh fax. The Cajun looked up when Mad Dog and Dale came in. "We've got an interesting lead here," La Roux said. "Old Snake Pissolt has a cabin in Horicon, just north of here. Belonged to his parents. ATF served a warrant up there a couple of years ago looking for buzz guns. We got people getting with the sheriff up there, telling him to sit tight till we get some air assets to make a flyby and see what kind of activity we got." La Roux paused. "I got a feeling about this . . . it would make sense they'd want to get out of town."

"So what are we waiting for?" Mad Dog said. He turned his back on Dale.

**NO OTHER OPTION**

Things were set. Jonny walked around the cabin, double checking the placement of the bodies, the explosive triggers, the pans of gasoline set out in each room, the trip wires. He looked in at Sherry, curled on the bed, her hooded head turning slowly from side to side as she struggled against the haze brought on by the Percodans and the whiskey he'd forced on her afterward. He watched her grow still. Poor bitch, he thought. At least it wouldn't hurt.

Jonny checked the timers once more, then stepped out into the night. It was clear and the sky was full of stars. This far from the big city, there was little nighttime illumination to wash out the brilliance of the night sky. He stood and stared up for a few moments. The house was dark behind him. He smelt the gasoline fumes and shut the door firmly. He pushed Lee Harvey's Harley Sportster to the end of the driveway, ran alongside it and jumped on, coasting down the long incline of the road till he was well away from the other houses. Then he started the bike. It handled well, even with the heavy canvas duffel bag tied on the back.

It didn't take long to get back on the Interstate for the ride back to where the 4Runner was hidden. It was a good long ride; little or no traffic, only the light of the Harley boring through the dark, the night air on his face, the rise and fall of the gentle hills of Wisconsin and the steady rumble between his legs, and his only company the thoughts he thought when he was alone at night.

**1.17**

Dale stood in the dark with the Fugitive Apprehension Team and looked up the driveway at the smoking, popping ruin that had been Snake Pissolt's family cabin. The fire department trucks, the ATF investigators, the Explosive Ordnance Disposal Unit from the Wisconsin National Guard at Fort McCoy, and cops from every local jurisdiction all stood at the end of the driveway out in the road. They'd been ordered back by the fire scene commander after one of his firemen had discovered yet another trip wire.

"It's going to be days before this is all sorted," Jed said. "First all this has to cool off. Nobody's going near it till then. Then EOD and ATF have to go through and make sure all the devices have been identified and rendered safe. They don't know how much explosive might still be in there."

"Are we sure he's dead?" Edgar said. "Was there enough left of him to make an ID?"

"Not much doubt, but it'll be a couple of days to be sure," Jed said. "What's left of him and the other bodies are still in there. The scene commander was sure there was nobody left alive before his guys fought in far enough to see some trip wires. Good thing we'd tipped them off. There's body parts all over the fucking place. They've been picking pieces out of the road and bushes. The fire chief is real clear about not risking his guys to recover bodies till the site's been cleared. They did find this."

He handed Dale a plastic evidence bag. Inside were the bent, burnt, and twisted remains of a Browning High-Power, the magazine well blown out where the ammunition had cooked off. "Recognize that?"

Dale looked closely at what was left of the pistol. "Yes," he said. "I recognize that." He handed the bag back to Jed.

"So what do they figure happened?" Tommy La Roux asked.

"The place went up around eleven PM," Jed said. "About an hour before we got the choppers up here."

"I talked to the scene commander and one of the ATF guys," Dale said. "There were pans of accelerant, probably gasoline, as well as explosives and trip wires. They were hardening the house for an assault when everything went up."

"With gasoline in pans? What's that for?" Mad Dog asked.

"You come for a hard case," Dale said. "You bust a door or window and what do you put in?"

"A flashbang," Mad Dog said.

"And you train to do what as the flashbang goes off?"

"Run right in," Mad Dog said, understanding.

Dale nodded. "Right into a fireball. The flashbang sets off the gasoline. Besides burning you, even if you're wearing Nomex, it'll distract you enough to miss the trip wires."

"How do you figure they set it off?" Edgar said.

Dale turned away to look at the still smoldering wreckage. A sharp crack from the ruin pile caused everyone to flinch. "I don't know," he said. "Could have been old dynamite, a mistake with the detonators, anything. We'll just have to wait and see."

"You all can wait and see," Edgar said. "That son of a bitch is dead and good riddance. I think it's Miller Time."

The generator on one of the fire trucks died and shut down the floodlights. The light from the smoldering fire flickered red on Dale's face.

# PART 2

Nina made her way through the maze of beige cubicles that divided up the Detective Division. Small signs led the way: Homicide, Robbery, Burglary, Sex Crimes, Street Crime. The other detectives, some in bad suits, others in street clothes, stood to greet her.

"Good work, Nina! Saved the State the cost of the trial."

"Hey Ace! Finally got on the scoreboard, huh?"

She grinned and gave them a thumbs-up. Herb stood up from his desk, walked around to the empty desk facing his, and ceremoniously pulled back her battered stenographer's chair. "Your seat, madam."

"Thank you, garçon," she said as he pushed in her chair. "Is that the evening's special splashed all across your tie?"

"Yes, madam. The finest Hardee's Breakfast Biscuits. Quite piquant, with a tart little sauce."

Nina laughed. "Where's my coffee, you goof? Where's Robbie?"

"Right behind you, Nina," said Robbie, the slim and bald male administrative assistant who rode herd on the unruly detectives. "I'm so glad you're back. Here you go," he said, handing her an oversized ceramic mug. "Caribou French Roast, done in a clean pot with fresh water, just a dollop of half and half and one sugar."

Nina wrapped her hands around the big mug and put her face into the steam. "Hmm," she said. "Robbie, I've missed you." She smiled up at the handsome young man, his shaven head gleaming under the office lights. "I wish you liked girls. I'd take you home in a minute."

"Well, if I ever decide to go *there*, you'll be the first to know," Robbie said. "That is if Sergeant Dunn here lets me near you."

Herb mock-threatened Robbie with one big fist. "Go on, get outta here..."

Robbie retreated, laughing, to his desk and its neatly stacked piles of investigative folders. "Welcome back!"

Herb sat down and leaned back in his groaning chair, kicked his feet up on the desk and gazed with great satisfaction at his partner. "How you doing?"

Nina sipped her coffee and waved to some other officers returning to their work areas. She studied her partner with affection. "I'm great, handsome. Worked out, caught up on my tan, read, even got laid. All in all, not a bad couple of days."

"Who's the guy?"

"I never asked."

"Jesus, Nina!"

Nina grinned over her coffee cup. "Got you. Don't ask if you don't want to know. What we got cooking?"

Herb dropped his feet and sat forward. "Not a lot. The Sanders and Anderson cases are coming up, we'll have to get ready for court on those. Catch up on your mail and we'll go over it later."

Nina nodded and turned her attention to the paper spilling out of her inbox. The stack of open cases was undisturbed. Herb knew better than to rummage through her organized files unless she was there to guide him. She quickly sorted through the various correspondence: internal memos, an administrative note pleading for officers to stop taking sodas from the malfunctioning machine on the third floor, a new parking sticker for her civilian car, a stack of NCIC and DOJ alerts. She flipped through those, then stopped and read with interest the alert detailing the escape and criminal history of Jonny Maxwell.

"Did you see this?" she said, holding up the black and white notice with Maxwell's picture. "Did you read about this guy?"

Herb looked up and nodded. "Yeah. Major league bad guy, that one. He blew himself up a couple of days ago."

"What do you mean?"

"Don't you watch the news?"

**MARCUS WYNNE**

"Not for the last couple of days."

"This guy Maxwell, the Green Beret. He robbed an armored car with a biker, Satan's Outlaws. They whack a couple of security guards, shoot up a Milwaukee cop, blew up a couple more with a booby-trapped car. U.S. Marshal's SOG tracks them up north of Milwaukee to some little town, but before they can take the guy he blows himself up by accident with a bunch of stolen explosives. He was booby-trapping the cabin they were hiding in and booby-trapped his own self," Herb said. He added with some satisfaction, "Killed him and his partners in crime very dead."

"This guy had some history," Nina said.

"Fuck him," Herb said. "He's a crispy critter now."

Later, after their meeting with the district attorney on the Sanders and Anderson cases, Nina and Herb prowled the Minneapolis streets in their unmarked Crown Victoria. Herb drove and Nina watched. Cruising with her partner was Nina's favorite route back to her on-the-job mindset. She studied the street the same way she'd learned as a uniform, watching for the people who watched them too closely or not closely enough, for the sudden shifts in body language, the turning away, the touching of the waist or hip or the burying of hands in pockets. Nina was a street animal at heart. She loved being out on the bricks catching bad guys, playing the game.

They cruised the West Side University area, through Seven Corners, across the Washington Street Bridge, and stopped for a coffee at Maxwell's, a cop hangout. Then they drove through downtown and the Warehouse District with all its clubs, restaurants, and coffee shops. The expensively dressed people hurrying from building to building clutching their Starbucks cups fell behind them as they drove up into the huddled black ghetto on the North Side where gang-bangers stalked away at the sight of the unmarked squad and daring children shouted "Five-oh!" and "Hello, Mr. Police!"

"How's the eye? You getting it back?" Herb said.

"Never lost it, old man."

"Funny thing is, I believe that."

Nina didn't know why that was so. More to the point, she didn't really care as long as it kept working. She'd always been alert to nuance. Maybe it was growing up in a household thick with tension and her need to understand the subtle silences between her parents. Maybe it was being a woman, understanding at some preverbal, unconscious level the song and dance of body language and intonation that spells out the real communication most people try to hide beneath the words.

She just knew to trust her intuition, that urgent feeling that became a soft voice from behind her right ear.

And though it wasn't any one thing that was happening or unfolding on the street in front of her, there was something urging her to look harder, to look twice, to keep looking around. Maybe it was the hyperalertness the psychologist had talked about, maybe a little depression with the anniversary of Uncle Ray's death coming up, or maybe it was just a case of off-rhythm PMS. But something was up. Something was coming their way.

Jonny Maxwell—Billy Martin to his neighbors—walked through his new apartment. It was small. One bedroom in the back, with a window that opened out into an alley. A good-sized kitchen, a bathroom with tub and shower, a small front room. Windows in all the rooms that opened out onto the side alley or the backyard. His front door opened into a hallway that led to the building's back security entrance. Behind a service door were washers and dryers; past them was a short hallway leading to storage lockers and an unused service door that opened out onto the alley. From the alley, there were at least six different driving routes out of the area on the two streets connected by the alleyway.

It was a great safehouse, one of the best he'd ever had.

The neighborhood was a mix of rental housing and single residence homes, with lots of transient foot traffic between the trendy shops that anchored the neighborhood, and the bike and foot paths at the bottom of the hill that connected the Chain of Lakes. As a flight attendant traveling constantly, no one, even if they noticed, would comment on his prolonged absences. Not that he planned to be here long. There was almost a half-million dollars stashed in neat bundles hidden in the suspended ceiling, in a duffel bag behind the bedroom door, and stashed in a lockbox in a privately owned vault company's main vault. Was it enough? He wasn't sure. He needed to lie low, watch his trail, and make sure that no one was sniffing for him. And he had yet to decide where to go.

It would be easy enough to go back to Central or South America, but the U.S. government had its tentacles into everything down there. Sooner or later, he'd run across someone who would know someone who'd want to pay him a visit. He'd rather disappear completely and that would cost: for plastic surgeons, if he went that route, but most of all for the ability to live without leaving traces, to pay cash and subsist well, but quietly, below the horizons of the searchers that might come someday.

There was Africa. Jonny had met some South Africans, mercs, good solid Afrikaners of Dutch descent who knew their business in the bush. Mercenaries had become one of South Africa's biggest exports. He'd have to steer clear of the big outfits, like Executive Outcomes—too many connections with government organizations. With enough money, he wouldn't have to work, and there was plenty of hunting in Africa. Maybe South Africa, maybe Zimbabwe or Uganda. A man with plenty of dollars could avoid questions and the American intelligence infrastructure was full of holes down there. That was a better possibility than Asia. Jonny didn't relish the thought of disappearing into the Golden Triangle and living at the whim of opium lords like Khun Sa, despite their willingness to take in men of his background. Better that he go his own way, make it someplace else.

He stood in his bathroom and studied his face in the mirror. After his return, a few minutes work with the hair cutters and a razor had restored the buzz cut, goateed hipster in his white T-shirt and black Levi's and Doc Martens. Jonny tried on faces. First he smiled, relaxing his eyes and letting the ends curl up with the rest of his face. Then he frowned. Then he let his face grow still. He needed work, he decided, especially on the relaxed face. Too much of the watcher and the hunter there. The CIA instructors and psychologists had warned them during their advanced training how the internal mental processes that made them effective hunters marked them out to other hunters. Jonny remembered one time in Annapolis, when he'd been walking the streets alone on a busy Sunday afternoon. He'd stopped to have a beer in Ego Alley, one of the bars down near the waterfront. His neck had gotten that little tingle he felt when someone was watching him, and he looked up to see a couple of off-duty SEALs giving him the operator's knowing look.

He shook himself out of his reverie and decided to go for a run. The constant action of the last few days, too much driving and too much sitting, had left him feeling tense and out of shape. Besides, it was the end of the workday and all the women would be out.

Time spent in reconnaissance was never time wasted.

Jonny started out easy. He'd clocked the distance; once around Lake Harriet was 2.7 miles, once around Lake Calhoun was 3.2; around them both was just over six miles, which was his normal training run. The wide paths were full of runners, walkers, strollers, dog-walkers; men, children, women of every shape, age and color, beauties and the not so beautiful, the haughty and the friendly. Most of the serious runners, the men anyway, looked like seventy-five-dollar haircut button-down shirt Yuppie types. Jonny blew by them easily, leaving them looking curiously at the hellishly fit creative-looking guy who whipped by them. A few tried to match his pace but fell behind quickly.

It was satisfying to leave them behind and settle into his solo rhythm, the long stride and smooth glide over the pavement, the sweat starting now, first a beading, then the flow as his pores opened up. And while he ran, he scanned. A woman was just ahead of him as he curved around Lake Harriet toward the band shell; she was a good runner, he could tell. She had the long stride, the upright stance, and the easy relaxed arms of a coached long distance runner. As he drew alongside, he took in her long, muscled tan legs, the lean mid-section, the small, firm breasts.

"Good pace you're running today," Jonny said.

"Thanks! You too ... what are you at, six minutes?"

"Yeah, easy training today."

"Are you racing?"

"I didn't know we were."

She laughed. "I mean, are you training for one, like Grandma's or Duluth?"

"Hadn't thought about it."

She had a good laugh and a strong, lean face, with green eyes that sparkled when she looked over at Jonny. "You should, if this is your easy training pace!"

Jonny said, "You run out here every day?"

"Yep. Every other day with my running club."

They drew near to the road connecting the two lakes.

"Well, I get off here," Jonny said. "I'm Billy."

"I'm Rachel," she called, waving as he crossed the road. "See you around!"

"I'm sure I will," Jonny called back. "Have a good run."

It was that easy.

**MARCUS WYNNE**

Jed sat straight, his feet together, in one of the big armchairs in Dale's hotel suite. "There's some inconsistencies in the scene I don't get. Maybe you can help me sort it out," he said.

"Is there a final ID?" Dale said.

Jed shrugged. "The coroner's working on it. We've got the Bureau and the Department of Defense labs helping out. Maxwell was hunkered right over the primary device when it went off, so there isn't much of him to piece together. I don't think there's much doubt about him. What bugs me is Pissolt. It's clear he was killed *before* the blast. He was bagged up in plastic just like chicken for a picnic. Why would Maxwell do that?"

"Maybe they had a falling out over money. Or the girl."

"I can't see Pissolt being too worried about the girl. Some of the money was recovered, but there's a lot missing, probably burnt. We found some lockbags with ash residue. Okay, if they had a falling out over money and Maxwell kills him, why bag him up?"

"I don't know. I can speculate all day—maybe he didn't want him stinking the place up, maybe he was going to dump the body someplace to put us off the track . . . hell, I don't know, Jed. How does it matter anyway? He's dead now."

"Yeah," Jed said. "There's that. I don't like to leave loose ends dangling. It just bugs me, is all."

"He might have wanted to clear up his own loose ends. Take care of those two, leave them there or dump them someplace, leave nothing but a dead end at the cabin for you. If SOG had hit that place, you'd have been putting all of them into bags."

Jed's face grew even flatter as the muscles smoothed out. "I hear that. So. Are you through here or what?"

"I want to wait till the coroner gives the definite ID. Then I can say my job is done."

"Everything we've found indicates those bone fragments came from Jonny Maxwell. The remains of his clothes, his guns and IDs, the money, the body characteristics . . . the coroner is ninety percent sure. If we could find more of the skull, that would take us all the way, or if you guys had DNA on record someplace . . ."

"I already checked. He was supposed to have been typed, but either got overlooked or his records lost. Not everybody in the military is in there yet."

Jed sighed and held up his hands. "Then we'll cultivate patience. But I tell you, Dale. He's dead."

After Jed left, Dale made himself a cup of coffee with the in-room brewer, dressed it heavily with cream and sugar, then pulled an overstuffed armchair in front of the window. Milwaukee's General Mitchell International Airport's runways were directly across the street. The airport hosted a Wisconsin Air Guard Unit, so between the DC-9s and B-727s, an olive drab C-130 or C-123 would sometimes lumber by. He'd made his first parachute jump at Fort Benning from a C-123 a long time ago.

He wondered what it would have been like if he'd been the one on the run. Unlike Jonny, he had family: a younger brother in Illinois, an uncle in Seattle. Like Jonny, both his parents were dead, his mother of breast cancer when he was a teenager, his father in a car accident outside of Reno six years ago. He had old friends in North Carolina and Washington, D.C., a few others scattered across the country. He had places to go where they'd take him in, where they wouldn't turn him away.

Not like Jonny.

Jonny had no one outside of Special Forces and DOMINANCE RAIN. Without them, nothing and no one. The humiliation of the trial and the exposure of his crimes had driven them all away. The final wedge between Jonny and his past was Dale on the stand. He could have pled ignorance, Dale supposed, could have said he didn't recall anything, said he hadn't suspected.

But it had to be done. Jonny was way off the reservation. Then, as now, it had taken Dale to bring him down. Deep down inside, Dale hid a shame-filled satisfaction at seeing Jonny brought down— then and now. The great Jonny Maxwell. Who turned out not to be so great after all. Whose lectures on mental discipline had turned out to be empty words.

Dale thought of what Special Agent Nakamura had said about structure. What that guy didn't know would fill a big book. Special operators build structure within structure, that's what they do. The regular military is built on being a cog in the big machine that looked out for you and told you what to do. Special operators lived, fought, and died in small units or alone, out on the sharp tip of the spear. It's one thing to be brave and optimistic when you're one grunt in a division of more than ten thousand other grunts; it's another thing to be brave and do your job when you're alone and exhausted, with no one to support you, to talk you through, to watch your back—or to tell anyone what you really did. The only thing you had for certain is what you build inside to sustain you. The structure no one else saw, the one you built and carried around in your head. When it came down to it, you were always alone. That had been hard to learn.

Watching Jonny had taught him how.

Dale slammed his coffee cup down on the windowsill and went to the bed and began to pack his bag. The cell phone he'd borrowed from Jed when his own had died rang from the bedside table.

"Miller," he snapped.

Ray Dalton said, "I interrupt you?"

"Boss."

A long silence. "What's the word?" Ray said.

"It's not official yet. But it's him. Caucasian male, right-handed, right size and weight, wearing his gear and carrying his ID . . . it was Jonny. They'll announce it on the record soon."

"Hard to believe he'd go like that."

"I think maybe he wanted to."

"I thought that too." Ray paused as though waiting for Dale to say something. After another long silence he said, "Come on home, son. Get on the next plane. I'll have one of the boys pick you up."

**NO OTHER OPTION**

Dale thought Ray's tone was too careful. "I'd better stay till all the loose ends are swept up. I'll see it through."

"Do you think it's necessary?"

"Better to be sure."

"What's your gut tell you?"

"What's yours tell you?"

"All right. Do what you think needs to be done. Be sure. Then take a couple of days admin if you want. Take your time. We've got plenty of work to do when you get back."

"I'll let you know when they get final with it. I'll see you in a couple of days."

"Dale?"

"Yeah."

"You did the right thing. It was a hard job and you did it well. Not that I expected any less from you. The hard things are what we do. Remember that." Ray paused. "We'll talk when you get back."

"Right. Miller out."

"Out here."

Dale pressed the END button. The room felt as though it was shrinking around him. It was time to get out.

The Minneapolis night life was different. In the light of day, every-thing—the blue waters of Lake Harriet, the sharp snap of sails as boats turned in the wind, the tanned and healthy pedestrians—seemed so clean and midwestern. At night the city was different; its rough edges showed. In the Warehouse District downtown, there were bright streetlights and well-dressed people crowding the clubs and restaurants. On the fringe of the night crowds that overlapped the sidewalks into the street were the sharp-eyed men and women who might prey on the unwary, who evaluated each passerby with the seasoned eyes of the urban predator.

They left Jonny alone.

Jonny cruised the sidewalks like a shark among the penguins. The physical confidence he moved with set him out. It wasn't just the easy physicality. Lots of athletes, and there were many others on the street, had that. It was his willingness to hurt that the predators saw in his faintly insolent, well-concealed look that lingered just a little too long in the eyes, in the solid shoulder bump he gave when he passed the other pedestrians, players, and citizens on the sidewalk. It was quiet but it was clear: "Don't fuck with me."

The diversity of the club scene surprised Jonny. There were so many different clubs in such a small area: South Beach was a dance club packed with blacks and Asians; First Avenue was young wanna-be metalheads; The Blues Alley a mix of young and old, blue and white collar. And it seemed as though the patrons of each club made their way to all the other clubs in the course of an evening.

Some of the people out on the street were transients and runaway teens, many of them girls. Jonny didn't care for those; he disliked the dirt and smell. He liked his bodies clean and well taken care of. He never saw their faces once he made ready to use them. He liked them like that girl Rachel, the runner. He'd filed her away as a possible, but she was too close to home. The better hunting grounds were farther away.

And there was good hunting here. He liked what he saw. There were lots of women with the well-tended, muscular bodies he liked, out alone or in small groups. During the day he saw them running or blading or biking around Lake Harriet; at night he saw them out down here prowling for drinks and fun. Most of the men out were walking in convivial frat boy huddles, looking but rarely daring to speak to the women. Two big college age boys came toward Jonny, and he smiled a dangerous smile that caused them to split apart and give him plenty of room.

Shy boys. They didn't know what they were missing.

Down the block on Hennepin, almost to the big bridge over the river, the new Federal Reserve Bank building stood. The construction was almost complete and bank operations had already commenced. Jonny walked down the street that paralleled the building complex, noting the armored exits where the trucks would come out, and the comprehensive camera coverage provided by the pan, tilt, and zoom cameras bristling from the building like the pimples on the face of a frustrated boy.

He'd be back here.

Farther down the street was a lonely neon sign above a brightly lit window. ICHIBAN—A JAPANESE RESTAURANT. Jonny looked in the window at the tables filled with chattering people. There was an open seat at the sushi bar in the back. He went in and let the wash of light and smell and chatter flow over him for a moment, then slipped between the tables to the host station.

"Hi, how many?" the Japanese man at the podium said.

"Just me, for the sushi bar, if that chair's open," Jonny said.

The Japanese host, whose name tag said TORI, looked around and checked his little chart. "There's two empty, go for it."

"Thanks."

**MARCUS WYNNE**

Jonny slid onto a low-backed stool chair and nodded to the sushi chef.

"Irrashi!" the sushi chef said. "What can I make you tonight?"

On Jonny's left was a beautiful Asian girl in a short, backless black dress and wearing the ridiculously high platform shoes that were in style. Her hair was cut short in a close helmet. She was some kind of mix, not Chinese or Japanese and far too fine-boned to be Korean—maybe Thai or Laotian in her middle to late twenties. She was nibbling delicately at a spicy tuna roll while flipping through the pages of what appeared to be a large comic book.

"I'll have one of whatever she's having, a futomaki, a salmon skin handwrap, and two mirugai. A Kirin, too," Jonny said.

The Asian girl gazed at him. It was the disdainful look of a beautiful woman who was fully aware of the impact she had on men, and was bored by it.

Jonny gave her a little raise of his eyebrows as though to say, 'So?'

"Hi," he said.

She turned away from him and returned to the pages of her comic book. She had one nostril pierced with a tiny blue sapphire mounted on a post. The blue stone caught the light from the track lighting above and glimmered in Jonny's eyes. Her skin was smooth and flawless and radiated warmth. She was alone. The couple on the other side of her were engrossed in their own conversation and paid her no attention.

"What are you reading?" Jonny asked.

She looked at him expressionlessly. "Manga," she said. "Do you know what that is?"

"Japanese comic book," Jonny said.

"Hmm," she said. "I prefer graphic novel."

Jonny smiled in barely veiled contempt. He felt the anger warming him; he banked it slightly with satisfaction, pushing it away for later. The sushi chef set his order down in front of him. He stirred soy sauce into his wasabi and said, "Same thing, isn't it?"

She pushed the book at him and pointed to the open page. "Does that look like a comic book to you?"

The artwork was beautifully done. A woman with hugely stylized breasts and an impossibly thin waist was bent over a leather armchair. Her head was hooded in a white leather mask. Behind her

**NO OTHER OPTION**

stood a fiercely grinning samurai, his kimono opened and an enormous phallus protruding, the tip just touching the naked buttocks of the woman. His swords were on the floor at his feet, the short one unsheathed among the ripped and sliced shreds of the woman's undergarments. It was strikingly done, in shades of purple and blue, set in a room with a huge French window through which gleamed a bright and shining moon.

It was one of the most beautiful things Jonny had ever seen, far away from the pornography he'd enjoyed as a boy. He looked her directly in the eyes, paused a moment, and said, quite honestly, "That's beautiful."

There was a sudden caution in the woman's face, a sudden caution followed by interest.

"You think so?" she said. "Why?"

"What do you think of it? You're the one reading it."

The tip of her tongue flicked to her lip, then away. "Most men find it . . . arousing. I don't often hear them say it's beautiful." She let her hand linger on the page. "It is beautiful, though . . . incredibly erotic."

The two studied each other for a long moment. She spoke first.

"My name is Annie. Annie Ma."

"You're Laotian?"

"Yes, my mother is Hmong. My father was white, a soldier."

"Ah," Jonny said.

"And you are?"

"Bill."

"What do you do, Bill?"

Jonny turned to his food. "Right now I'm eating sushi."

She was silent for a moment.

"Where did you learn to do that?" she said.

"Where did I learn to do what?"

"To be so hard. And to conceal it so well."

Jonny looked up from his sushi and studied her carefully. She was fully engaged and alert, watching him, listening carefully for his response.

"I don't know what you mean," he said, gauging her.

She rested her elbow on the counter, draped one immaculately manicured hand, her nails a lustrous red, across the manga page and its picture.

**MARCUS WYNNE**

"Like that," she said. "Anger, caution, you hide it so well. What do you do?"

"You an amateur psychologist? Counselor to the secretly crazy you meet in sushi bars?"

She smiled for the first time. Her teeth were small and fine, like pearl corn. "I just find you . . . interesting. Are you an actor?"

"I'm a flight attendant."

"Oh, I don't believe that."

Jonny shrugged and busied himself pouring his Kirin into the iced glass the waitress brought him.

"What do you find most beautiful about this scene?" Ann asked.

Jonny ignored her and dipped his futomaki into the wasabi paste. The spice brought a mist to his eyes and a flush to his face, which helped to conceal his mounting anger. He sipped his beer, slowed his breath, and made a promise to himself about this woman.

"I just like it," he said. "I don't think much about what I like. I know it when I see it."

"You see it and you feel it, then?"

"What do you do?"

She touched her ear, traced the line of her jaw and down her neck.

"I'm an artist."

"Painting, that kind of thing?"

"Yes."

"What do you like most about that drawing? You like it as an artist?"

She took her last piece of spicy tuna roll, placed it between her teeth, and took a neat bite, chewing and swallowing before she answered. "I like it as a woman. I appreciate it as an artist." She wiped her fingers delicately on her napkin. "The energy. The danger. The excitement of such total . . . submission. Strength. The pleasure of being taken. The pleasure of giving such . . . pleasure . . . to the taker."

Jonny looked at her and let his mask slide, just a little, to give her some of the fierce light he kept banked behind his eyes. "You like it as a woman?" he said. He took satisfaction in the way her cool composure shook under the intensity of his cruel, measured gaze. "I don't think you know anything about that."

She looked away, then stood and fumbled with her purse. She

**NO OTHER OPTION**

set a handful of bills on the counter and walked quickly away, turning sideways to squeeze past several customers waiting at the host stand.

The sushi chef fixed a hard look on Jonny. "What's up with that?"

Jonny shrugged, dipped another futomaki in the wasabi. "She's crazy."

"No," the sushi chef said. "I saw that look you gave her. What's wrong with you? You crazy?"

"No," Jonny said. "I'm an artist."

The sushi chef shook his head and waved the waitress over. "Get him his check," he said.

"I didn't ask for the check," Jonny said.

"I don't want you in here. She's a regular. You're not. Finish up and get out."

Jonny set the piece of sushi he'd been eating down and wiped his hands. "I'm not done with my meal."

"You're done. Tori!" the sushi chef called to the host. "Get this guy's check."

Jonny held up his hand, stood, and pulled out a roll of bills. He counted several off and threw them down on the counter.

He walked out, bumping several customers, who looked after him and wisely offered no protest. Out on the street, he took several deep breaths through his nostrils, holding for a count of four, exhaling for a count of four. He took satisfaction in the reassurance of discipline and control when his heartrate began to subside and the dull pounding in his ears began to moderate. A late-model Volvo sedan slowed as it passed by, and he saw Annie Ma behind the wheel looking at him, hesitating, then driving slowly on. 978 LVE. Jonny looked up and visualized the numbers and letters, memorizing them. For $4.95 at the Department of Motor Vehicles, he'd have the registration and the address. Midwestern efficiency. It was a beautiful thing. But right now he needed something. He had some things to work out.

"This is different," Herb said. "Real signature case."

Nina nodded as she went over the handwritten notes she was compiling for the typist. They'd just spent two hours with a victim from the night before, working through the detailed pro forma interview the FBI's Behavioral Science Unit had developed for local law enforcement to capture all pertinent information on a sexual predator.

"Real winner, this guy," Nina said. She glanced over her notes. "Check me on this, Herb. Twenty-three-year-old victim. Recent grad from St. Olaf's. Out celebrating her job offer from, um, Salomon Smith Barney. Perp surprises her outside her apartment door, in a secured building with a secured garage. Uses fucking pressure point techniques to gain compliance. Ties her to the bed with sashcord brought to the scene. Hoods her with a pillowcase. Rapes her and tape-records it. Takes a break and helps himself to a sandwich from her icebox, comes back for round two. Then he interrogates her? Asks her if she gets pleasure out of the whole thing?"

"It's like he was genuinely curious," Herb said. His face was set and hard in a look Nina knew well. "Sick fuck."

"He doesn't cut her, beat her, or get more violent than he has to—except when he starts asking her about whether she got pleasure from being raped?" Nina said. "That's the word he used. Pleasure. That seemed to really set him off. And then when she finally snaps and starts screaming about how she doesn't get any pleasure at all, then he just leaves her?"

"Girl had guts," Herb said. "She was lucky. I'd of expected this guy to go all the way."

"He could have, but he didn't. You know what I'm thinking on this?"

"What?"

"That Green Beret rapist? The one who blew himself up?"

"Yeah? What about him?"

Nina dug through her inbox. She pulled out the Jonny Maxwell bulletin and handed it to Herb. "Look. Same MO and signature. Skillful stealth entry, easy control of victim, sashcord brought to the scene, hooded victims with pillowcase, tape recording. Same MO, same signature. I'm thinking same guy."

"This guy is dead, Nina. It was on the fucking evening news."

"So maybe he had a partner at one time, or celled with somebody who picked up his tricks. Let's call the marshals and see who his known affiliates were, find out who he celled with. Maybe we got a recent parolee up here."

Herb nodded. "I like it. You're my gal, Nina. I'll give them a call."

"No, I'll call. I'll get more with my sugar than you'll get with your stick. You go buy me lunch. I want the number two special with egg roll. Go. Get out of here. Fetch me food."

Nina phoned a female U.S. marshal she knew in the St. Paul office, who was able to give her some background on the Jonny Maxwell fugitive case and the unlisted cell phone number of the inspector in charge, Jed Loveless.

**MARCUS WYNNE**

## 2.6

Jed looked down the long breakfast table he shared with his task force in the dining room of the Manchester Suites hotel. "It's down to me now, boys. I've been to see the coroner. The final results aren't conclusive—they couldn't find enough of the late Jonny Maxwell to give a one hundred percent positive ID. We decided to settle for the ninety percent we got." He paused, and looked at Dale. "The son of a bitch is dead. Blew himself up fixing a nasty for us. Good riddance, case closed, do not pass go, return home."

"So it's over?" Dale said. "We're done now?"

"Yes, Dale," Jed said formally. "It's over." He looked at his marshals and said in a lighter tone, "So it's time for a few drinks, courtesy of Willie Mac, over at the Airport Club."

"Drinks?" Edgar said. "Oh, okay. Maybe just one."

"Shut up, fool," Tommy said. "They got food at this club?"

"They got food, they got big-tit naked dancers, they got drinks, and it's all on the Milwaukee Police Department," Jed said.

"I got to think about a career change," Dale said. "You guys got the better benefit package."

Edgar snorted.

"Ignore my partner," Tommy said. "Let me buy you a drink, young Mr. Miller. I'll tell you some lies and you can continue not telling me a goddam thing."

That made all of them laugh, even Edgar. They left the breakfast room for their rooms.

"Remember to bring me my cell phone and charger," Jed said to Dale. "That is if you're all through running up long distance calls on my dime. You check in with your people?"

"I'll need to call them, let them know."

"You do that." Jed turned to catch the elevator behind Tommy and Edgar.

"Hey, Jed!" Dale called.

The old marshal turned. "Yeah?"

"Thanks."

"For what?"

"Never mind. Meet you in the lobby in what?"

"I got to make some calls. Give me forty-five minutes."

"Roger that."

In his own room, Dale plugged the cell phone charger into the wall and reinserted the Motorola. He fussed with the coffeepot to make another cup. Just as he settled into the armchair, the cell phone trilled.

He answered. "Miller."

"This is Detective Nina Capushek with the Minneapolis Police Department. Jed Loveless, please." The woman's voice was crisp but pleasant.

"This is his phone, but he's not available right now. I'll see him in a few minutes. Can I give him your number?"

"Are you working on the Jonathan Maxwell fugitive case?"

"I was," Dale said. "The case is closed. Maxwell's dead. Why?"

"I heard he was killed. Look, I'm in Sex Crimes. We have a case with an MO and signature real similar to Maxwell's. We're wondering what you can tell us about any possible associates or cell-mates that might have been recently paroled."

"I'm not the one you should talk to. Let me get your number and I'll have Jed call you."

"Hey look," Nina said. "I know how you guys are about your cases. Talk to Stephanie Bokash in the St. Paul office if you want some history on me. I just need some help here, okay? Cop to cop?"

"I'm not a cop."

There was a long silence. "Okay," she said. "So what are you? The official phone answerer or what?"

"I'm a consultant with DOD. Came to help out with the profiling."

**MARCUS WYNNE**

"Well then, you are the guy I should talk to. Can you help me out?"

"I doubt it, but I'll do what I can."

Nina told him about the case.

"When did this happen?" Dale said.

"Last night. Some similarities, huh?"

"How did she describe him?"

"Never got a good look at him. Very strong, in shape. Knew some kind of martial arts stuff."

Dale was silent as he absorbed that. His mind spun with the possibility.

"That bring up anything?" Nina pressed. "Any of the guys Maxwell hung with, celled with, anything?"

"No. He didn't have any real associates. His new ones, they all died with him."

Nina sighed. "Well, this is a dry hole sucking. If you or Loveless come up with any ideas, give me a call at 612-555-4988. You'll get my voice mail if I'm not here. Thanks for the time."

"Is this the first case like this you've had?" Dale said.

"Yeah. Why?"

"It's nothing. I'll tell Jed you called. If he's got anything else for you, he'll call you back."

"Whatever. Thanks." Nina hung up.

Dale flipped the cell phone closed and slid it back into the charger. He took out his pocket atlas and studied the distance between Milwaukee and Minneapolis. He leaned back in the chair, his coffee forgotten, and thought through the implications of the phone call.

"Oh, Jonny," he said. "That would be a good one, wouldn't it?"

He made a short call to Northwest Airlines, then threw his gear into his bag and went down to the lobby and checked out. When Jed and his marshals came out of the elevator, he was waiting for them.

"Here's your phone," Dale said.

"Thanks," Jed said. "Did you charge it?"

"Yeah."

"Ready to go?"

"I've got to take off," Dale said. "They want me back on the ranch and back to work."

**NO OTHER OPTION**

"You don't have time for a drink?" Jed said.

"Too bad," Edgar said.

"If I go now, I can catch the next plane," Dale said.

Jed held out his hand. "Take care of yourself. Stay in touch."

Dale shook with Jed, then Tommy, and nodded to Edgar. "You guys be careful out there."

"You too, Dale. Whatever it is you do." Tommy grinned and ran a hand through his hair.

Edgar shrugged and waved. He watched Dale go out the hotel lobby door and drive away in his rental car. "That's a strange boy," he said to no one in particular.

"You should talk," Tommy said. "Let's go get us some titties and beer."

Dale returned his car at the Express Aisle and went to the Northwest ticket counter. He'd timed it right. He was just able to catch the next flight to Minneapolis.

Something nagged at him after Detective Capushek's call, something he didn't want to discuss with Jed. Yet. Hunches were an important part of his job, and his training had built the ability to temper the nuances of intuition with judgment. And he was sick and tired of being the advisor, the man in the background with someone else setting the pace. He was a hunter and his secondary role in this operation chafed. Maybe it was over. But maybe it wasn't, and it was his job to be sure. A deception of that magnitude and the brazen cunning of it . . . how logical it would be for Jonny to cover his trail like that. And so much more believable than thinking Jonny would blow himself up.

He had the authority to act alone if he had to, so he could go and see for himself, walk the ground, look at the evidence. If it turned out to be nothing, then he could put it onto Loveless to help the locals with their search for someone who copied Jonny's methodology. And then he could take some time to decompress and see Minneapolis, which was supposed to be a nice town with good-looking women.

It was a short forty-minute flight from Milwaukee to Minneapolis. The Twin Cities were lush and green beneath him, crossed with rivers and spotted with lakes. With only hand luggage and the

DOD Special Agent credentials that let him take his pistol in the cabin with him, he was quickly off the plane and to the rental car counters, where he picked a full-size Le Baron out of the National Emerald Aisle. He studied the map the clerk gave him, then drove from the airport into downtown and quartered it as carefully as he would if he were making an initial foray into enemy territory. Satisfied that he could find his way around, he drove back out toward the airport and checked into a Motel Six for the night. After a light dinner, he went to bed early and slept surprisingly well.

The Sex Crimes Unit was housed in the main police headquarters, a hulking gray stone anachronism lumped down between the sparkling metal and glass corporate towers that surrounded it. The block was seedy. The only businesses were a few small bars and strip clubs. A long line of blue and white Minneapolis Police cruisers were parked bumper to bumper down the middle of the street. Dale parked in the open garage down the block and walked back. Inside, he asked two uniformed officers where the Sex Crimes Unit was. He went up two flights of stairs and came to a windowless door with an intercom set in the wall beside it. When he pushed the button, there was a loud hum and a tinny voice said, "Can I help you?"

Dale looked up at the video camera set above the door. "I'm looking for Detective Capushek."

"Your name?"

Dale held up his DOD credentials. "Master Sergeant Dale Miller. I'm with the Department of Defense. I spoke to her yesterday."

"Just a moment please."

There was a short silence. Nina Capushek's voice came over the intercom. "Miller? I'll be right down to let you in."

There were fast, sharp footsteps behind the door, which was yanked open by a woman in her late twenties or early thirties. She was younger than Dale expected and surprisingly good-looking. Big green eyes with only a touch of makeup, a serious expression, tall with long athlete's legs set off in khaki Dockers cinched close at the waist with a heavy leather belt. A Sig-Sauer P-228 was holstered behind her right hip in a speed scabbard, with two magazines set in racing pouches in front of her left hip. Her badge was clipped to the belt in front of her pistol.

"Miller?" She held out her hand. "I'm Nina."

"Dale," he said. She had a strong grip. Her nails were cut square and short with a clear polish.

"Come on down." She led him down the hallway. "I didn't expect you," she said over her shoulder.

"I had to come this way to get home," Dale lied. "I thought I'd stop by, see if there was anything I could do."

"Really?" Nina said. She led him into a long office off the hall. There were too many desks squeezed into too small a space. Police officers in uniform and in plainclothes worked and looked at Dale curiously as he followed her to where two old gray metal desks sat facing each other. She sat at one, gestured at a folding chair beside it for Dale.

"So," Nina said. "What do you think you might be able to do for me?"

"Look over your findings, see if there's some military training evident, something like that . . ." Dale began.

Nina cut him off. "You have a lot of experience as a sex crimes investigator, Sergeant Miller?"

"No."

She looked him up and down. "Is law enforcement your main function?"

"Not in that area."

"Not in that area. What area would your main function lie in?"

Dale was stone-faced and stymied. He hadn't expected this, and he could tell she knew it.

"Why are you here?" Nina said. She looked him right in the eye and he saw no intention of letting him off the hook. "According to you the Green Beret rapist blew himself up in Horicon. Case closed. You tell me that there's nobody who celled or associated with Maxwell, I believe you. Should I not believe you?"

Dale found Nina's directness disconcerting and her attractiveness distracting. Nina smiled as though she knew exactly what he was thinking.

"You're not any kind of cop, are you, Miller?" she said. "Something else. Green Beret? You work with this guy? Is that the track?"

Dale let the word be dragged out of him. "Yes."

"So let me ask you again. Why are you here?" She leaned

forward in her chair, rested her elbows on her knees. "Is this fucker Maxwell alive, is that why you're here?"

Dale held up his hand. "Whoa. Wait. Stop. I just came through here to see if I could offer some help."

Nina sat back in her chair and crossed her legs. She wore plain blue low-heeled shoes and swung one foot back and forth, slowly. "You know one thing I never really get used to?"

"What?"

"How everybody lies to the cops."

Dale flushed. He was surprised at his embarrassment.

"You drink espresso?" she said.

"What?"

"I like espresso. Especially this time of the morning." She stood up. "You look like you could use some. C'mon, I'll buy."

"I don't . . ."

"C'mon, Dale. It's Dale, right? Let me get you a nice double latte. It'll put lead in your pencil." She brushed against him, close enough for him to smell a faint clean scent, like pine, from her hair. "Let's go, soldier."

Dale followed her to the door. She paused and said to the athletic, shaven-headed man sitting at the receptionist desk, "Robbie? Be a dear and tell Herb I'm out for coffee with my new boyfriend, will you?"

Robbie gave Dale a long look up and down and held his thumb up. "You go, girl."

Nina laughed out loud, deep hearty laughter, as Dale followed her out, confused as all hell.

The problem with robbing armored cars was that he needed backups. Snake and his little support structure had been adequate for the Milwaukee job, but Jonny had selected them more for the deception potential they offered which, according to the TV and newspapers, seemed to have worked perfectly. Their actual performance on the operation was piss-poor and unprofessional, but that had all worked to his ultimate advantage. He held his Pentax ZX-5 steady and zoomed the 28–200 lens out and photographed the truck entrance of the Federal Reserve Bank. On his mountain bike, with his camera slung over his shoulder, he looked like one of the photographers, graphic designers, or art students that made Minneapolis a center for advertising and design. And the architecture of the new Federal Reserve Bank, combining the latest security design with a pleasing modern facade, made for interesting shadows for photo compositions, if anyone bothered to ask what he was doing.

This would be too difficult to do on his own. He pedaled off, weaving between cars and making his way back to the Cedar Lake Bike Trail. And what for? He had $476,000 stashed. That was more than enough to leave the country, get him what he needed someplace else. But then he'd have to decide where. Where would he go? He banked his bike between two concrete pillars, down a short hill and onto the wide smooth bike path that connected downtown with the paths around the Chain of Lakes. With the current exchange rates in South Africa, his $476,000 would give him 3,584,280 South African rands. That would be enough to set him up for years, maybe even for life if he was careful.

But he didn't want to be careful.

If he could take it to a cool million in U.S. dollars—not counting the operational funds he'd need to set up a new identity, pay for minor plastic surgery, commissions to get the money in the appropriate banking circles so he could move it easily—he could bank it and do quite well on the interest alone. He'd be free to do whatever he wanted. South Africa was wild enough, open enough, with enough instability that he'd disappear beneath those troubled waters without a trace. The U.S. would have a hard time tracking him there. Despite the U.S.'s recent efforts to better relations after the lifting of apartheid, the Dutchmen in Pretoria had long memories.

The bike path rolled along a stretch of isolated meadow between the old rail tracks and Cedar Lake. There were only a few other bikers and one Rollerblader, an attractive redhead racing along. Jonny admired the lean length of her torso. He'd want more of that soon, too. He pedaled harder as he thought of Annie Ma and her second floor flat at 2782 Emerson Street. It looked like a nice place from the outside. The thought of taking a look inside was one he relished as he worked up a sweat. He followed the bike trail around to the Chain of Lakes trail. It only took him twenty minutes to get back to Lake Harriet and his apartment, where he took his bike around to the back of the building. One of his neighbors from upstairs, Rich, was in the backyard grilling.

141

"Have a good ride?" Rich called out to Jonny.

"Yeah. Great. It's a good day for it."

"Get any good shots?"

"Couple of nice architectural shots and some street scenes. We'll see how they come out."

"I'd like to see them," Rich said. He was a graphic designer and web page designer who freelanced for several of the local ad agencies. "I'm having a few people over ... we're going to party out here a little. You're welcome to join us. We're grilling a little salmon and asparagus and having some Sam Adams."

"I might just do that," Jonny said. "I'm going to cool off first."

He took his bike inside, unlocked his apartment, and wheeled his bike into the front room. The apartment was minimalist: a TV and VCR, a bookshelf stereo system, a small sofa. A single table in

**NO OTHER OPTION**

the kitchen, a folding futon in the bedroom. Jonny had quietly worked a few stash caches into the walls of the bedroom closet, where the rifles and shotguns he had taken from Snake's cabin were concealed. He'd removed and then replaced the suspended ceiling panels after he had hidden small bundles of packaged bills up there. Snake's .45 was loaded and slipped down between the cushions of the sofa, a Glock 19 was in a kitchen cabinet, and the .357 stoked with Glaser Safety Slugs was in the bedroom. Jonny kept his third High-Power, forwarded from Seattle, with him. When he rode his bike he stashed it in his fanny pack.

After a quick shower, he sat on the sofa and scribbled notes to himself on a legal-size yellow pad. He listed his options and considered them for a while. He could go for the job by himself, which was possible, but very high risk and fraught with all sorts of uncontrollable variables. He could set about trying to find local backups, dip into the biker community with some of the leads Snake had let drop. Shifting targets was another possibility. He could locate some other sources for large amounts of cash. He flipped through the yellow pages to Jewelry Wholesalers. While they might not have lots of cash on hand, loose diamonds were easy to transport out of the country. He could go to Antwerp or Amsterdam and dispose of them, no questions asked, then take the money on to South Africa. That would require him to do a different and probably more prolonged workup.

A multiple approach might be the ticket. Maybe several smaller jobs: gather gem quality stones, hit some of the smaller proprietary armored cars that worked for the banks instead of the Federal Reserve. Or maybe he could work some connects into the drug community. The Twin Cities had a well-established network of high-level drug traffickers; they were behind the ownership of some of the clubs in the Warehouse District. They would have large amounts of cash. A lot of money laundering took place in the heavy cash flow operations of bars and restaurants. That might bear looking into. All told, he had an operational goal of another $750,000. With what he already had stashed, that would cover his million nut with a suitable surplus to cover operational costs. That shouldn't be too hard to put together.

A crew, though . . . that was an interesting challenge. It would enable him to make one or two major scores instead of a risky series of smaller payoff one-man jobs. Maybe at least a backup or two. He'd have to look into that. He heard laughter outside. Rich and two of his golf buddies were outside with three women. They were all suntanned and healthy, the women beautiful in the outdoorsy fashion popular now. Jonny looked at them hungrily, his face hidden in the shadows back from the window. He felt a pang of something, quickly repressed—envy, sadness, anger? How easily they laughed and joked together, talking about things of no consequence at all: golf, friends at the ad agencies, the travails of the freelancer's life. It seemed so easy for them. It wasn't a job, a cover, a mask . . . at least as far as he could tell, and he was a grand master at that game. That was good to remember. He was a grand master of the game. They didn't know that, but he did. The grand master of the game went into the bathroom, studied his face in the mirror. Smiled once, twice. Then he went outside to say hello.

**NO OTHER OPTION**

There was a street vendor with an espresso machine mounted in a cart parked in front of the police headquarters. Nina handed Dale his double latte, then turned her back to him as she sugared her own. "You date much, Miller?"

Dale said, "What does that have to do with anything?"

Nina listened to how his voice changed when his temper began to fray. Amused, she turned to look at him. She sipped her coffee and kept her eyes down for now. "You don't seem like you get out much. Mr. Business and all that. Very serious guy. Is that how you really are? Or is it just that you don't see many women in your . . . line of work, whatever that might be?"

The soldier busied himself with the latte. He sniffed at it, touched his tongue to the foam, then dumped three seconds' worth of sugar into it.

"Like it?" Nina said.

"It's okay."

Nina wandered away from the stand and felt him hesitate, then follow behind her. Good. "What exactly do you do?"

Dale sighed as she turned to face him, then propped herself against the low wall beside the concrete stairs of the front entrance.

"Oh, let me guess," she said. "It's classified Super Double Top Secret and you'll have to kill me if you tell me, right?"

He couldn't keep the serious face. "Something like that, yeah."

"Jesus, I don't know who's worse. You military guys or the fucking Feds. Sit down."

He sat beside her on the low wall. They watched the cops come and go out of the building. A large black man came shambling by, his baseball hat cocked at an angle, his oversized jeans and shirt hanging out. The black man nodded with elaborate courtesy to Nina, who ignored him, and kept on going down the block.

"Friend of yours?" Dale said.

"I might have busted him once. Don't remember what for."

"How long you been a cop?"

"All my life. My dad was a Feeb, my uncle Ray with ATF. Grew up with it. Been here nine years."

Dale was impressed and that warmed her.

"That's pretty fast to make detective, isn't it? Nine years?" he said.

"I had some time with Treasury before I came over. That helped. Got lucky early on with some good arrests. That helped too." She felt a half smile on her face when she looked at him. "How about you? Lifer? How long you been doing...whatever it is you do?"

"Thirteen years."

"How old are you?"

"Thirty-one. Why?"

"Went in right out of high school?"

"Yeah."

"Where was that?"

"Illinois. Decatur."

"I know where that is. Nice city, pretty lake. Got the smell of soybeans hanging over it all the time."

Dale laughed. "Yeah it does. Nice to walk down by that lake."

"We've got lots of lakes here. Land of Ten Thousand Lakes, you know. Nice for walking. You been down to the Chain of Lakes yet? Harriet, Calhoun, Isles? I live down there. Great walking and running, I do that every day."

"I've never been to Minneapolis before."

"Then we'll have to show you around."

"That would be nice."

"What would be nice," Nina said, "would be for you to quit

145

**NO OTHER OPTION**

dicking around and tell me whether Jonny Maxwell blew himself up or not. Because I suspect he or somebody he knows is running around my city. And I intend to put his ass away. And I'd strongly suggest that if you have anything of value to say, you say it now, before I go get the highest-ranking U.S. marshal I can find and ask him what the fuck a non-law enforcement advisor for a supposedly closed case is doing running down leads on a guy who's supposed to be dead."

She sipped her coffee and looked straight ahead, using her peripheral vision to note how he tensed up, his coffee cup frozen in midsip. He had a strong face, but there was still a lot of boyishness there. He'd be good at his job, good at the yes sir, no sir, all the way and then some sir, but probably a thinker too. Some ruthlessness there, carefully concealed. Arrogance too, the self-confidence of someone very highly trained and skilled who'd had the experience of using his skills in the real world to affirm his high self-opinion. She knew, without any false modesty, that those traits were in her face as well.

Nina was aware of her strengths and her weaknesses. She kept those weaknesses hidden away. But this Dale Miller . . . he had weakness in his face. He obviously didn't spend much time around smart women. Maybe he liked the big-boobed, big hair type that looked good on the back of a crotch rocket. She wondered how he got along with his father. Maybe that was what she saw in his face. Right now he'd recovered and was glaring at her, a no-holds-barred "Fuck you" written in every line of his face.

"Well?" she said.

Dale got up and dumped his coffee into the bushes. "I made a mistake here."

"Too late to walk away, Dale," Nina said. "You got something on your mind, something you haven't brought the marshals in on— am I right?—and I know those boys . . . they don't take lightly to being left in the dark. Neither do I. Neither does any other cop. I don't imagine you do either, in your little secret world. So why don't we quit fencing? Tell me what you think. We can keep it right here between us. If it's something we've got to involve other people in, at least with me you'll have a say."

She watched his chagrin play across his face. She hid her amusement and the little stab of pleasure she got. Served him right for underestimating her. Now she'd see if he thought fast on his feet and did the right thing.

**MARCUS WYNNE**

"You're right," he said.

She pretended to be surprised.

"I've got some questions about your incident out here. I didn't bring it up with the marshals," Dale said. "I want to see what you've got."

"Questions about what?"

"I'm not fully convinced Jonny went down the way they think."

"Ah," Nina said. "Why didn't you tell them that? They're the pros. No offense, but I don't think you know shit about law enforcement."

"It's a long story. If it's him, and I'm not saying it is . . . then I want a clean run at him. I need to be part of the play. You understand that?"

He seemed surprised by what had just come out of his mouth. Nina saw the floodgate of emotion that had forced the words begin to swing shut.

"There's some background here I'm not getting," she said. "But believe me, we will get to it. You're saying there's some question whether Maxwell is actually dead? He may be alive in Minneapolis?"

"All this went down a six-hour drive away. I need to see what you got and to hear what this girl has to say. Then you and me, we'll talk some more. If all the pieces are there."

"Oh, we'll definitely be talking more, Mr. Dale Miller. Let's go. I want to get my partner."

"I thought we were going to keep this close hold?"

"We are. I don't know you well enough to have you watch my back."

Herb turned from the driver's seat and rested one thick arm along the back of the seat. His hand hovered near Nina's shoulder. "You carrying a gun?"

"Yeah," Dale said.

"Creds," Herb said in his no-discussion voice.

Dale handed the imitation leather folder with his DOD credentials over the backseat. Herb grabbed them from his hand. Dale rubbed his fingertips together, curled them into a fist, and set it on his thigh.

"These say you're authorized to carry weapons and conduct investigations relating to national security. Doesn't say anything about

**NO OTHER OPTION**

arrest powers." Herb tossed the credential case onto the seat beside Dale. "You know how to use that gun?"

"A little."

"Well, Sergeant Miller, make sure you don't take your fancy gun out when we're around. Just leave it in your purse or wherever you stash it."

"Herb," Nina said.

"You leave all that stuff to my partner and me," Herb said. His face was red and his eyes aimed at Dale like red-rimmed shotgun barrels. "You don't get in our way. You don't say nothing unless we ask you. Nothing. I won't have any civilian fucking up an investigation."

"I'm not a civilian," Dale said. His right index finger tapped twice, then once.

"As far as I'm concerned you are. You might be a shit hot secret agent or something, but this is police work. If Nina wasn't vouching for you and all this, I'd slam your ass into cuffs and send you back to the marshals for obstruction. I don't know what to think about all this and I don't like that. You're here on sufferance, get me? That means you sit where we tell you to sit and talk when we tell you to talk."

"Take it easy, Herbie," Nina said. "Dale's one of the good guys."

"I want all this shit out front," Herb said. "I said what I got to say."

Nina looked in the mirror. Dale sat crossarmed in the backseat. His stone-faced expression did nothing to conceal the flush of anger that boiled up his neck and across his face. Fair skin. He's not used to being talked to like this. But he's not used to running this kind of show, either. He'd take direction if it suited his purpose. It seemed odd that he would take off on his own like this, dump the marshals. She knew to be cautious when dealing with spooks, and Miller was some kind of military spook. Her father had told her of his dealings with the CIA, and there were plenty of police bar stories about the occasional encounter with the military operators who prowled the gray area between law enforcement and national intelligence like great white sharks.

They drove out to Minnetonka, a wealthy suburb on the shores

**MARCUS WYNNE**

of Lake Minnetonka, one of the largest lakes in Minnesota. The house was large, set back on a long cul-de-sac well off the main road, bordering a marshy nature preserve. The other houses on the street were in the same style: big yards, neat lawns with children's toys scattered across them, two stories, a good view of the nature preserve. BMWs, Land Cruisers, Range Rovers, and Jeep Grand Cherokees were parked in the driveways and garages.

The man who answered their knock was tall and well dressed in a battered but expensive polo shirt, khakis, and dock shoes. "Can I help you?"

"Mr. Martin, I'm Nina Capushek from the Minneapolis Police Department, I spoke to your daughter earlier?" Nina led gently. "I need to speak to her for just a few minutes?"

"She's resting," Mr. Martin said. "Is this necessary? Do we have to do this right now?"

"I'm sorry, sir," Nina said. "It's important we speak to her. We wouldn't disturb your daughter right now if we didn't think it was vital. To help us catch the man who hurt her."

Mr. Martin looked down. He looked beaten. "Of course," he said. "Whatever it takes."

He led them into the front room. It was a comfortable and lived-in room: a long deep sofa, two paired armchairs with a lamp between them, pictures of friends and family on the walls, bookshelves, magazines strewn untidily across a low coffee table.

"Please wait here," Mr. Martin said. "I'll get my daughter . . . my wife is with her now."

He went up the staircase and after a moment returned with his daughter. Lu Ann Martin was a pretty girl despite the strain that stretched skin taut over her facial bones. Nina saw that she was tall and athletic under the baggy clothes she wore. Her hair was pulled back in a tight ponytail with a red ribbon that seemed out of place. She looked at Nina and away from Herb and Dale. She took a breath and visibly gathered herself.

"Hi, Lu Ann," Nina said. She stepped forward and took Lu Ann's hand in both of hers. "Thank you for taking the time to see us."

"Would you all like to sit down?" Mr. Martin said. "Something to drink? Lu Ann?"

**NO OTHER OPTION**

"No, Daddy," Lu Ann said. "I'm fine."

Nina answered for all of them. "Thank you, Mr. Martin. We're okay."

She steered Lu Ann to the couch and sat beside her. "Lu Ann, we need to ask you a few more questions. Just a few things. It will help us find him and put him away. Can you do that?"

Lu Ann's look darted at the men, her father, back to Nina. She straightened herself out of her defensive slouch. "Yes. I can do that, Detective Capushek."

"Please call me Nina. It'll help an old woman feel younger."

"You're not so old," Lu Ann said.

"You have a kind heart."

Lu Ann shrugged, half smiled. Her hands knotted like trapped animals in her lap. Nina reached out and squeezed Lu Ann's hands.

"Okay?" Nina said.

"What do you need to know?" Lu Ann said. Her father moved beside the couch and stood beside his daughter.

"You were down at the Pickled Parrot with your friends," Nina said. "And you left there about twelve-thirty and drove yourself home. Did you see anyone follow you out of the bar, or the parking ramp?"

Lu Ann touched her hair and bowed her head. "No. Like I told you before, I didn't see him until I was unlocking my apartment door."

"Think back, Lu Ann," Nina said. "Was there anybody in the bar who sticks out in your memory? Anybody who might have heard you and your friends talking, anyone you might have spoken to even in passing?"

"I don't remember anyone like that. We were all just laughing, having fun."

Nina watched the furrows deepen between Lu Ann's eyes. "Okay," Nina said. "So when you got home, in the parking garage . . . did you notice anyone there? Maybe someone leaving or just getting back?"

"No."

"So you're at the door of your apartment and . . ."

Lu Ann stiffened. She folded her hands in her lap. Her knuckles were white. She drew a deep breath and said, "I was opening my apartment door. I never saw where he came from. He was just there. He squeezed my neck from behind and he whispered in my ear,

**MARCUS WYNNE**

'Quiet. Just be quiet and you'll be okay.'" Lu Ann shuddered and her eyes filled with tears.

Nina waited.

"Then he pushed me inside and shut the door," Lu Ann went on. Her voice shook. "He was so strong . . . I could tell he worked out. There was nothing I could do. He just held me there with one hand . . . he asked me if there was anybody else at home. Then he did something to my neck, it hurt so bad I couldn't speak, I couldn't stand. He went into each room looking around. Then he took me into the bedroom. He had a little satchel, like a courier bag. He took a pillowcase out of that and put it over my head."

"You never saw his face?" Dale said. Nina shot a glare at him and Herb put a cautioning hand on his arm.

Lu Ann looked up at Dale. "No, not really. He never let me turn around, not until he had that pillowcase on my head."

Nina took Lu Ann's hand again and held it.

"Then he tied me to the bed," Lu Ann said. "It was like he'd done it before. He had the rope with him, he knew just how to hold me with his knee while he tied me. I couldn't move, couldn't say anything. It was hard to breathe with the bag over my face. He didn't say anything except 'Shut up.' He knew I couldn't do anything. Then he . . . then he cut all my clothes off with a knife and he raped me. He didn't say anything till afterward. He was setting up his . . . tape recorder. Then he . . ." Lu Ann began deep from the belly cries that twisted their guts.

Her father put his hands on her shoulders. "That's enough," he said. "This will just have to wait." He led his girl away, up the stairs.

"What happened?" Dale said.

"He tortured her for a while," Herb said. "Used those nerve locks like pressure point control. Asked her if she got pleasure out of it. She told him what she thought he wanted to hear. Apparently that pissed him off. He kept asking her, 'Do you get pleasure out of this? Does it please you to be taken?' Weird, sick shit. Then he stops and leaves her there. Neighbors never heard a thing. One of her friends comes looking for her when she doesn't show up for work, lets herself in with her spare key and found her. Still alive, thank God."

"You think he meant to kill her?" Dale said.

Herb's face was drawn with disgust. "Maybe. If he hasn't before, maybe he's getting ready to start. In case you hadn't noticed, he did a

**NO OTHER OPTION**

real good job of killing off part of Lu Ann Martin. That's her name, you know." Herb looked at the pictures on the walls of the laughing beautiful girl in a prom dress, in a swimsuit on a sailboat with her family. "We don't get too many of this kind here in the Cities. They're a rare breed. Most of the scumbags we deal with aren't this smart, this organized, or this cold." Herb fell silent as Mr. Martin returned.

"I'm sorry, but you'll have to leave," Lu Ann's father said. "I've given Lu Ann one of her sedatives and she'll be asleep soon."

Nina stood and offered her hand. Lu Ann's father paused before he took it.

"We're sorry to have bothered you both, Mr. Martin," Nina said. "Please keep in touch with our Victim Advocate about counseling for Lu Ann. We'll be in touch regarding the case."

"Did you get anything new out of this?" Mr. Martin said, anger creeping into his voice. "How many times must she go through this?"

Nina looked at Dale while she answered. "We don't need anything else, Mr. Martin. It helped our new investigator get the feel for who we're looking for. We have to go there to get what we need to find this guy. You want that, don't you?"

"Of course I want that. But I want my daughter back, too. You understand that, don't you?"

"Yes, sir," Nina said softly. "Yes sir, I do. Completely. Thank you, and please thank Lu Ann for us."

The three were silent as they left the house and went back to the squad car.

"Herb, you drive, okay?" Nina said.

"Sure." Herb squeezed behind the wheel.

Dale sat silently in the backseat.

"Your first time?" Nina asked him.

"First time for what?" Dale said.

"First time seeing what rape does."

". . . I knew a woman who'd been raped."

"Not quite the same thing talking to them so soon after, is it?"

"No."

"This is what we do," Herb said. "Day in, day out."

"I couldn't do this," Dale said. "I don't know how you can."

Herb looked at Dale in the mirror, then looked back at the road.

"I'd want to kill these guys. All of them," Dale said.

Herb and Nina looked at each other and said nothing.

**MARCUS WYNNE**

## 2.9

Jonny Maxwell went out walking, after midnight, in the moonlight, with the hunter's rush full on him. The busy intersection of Hennepin and Lake, and the bright lights of Uptown were behind him, two streets over. Here on Emerson Street it was darker, farther between streetlights, only an occasional glow from windows that flickered, then went dark; a moment's brief illumination from a passing car, the driver looking incuriously at the athletic man strolling along, just another young, hip Uptown citizen on his way home from Liquor Lyle's bar or a late movie at the Uptown Theater. The dark, the dark, it was a little song in Jonny's head. He'd always been at home in the dark, always had been, always would be. He let his face down, let the hunter out to peer through his eyes, tracking and seeking, to add a flex and bounce to his stride, his courier satchel over one shoulder full of little treats to share with Miss Annie Ma, artist and woman.

Jonny walked slowly past 2782 Emerson. The building was an old converted brownstone, two stories high, not unlike his. This one had been converted to condominium apartment flats, two to each floor. A short walk up to the secured door, brightly lit; a rear access door, also secured by a buzzer intercom system. There were big, roomy windows on all sides of the building, including the dark narrow walkways that separated the converted brownstone from its neighbors on either side. The night before, on his target reconnaissance, Jonny had shot out the side lights on the north side of the building with a $CO_2$ pellet pistol. Annie Ma's apartment was second floor, north side.

Annie Ma sat in a wooden spindle chair in front of her easel, surrounded by candles. Inconstant light flickered across warm wall tapestries in southwestern colors and patterns, throw rugs—Navajo, Iranian, a Turkish kilim—scattered in an irregular but pleasing pattern across the floor. She was barefoot, one foot curling, over and over, into the thick carpet, the other foot perched delicately on the cross brace of her chair. Annie leaned forward, intent on the details she painted in with the tip of her finest brush. It was a large canvas, dominated by a stylized, harsh face, with lots of red and black and russet— an abstraction of a face that came to her in her dreams, that pressed on her consciousness in a way that no face or anything else had ever done. Fear. Longing. Hatred. Curiosity. All those things were in her painting, in the stylized rendition of the face beneath the mask of the man she'd met briefly in the sushi bar, the man who said his name was Bill.

She had taught herself not to look too long at the whole of the face, at the whole of the canvas, to instead trust her intuition and look closely for the small details, filling them in with the right color and the right line, trusting her other than conscious mind to build the details up into the totality of the image that burned behind her eyes and filled her dreams at night. Annie had the gift of seeing, as do so many artists, the gift of seeing through, and that gift, like Cassandra's, was both a blessing and a curse.

She knew he would come for her.

Annie knew nothing of real violence, but she understood caution. She felt the draw of the man she called the Demon Lover in her painting. She felt the violence that came off him, the tried and tested . . . ease . . . with which it radiated from beneath his mask, like heat from molten metal in a crucible. Annie and her neighbors were good about making sure the doors stayed shut and locked, and they looked out for one another. She felt safe in her home. But in the sure keen way of the hunted, she felt the presence of a hunter pressing down on her from somewhere not too far away.

"I go out walking, after midnight, in the moooooonlight . . ." Jonny sang the old Patsy Cline song just under his breath as he rounded the block. He was almost gleeful. This was the part he loved best:

**MARCUS WYNNE**

the stalk, the hunt itself. The sex was justified by the stalk. He earned his release through the exercise of his skill. This would be good, he promised himself as he slipped into the dark alley between Annie Ma's building and the next, shadowed from the moonlight that fell evenly on the street. He slung his courier bag lengthwise across his back, then took a grip on the bricks protruding at regular intervals up the wall. The sticky soled climbing shoes he wore smeared into the brick and mortar giving him plenty of toeholds. Jonny pulled himself up easily, scaling the wall between the big apartment windows, as silent as an apparition scuttling up the side of the building.

Two floors were easy. He rolled smoothly over the raised parapet onto the flat roof. He moved slowly and quietly across the roof, through the little forest of protruding antennas and ventilation pipes and ducts, to the roof access panel. The access panel was a three-by-three-foot square of metal with a handle welded on it. It came up several inches and then stopped, locked on the inside with a padlock, just as it had been on his dry run. The panel was hinged on the outside with two large metal pins stuck through tarnished brass hinges. Jonny took out a spray bottle of Break-Free lubricant and sprayed it liberally over the hinge joints, making sure that it ran freely around the gaps and into the interstices of the hinge. He waited  a few minutes, then took a ball peen hammer and cloth-padded punch from his bag and gave each hinge pin a light tap. The pins moved slightly, enough to introduce more lubricant. He waited some more, his mind empty, processing the information his senses brought him: the subtle vibration of the roof beneath his feet; the steady hum of air conditioners; a slight breeze from the west, cooling across his sweaty brow; voices from an open window in the next building.

Finally he tapped free the hinge pins and lifted the access panel. It swiveled on the padlock, but raised up enough to let Jonny squeeze through and drop quietly into the back service stairwell of the building. The service stairwell came to the back door of each apartment and terminated in the basement, where it led to the back entrance and out into the small parking lot. Behind each doorway was a small landing where the tenants stacked trash cans, empty appliance boxes, bicycles, and other apartment miscellany.

Jonny stood on Annie Ma's back doorstep, listening.

———

**NO OTHER OPTION**

Annie slid another CD into the rack and reinserted it into the player. John Coltrane's "After the Rain" filled the room. She adjusted the equalizer and turned the volume up. She sat in her wooden chair, her eyes closed, and let the sound fill her, sway her in her seat. There was a stillness inside her, and she let the music seep into that quiet empty space and fill her. She pulled her hair back with one hand and rolled her neck to loosen it. She felt a sudden chill and the fine hairs on the nape of her neck rose. From behind her, so close she could smell his body and feel the heat from it, the man she knew as Bill said, "Nice painting. Interesting likeness."

"I'm glad you like it," she said. Her heart pounded, yet her voice remained calm. "I think it . . . captures you." She didn't look at him when she spoke.

"How so?" Jonny said.

"May I turn around?" Annie said.

"Not yet," Jonny said.

"Of course," she said. "In the sense that it shows the real you. The one you keep hidden away." The anger coming from him was palpable; it was the heat of his body magnified. She felt it on the back of her neck, like hot breath; it made the slightly sweaty smell of him stronger. "I mean you no disrespect when I say that," she said carefully. "Do you understand that?" She sensed the control in him.

"What do you see?" he asked.

"Control. Discipline. Incredible strength. Anger. Rage. Sorrow. Longing. Frustration. Desire." She paused. "What is it you want so badly?"

"Don't you know?"

"I can give you . . ."

"I take. You don't give. I take."

"I would give."

"You don't give!" Jonny hissed. "You don't give. You never give."

She was silent, her head bowed in submission. Her thin shoulders trembled. "I . . ." she began.

"Shut up," Jonny said flatly. "Silent. Nothing."

She heard him open something, a bag or a satchel, and then he slid a pillowcase over her head. Despite herself, she panicked and reached up to tug at the cloth so tight on her face. He cinched it tighter around her neck, choking her, and jerked it sharply back, like a dog on a leash.

**MARCUS WYNNE**

"No," he said. "Don't move unless I tell you to."

She dropped her hands, sucked frantically for air, pulling the thin material tight across her nose and mouth. Jonny bunched the pillowcase tight in his fist and lifted her to her feet. She went on tiptoe, her hands held down by her side. She couldn't see, could only sense where she was by the feel of the carpet beneath her feet, then bare floor, then carpet. She gasped in pain when she was thrust hard against the doorjamb of her bedroom, then felt her bed against the back of her legs as he forced her down.

"Put your hands above your head," he said.

Jonny tied her hands quickly and expertly to the headboard. He ran his hands over her body. She was naked under the extra long oxford shirt she wore. She was thin, but surprisingly full and soft in her breasts. He pulled the CQC-7 from where it was clipped inside his waistline and snapped open the serrated blade, lifted her shirt with the tip and studied her pubis. Annie felt the air against her skin. She closed her eyes and ceased straining against the cords. She took a deep breath and relaxed. She felt the cold steel against her thigh, then the point pressing on her. She opened her legs. She felt him still and silent above her; she could feel his gaze on her.

He ran his hands over her breasts, let his fingers linger in the deep notch between her clavicles, then hooked one hard fingertip deep into the notch. Annie choked and her torso jerked upward, then down as he released the pressure. He massaged the nerve center gently as she recovered her breath.

"That's the jugular notch," he said. "There's more."

"I'm sorry," Annie said. "I want to do it right for you."

"You want to do it right?"

"You already have the control," she said. "The mask, yes . . . but I can do more. I can play the part. Tell me how you want it, tell me exactly."

"You want to do it right," he said, softly.

"I don't want to call you . . . Bill," she said. "It doesn't feel right. What should I call you?"

Jonny's finger lingered at the jugular notch. She stiffened, then relaxed again. The thin hair of her pubis drew him. "I don't want you to call me anything at all," he said.

"I think you do. I think you want to hear me call your name. I have a name for you. A name to go with my painting."

**NO OTHER OPTION**

"What do you call your painting?"

"I call it the Demon Lover."

Jonny unbuttoned her shirt slowly and ceremoniously.

"You want to fuck a demon, girl? Is that what you want? Is that what you think about?" he said.

She was silent. Jonny watched the tremor of her muscles play across her flat abdomen, the golden gloss of her skin sloping flat between her hipbones. He tapped his fingers on her flat belly, stroked the hair of her pubis.

"You remind me of my father," she said.

Jonny was still.

"He was like you. He was a Green Beret, Special Forces."

"What do you mean, he was like me?"

"He was strong. He was angry all the time when he came to see me. Not at me, at my mother. Sometimes he sent money. He looked after us. My mother was afraid of him, but he was always good to me. When he died, his insurance money paid for my college."

"How did he die?"

"Agent Orange. He got sprayed when his team was in Laos or near the border, I forget what he told me. He sent me his beret when I graduated from high school. I still have it, there in the closet."

"What do I care about a Green Beret?"

"You're like him. The way you do things, the way you are ... something about you is like him."

Jonny stepped away from the bed and opened the closet door. Hung on a nail on the back of the door was a battered old green beret, molded and shaped to a head and still holding the shape. The tarnished crest was centered on the old Seventh Special Forces Group flash. Jonny took the old "blanket" and turned it over. Ken Symington was written inside with ink on the sheer silk label. He set it on top of the dresser, closed the closet, and turned to study Annie Ma laid out on the bed.

"What are you doing?" she said.

"Why do you think your father was like me?"

"What should I call you?"

"Call me ... Jonny," he said. He pulled her shirt back over her, but left it unbuttoned. "Tell me why."

**MARCUS WYNNE**

Kieran's Irish Pub was just down the street from City Hall and directly across the street from the police headquarters building. Nina and Dale sat at one of the tables beside the long windows, where they could look out at the cops coming and going from the gray building across the street.

Nina sipped at a pint glass of Guinness, then licked the foam off her upper lip.

"You got a girlfriend, Miller?" she said. "Some nice girl at home to darn your socks?"

Dale swirled his Bushmills on rocks and shook his head no. "I don't have time for one. What about you?"

"I got a nice place down by the water. It's beautiful on nights like this . . . moon on the water, people strolling in the dark . . . Finish your drink. We'll go down there."

"Where's your partner?"

"Had to get home."

"He doesn't seem like the family-man type."

"You don't know shit, Miller. He's a family man, a great cop, the best partner I ever had, and he's my friend. My friend. You got any friends? You don't seem like the friend type."

"Do you ever ease up? It was an observation, period. I didn't mean to offend you."

"You got any friends?"

Dale took a big swallow of his whiskey. His eyes watered.

"Yeah," he said. "I got friends."

Nina made a small smile.

"You get much? Sex, I mean."

Dale stood up and set his glass down gently.

"I don't need this shit."

"Sit down," Nina said. "Really. You're embarrassing yourself."

Several tables over, a man and a woman watched them and spoke to each other out of the sides of their mouths.

"You hate all men, or just military men?"

Nina laughed.

"Sit down, Dale. Finish your drink. I'll quit picking on you. Really. You're not going anywhere without me and I haven't finished my drink. And we haven't decided yet what we're going to tell the marshals."

Dale sat down. He left his drink alone.

"You're a good soldier, aren't you, Sergeant Miller?" Nina said, lowering her voice. "Do the right thing, yes sir, no sir, three bags full. What *should* we tell the marshals? I've heard about Jed Loveless. That's a hard, bad-tempered old man-chaser there. We bring the marshals in on this, tell them, hey, your buddy Dale Miller got a bug up his ass and oh, by the way, he turned out to be right and didn't tell anybody he was *supposed* to tell . . . just showed up at a MPD detective's desk with a wild ass guess . . ."

Dale shrugged and picked up his drink. "Do what you think you gotta do, Capushek. They send me home, I go home. But I'm more likely to be on this case than you are, you go that route."

"Good boy. You're smarter than you act. You figured that out all by yourself. So since it's just us girls here, let's make a deal, you and me, Mr. Mystery Commando. Oh, by the way, you'll probably get a call soon—we did check your creds and the very official-sounding boy on the phone seemed concerned that you were in Minneapolis instead of on the plane back to wherever you hang your gun belt. But we covered you. Said you got stopped for a traffic safety violation and you ID'd yourself to the officer. So you can tell them you're here checking out the Minnesota girls to see if they're all they're supposed to be."

"Ice queens? Stone-cold bitches?"

Nina laughed and raised her glass in a mock toast. "Good one. You might turn out to be okay, Miller. We play our hand right, we'll have a full week or so before your folks start wondering where you are and asking the marshals to return you posthaste."

"At least that. I told them I was taking some personal time."

"What's your story? With this Maxwell?"

"I'm not positive it's him."

"You sure seem positive."

"There's that coroner's ID."

"No DNA match, no blood match...hard if not impossible after fires. Not enough left of his head for a dental match...everything hinges on him having those IDs, personal effects, so on, right?"

"Right."

"Sounds iffy to me."

Dale swirled the dregs of his drink to avoid looking at her. "I don't know."

"Want him all to yourself, huh?"

"Why do you say that?"

"I've been there. I know what that's about. But if you want him, you're going to have to get him with me. Nobody does women like that in my city."

"First we have to find him," Dale said. He stared through the faint reflection of himself in the window glass at the people on the sidewalk outside. "First we have to find him."

Nina turned her unmarked squad at the corner of Hennepin and Washington. Once across the Washington Bridge, she bore to the right and picked up First Avenue and motored slowly through the bright-lit Warehouse District. The streets were packed with people. The nightclubs, restaurants, and bars were full. In the balmy night, men and women strolled, some alone, others arm in arm.

"Where are we going?" Dale said.

"I'm giving you the tour. This is a great city at night."

Nina passed Loring Park and turned right at the Walker Art Center and drove slowly through the back streets till she came to Lake of the Isles Parkway. The lake was flat and still under the moonlight. She slowed the car near an old stone bridge on the Parkway.

"Look," she said.

The Minneapolis skyline was mirrored in the clear waters of Lake of the Isles. The skyline glowed with its own light and the

**NO OTHER OPTION**

light of the moon. The image on the water was as still as a photograph.

"It's beautiful," Dale said.

"I don't hear many men use that word."

"Beautiful? Why?"

"I don't know."

They drove around Lake Calhoun and then to Lake Harriet. Nina parked her squad near the band shell. The band shell's backdrop was evenly spaced with long panels of clear glass so the audience seated in front on the grass and benches could see the lake through the band shell. Sailboats were tethered at a small pier. The steady clink, clink, clink of the anchor chains carried far across the water. A few people walked on the lakeside path.

"Let's walk," Nina said.

"Sure."

They followed the meandering paved path beside the water. Nina shoved her hands deep in her light blazer pockets and hunched her shoulders against the breeze.

"Are you cold?" Dale said.

Nina leaned her head back and greedily breathed the air in. "I'm fine. That's so good. It smells free here."

"I never thought of it like that."

"You ever been free, Miller?"

"I don't know what you mean."

Nina stopped and put her hand on Dale's arm, her fingers curling around his thick bicep for balance as she checked the sole of one shoe. She smiled out at the water.

"That's a true thing you just said. What I mean is, have you ever felt really free? Felt like you didn't owe anyone anything, like there was only you to think about and there wasn't one single thing you *had* to do, that you could turn in any direction, do anything, go anywhere, away from everything you'd ever done to someplace new and exciting you'd never been?"

Dale took his time answering.

"I felt like that once. When I was a kid. I was backpacking in Glacier National Park with my dad. He got tired and decided to stay in the valley, but he told me I should go up the mountains for a night out on my own. I went up this long mountain pass. By myself. Nobody else was on the trail. It was hard, but it was good. I got to the top of that pass and looked back at how high I'd climbed. Then I went on over the pass, and looked down at the long valley on the other side, all these mountains around it . . . I felt free then. I could go anywhere. I had everything I needed on my back. No obligations . . . I was free. Then."

"Only then? Never since?"

"Not in the same way you say. Obligations." Dale shrugged. "Duty."

"Aren't you ever off duty? Do you ever put all that Army stuff aside and just be Dale Miller? Are you somebody without the Army? What do you do when you're not being the Army's Sergeant Miller?"

"I backpack, camp. Like I did when I was a kid. I like to travel. See new places and things. Meet people."

"Meet people. Women?"

"Sometimes."

"You ever keep any of them around, or are you the love 'em and leave 'em type?"

"I've kept some."

"Some? Tell me about one."

Dale shrugged. "Not much to tell."

"Ever live with one?"

"Yeah."

"Tell me about her."

"She was in advertising. An executive. She was the daughter of an officer I worked with. We met at a party he had during Christmas."

"What was she like?"

"She was a good woman. Good-looking, good job, had her own life. You'd have thought she'd be used to the lifestyle, growing up in a military family. But she hated it, all of it. Took a while for it to come out, but it did. Didn't like the travel, didn't like what I was doing . . ."

"What were you doing?"

He continued as though he didn't hear her. ". . . didn't like having guns in the house, didn't like my friends . . . It's like we were in two different countries, living on the border with one foot in each other's world."

"Sounds like living with a cop. What do you tell women you do?"

**NO OTHER OPTION**

Dale looked up at the moon. "How do men act when they find out you're a cop?"

Nina stopped and turned to face the water. "I don't tell civilians I'm a cop."

"Why?"

"Because what I do on the job is for them. What I do and want off the job is for me. I don't have to give them that."

"What if you have to be a cop when you're off duty?"

Nina gave a tiny snort. "Then I do my job. But I'm long past jumping into every little thing just to flash my tin. That's what cell phones are for."

"I don't think I'd deal with your job very well. I'd want to go off on the assholes you got to deal with."

"Don't think I don't. And no, I don't think you'd handle it very well. Nothing against you, you seem like a good human being. But this world isn't as black and white as your military world is. You get a clear target, you got your orders, you go do what you got to do. Us, we deal in the gray world. Out on the street it's never that clear. Everybody lies. It's up to us to sort it out, find out who has to answer, then make sure they do. That's what we do."

"I'm starting to understand that."

"That's why this thing is so hard for you. You're not fooling anyone but yourself. This isn't so cut and dried, is it? You've got your orders . . . just like Colonel Troutman to Rambo. But you don't know the truth, do you?"

"Do you?"

"I don't know what you and Maxwell did together. You've got a lot of dark history in your face. I do know he's out there. And you're going to help me make him answer for Lu Ann Martin. He goes down for that."

Dale stooped and picked up a stone. He threw it as hard as he could out into the water. The ripples rose from where the stone fell. "I don't want to think about this anymore tonight."

"I understand that." Nina tucked her hands into the crook of his arm and gently tugged him toward the car. He tensed under her touch, then relaxed.

"Are you free tonight?" Nina said lightly.

"Yes. Yes, I am."

"Want to get lucky?"

**MARCUS WYNNE**

**2.11**

"He was like you," Annie said. "I dreamed of him the way I dreamed about you. He'd gone away when I was very young, but I would remember things about him. He was hard, hard . . . his body was hard when I pressed against him. His voice was so hard when he spoke to my mother. I felt as though I were watching the two of them through a pane of thick glass. I could feel the vibrations of their words in the palms of my hands, pressed flat against that windowpane in my mind. He was watchful, like you. He'd turn this way and that when we were out, always looking for something. I never knew what it was he looked for. I remember I was always afraid that he would find it. He made me afraid. I remember that. He was my father and he loved me, but he made me afraid. It was like being too close to a lion in the zoo, being behind the bars and in the cage, the lion just watching you, not hungry, not hunting you, but watching you all the same."

Annie's heart pounded. The thin skin stretched tight across her breastbone, in the valley made by her breasts, beat with her pulse. The cotton pillowcase across her face rose and fell with her voice and her breath. The material had settled, outlining her eye sockets and the fine bones of her skull.

Jonny was still. The knife was still open in his hand. He lay the palm of his other hand between Annie's breasts, flat against her breastbone, and felt the beat of her heart.

"Why did you say that to me? In the restaurant. About the picture," he asked softly. "Tell me why you said that."

"Because it was true."

"Because it was true?"

"Yes."

"Did you think you could play with me?" he asked, running his hand down the flat of her belly, resting it over her mound.

"No. I wanted to . . . speak to you. You made me afraid."

"You should be afraid."

"I am. Of myself. And of you."

"Are you playing with me now?"

"No." She shifted on the bed. "How do you want me?"

Dale stood beside the tall front windows of Nina's condominium and looked down over Lake Harriet and the long reflection of the moon on the water. Nina stood close behind him. He felt her body heat radiating through the thin material of her blouse.

"I like your place," he said.

"Uh hmm."

Dale's muscles were hard with tension. Nina grabbed his belt from behind and turned him away from the window. He was only half a head taller than she was. She took him by the back of his neck and bent him to her. She was amused by how he stood there, his hands dangling at his sides, while she kissed him.

"That wasn't so bad, was it?" she said.

"No."

He kissed her and she felt him wanting her. She pulled him to the big green armchair. She pushed him down into the chair, then straddled him, fully clothed. His face was level with her breasts. He gripped her waist and felt the pistol holstered there.

"Do you need that?" he said.

"Maybe." She opened her shirt and put his face between her breasts. She reached down between her legs and tugged at his belt.

"I haven't decided yet," Jonny said. "I'll let you know."

He stood, and walked slowly through the room, looking at all she had: paintings, a gold patterned scarf pinned on the wall, a Japanese wedding kimono hung on wooden dowels, photos in antique picture frames. That green beret. He stood at her dresser and ran his hands through the jewelry tossed into an antique crystal punch bowl. An old set of silver master parachutist wings. Like his. He weighed the wings in his palm, slid the protective brads off the prongs on the back, felt their sharp tips. Jonny turned and looked at Annie Ma, spread out on her bed for his pleasure.

"Jonny?" she said. "Jonny?"

"Let's go in the bedroom," Dale said.

"I'm fine right here."

"We can..."

"Shhh." Nina pulled off her blouse and threw it on the floor. She stood before him. Her pale skin glowed around her beige bra. The butt of her pistol sloped sharply in to the cut of her waist above her hip's swell. She drew her pistol, held it muzzle down, and turned away for somewhere to set it down. Dale stood, hobbled by his pants, and she pointed the Sig-Sauer at him.

"Down, boy," she said.

"Don't point that at me," he said. He reached for the pistol but she stepped away.

"Don't touch my weapon."

"Nina..."

"Take off your clothes."

"What?"

"You heard me."

Dale sat down and took off his shoes.

"That's right," she said.

Jonny opened up the dresser drawers. The top drawer was filled with lingerie in red, black, and beige. Nice stuff. In the second drawer was a bloodred velvet bag. Inside was a plastic bag full of marijuana, a small pipe, and a packet of rolling papers.

"Where do you get your smoke from?" Jonny said.

"I don't know what you mean," Annie said.

"Where do you buy your dope?"

"From a friend...he works at First Avenue. Another artist."

"What, a musician?"

"No, he's a painter. He does security there."

Jonny laughed. "That's good," he said. "Where does he get it from? Who's his supplier?"

**NO OTHER OPTION**

"I don't know. I never asked."

Jonny closed the drawers, walked to the bed, sat down. He traced the outline of her belly muscles with his fingers. She trembled, just slightly, and that aroused him. He slipped a finger into her, watched how she gasped and trembled and then became still. He took his finger out and smelled it.

"So how are we going to be, Annie? You and me. How are we going to be?"

She was silent.

"You know what I'm thinking about, don't you?"

She said nothing. He watched her belly rise and fall as she fought to control her breathing. The thin cotton of the pillowcase rose and fell with her breath. The material around her eyes became dark with moisture.

"Your daddy was like the lion in the cage, Annie," Jonny said, running his hand down the front of her body from collarbone to pubis in long strokes. "And you were in the cage with him, remember? But you got to get away, mommy saw to that, didn't she? No mommy here today, Annie. Just us. You and your demon lover. Isn't this what you were talking about in the restaurant, Annie? What you were so quick to talk about, something you don't know anything about—yet. The pleasure of being taken, you said. Pleasing the taker, you said. We'll see about that."

He stood and took off his clothes, taking his time about it. He looked down at himself, at his penis pulsing with his heartbeat. Jonny got on the bed, poised himself on all fours above Annie. She was crying audibly now.

"Shhh," he said, pressing his finger to her lips through the pillowcase. "Shhh, Annie. Nothing to cry about yet. You're in the cage this time, Annie, and the lion is out, and he's come home with you. I'm nothing like your daddy, Annie. Nothing like him at all."

"Yes you are," she said. "You're exactly like him."

Nina set her pistol on the floor and kicked off her shoes. She unbuckled her belt and stepped out of her slacks. The spare magazines and cuff case made a hollow sound on the wooden floor. Her bra unsnapped from the front. She hooked her thumbs in the waistband of her panties and took her time wiggling them off. Moonlight silhouetted her. Her breasts rose and fell, rose and fell. She knelt in front of Dale in the chair, put her hands on the armrests and bent her head forward like an obedient child and took him in her mouth. When he was hard again, she stood and straddled him in the chair, slipping him up into her with one hand while she balanced herself by gripping his neck. When he raised his hands to hold her, she pushed them away.

"No," she said. "Don't touch me."

She felt him flag, and then stiffen again as she twisted and turned on his lap. She rode him up and down till he started to flex harder and faster, almost there, then she slowed, slowed more, then swung her leg up and stood.

"Ah," Dale gasped as he slipped out of her.

She turned away from him, bent at the waist, and grabbed the arms of the armchair across from him. She looked back over her shoulder at him and said, "Fuck me."

"Did your daddy do that?" Jonny asked. "Or did your daddy do this?"

She was dry and it pleased him to force his way into her. He felt her willing herself to relax, to not resist, and it angered him. He jammed his thumb into her rectum. She cried out and bucked beneath him.

"Yeah," he said throatily. "Like that."

"Harder," Nina urged Dale. "Harder."

"Don't! Please don't!"

"We're just getting started, Annie."

Dale caught a glimpse of himself reflected in the window glass, the long spill of moonlight across the floor illuminating him as he stood behind Nina, thrusting and thrusting into her, her thrusting back, and it seemed as though the light from the floor rose up through his feet and pelvis to flood the veins behind his eyes with a brilliant light.

This wasn't going to be enough, Jonny knew, with a twisted certainty that had been in him for a long, long time but was only now fully grown and nurtured. She was weeping beneath him.

"Daddy, please don't," she was whispering. "Please don't. It hurts. Please, Daddy . . ."

He hardened even more as his hands wrapped around her thin neck.

Nina knelt on the floor and hugged the chair to her breasts.

"What is it?" Dale said. He knelt beside her, put his hands on her shoulders.

"No." She shook her head and shrugged off his hands.

"Are you okay?" he said.

She hugged the chair tightly and nodded yes.

Jonny knelt beside the bed. Sweat cooled on his naked body. The woman was still and limp. Jonny had never before seen a woman dead by his hands. He'd seen dead women in Beirut, in the Kurdish camps in northern Iraq, in the camps in Guatemala. But even Sherry had been alive when he left her. He stared at the fine downy hairs on her thigh, still struggling to rise as though to catch the last breath she'd gasped under his hands. He blew softly across her leg and watched the tiny, minuscule ripple of the golden peach fuzz. So pretty.

She got up without speaking, went to the bathroom, and then into the bed. Silent. Nothing else. Dale stood naked and watched her and let her go. She huddled up, her back to him. He went to the window and looked out. The moonlight washed over him. He closed his eyes and felt the light on him, like standing in the sun and then moving into deep shadow. Like a shower of light, delicate on his skin, on the fine hairs that rose as his sweat dried.

"Will you come in here?" Nina said. Her voice was uncertain.

"Yes," Dale said. "In a minute. I want to look out."

He stared out at the waters of Lake Harriet, with the moonlight spilling across it like a white scar. A chill rose up his spine. He went to Nina in her bed.

Jonny sat cross-legged on the floor, sorting through a variety of photographs in a large ornately decorated shoebox. Pictures of Annie in costume at a Halloween party, Annie with friends. Annie with her father. He studied the man's face. Long boned, deep grooves on the

**MARCUS WYNNE**

cheeks around the mouth, cross furrowed forehead, dark tanned, a pale scar like a thick worm curled on his right temple. He set that photo aside. Here was one of Annie surrounded by friends at a nightclub. Several of the men wore black polo shirts with SECURITY printed on them. He looked closer. It was the First Avenue nightclub. The one with his arm wrapped around Annie, his shirt had the name Tony embroidered on the breast.

**2.12**

"We had another one last night. This one's dead." Herb spoke only to Nina and ignored Dale, who stood beside their desks.

"Have you had your coffee this morning, Herbie?" Nina said.

"Quit fucking around." Herb stalked off, adjusting his shoulder holster.

Dale set his coffee cup down on Herb's desk. "Is he always like this?"

"Especially when I've been getting some." Nina was cheerful and alert, different than she had been in her moonlit apartment six hours before. She laughed when Dale looked around to see if anyone had heard her.

"Don't worry, Deputy Dawg," she said. "Your secret is safe with me."

"What about yours?"

"Nobody would believe you."

Nina always thought the crime scene added another level of violation to the victims. The room full of strangers—paramedics, coroners, uniformed and plainclothes police, neighbors—the intrusive camera-men flashing, angling and circling over the body askew with all dignity robbed away. Strangers rooting through drawers, examining pictures, holding up lingerie . . . It was an invasion to solve an invasion, an effort to wring from silence and aftermath some semblance of the story, to put together the pieces of what had happened, to make the silence of a private place speak for the dead. As a senior detective, Nina had rotated into Homicide and spent her time with the murder police. Each scene had the pathos of something ended in a squalid fashion. She never got used to it. No one ever really did, despite the easy patter they all used to insulate themselves.

This one was hard for her. When she entered the apartment, she had an immediate sense of the woman who'd lived there. There was a sense of beauty, of fun, of erotic sensibility in the decor. Something else had come into this place and left a lingering vibration, dark and dangerous. The diminished body of the young Asian woman gave her the queasy feeling she'd taught herself to hide.

The homicide detective in charge of the scene was a wiry and diminutive Italian, Tony Rocelli. "Hey, Rocco," she said. "You caught this one?"

"Nina, how you doing? I didn't see you since that shoot. I heard you come out all right," Rocelli said. He nodded to Dale and said to Herb, "Who's your pal?"

"He's all right," Nina said. "He's working with us."

Dale held his hand out. "Dale Miller."

"Rocco," Rocelli said. His palm was smooth and hard. He was very strong. "You a cop?"

"He's an investigative consultant with DOD, helping us out," Herb said. He didn't look at Dale when he spoke. "Forensic psychology shit."

"No kidding?" Rocelli said. He looked at Dale with interest. "I better watch myself around you, then. My old lady is convinced I'm crazy and I don't need to encourage her."

"What you got, Rocco?" Nina said.

"Asian female, age twenty-eight, name Annie Ma. Rape and strangulation, death ten thirty P.M. according to my friend Mr. Dahlquist from the Medical Examiner's Office." Rocelli nodded toward the husky middle-aged blond man standing beside the bed writing notes on his clipboard. "I saw the scene, I thought about that case you're working, the kid from Minnetonka. We haven't bagged her up, thought you'd like to see it fresh."

"Who called it in?" Nina said.

"Friend from work. She was part-time down at the Walker, in

the curator's shop. Did framing, exhibit layout, all that. Museum tech they call them. She didn't show up. Her friend says she'd been real hinky lately, bad dreams and shit. Said she was afraid of something."

"Of what?" Herb said.

"Didn't know. I'm going down to interview the friend. Want to tag along?" Rocelli said.

Herb looked at Nina. "Yeah. I'm with you, Rocco."

Nina nodded.

Dale stood beside the bed. The medical examiner wrote careful, neat notes onto the forms clipped on his board. Dale had looked upon the dead before. He'd killed, as a soldier, and seen men die around him. But he'd never seen a murder scene before. It chilled him to see the waxiness of the once beautiful girl's skin, the discoloration of her eyeballs, and the grimace on her face below the peeled back pillowcase. Her neck was as thin as a child's. It was discolored with the deep, unmistakable bruises of a man's hand, livid in the puffy flesh. She was empty, an emptiness made more vivid by the living men and women working around her.

"Dale," Nina called. "Look at this."

She knelt on the floor and used a ballpoint pen to flip over a series of photographs scattered on the floor. Some of the photos were old, yellowed, and curled, of men in jungle fatigues standing in front of a sign somewhere in the jungle.

"Who do you think this is?" Nina said. She pointed the pen at a face that appeared again and again in the old photos.

"It's her father," Dale said in a thick voice. "Look over there." On the dresser top was an old green beret, a set of silver master parachutist wings resting on top of it, and a photo of the young Annie Ma and the man from the old photos. "Her father was SF."

Nina's hands were light on the wheel as she drove nimbly through the traffic on Hennepin Street. Dale had been withdrawn and quiet since he'd seen the crime scene and the pictures of Annie Ma's father. He tapped his fingers on his thigh again and again as he looked out the window, his head panning as though he expected to spot someone he knew any moment.

"What do you think makes a man go bad?" he said.

"You thinking about Maxwell?" Nina said.

"Yeah."

"How do you know he went bad?"

He looked over and raised his chin at her. "I don't get you."

"Maybe he was bad all along and you just didn't see it. Seems like nobody else saw it either, from what you say."

"I haven't been able to get around that from the beginning," Dale said. He spoke as though his mouth were dry. "I worked with this guy for years. He saved my life, other people's lives . . . I just don't understand how he could do . . . all this. The thought of it makes me sick."

"Reality check, Sergeant Miller," Nina said. "You think that rapists are all big bad ugly unshaven motherfuckers in long trench coats? I've popped priests, CEOs, doctors, lawyers, and an Indian chief. That's no shit. What's bent in these guys is inside. You got to look into their eyes to see what's dark inside. Sometimes it's real subtle, just a feeling you get. The way a guy looks at a woman when he thinks she's not looking. Or how he *won't* look at her. It's all about anger, and some people are really, really good at hiding it away. For a long time. Evil grows. Sometimes it's just a little seed of something, and then some shit comes up, some kind of hard time or hard circumstance in their life, and it's like watering that seed. Then it all comes out.

"Your Jonny, something happened to him a long time ago. He was probably just a kid. But it festered and grew in him since then, and the pressure you guys are under in your job . . . well, you got to have a release. Sex is a pretty good one, as you may have noticed. And that stuff will always find a way out."

"I don't know how you do this," Dale said. "Hang out in these guys' heads. Just what I've seen . . . don't you ever just feel like blowing them away? Just take care of business and sort it out yourself?"

Nina puckered her lips as though she were kissing a thought good-bye. "We'll talk about that some other time. I got to go see my boss, there's this press thing I gotta do. About an old case. You might find it interesting. Just hang tight while we do this thing, then we'll go find Herbie and Rocco and see what they got from the girl's friends. We're going to find Jonny Maxwell. And we're going to do it quick. We're running out of time before somebody comes looking for you."

**NO OTHER OPTION**

## 2.13

"Today I'm Jonny Walker," Jonny thought as he walked along the Mississippi River walkway. He followed the path to the Stone Bridge and crossed the river to the shaded walks on Main Street near Riverplace. Fragments of thoughts and images—Annie Ma, the photos of her father, the battered old green beret she kept—skipped like a broken record, leaving blanks in the humming that came and went inside his head. His awareness shrunk to just outside his skin; he bumped into people he didn't see until they'd touched him.

He stopped in an open-air bar-café and ordered coffee, then changed his mind and asked for a beer. The waitress looked strangely at him before she walked away. He watched her go, empty of the anger he would normally have felt. Annie Ma had drained that out of him and he felt nothing in its place.

He felt nothing. He had nothing.

Then he felt a tiny twinge of something close to panic.

He had his training and his mission, he reminded himself. He wasn't empty. He wasn't a bag of skin around a hollow space ringing with recrimination. He had what he needed, he had what he wanted. He had something to do and someplace to go, a mission to complete.

He wasn't empty. He wasn't nothing.

He looked up at the sky and gauged the hours till nightfall. He had time to kill before he went hunting. He stood up and walked away, throwing a few bills on the table as the waitress returned with his beer.

She picked up the money and called after him, "Don't you want your beer?"

He waved his hand good-bye without looking back.

Back in his apartment, Jonny slouched on the couch and flipped his remote through 120 cable TV stations. WCCO had the five o'clock news. A press conference gathered on the steps of police headquarters downtown. Jonny turned up the volume. The pretty blond news-woman described the scene: the Chief of Police was awarding a Medal of Valor to a woman detective from Sex Crimes who'd killed a child molester in a shoot-out. The camera panned away from the anchorwoman to the podium set up on the stairs. The detective was good-looking. Real good-looking. The chief said something, and then the camera panned away, and on the edge of the crowd Jonny got a glimpse of Dale Miller turning his face away from the camera.

Jonny's emotional response was neatly sliced off as though a clear veil of icy glass had fallen into place within his skull. One part of his brain noted his sudden rush of surprise and fear, while another part began to tabulate his options.

Dale. He hadn't seen him since the trial. Jonny never put him on his visitors' list, never got any mail from him. Dale. Here in Minneapolis. No coincidence, that. He was here hunting with the police.

How quickly things could change.

The hunters were here, men who knew him and knew how to hunt him. Things were going to have to happen faster than he'd planned.

The news went on to other things. Jonny flipped back and forth between the local channels to see if he could catch a repeat of the ceremony.

Dale. It had been him. No doubt.

Jonny turned off the television and stood by his window. He stared out at the small lawn and garden tended by his neighbor across the hall. Two sparrows landed, fluttered their wings, then flew away.

Dale.

Rocco Rocelli yelled across the cubicles in the Detective Division. "Yo, Nina! What the fuck? You don't tell anybody you're getting an award?"

"Surprise for me too, Rocco," Nina said. "Herbie knew, but did he tell his partner? Noooo."

Dale trailed behind her. Nina held the plaque the chief had presented her under one arm while she took a sheaf of pink message forms from Robbie with the other hand.

"Congratulations, Nina," Robbie said. "You deserve that."

"Thanks, Robbie," Nina said. She kissed him on the cheek and said, "Hey, what do you think of my new squeeze?"

Robbie camped and looked Dale up and down. "Uh huh. Oh, yeah."

"Dale, don't be teasing Robbie. You're mine." Nina tugged at Dale's shirt and guided him into the spare folding chair beside her desk.

"You don't give much away, do you?" Dale said.

Nina leafed through her messages. "What do you mean?"

"Did you know about that ceremony when we were talking earlier?"

"Not exactly. But I am a defective, at least on my good days, and I detected it. Now what the . . ." Nina studied one of the messages. "Robbie! Come here for a minute."

Robbie came to her desk. "Yes, Nina?"

"What's this?" She handed him one of the pink message forms.

"Oh, that was for your friend," Robbie said. "He called in for you, he asked first for Detective Capushek. Then he wanted to know if Dale Miller was around and I told him that Dale was with you. He didn't leave a number. He said he'd get back to you soon."

Nina's eyes narrowed as she looked at Dale. "He said his name was Jay?"

Robbie looked at the note again. "Well, I asked for his name and he said just sign it Jay. Is there a problem?"

"J as in the letter or Jay as in the bird?" Nina said.

"I don't know," Robbie said. "Is there a problem?"

"Get the exchange people and find out where this call came from. Now." Her light manner was gone.

Robbie hurried off. Nina said to Dale, "Who knows you're here?"

"Nobody." Dale checked his Skypager and scrolled through his recent messages. "And there's no message from my people to me. They'd page me."

"I think your boy saw you on the newscast. Just now."

"I wasn't . . ."

"You were. On the edge of the crowd. The cameras must have picked you up. What was I thinking?"

"Jonny?"

"We already had our reality check this morning, Dale. Do you have any doubt at all that this is from your buddy Jonny?"

Dale closed his eyes for a long moment. He wished he could keep them closed forever. "No," he said, looking at Nina.

"Well, then."

Robbie hurried back to them with a slip of paper. "Here, Nina. It was from a pay phone in City Center. The number's there."

Herb walked in behind him. "What's all this?" he asked, slapping his frayed notebook against his thigh. Nina told him. Herb picked up his desk phone.

"I'll get the techs over there now to pull prints," Herb said. "By the way," he said to Dale, "we got lots of prints in Annie Ma's apartment. The guy didn't wear gloves this time. Those prints are going to the Bureau. If it's who we think it is, there's going to be some bells and whistles and a ton of shit heading this way."

"It may be settled before then," Dale said.

"Whatever," Herb said. He turned his back to Dale and punched in numbers on his phone. "I don't like all this."

**NO OTHER OPTION**

Herb barked orders into his phone. Nina led Dale away. She took him into an empty interview room and shut the door. "Full disclosure," she said. "Why did he call you?"

"I don't know," Dale said. He looked everywhere in the room except at her.

"You must have some idea."

"No."

"Dale," she said. "What is it between you two?"

"I told you we worked together."

"What else?"

"We were friends."

"I knew that. Why would he think he could contact you? Does he think you're here to help him? Are you?"

"He would want me to know he knew I was here."

"Hmm." Nina digested that. "What happened with you two when he went down?"

"I was called to testify."

"Did you?"

"Yes."

"What was that like for you?"

"How do you think?" Dale said. "How'd you like it if you testified against Herb?"

She paused. "I never would."

"Never say never, Detective. What if you found out he was a rapist? For real? Even though you couldn't believe it, even though you worked side by side . . . what if he was? What if he raped children? What if for all your high and mighty investigator skills you never saw it right in front of you? Or you did and didn't want to say?" He forced himself to slow his breath and collect himself. "What then?"

"Okay," Nina said. She looked on him with a measure of sympathy. "I get it, now. That was a hard thing to do. Harder to live with, after."

His glare was fixed on the bridge of her nose. "You live the life, you walk the walk, you get the lessons sinking in all the time. Everything we do is training. That's why we'll be the ones doing what needs to be done."

"Who said that?"

"We better get back, Detective. You just ran out of time."

**MARCUS WYNNE**

Da da da da da THUMP. da da da da da THUMP. da da da da da
THUMP. The hypnotic beat of bass and drum from the band was
punctuated by the slam of heavy booted feet on the dance floor.
Flashes of light from ceiling-mounted spotlights whirled crazily and
cut through the smoke-filled air. The black-painted walls were decorated with murals drawn from heavy metal fantasy. At night in
First Avenue, the clothing was black, the hair black or shock blond,
tongues, noses, and cheeks pierced. Pale young bodies slammed in
unison to the beat. Jonny prowled and felt his age. There were a few
others too old to be full members of the generation stomping out
their defiance: one pathetic middle-aged guy trying too hard to be
hip in his knee-length shorts and tie-dyed shirt; two men with wolfish looks searching for young flesh; a woman with a gray ponytail
over one shoulder, taking it all in, leaning against the wall, her arms
crossed on her black T-shirt.

Jonny prowled.

There was a lot of security. Young muscled men, boys really,
in a semi-uniform of black T-shirt with SECURITY stenciled in white
across the chest and back, black or blue Levi's, and heavy Doc Martens. Some had knives or short collapsible batons tucked into their
pockets. Two had cans of Mace in leather police holders laced onto
their belts. They looked at Jonny and then away, the way young
sharks steer clear of a great white swimming lazily through their
waters. One of the men, a supervisor of some sort, leaned back against

the wall, watching everything. The others came to him, spoke for a moment, then left. Jonny got closer. It was the boy from Annie Ma's picture, her friend, Tony.

Jonny got a tall Budweiser at the bar. He drank from the bottle as he worked his way along the edge of the dance floor and leaned against the wall beside Tony the security supervisor.

"Busy in here," Jonny observed. "Is it always like this on a weeknight?"

Tony shrugged. "Sometimes. The band has a following."

Jonny sipped on his beer. Tony pretended to ignore him. The boy had paint under his nails, and hands surprisingly callused and scarred for someone in the arts.

"Who did the murals in here?" Jonny asked on a hunch.

"I did," Tony said.

"No shit? All of them?"

"No," Tony said, opening a little. "The big one on the wall there, the one with the mermaid and dolphin motif in it...I did that one."

"That's the best one in here. That's a work of art, really."

"Thanks."

"No, really. Do you do that professionally? Murals, faux finish, that kind of stuff?"

"I've done some. You in design?"

"No, I just like it. Do a little photography."

"What kind of camera do you shoot?"

"Pentax, the ZX-5. Really nice, lightweight, got autofocus and autoexposure if I need it, but all the manual stuff too, built in metering. Handles really well. I like it a lot."

"Those Pentax, they'll take all the old K-mount lenses?"

"Yeah. You don't have to start all over with lenses when you upgrade."

"That's cool. I shoot Nikon. I'd like to upgrade to one of the newer cameras, but it sucks to have to start buying lenses again."

"Nikon is good. That's real professional stuff."

"I'm Tony," said the young security man, holding out his hand.

"Yeah, I saw," Jonny said, gesturing with his beer at the name stenciled on the T-shirt, then shaking his hand. "I'm Jonny."

------

**MARCUS WYNNE**

Tony and Jonny stood in the alley behind First Avenue. The thump of the bass line was audible even through the worn brick walls. Jonny took another hit off the thin joint Tony offered him.

"This is pretty good smoke," Jonny said. "Where you get this?"

"Guy I know brings it in. He's got good connects in northern California for the best Humboldt smoke."

"Suppose I want to buy some?"

"I can take care of you."

"I mean suppose I want to buy a lot?"

"What's a lot?"

"A lot."

Tony shrugged. "If you were serious, I'd talk to him about it. You'd have to be serious, and that means you'd have to show me some long green, you know what I mean?"

"I can do that," Jonny said. "I'd like to get into the business, move some into the people I work with, you know? I got some money from a settlement, pretty substantial settlement. You help me out, I'll make it worth your while."

"Maybe. This guy is really paranoid. He's into guns and security, got a bodyguard, the whole real deal. He lives large."

"He's not some gun wacko, is he?" Jonny said. "Those guys  make me real nervous."

"Yeah, he's into it. He's all right, just always looking for the edge. Money, guns, dope. He had a close call with some bikers tried to rip him off a couple of years ago, so he's been paranoid ever since." Tony laughed. "But this isn't exactly L.A. Pretty tame around here."

"I hear that," Jonny said, passing the joint back. "So when do I meet the guy?"

"Soon as I see the color of your money."

"Tonight too soon?"

"I work till three-thirty. After we get done closing up the club and take care of the count, hell, I'm up till the sun comes up. I'm a Lost Boy. Where you live?"

"Over by Harriet."

"Yuptown?"

"Linden Hills."

"Oh, that's sweet. I go to the Co-op over there sometimes. Cool. I got to get back in."

Jonny paused before the open door and stared up at the night sky.

**NO OTHER OPTION**

## 2.16

"What is this!" Jed Loveless bellowed. He threw the thin sheaf of papers he'd been reading down on his desk, stood and kicked his trash can across the office.

The other marshals who shared space with him were surprised into silence until one said, "Home team lose, Jed?"

"Get La Roux and Harris in here, now! Find them and get them in here. And Mad Dog from SOG too. Hurry up! Is everybody deaf?" Jed shouted.

Jed picked up his trash can and replaced it beside his desk. He rubbed his forehead furiously with one fist. Then he picked up the sheaf of papers routed to his desk informing him that fingerprints found at a crime scene in Minneapolis were a positive match for one Jonathan Harding Maxwell, a fugitive case assigned to his Special Task Force. A note attached to the routing slip said questions should be directed to Detective Nina Capushek, Major Crimes Unit, Minneapolis Police Department, or Investigative Assistant Robert Holm, or DOD Liaison Officer Master Sergeant Dale Miller.

Ray Dalton leaned back in his chair and steepled his fingers. On the wall was a Japanese ink brush painting of an iris, given him by a grateful member of the Japanese Intelligence Service after Ray's tour in the Tokyo embassy. He liked to study the peaceful, graceful lines of the flower when he had to think. He had a lot to think about right now. The Marshals Service was in a major uproar, demanding to know what Dale was up to, and Ray, after his soothing assurances of some miscommunication, had no answer to present to his bosses. This called for finesse, the velvet touch. Or the iron fist he kept inside his velvet glove.

He picked up the phone and punched in the number for the communications center. "This is Dalton," he said. "I want an emergency recall put out on Dale Miller's beeper. Use the locate. I want him found and called in. Recall the Bravo split and put them on standby for deployment. When Roger gets in, send him up here. Thanks, Charlie."

Ray hung up the phone, leaned back in his chair, and admired the artistry of the Japanese. He didn't dwell on the need to kill at least one, perhaps two, of the best men he'd ever fielded.

"Well, the shit's hit the fan," Nina said.

"Couldn't be helped," Herb said. He wouldn't look at Dale. "Those prints had to go in and they did. We didn't know they were flagged. And it removes any doubt about who we're dealing with."

He finally glared at Dale. "Why would he do this? Leave his prints all over the place like that?"

"He wants us to know he's here," Dale said. "It's his way of telling us, first his little call and then this. He wants us to know that he *knows* that I'm here. That it's a different game now."

Dale held his pager up in his hand. The red message light blinked steadily. "They're going to take this away from you, Herb. As soon as I return this call, I'm off it. The marshals are on their way and your chief is going to be read the riot act. You are going to be sitting on the sidelines and the Feds are going to take the whole show over."

"They have to cooperate with us ..." Herb started.

"Federal case," Dale said flatly. "With national security implications. Can you spell DOD? FBI? U.S. Marshals?"

"Let's go," Nina said. She stood. "We're out of here."

"What?" Herb said.

"Except for you, Herbie boy. You're going to hold down the fort. I'm going to lose our soldier boy and then I'll be back to take the heat with you. We're not giving up this case. Until I'm ordered by the captain or the chief, I'm not changing a thing. We clear on that?" Nina's voice was cool and relaxed, the same way it was when

**NO OTHER OPTION**

she was telling the shooting team about capping MacDouglas, Herb thought.

"Go then, get out of here," Herb said. "Go on."

"Where we going?" Dale asked Nina as they drove away from the headquarters parking lot.

"My place," Nina said. "You can stay there till you figure out what you want to do about your people. I'll just say I don't know where you're at. You still keeping that hotel room?"

"Yeah."

"I'll tell the marshals I left you off there. I'd suggest you just lie low and avoid this heat and get your head around what you need to do to keep your bosses happy. That's if you intend to stick around and see how all this comes out?"

Dale's pager buzzed again.

"You ever going to answer that?" Nina asked.

"Sooner or later," Dale said. "Just not right now."

Nina took the freeway to Thirty-sixth Street and down to Lake Parkway. After winding her way round Calhoun to Harriet, she pulled in front of her condo. "Here's the key," she said, taking an extra from her key ring. "Make yourself at home."

Dale watched her drive away in the thin traffic on the parkway, then let himself into her home. He stood for a moment in the entranceway and let the sense of the house roll over him. There was a faint scent of jasmine, a hint of perfume. The air was cool inside. He went into the kitchen and looked in the refrigerator. He sat at the kitchen table and held his pager in his hand and stared at the blinking red light.

He thought of calling from somewhere else, but he no longer cared if they knew where he was. The tracer in the pager told them minute by minute anyway. Let them find him. He picked up the phone and entered the toll free number of the Operations Center.

"Hello?" said the brisk male voice on the other end.

"This is Miller. I authenticate Star Wars 99, royal rules dominion."

"Hello, Miller. Authenticate Star Wars 99, royal rules dominion. Your line is not secured," the voice said. "Lot of people want to talk to you, Miller, but the boss has first dibs. Do you have a portable crypto?"

**MARCUS WYNNE**

"No."

"Stand by for a nonsecure line to the boss. I'll let him know. You okay?"

"Yeah."

"Stand by."

There were several clicks and then the clear tinny hum of whatever electronic magic the best gurus at NSA could dream up to make a call from an unsecure phone into a secure one as leakproof as possible.

"Well, son," said Ray Dalton. "It seems we have a few problems."

"We do."

"What's going on with you?"

"I followed a hunch and it paid off."

"Any particular reason you couldn't tell me that before I got a series of heated phone calls today?"

"It was a hunch, Ray. I'm clear on it now, and I've run him down. Time to see it through."

"I'm sending Roger Magritte to Minneapolis," Ray said.

"Why?"

"Because you need some help."

"I don't need any help. Not from Roger or anybody else. I need to be the one to finish this."

"You're going to."

"With Roger looking over my shoulder? Is that it? You worried about me in that way, Ray? I don't like that. I don't like where this is going."

"Get used to it," Ray said, the steel in his voice rising. "And stay in touch. I want to hear from you, personally, every single day. You've got a job to do and you've kicked over every table in the china shop on the way. Get it done. Take care of business."

"I will," Dale said. He hung up the phone and went to the window and looked out at the lake.

Ray gently set his phone back down in the cradle. In a big leather armchair across from his desk, a wiry, compact man with tightly curled black hair, boneless and relaxed as a cat, smoked a thin brown cigarillo.

"Well," the wiry man, whose name was Roger Magritte, said. "How do you want me to handle this?"

**NO OTHER OPTION**

"Reel him back in," Ray said. "Make sure he's okay. And if you get a clear shot on Jonny—take him out. This has gotten out of hand."

"You know Dale isn't going to take this well. I may have to run parallel to him."

"You stick close to Dale. That's as much your job as seeing to Maxwell. I can't afford to lose Miller over this shit and we're right on the brink of way too much exposure as it is."

"Okay, boss." The best solo assassin in the U.S. government unwound out of the chair and ground his cigarillo out in Ray's ashtray. Roger adjusted the Kramer Speed Scabbard holding his Glock 19 behind his hip. "I'll take care of business. I'm on the next flight out."

"Go," Ray said. "You got the green light."

**MARCUS WYNNE**

**2.17**

The U.S. Marshals Special Task Force was lined up on one side of the long table in the conference room beside the office of Chief Martin Thomas of the Minneapolis Police Department. Mustered on the other side were the chief, Captain Martinson, who oversaw the Major Crimes Division, the city attorney, and the investigative team of Herb Dunn and Nina Capushek.

"Where is that son of a bitch Miller?" Edgar Harris demanded.

"Put a sock in it, cowboy," Nina said. "He should have kept you informed, but that's not my problem. Things happened pretty quick out here. And it seems Miller did a whole hell of a lot better job following up than you all did."

"That's enough," Jed Loveless said.

"*You* don't tell *me* enough, Loveless," Nina said. "Keep your dog muzzled and on your side of the fence. I'll worry about me."

Jed looked at Chief Thomas and Captain Martinson, who both stared coolly at him and made no move to silence the angry young detective.

"Okay," Jed said. "Let's start over. We got some hard feelings on our side . . ."

"Which don't have anything to do with us," Nina said.

"Okay, which don't have anything to do with you. You're right. We're wrong. Edgar?" Jed said.

Harris sat back in his seat, puffed out his cheeks, and exhaled loudly. "I apologize," he said in a flat monotone. "I was out of line."

"This is not a good situation," Jed began. "We've got a serious problem . . ."

"Which might just get worse, Inspector Loveless," Chief Thomas said. "That, of course, depends a great deal on you. The Minneapolis Police Department isn't going to tolerate this kind of high and mighty . . . crap, no matter what you say. You want to get a U.S. attorney involved, try to throw some weight around, you go right ahead. In the meantime, my detectives, *my* detectives, will continue with their investigation. They are in charge of the investigation. As for yours, well, if you'd been doing your damn job you would have had this son of a bitch before he showed up here to rape and murder. You want to push this matter, I guarantee that you'll be explaining *that* on the evening news."

"I don't appreciate, nor do I deserve, that threat, Chief," Jed said, struggling with his own temper.

"It's a promise, Loveless." The chief stared at the senior marshal. "We all want to catch this son of a bitch. You had your chance and you blew it. Don't you ever come into my department woofing that kind of shit again. You want to play, you play backup. If my detectives *allow* it. And I will support them one hundred ten percent. You want to muscle the play, you get the U.S. attorney and whoever the hell you want from the Justice Department down here. We can hold a joint press conference out on the steps. Minneapolis gets this guy, period. When we're done with him for what he's done here, you can have what's left."

Jed held his hands up in surrender. "All right," he said. "All right. I'm going to talk to my bosses. Maybe they can get you to reconsider this. We're coming in, one way or the other. It's ridiculous for us to be sitting here while this asshole is out running around. We need to get past this."

"We are," the chief said. "You want to play, you play second string. My detectives call the shots. If they want, they can let you in. But Minneapolis takes him. We get the shot. We're done here." He stood and walked out of the room, followed by Captain Martinson and the grinning city attorney. Nina and Herb remained at the table and stared across at Jed, La Roux, and Harris.

"Well, boys," Nina said. "What's it going to be?"

Herb had his Doctor Death face on and was staring down Harris. "You got something you want to say?" Herb said.

**MARCUS WYNNE**

"Yeah," Edgar said, pointing at Herb's shoulder holster. "What kind of cut-down hog leg you carrying there?"

Herb snorted in derision.

"Wow, that looked like an attempt to build rapport, don't you think, Herb?" Nina said caustically.

"Hey, Nina, can we put this behind us?" Jed asked.

"Hey, Jed, sure we can. Just save the saccharine role play shit they taught you in 'Managing Local Agencies 101' for the starry-eyed yokels in Bum Fuck Mississippi. Around here, we don't roll over when somebody says Fed," Nina said.

"Would you be willing to tell us what you've found out so far if we ask politely and say please?" Jed said.

"Sure. You guys let Jonny Maxwell lead you around by your dick and convince you that he was dead. He came over and raped at least two women and murdered one of them. Now you guys come muscling in here, trying to take over my investigation to cover your own fuckup. Which my boss ain't gonna allow. And if you try it again, you'll be on the front page of the *Star Tribune* in twelve hours and on the evening news in three."

"What's Miller's role in all this?" Jed said.

"Ask him."

"I would if I could find him. I'm considering filing obstruction charges on him," Jed said.

"That's a laugh," Nina said. "He's the most organized one of your whole task force."

"Can we get on with it?"

Nina stood up. "Nothing to get on to, Jed. Me and my partner, we're going to go detect some and catch this guy who's been rubbing your nose in your own shit for the last little while. As far as I'm concerned, you can all sit here till we bring him in. Later."

Herb followed her out of the room, favoring each man in turn with his hard look.

"Well, this is just delightful," Tommy said. "Simply fucking piquant."

Harris laughed. "That's pretty good. Piquant."

"Shut up," Jed said.

**2.18**

Roger Magritte looked out his window and watched the Minneapolis–St. Paul International Airport rise up beneath the descending 747. It was a green city; trees and rivers ran through and around the city center, with its glass-faced skyscrapers rising high above the streets. Roger admired the neatness and organization. He was a neat and tidy and organized man. His credentials as a special security agent for the U.S. Department of Defense had gotten him through security and onboard the aircraft with all his weapons and other gear, which was stowed in a black Cordura bag tucked neatly beneath the seat in front of him. The bag contained a change of clothing, a trauma-level first aid kit, a water bottle, a small utility kit, a tiny and very expensive satellite cellular phone, spare ammunition, and two small HK MP-5K submachine pistols. Money, credit cards, and a laminated plastic card with his blood type and a toll-free contact number were in a small pouch hung round his neck and concealed beneath his nondescript button-down blue oxford shirt and khakis.

Roger carried the same and dressed the same wherever he went. He found it made packing and traveling easier. A book lay in his lap, his finger marking his place as he watched out the window. *The Warriors*, by J. Glenn Gray, a philosophical treatise on the philosophy and psychology of the soldier. Roger was interested in how people's minds worked, especially his own. He spent a great deal of time talking with the unit psychologist and reading psychological journals. He liked people and enjoyed talking with them. Some of the best conversations he'd had were with targets before he killed them. Nothing sadistic to it in his mind—it just seemed a hidden blessing in the often arduous task he was given, to be able to discuss the ramifications of imminent death with someone facing the immediate prospect.

He hoped to have a discussion with Jonny before he killed him.

They'd not spoken much when they had worked together. Jonny's bent as a loner became more pronounced in the time before he was caught and tried, and Roger had come aboard just before that, out of the Agency's paramilitary cells in the Special Operations Division. He'd done a short tour in the Navy on SEAL Team Eight, gotten his languages, and then left to join the CIA, where he'd risen to be a star in the Special Operations cells. He'd attracted the eye of Ray Dalton, after Roger had pulled a major coup by infiltrating a Paris-based, Algerian-staffed, and Saudi-funded (courtesy of the renegade Saudi Osama Bin Laden) terrorist cell and killing all five of the operational members and one of the support team. The French DGSE had been blamed for the bloody operation, for which they were publicly glad to take credit for and privately outraged that someone (they suspected the Israelis) had trumped their own concurrent operation. Ray recognized the peculiar genius evident in that operation and poached the young operator for DOMINANCE RAIN, where Roger settled comfortably into his niche as a singleton operator with a specialty in "extra-judicial resolution."

Roger filed off the plane with the other passengers, nodded politely to the flight attendants and flight crew as he went down the jetway and disappeared into the crowd.

**2.19**

Jonny Maxwell sat in the Irish pub across the street from the Minneapolis Police headquarters building and listened to the folk singer do his sound check.

"Oh, Danny boy, the pipes, the pipes are calling . . . ," the singer sang. He was short and fat and black-haired with a sweet voice, and he smiled and nodded to Jonny as he sang.

Jonny nodded back and tapped his finger to the music. The soft sounds soothed him, though the late afternoon light was hard on his eyes after the few hours of sleep he'd managed. He sipped appreciatively at the Guinness the bartender had set him up with. He'd never been much of a drinker, but the lazy afterglow of the marijuana he'd smoked last night made the sweet Guinness taste all the better. He'd have to watch himself; he'd been drinking more lately.

An hour passed. The side door across the street was where most of the police officers came and went, probably to avoid the office smokers—some of them brass—huddled on the front steps. No sign of the woman detective he'd seen on television, or her "partner"— Dale Miller.

Young Dale. Jonny had drawn him here like an old magnet to new steel. What would he say if he walked into the bar, saw him sitting in the window, a beer in his hand? Would he even recognize him?

Dale. They'd laughed at the same jokes, run sweating in the same operations. And then his arrest and the trial slammed a door as impenetrable as any prison's between them. Dale on the stand . . . he could understand how that came to be. But underneath the visible vacillation and conflict on the stand, something else, something like a hidden satisfaction at seeing him brought down . . . He'd never seen that coming. He knew the others, Roger Magritte especially, quietly nursed grudges at his aloofness and the special missions and the perks that came with them. But he'd never seen that in Dale.

He'd given Dale the best he had. Everyone saw that.

And everyone saw what Dale gave him in return.

He might have tried to contact Jonny after the trial. He wasn't sure, he'd kept his visitors' list empty and took no calls. He thought it was better that way. At least that's what he told himself. What would he say? "Hey, Dale, how you doing? Ratted out any friends lately?"

Ray Dalton had come. Jonny took the cigarettes he offered, listened without comment to the old man's attempt at breaking through the barrier of silence.

Finally, Ray gave up. "Just keep your mouth shut. Do your time. Down the road, maybe, we might be able to do something. I'll make sure you get some extra money in your commissary fund, or anything else you want. But keep your mouth shut. I don't think you want to hurt your people anymore. We'll be watching you."

Jonny watched him leave the visiting room, the old man as straight and erect as he had always been. He got the message; he could read between the lines as well as anyone. Locking him up didn't translate into locking up what was in his head. Targets. Operations. Procedures. Tactics. Equipment. Information that would wreak a fine havoc in the wrong hands. How would the American public and Congress respond if the details of the numerous assassination operations mounted by DOMINANCE RAIN hit the front pages of the major newspapers? There was still a standing Executive Order prohibiting assassination. Lawyers' talk, all of it. Assassination wasn't assassination if the target posed a clear and present danger to the national security. It wasn't assassination if he wasn't a head of state. It wasn't assassination if you didn't aim your .50 caliber rifle at him, but at his equipment. Like the ballpoint pen in his pocket or the phone in his hand or the crosspiece of his eyeglasses. It wasn't assassination if you tampered with his plane, his car, or the syringes in his doctor's office.

It wasn't assassination if you killed a dangerous escaped convict.

Jonny caught the bartender's eye and pointed at his glass. The bartender took a fresh glass and eased the tap slowly, allowing time for the beer to settle and the head to form before he topped it off.

"Thanks," Jonny said, shoving loose bills across the bar.

What would he do when Dale walked out across the street? Take him out fast and hard with the pistol he concealed beneath his light jacket? Eliminate the only chance the police had of getting close to him before he got his money and was gone? Or say, "Dale . . . how you doing? Join me for a beer," and stand and see what he would do?

That was an interesting thought. What would he do?

He remembered a scratch job they'd done together in South Africa, taking out a Chinese nuclear engineer who'd come to evaluate the Pelindaba nuclear facility that Nelson Mandela was selling to the PRC. It wasn't a straight up shoot on sight mission; it had to appear to be an accident, preferably one that would attract press attention  and discredit the PRC, who wanted a tight lid kept on the sale.

A Special Operating Group from CIA's Special Activities Section had done the close target reconnaissance, and then a three-man element from DOMINANCE RAIN slid into place, and was briefed to do the job. The engineer had a dangerous and ultimately fatal fascination with black women and sex in semiprivate settings. The operators took advantage of his weakness when they developed the final plan, which involved two attractive Tanzanian hookers picking up the engineer and taking him out to a minivan taxi parked behind the hotel for sex.

Then the DOMINANCE RAIN shooters would kill all three in what would appear to be a botched car-jacking, one of the dozens that happened each day in Johannesburg.

It was primarily Roger's plan—it had all his earmarks: deceptive, convolute, and ruthless. Dale had balked at the requirement to kill the two prostitutes.

"It's not necessary," Dale said.

"How else are we going to close off that loophole?" Roger said. "They know the cutout." The cutout was a local CIA contract employee who'd brought the two hookers in. "You want to compromise him to save two hookers who are probably going to die of AIDS in a year or so anyway? We're doing them a favor."

"They're not targets," Dale said.

"Collateral damage, Dale," Jonny said. "You got a better idea?"

"We could let them get away when we go for the van," Dale said. "Run them off. We'll be masked anyway."

"You think they can't tell three white men, even under masks?" Roger said. "Jonny, talk to him."

Jonny shrugged. "He's right. They'd know, and National Intelligence could put it together. These Dutchmen aren't stupid."

"How is it going to get to them?" Dale countered. "They think they're doing the local a favor by fucking his Chinese buddy. They don't know anything else. They're going to get the hell out of there as quick as they can. They got paid already. They're not going to run to the cops—they're hookers and in for nothing but a long night of giving it away for free for the on-duty cops at the jail if they get arrested. It's not necessary. We can just walk up, do it, and tell them to get the hell out of there while we fiddle with the van."

"I don't like it," Roger said. "Let's stick to our plan."

"It's your plan," Jonny said. "I don't have any problem with what Dale says. We can go with it."

Roger conceded, grudgingly. And the job went off as planned, with one small hitch. The three had moved on the van, Roger to cover the hookers, Jonny on rear security, and Dale on the trigger for the Chinese. Two fast 9mm rounds to the head on the walk-up, visual verification that his brain pan was open, turn to walk away. Roger was drawing down on the hookers instead of shooing them away. Jonny bumped him hard with his shoulder, spoiling his aim.

"What we said," Jonny whispered.

The women ran away and never looked back. But Roger glared at Jonny for a long moment before he concealed his pistol beneath his shirttail and followed Dale down the alley where their own vehicle waited.

Less than a minute time on target. Par for the course.

Dale didn't have any problem taking out the Chinese scientist. That was the job. But he didn't want to kill the hookers.

Jonny smiled.

He stood up and pushed his remaining bills and change across the bar top for the bartender. He turned his back on the window and walked through the bar to the exit door that opened out on the side street away from the police building.

Jonny stepped out into the early evening. There were more people on the streets, coming from work, hurrying to happy hour at one of the bars, rushing to the buses to get home. He slipped smoothly into the crowd, his back to the police building, walked away and never looked back.

"Ron, this is Jonny," Tony said. "He's the guy I was telling you about."

Ron looked Jonny over and Jonny looked him right back. Ron Pierce was a tall man, once strong but now soft around the edges. The muscle folded into fat at his waistline and his biceps were flabby. Jonny bristled at the indolent way he held his hand out to shake. His grip was weak and quick.

"How you doing?" Jonny said. He smiled, his eyes hidden beneath his Wayfarers. "Quite the place you've got here," he said, gesturing at the sprawling ranch and its outbuildings. Pierce raised llamas and dwarf donkeys for the exotic pet market. It was a good way to hide the cash he had rolling in from his extensive marijuana sales. Last night and early this morning, over too much coffee, a little speed, and some more smoke, Tony had told Jonny that Pierce brought the dope in on semitrailers, which were off-loaded in his facility. Then the bundles were broken down and shipped out to dealers like Tony, who broke them down some more for their customers.

"It's not bad, is it?" Pierce said. "Let's walk and talk some. I've got to see my animals."

Tony and Jonny fell in behind Pierce as he led the way down the gravel road toward a long outbuilding.

"I've got one of my llamas ready to foal here," Pierce said. He opened up the heavy barn door and led them inside. A long line of stalls faced each other across a wide concrete walkway slick with water that smelt of disinfectant. A skinny blond man in his early twenties, eyes huge behind thick glasses, looked up from where he sat on a stool in front of a fuse box, a circuit tester in his hand. A Beretta 92FS pistol was holstered at his waist on a pistol belt that drooped off his thin hips. He looked like Barney Fife. Beside him was a big dog, a Doberman blend, who studied Jonny intently.

"Security," Pierce said.

Jonny pretended to be impressed. "Pretty tight, it looks like," he said.

"Oh, yeah," Pierce said. "We know how to take care of business out here."

"Looks like it," Jonny said.

They stopped in front of one stall, where a llama with a huge, distended belly came to the wooden rail and nuzzled Pierce's hand.

"Hi, darling," Pierce crooned. "How's my girl today?" He looked at Jonny. "You like animals?"

Jonny said, "I don't think about it much."

"I like them," Pierce said. "They don't try to fuck with you, they know what's what. In return for care, they just love you. Don't ask for anything except something to eat and a place to sleep." He petted the llama's nose. "Not like people."

Pierce walked back outside into the sunlight. Bits of wet straw clung to his expensive cowboy boots. He hitched his pants up, self-consciously adjusting the four-inch Smith & Wesson 686 revolver holstered beneath his open shirt.

"Tony says you're interested in doing some business," Pierce said.

"If the price is right," Jonny said. "Your product is pretty good. I'm interested."

"What kind of weight are you looking for?"

"Couple hundred pounds. To start."

"You got that kind of cash, huh?"

"Yeah, I do."

"Hm." Pierce walked off and gestured for Jonny and Tony to follow. The owl-eyed security guard trailed behind them, after telling the Doberman to stay.

"Watch out for the llama shit," Tony muttered. "It's all over the fucking place."

"Yeah," Jonny said, stepping carefully. "Where we going?" he called after Pierce.

"Show you my shooting range," Pierce said. He led them around the sweep of one wing of the house and down an incline behind the house. There was a long scrape of smooth plowed earth, banked high on either side with dirt. Three hundred yards down were a row of human silhouette targets. Closer, at the fifty, one hundred, and two hundred yard lines were scattered silhouettes set up on wooden posts. Off to the side of the five shooting positions was a shorter bermed range for handguns, with a pneumatic-powered metal plate rack and a combat B-27 silhouette with a neat cluster of holes in its center.

"You like to shoot?" Pierce asked Jonny.

"Guns scare me," Jonny said. "I don't like them at all."

Pierce curled his lip. "Watch this," he said. He drew the .357 revolver smoothly, locked into a strong Weaver stance, and put six rounds in the X-ring of the B-27 rapid fire. He flipped the revolver over into his weak hand, opened the cylinder and punched the empties out, then slammed a speed-loader into place, brought the revolver back up, and put six more rounds into the X-ring. He grinned at Jonny and said, "Not bad, huh?"

Jonny studied the neat group and shrugged. "I wouldn't know. I heard once that a smart man got more with a lawyer and a briefcase than with a gun."

Pierce stared hard at Jonny, then laughed. "Yeah, that's no shit. Come on up to the house. We'll talk."

The quiet security guard with the overly large pistol watched them go up to the house. He wondered if he was the only one who'd noticed that the big guy, who said he was scared of guns, hadn't flinched at all through the barrage of twelve full-power .357 loads.

They sat in Pierce's vault room, a fifteen by fifteen room with a sunken floor, no windows, and the best bank vault door Mosler offered. A variety of automatic weapons, pistols, and other militaria hung on the walls. The low padded benches in the room were storage lockers, whose tops lifted up to display more guns, cases of ammunition, and in one, a case of M-26 fragmentation grenades.

"So besides the dope, I got guns, in case some of your friends are interested," Pierce went on. "Lots of guns. Mostly assault rifles and pistols, but I got some other real good shit. Check this out," he said. He handed an Ingram Mac-10 with an attached Sionics suppresser to Jonny. Rollmarked and highlighted in white paint above the magazine well were the words "Property of U.S. government."

"You're looking at serious time with this shit," Jonny said, handing back the Ingram.

"Why do you say that?" Pierce said.

"I'm only interested in the smoke. Not guns. I don't need that sort of complication in my life. That's your business, not mine."

Pierce took the weapon back, ran his hands over it. "Whatever."

"So when can I get my dope?" Jonny said.

"Right now, you got the cash on you," Pierce said.

"Sorry, I'm a little short. That makes for a bigger bundle than I like to carry around. I can go get it and come back."

"I can bring you back out if you need to," Tony said. "I don't have to be down to the club till nine tonight."

"You can find your way back out here, can't you?" Pierce asked Jonny.

"Sure," Jonny said. "Give me your phone number and I'll call you before I come back out. Or do you just want me to call from the gate?"

"Whatever," Pierce said. "Just make sure you come alone. I don't let just anybody come out here."

"Sure," Jonny said. He smiled. "No problem. I'll come alone."

## 2.20

Roger Magritte ambled along the Lake Harriet footpath. He carried compact Nikon binoculars in one hand and a birding book in the other. Occasionally he'd stop and train his binoculars on the grebes, ducks, and loons out on the water or follow one flying overhead. He stopped a hundred yards away from the front steps of Nina Capushek's condominium and focused on her front windows. The phone track from DOMINANCE RAIN led him to Detective Capushek's home; the GPS signal from the special pager Dale wore located him within one meter anywhere on earth. Roger knew exactly where Dale was, but he didn't want to press him yet. He didn't understand why Ray had put Dale onto this project, given their history. But now that he had the assignment, it really wasn't important. He'd gather his own intelligence and make his plays based on what he decided was best.

He walked back to the band shell and the pay phones there. He dropped in his quarter and dialed Nina Capushek's number. The phone rang four times and then the answering machine picked up.

"Hello, Dale," Roger said. "It's Roger Magritte. Would you pick up, please?"

There was no answer.

"Look, we should talk," Roger went on. "I don't want to complicate things. We're going to have to talk and, shit, man . . . we work together. Let's take care of business."

The phone clicked on the other end. Dale came on the line. "Where are you?"

"At the band shell next to the lake, just down the street."

"I'll be there in five."

The two men strolled slowly around Lake Harriet, exchanging appreciative glances with the attractive women passing by.

"These northern gals are a well-kept secret," Roger said. "I think Minneapolis, I think cold and chubby girls in flannel shirts."

"It's been a while," Dale said.

"Not that long. We worked that Angola thing and that was, what? A year ago?" Roger held out a plastic-wrapped cigarillo. "Want a Cubanito?"

"No. You been down there this whole time?"

"There and SA. Took some downtime to cool off after the job, got a game guide and did some hunting on one of the preserves just outside of Kruger."

"Get anything?"

"Nothing I could bring back." Roger drew on his cigarillo and ignored the disapproving look from a passerby. "What do you want to tell me about all this, Dale? The boss told me some. I knew Jonny, I know you. What the fuck, over?"

Dale sighed. "It's a pigfuck. FUBAR from start to finish." He gave Roger the rundown, leaving out the details about Nina and him.

"Ray should never have put you on this," Roger said, not without sympathy. "It's wrong. Just complicates things."

"He has his point. Who knows him better? Not you. I'm on it and I'll stay on it."

Dale delicately tapped his cigar and let the ash fall onto the grass. "I don't think that's the best course. Better that you back off, better yet go home. Get your head right, drink some beer. Let this play out. We'll get it squared away."

"How?" Dale said. "You going to put him down? That's the mission, right? It never was about bringing him in, is that what you're telling me?"

"That's right, Dale. It never was. And you're right. I'm here to put him down." Roger lowered his voice as they passed an elderly couple walking slowly along the path. "You knew that going in. Don't fool yourself."

"What about me?" Dale said. His voice dropped to a dangerous murmur. "Ray give you marching orders on me?"

**NO OTHER OPTION**

Roger stopped and took his time blowing a smoke ring. It held together in the air for a few seconds, then came apart. He looked at Dale. "He wants you back in. Either here or at home. I'm to get the job done any way I see fit. I'm talking to you now, bringing you in, out of respect." He shrugged. "I'll admit I'm curious. I want to see how this is for you. Hunting a friend . . . but if you insist on staying in the game, you're hunting with me. Partners. Like it or not. We've got history together. I don't know why you think you have to do this all yourself. You trying to punish yourself, do penance for being Jonny's friend? We all felt like that, even though none of us were as close to him as you were. You're not responsible for what went on and what goes on in Jonny Maxwell's head. He is. He's the only one responsible."

**2.21**

Ron Pierce's pie-eyed "bodyguard" supplemented his meager income by moonlighting as a Confidential Informant for the ATF, who had a deep and abiding interest in his employer. Harold Ragborne was a bitter ex-con who'd taken a five-year fall in Stillwater for Pierce. After he was paroled, Pierce offered him work as a security guard on his estate. It made Pierce feel as though he'd looked after Ragborne for taking the fall, and helped him forget that it was his own incompetence that landed Harold in prison in the first place.

But Harold hadn't forgotten. He carefully concealed his bitterness and desire for vengeance and set about knocking Ron Pierce off his pedestal. That's what brought him to a federal safe house in the suburbs of Minneapolis, shared by FBI, DEA, ATF, and even on occasion by the snooty out of towners from CIA. His controller, ATF Special Agent Dean Hardaway, sat on the couch beside Harold and took notes.

"It's either drugs or guns or both," Harold said. "This guy, he's got big bucks. He's from out of town, got some connection for moving stuff through the airlines."

"So who is this guy?" Hardaway said. "Who's the guy?"

"I don't know nothing but his first name," Harold whined. "And that he's got the cash, and the deal is going down tonight. Ain't that enough?"

"So give me the name."

"Jonny," Harold said. "Jonny something. He's connected with

First Avenue some way. That Tony guy, the head bouncer, he brought him up to the house."

"We're going to have to take a look at Jonny," Hardaway said with satisfaction. "Might just be tonight, too, Harold."

"Look, I don't care what you do. I got to be back at the house by six. You got my money?"

"Don't worry, Harold," Hardaway said. "We'll take care of you."

Dean Hardaway despised his supervisor, a rat-faced former Marine named Kevin Beale. In the weekly staff meetings, the barely restrained loathing he felt for Beale welled up and pushed his blood pressure right up against the red line.

"You haven't filed the CI contact reports on the Pierce snitch," Beale said. He loved to pose questions and then chip away at his subordinate's answers.

"That's right, Kevin, I haven't," Hardaway said. "I've been in this highly important meeting instead of working my case."

The other agents at the conference table grinned down into their notes.

Supervisory Special Agent Beale glared at Hardaway. "You'll get them done and on my desk before you go out to cover this meet." He looked down at his own notes to hide his discomfort. "Who's backing you up?"

"Mitch," Hardaway said, nodding at his partner, Mitch Kojira, who dropped him a slow wink.

"All right then," Beale said, standing up. "Let's get it done, people." He led the way out of the conference room so he wouldn't have to see the looks his agents exchanged.

"Deano, Deano, one of these days Beale is going to be gone and you won't have anybody to fuck with anymore," Mitch said, poking his partner in his paunch.

"I'll have you then, Chinaman," Hardaway said. "I hope you don't have any plans for dinner."

"Why not," Kojira said wearily. "I haven't been home for dinner in a week, my wife won't have sex with me, and my kids are probably selling dope out of the garage. Why shouldn't I go sit in a car with you someplace and watch mopes play with each other?"

"You want to be there when we make Pierce. I hate this cocky

**MARCUS WYNNE**

rich son of a bitch. He spends more on animal feed than I made last year," Hardaway said.

"What's the deal?"

"My little snitch, Harold the Ragman, tells me Pierce has a buyer for some guns and/or some dope. A guy named Jonny, no last, got connections for moving guns and dope through the airlines. Meeting with Pierce later on tonight to make a first buy."

Mitch said, "Let's go out for a smoke."

"I thought you quit."

"I have. Didn't you notice?" The two of them went out the front door of the Federal Building into the late afternoon sun. Mitch lit his cigarette and nodded to the other smokers on the steps. "What else we got on this Jonny? No last name, no picture, what?"

"Nothing. Figured we take the long lens out, see if we can get some pictures of him out at Pierce's. We got that good hide off that road on the hill overlooks his corrals. Harold is going to work him some, see if he can get a name, some other stuff," Hardaway said.

"You going to bring DEA in? They could lend us some bodies . . ."

"Nah. They're all tied up on a bust tonight in Bloomington. I talked to Bruce over there, he said get pictures and share info, they'll find Jonny next time."

"Sounds easy enough," Mitch said. "You don't got a specific time?"

"Supposedly after dark."

Mitch ground his cigarette out in the overflowing ashtray set out on the front steps for the building's smokers. "Goddamn no smoking policy," he groused. "All right. Let's draw our shit and go get it done."

Herb and Nina drove aimlessly through the North Side. Four teen-
agers in baggy jeans and leather car coats turned and went back
inside their run-down house when the squad cruised slowly by.

"We've got nothing, Herb," Nina said. "Nada. Zip. Zero."

Herb looked over with concern. His partner was slumped
against the door of the squad. "Dale got any ideas?"

"I think his people have muzzled him. The marshals are all
over his boss and they'll be all over him if they find him."

"Nina."

"So he's been at my place. He still doesn't have any ideas."

"Damn."

"Yeah." Nina stared out the window, not seeing the street. "You
got any ideas, Herbie? Something we can scrape up ourselves."

"Only what I should have said from the get-go. Let's sit Dale
down and pick his brain. Figure out how this guy thinks. He must
know we're right on his ass, he knows Dale is here. He's either gone
or getting ready to get gone. If he's gone there's nothing we can do.
If he's getting ready, there's something he's doing, someplace he's
going, where we can collar his ass."

"You ready to listen to him now?"

Herb flushed and picked his words carefully. "So I was wrong.
Okay, I was wrong about him. I should have listened to you. I don't
like him and I don't trust him and I think that whatever you got
going with him is clouding your judgment. There. That's said. But

I see now he's the best chance we've got to deal with this sick twist Maxwell. I'm ready to do what I got to do, including eating fucking crow if it makes you happy and gets you off my ass. All right? Anything I left out? Maybe you'd like me to park the car and kiss your ass right here in the middle of the street?"

"That would be sweet, Herbie," Nina said. "But I haven't changed my panties in two days and I wouldn't want you to be overcome by so much essence of pussy."

Herb's mouth hung open. He laughed, reluctantly at first, and then fully. "You're a sick girl . . . essence of pussy . . . you're a sick, sick girl . . ."

Roger sat in Nina's big green armchair while Dale paced restlessly in front of Nina's big window overlooking the lake. Roger studied the yellow legal pad he held on his lap. "Why do you think he called you at the police station?"

"Maybe he wanted to talk. Or wanted me to bring him in. Or maybe just throw down on me, I don't know."

"The police traced the call?"

"Pay phone down the street. City Center, the big shopping complex on Hennepin? No prints on the phone, no security cameras, nobody remembered anything."

Roger nodded. "Of course not." He tapped his pen against the pad. "I checked all the identities he's ever run—the ones we know about—and there's no activity on any of them except for the one he ran in Milwaukee. Nice deception plan, there." Roger leaned back in the chair. "I like this chair. He's got something going here. It's not the women . . . he must be getting money together. He took down that bank in Milwaukee . . . another robbery? Cash to get out of the country and set up someplace?"

Dale propped one foot on the windowsill and rested his elbow on his bent knee. "The cops think he's getting ready to bail."

"Then why call you?" Roger said. "Say good-bye or what?"

"Maybe he wants me to bring him in."

"I don't think he wants you to bring him in."

"No. I guess I don't believe that either."

"So maybe we should set up a meet."

Dale dropped his foot from the windowsill and turned to Roger. "What?"

"He saw you on TV when this cop gets her award. Maybe we should dangle you. Get him to call again. We could pin him that way."

"That's good," Dale said. "Let's get Nina in on this."

"Is that the best idea? I don't like it. From what you say, she's too sharp, she'll put it together."

"We could still bring him in."

Roger snorted in disdain and turned his head away. "That's not what we do, Dale. You know that. Look, I think it would be better if . . ."

"No. I'm in. All right. If we play it right, the cops would be the ones to . . ."

"Suicide by cop isn't going to work with Jonny. And I don't think that's what he's looking for, do you? How many cops are you willing to see killed before one of them gets lucky? He taught you, man. You saw what he did in Milwaukee. You think these cops are up to that?" Roger said.

"No." Dale paused. "They're not. But they could draw him into the open. That's what I mean."

Roger drummed his fingers on his thigh. He gazed, half smiling, at Dale.

Dale turned away from that knowing look. "I'll make the call. You better go." He picked up the cordless phone and turned to look out the window as he dialed.

Roger got up and went into the kitchen. He glanced quickly at Dale, whose back was still to him. Then he placed a tiny one-by-one-inch box underneath the edge of the kitchen table. The sticky adhesive on the top of the box held it firmly against the wood, hidden behind a thick leg.

"Hey," Roger called softly to Dale, "I'll let myself out."

Dale sat across from Herb at Nina's wooden kitchen table. The smell of fresh coffee rose from the Melitta drip where Nina poured boiling water through the filter. The two men glared at each other.

"Do we need to hash this out or are we going to put it aside?" Dale said. "I'm sick of this and I'm sick of you."

"Likewise, Army boy. But we need each other now, don't we? So we'll just have to put it aside and be done with it."

"Enough already," Nina said. She set cups of fresh coffee down in front of her two men. "What did your people say?" she asked Dale. "Are you off this?"

"I'm still on," Dale said. "I lost ten pounds of my ass, but I'm still on. What's up with Loveless and the marshals?"

Herb laughed. "You won't be asked to dance anytime soon. The 'Fugitive Task Force' is sitting and stewing in the Holiday Inn. Stymied," he said.

"Stymied?" Nina said. "You reading Word of the Week or what?"

They laughed and drank coffee.

"I've got an idea," Dale said.

Herb grinned. "Oh, oh."

Dale set his coffee cup down and leaned forward, looking back and forth from Herb to Nina. "He tried to get hold of me once, right? So maybe he'll do it twice. Is there a way you can get me out front, not a media interview or anything like that, but maybe you two in a press conference with me in the background. Like say you're looking for help from the public on these cases, get a phone number out . . . I think he might call in. You've got the equipment to do quick traces. I could try to set up a meet if he called . . ."

Herb and Nina looked at each other at exactly the same moment. Then Herb nodded in agreement. "That's not bad. We could do a press statement about the rapes, ask for help. We release it right we'll get the press and TV there, get it on the six o'clock news and the morning paper. Set up a hotline number, get the operators to sort the nutcases out and forward any viable calls to our cell phones . . . that could work. That could work good."

"So what do we have to do?" Dale said.

"We'll take care of it," Nina said. "We'll have to get the marshals straightened out, I'm thinking." She looked away, lost in her thoughts. "Yeah. We'll get this straightened out."

After a series of hasty phone calls, Nina hung up the phone. "Here's the deal. We go on the six o'clock news with all three of the majors with a brief spot asking for help in the Ma case. We couple it with safety and awareness tips for women. Me and Herb in the foreground, you in the background, you defer all questions to me, you're just another detective assigned to the case. We follow up with a meeting with the *Pioneer Press* and the *Star Tribune* and a quick photo op to get our pictures in tomorrow's paper. Contact number to be staffed downtown with an immediate bounce to a cleared cell phone, automatic trace on any call that gets bounced to us. That's anybody who mentions or asks for you." She paused. "What do you think? Did I miss anything?"

"I don't think so," Dale said. He looked at Herb. "What about the marshals?"

Herb grinned and tugged at his tie. "The chief says they can read about it in the papers."

On a park bench beside Lake Harriet, directly across from Nina's apartment, Roger held his laptop on his lap. He looked just like any other overworked businessman checking his e-mail or catching up on correspondence during his lunch hour. Anyone who saw the single earplug running from the computer to his left ear would think he was running a music CD. He was listening to the audio file downloaded to his computer in real-time from the wireless receiving/recording device built into the computer bag that held his laptop. All of the conversation in Nina's kitchen was clearly recorded into his machine, transmitted from the tiny bug he'd planted beneath the kitchen table. He'd heard what he needed to hear. It was enough to plan on. It was shaping up to be a beautiful night. He had time for a good run around the lake while it was still early.

Later, after his run, Roger lounged on the queen-size bed in his suite at the Residence Inn and read his book. He lay the paperback across his chest and stared at the ceiling and listened to the hotel sounds: the rattle of a car engine in the parking lot, doors opening and closing, murmurs and snippets of voice from the ventilation ducts. For some reason he felt uneasy. He set his book aside and moved, with the quick grace of the gymnast and swimmer he'd been, to the duffel bag set beside the dresser. He took out a small cleaning kit neatly packaged into a round tin, then stripped his Glock down and cleaned the spotless weapon, lightly lubricating each part with Break-Free. He worked the action several times, then stripped the rounds out of the magazines and inspected each one, setting each bullet on its base on the table to check for proper primer seating, then wiped each round with a silicone cloth and loaded it back into the magazines. He wiped the pistol down with the silicone cloth and reinserted it

**MARCUS WYNNE**

into the holster. He did the same with the two MP-5Ks and his fighting knife. He tested the edge of the knife on his forearm hair, which bore several bare patches, the silent badge of the knife fighter.

Roger looked out the window and checked his wristwatch. He was ready.

# PART 3

**3.1**

Darkness grew in the summer sky. In the back bedroom of his apartment, the curtains drawn against the lingering light, Jonny Maxwell studied himself in the full-length mirror behind his door and put on his game face. A part of him noted that he'd been doing that more and more often, looking at himself, as though he'd never really seen his face. Or maybe it was the new face emerging from beneath the lines and bags and small muscular tics. His eyes were darker now, and while he had always been lean, it seemed as though something inside him was burning away what little extra flesh he had. The bones were prominent beneath the smooth skin of his shaven scalp and cheeks. His goatee had sprouted a gray streak rapidly turning white. He held his hand out and studied his fingertips. A slight tremor at the very tip. He willed it still.

That worked.

Stacked in the corner were three large duffel bags, carefully packed with his few belongings. In a smaller duffel were camouflage hunter's overalls, a drop holster for his High-Power, a black balaclava, plastic flex-ties, a small butane torch with cylinder, a roll of duct tape, and an Eagle Arms assault chest pouch holding eight fully loaded magazines of 5.56 for the M-4 carbine that leaned against the duffel bag. Tony, the bouncer from First Avenue, lay full length on Jonny's bed, the covers pulled up over his fully clothed body as though he were sleeping. Jonny had neatly broken his neck at the fourth cervical vertebra and worked the fragments back and forth to sever the spinal cord. Death had been nearly instantaneous and the only immediate problem was the stink from Tony's bowels emptying into his Levi's. Jonny sprayed air freshener in the room and lit a scented candle and set it on the nightstand beside the bed.

Before he'd died, Tony had called Pierce, told him he'd seen the money and set the meet for around nine or ten that evening. Pierce said he'd be watching TV, and right after Tony had hung up the phone and turned his head away, Jonny had broken his neck, just like that. It was irreversible now, Jonny thought. And so it should be, for the decisive man. Pierce had money in the house, lots of money, enough for Jonny to get out of the country. If he didn't have as much as he'd claimed, the guns and drugs would be sufficient. They'd leave with Jonny. It would be a long while before anyone responded to Pierce's residence and by then Jonny would be long gone, maybe even out of the country.

So it was all set. All he had to do now was do it.

"God, I hate this son of a bitch," Dean Hardaway said, looking down over the expanse of Ron Pierce's property. "What he spends on lawn fertilizer I could put my kids through college with."

"He doesn't pay for fertilizer, man. He uses llama shit," Mitch said, twisting in his seat and readjusting the window mount for the 600x telescopic lens mounted on his camera. The two ATF agents were seated in a federal issue shit-brown Ford Taurus on the one hill that overlooked Pierce's property. A winding dirt road led them to a little overlook, just tight enough for one car to squeeze into. While it would be visible if someone glassed it with binoculars from the ranch, Hardaway had never seen anyone looking up this way and favored the spot for home surveillance of the mope he most loved to hate. The car was jammed with surveillance paraphernalia: several camera bodies with long lenses, a night vision scope, high speed film in coolers, raid vests thrown over the backseats, two shotguns, thermoses, and a bag of cooling burgers from Burger King.

"For the money we paid for this lens, it doesn't gather light for squat," Mitch groused, squinting through the camera's viewfinder.

"We're too far. Use those binoculars or the night vision scope."

"Too much flare from the barn lights. Can't see anything around the house with the night scope."

"I wish these mopes would get here," Dean said. "My ass hurts from too much sitting."

"Tell it to somebody else, man. Or put in for worker's comp."

"Worker's comp." Dean laughed. "I should. I'm getting piles."

"You could lose some weight. That might help."

"Whatever. Watch the ranch."

Hardaway pulled a plain cheeseburger from the bag and bit into it while opening a thermos of hot coffee. "You want a cup?" he asked his partner.

"Nah. It'll just steam up this lens some more."

"Whatever."

Hardaway munched away contentedly. The police radio mounted below the dash crackled quietly. The Orono and Shakopee Police Departments had zip to do, especially on a weeknight, so the only calls he heard were routine radio checks and a couple of traffic stops. Occasionally a call would jump the receiver over to the ATF internal net, where he heard some of his fellow agents working a surveillance on the North Side of Minneapolis, trying yet again to pin the local Hell's Angels chapter with arms dealing.

"There's our snitch," Mitch said. He picked up his small microcassette recorder and spoke into it. "2213 hours, CI goes from CI residence to main house." He set the recorder down. "Wonder what he's doing? Maybe Mr. Jonny ain't showing up."

"He'll show," Hardaway said around a mouthful of sandwich. "Guys like him always do."

The best approach would be over the fields, through the low river bottomland bordering the cleared area Pierce had bulldozed for his firing range. That meant a longish drive out of the way and risking attention from parking his car on someone's property. During his reconnaissance, Jonny had seen a few pull-offs that were possible hides for his vehicle, but the best was a semicleared dirt road that led to a level building pad, where someone planned a home. The road was blocked off with a chain and padlock between two posts across the road. He got out of the 4Runner with a set of bolt cutters. He left the door slightly ajar, having taped the door release light switches closed to prevent sudden flares of light. Jonny knelt and examined the chain, cut carefully through one side of a lone link, then unlinked the chain. He drove in over it, then carefully linked the chain back together again. He drove twenty yards farther, around a slight turn, where the lights of passing cars wouldn't hit the reflecting surfaces of his vehicle, and shut off the engine.

Night was best, he thought, as he stood next to the 4Runner and listened to the tick of the cooling motor and the early sounds of nightfall. Crickets. Leaves rustling, high in the trees. Frogs, from the river bottom. An occasional splash, as a fish or a turtle sprang for the mosquitoes buzzing close to the water's surface. Night was best.

He took his gear out of the duffel and dressed quickly, setting his gear pouches into place, checking the loads in his rifle and pistol, settling the light rucksack into place. The camouflage cream went on easily, breaking the outline of his face and the gleam of his skin with dark shadows. The balaclava was rolled up as a cap on his head. He hit the flash button on his red-filter flashlight and checked his reflection in the truck's side mirror. He was ready.

It was comforting to be alone in the dark with his gear and his guns, with a job ahead of him. This is what had always sustained him. A man, alone, in the dark, doing what had to be done. "Is that right?" said a nagging small voice inside his head. "Is this the job you were meant to do?" Something that had grown darker and larger inside him answered with a hissed "Yes," and he heard himself mouth the word. He paused for a moment, listened to the night, gathered himself, and focused again.

Six steps and a pause to listen, then six steps again and a pause to listen. Old habits die hard because they keep you alive. He doubted Pierce had patrols out, and what he'd seen of his "security" made him skeptical of their ability to perform a fixed guardpost function, let alone a patrol. The lights around Pierce's house, corrals, and outbuildings shone a bright nimbus against the night sky. Jonny followed the water drainage, part creek and part agricultural drain, that led from the river toward the buildings. He moved quickly and fairly quietly along the game path that bordered the creek, trading silence for speed. There had been no other vehicles on the isolated road as he had come in, and it wasn't hunting season, so he wasn't likely to encounter poachers, fishermen, or young lovers out for the night.

He came to the edge of the cleared area where the shooting range began and knelt in the brush and studied the house and the lighting. He looked behind him and saw only the dark silhouettes of the trees and the fields. The way the ground sloped, he wouldn't be highlighted against the sky, and anyone looking out from the brightly lit house or outbuildings would see only solid black. Jonny decided to risk walking straight in along the edge of the range. He'd only be a few steps from concealment if he saw or heard anyone. He could stage from the edge of the range line along a shadowed approach directly to the house. The butt of his M-4 tucked into his shoulder, he stepped out and walked briskly toward the house.

"Let me see that night scope," Mitch said to his partner.

"I thought you said there was too much flare," Hardaway complained as he twisted in his seat and reached back for the case that held the night vision scope.

"Got to be better than this camera lens. Wish we had that IR set up."

"That's too hard to work with. You want to spend your time playing with it, be my guest," Hardaway said. He handed the night vision scope to Mitch. "Here. Let me know if you spot any naked broads."

Mitch took the scope. "Didn't he have some broads out here a couple of weeks ago? Jerry told me about that."

"Yeah. Looked like some high-buck big-tit hookers. Didn't get no action shots, if that's what you're asking."

"Figures."

Mitch dismounted the big camera lens and put on the night vision scope and cranked it up. He swiveled it back and forth on the window mount. "Hey, this ain't so bad," he said.

"See Harold anyplace?"

"No. I didn't see him come out. Not unless he went out the side over by the range."

"What for? They ain't gonna do no night shooting. They're laid up with the TV and some beer."

"Yeah, I imagine so," Mitch murmured, slowly scanning with the big lens. "What the . . . ? There's somebody out on the range."

"What?" Hardaway scrambled for his high-power binoculars. "Where?"

"Wait a minute . . . I lost him, hang on, looked like Harold walking out on the edge of the range . . . yeah." Mitch tensed. "Looks like . . . somebody carrying a long gun, rifle or shotgun, walking along the edge of the range . . . he's down behind the firing points. I can't see him."

"Was it Harold? Who is it?"

"I don't know who it is. Shut up and let me work. Put your glass on the near side of the berm and I'll glass back and forth toward the house. It's got to be either Harold or Pierce walking out there, maybe they saw something from the house."

"Maybe," Hardaway said. He looked down at the radio, then touched his holstered pistol with his elbow. He pressed the binoculars tight to his eyes and scanned slowly and carefully, back and forth, looking for the man with the gun. "I don't like this," he said.

"Yeah? You think?"

"I don't know for sure. I wonder if that could be our Mr. Jonny coming to visit old boy Pierce."

"Think it's a rip?"

"Maybe . . . hard to say. Harold didn't seem to think so. One guy by himself taking on Pierce and Harold with all those guns in there? Pretty ballsy, if that's the case. Must just be Harold or Pierce out looking around."

"Didn't look as big as Pierce," Mitch said. "Think we ought to call it in, get a couple of the guys out here just in case?"

Dean thought for a moment. "No, let's sit on it for a while. If it starts to look hinky, we can call for the locals to do a drive-by and check things out."

"You sure?"

"Yeah. Probably nothing anyway," Hardaway said.

Mitch looked at his partner. "You don't sound convinced."

"Just watch for the guy, huh?"

Jonny made his final approach slowly and cautiously. He took a step, stopped and listened, then stepped again. Pierce didn't let his big dog run free at night because of the other animals, but Jonny wanted to make sure that the dog wasn't out back taking a dump. He stayed in the shadows, his eyes slitted with concentration, carefully studying each fold of ground, each finger of shadow, as he inched closer to the house. The door he wanted to make entry through was the side door they'd gone through after Pierce's shooting display earlier today. The door gleamed like the light at the end of a dark tunnel, throbbing as his heartbeat increased and the pounding of his chest seemed to rise up and pulse behind his eyes. He rolled the balaclava down over his face. The buttstock of his carbine was locked into his shoulder, his stockweld tight, the tip of his nose almost against the charging handle, both eyes open wide to expand his vision beyond the narrowness of the sight. Where his eyes went, his muzzle went. He stayed in the shadows, skirting the light, looking in the windows, safe in the knowledge that anyone looking out would only see black upon black beyond the safe splash of light thrown by the house lights. In the front room, through its big windows looking out over the fields and part of the shooting range, Jonny saw Pierce sitting on the leather couch, watching his wide screen TV, having a desultory conversation with the raggedy little security guard, who sat in a kitchen chair with the back turned front, a Coors in his hand. The big Doberman slept on the floor at Pierce's feet.

Jonny moved fast, picking up speed as he tracked in on the side door. He entered the splash of light, stepped lightly onto the concrete doorstep, tested the door, and found it unlocked. He eased the door open, ducking his muzzle so it wouldn't catch, and went through.

"Did you see that? Did you see that?" Mitch said.

"See what?"

"Somebody just went in the side door. Had a long gun, sure as shit."

"Get a make?"

"No."

"Fuck!" Hardaway shouted in frustration and indecision. He put his binoculars on the house.

"Should we call it in?"

"What for? We haven't seen anything yet. It'll just blow our surveillance and for nothing!"

"Deano, this could be a rip," Mitch warned.

"Yeah, well, if that guy's got the balls to go in by himself and take off Pierce, let him. If that's what's going down, we'll take him on the way out."

"You're the one who said you had a bad feeling," Mitch muttered unhappily.

**NO OTHER OPTION**

It was like the muzzle of his rifle was pulling him through the door and then quickly down the hall and sharply to the right into the front room where the dog had sprung to its feet and begun to dash at him, its claws scrabbling for purchase on the slick polished wood floor and the first round hit it in the side, quartering its body and breaking the far hip, and the second round broke its chest, and the third round spilled its brains, the high-powered round punching right through the thin skull and continuing on into the floor and another one ricocheting with a deadly whine off the rock fireplace and then the muzzle tracked onto the skinny little bodyguard who had dropped his beer can, and to give him credit was fumbling for his weapon, before the double tap to his chest spilled him backward, bloody spray from his front and back as the exiting rounds tore hand-sized pieces of bone and flesh out of him, and Pierce's jaw dropping, his eyes wide with fear as the rifle cut across his face, and then Jonny grabbed his hair and yanked him to the floor, kicked him into position and pressed the hot muzzle of the hungry rifle to the base of his skull and said, "Hi, Ron."

"Jesus! Jesus! You see that?" Mitch stammered.

Both agents heard the sharp crack of rifle fire. They couldn't see directly into the front room but they saw the muzzle flash. Hardaway was already on the radio, coordinating a response between the ATF units downtown and the local police department.

"They're going to come heavy and quiet," he said. "Orono and Shakopee are on their way, running silent. Our guys are on their way, but they've got to come all the way from the North Side. We'll stay put and have them block the road out. Once they got that, we'll get closer in case he tries to go cross-country again. The Sheriff's Department is going to block off those back roads there."

"Yeah," Mitch said with satisfaction. "We got this bitch boxed."

Pierce had wet his pants, Jonny noticed.

"This is how it goes, Ron," Jonny said evenly. "You tell me who else is in the house."

"No, nobody is here, just me and Harold, that's all!"

"Ron, I'm going to have you put your hands behind your back right now. Now!"

**MARCUS WYNNE**

Pierce put his hands in the small of his back. Jonny pulled out two flex-ties he'd looped into a double link, put them over Pierce's wrists, and cinched them tight. Then he slung his rifle, pulled out his duct tape, and wrapped several layers over the cuffs. He taped Pierce's ankles and knees together, then grabbed the big man by his hair and yanked him up roughly and threw him onto the deep couch. The urine stain at Pierce's crotch covered the entire front of his pants and ran down his left leg.

"Too much beer, Ron," Jonny said. "Not good for you." He nudged Harold's body, then the dog's, with his boot. "That was a good dog," Jonny said regretfully. "He really went for me. I hate to kill a good dog."

"What do you want, what the fuck, what..."

"You have some money around here, Ron. I want it. I want some of the guns you've got. Not everything, just a few things to see me on my way. Give me what I want, I go away and leave you here. Somebody will come along and let you go eventually."

"You're going to kill me!" Pierce said. His face collapsed and he began to snivel like a small child. Jonny looked at him with disgust.

"You were never in the service, were you, Ron?"

"What?"

"You never been in the service, got any trigger time, did you? You ever shoot anybody?"

"No."

"I didn't think so. Where's the money?"

"You're going to kill me!"

"Ron, you have just seen that I'm perfectly willing to kill people who try to hurt me. Your boy there would still be alive if he hadn't tried to John Wayne me. Now if you give me what I want, I'll walk out of your life and you can go back to believing that you're a big tough gunman and ain't nobody but you and me going to know different. Where's the money?"

"You don't need to kill me. I'll tell you where it is. I can make it worth your while not to kill me."

"I'm not going to kill you, Ron. Give me what I want and you can live. All I want is the money—and you can always get more, right? You got lots in the bank. I don't want that. I just want what you have here, a few guns... that's all I need."

**NO OTHER OPTION**

Jonny's voice was soft and reasonable, in frightening contrast to the violence he'd entered with. Ron Pierce hadn't put the voice together with the cold brown eyes staring at him out of the black balaclava.

"My bedroom," Ron said. "Under the carpet there's a safe. It's not locked now."

"You stay right there, Ron. I'll be right back."

Jonny went into the bedroom. Under an expensive Turkish kilim prayer rug he found a heavy round plug safe set in the floor. Inside was a short-barreled .357 loaded with Glaser Safety Slugs. He pocketed that. There were several Polaroid photos of a naked Pierce cavorting with two young Asian girls. And eighty thousand dollars in neat bundles of $100 bills. Not bad. Jonny dropped the cash into his duffel and returned to the front room.

"Where's the rest, Ron?" Jonny asked. "Guy like you, I know you keep more than this around the house. Oh, by the way, nice pictures." He threw the Polaroids onto Pierce's chest. "Where's the rest? In the gun room? Let's go in there, shall we?"

He dragged Pierce by the hair into the open gun room and flung him roughly down the two steps from the vault door to the carpeted concrete floor.

"Where's the rest, Ron? Where do you keep the rest of the cash?"

Pierce wouldn't look at him. He spoke to the floor. "There isn't any more. I was expecting somebody to bring me some tonight, I don't have..."

Jonny kicked him at the base of his spine, then again on the outside of his thigh. "You're a poor liar, Ron. Let me teach you something about lying."

Jonny set his rifle down and opened his rucksack. He took out the butane mini-torch. He clicked the electric igniter and fine-tuned the hissing blue flame to a brilliant point. Pierce opened his mouth to scream and Jonny kicked him hard in the stomach. He cut off the torch and set it aside, then took a pillowcase and a rag from his bag. He stuffed the washrag into Pierce's mouth and slapped duct tape across it. Pierce's nostrils flared as he sucked air violently through his nose. Jonny bagged Pierce's head in the pillowcase, then reignited the torch. Pierce thrashed violently. The big man, soft as he'd become, was still hard to hold down. Jonny straddled him, rode him easily, then touched the tip of the flame to Pierce's shirt, right above the soft skin of his nipple. Pierce convulsed and Jonny stumbled off him, holding the torch carefully away.

"Guess I'm going to have to hog-tie you, Ron," Jonny said. "Unless you want to tell me what I want to know...nod yes you want to tell me, Ron..."

Pierce's whole upper body went back and forth, up and down.

"I take that to be a yes, Ron. Now just hold still for a minute, let's get that bag off your head..."

Jonny lifted the bag and tilted Pierce's face up. The man was crying and great plugs of mucus were hampering his ability to breathe through his nose.

"There, there," Jonny said. He wiped Pierce's nose with the pillowcase. "Is that better? You want to tell me what I want to know, Ronnie?"

Pierce nodded. Jonny stripped the tape off and pulled the wash-cloth out. The big dope and arms dealer wept like a child and sucked in great gasps of air.

"Over there," he cried. "Over there, the green cushion, under that."

Jonny lifted the green cushion off of the wooden bench seat and found a push-button keyboard set flush in the top of the bench.

"Combination, Ron?"

"Ninety-nine, star, seventy-seven, pound, eight, star," Ron said.

"Fancy," Jonny said. He punched in the combination and the panel clicked and raised slightly. He opened it up and saw a stack of $50s and $100s, all neatly bundled, a stack about two feet high. "How much is here, Ron?" he asked as he began to pull the bundles out and put them into his duffel bag.

"There's two hundred seventy-five thousand dollars there."

Jonny filled his duffel bag. It was considerably heavier now, and he was grateful for the straps that would fasten it to his small rucksack. On the wall was a M-203, like the carbine he was carrying now, except that this one had a grenade launcher mounted below the rifle barrel.

"This for real, Ron? You got any eggs for it?"

"In the blue cushion cabinet," Pierce said weakly.

Jonny inspected the M-203 and did a quick function check on the rifle. He'd have to sight it in, check the zero someplace, but then it would be just fine. He liked the M-203. There were seven bandoleers of grenade projectiles for the launcher in the cabinet. He strung all seven across his shoulders and strapped the 203 between the back compression straps of his rucksack. He pocketed a few of the fragmentation grenades he'd seen earlier, just for good luck. There was a box of 9mm Corbon +P+ that went into his bag, too.

"Guess that's all, huh, Ron?" Jonny said cheerfully.

"You're going to kill me, aren't you?" Ron said in a flat, broken tone.

"Yep," Jonny said.

And he did.

**MARCUS WYNNE**

The first unit to arrive in response to Hardaway's backup request was an Orono PD cruiser that shut down all its lights and glided quietly to a stop outside the barred gate entrance to the Pierce property. Hardaway picked up his handset and called the squad.

"Squad 642, ATF. We see you. Hold there for more backup. We're on our way down." He turned to his partner and said, "Okay, buddy. You bail out here with the handheld and the night vision. I'll go down and get this squared away."

Mitch rolled out the door, checked his handheld radio, then took the night vision scope. "Hand me my vest, will you?" he said.

Hardaway handed him the blue vest with ATF emblazoned in yellow across the front.

"Be careful, Deano," Mitch said.

"We got this guy," Hardaway said, excitement on his face. "We're gonna roll him up."

"Don't play with this guy. Break the shotgun out," Mitch called after his partner as he started the vehicle.

Hardaway drove down quickly to meet the Orono cop, a young officer in his mid-twenties named Rand.

"What you got?" Rand said.

"We got a surveillance rolling on this guy Pierce. Some mope went in with a long gun, shots fired. Nobody's come out yet. We're figuring rip-off," Hardaway said.

"Just one guy?"

"Yeah, with a rifle it looked like. Had a couple of shots fired inside. My partner is up on that hill with a night vision scope and a handheld. He can see the whole place. What I want to do is, when the other backup gets here, is block off this road and the country road back of this place. This guy probably walked in across that field from there. Then we'll go in close and quiet and take him on the way out. I got an entry team from ATF coming in now with the Sheriff's SWAT guys in case it turns into a barricade," Hardaway said.

"No offense, Agent Hardaway, but I don't think we should be going in there. We should just set up the perimeter and let the SWATs go in," Rand said.

"Hey, I know that's what they teach you in the Academy, but this is one guy. We go in quiet and get the jump on him, then we can get the scene squared away and we can all go home, okay? It's been a long fucking night. Let's just get this done."

"You want to go in there, you go right ahead. I'll back you up right here, but I don't think we should be going in there."

"Fine. You get the responding units squared away. I'm going over this fence and see if I can get the gate opened," Hardaway said impatiently.

"You do that," Rand said with barely contained insolence. "You go right ahead, Mr. High and Mighty Federal Agent," he continued under his breath as the overweight and out of shape agent strained to get over the rock wall.

The cruiser's radio crackled as yet another squad from Orono, another from Loretto, and one from the Sheriff's Department pulled up, lights dimmed, the officers craning their heads out their windows and asking, "What's going on?"

Jonny paused just outside of the circle of light around the house and listened. He saw a flare of light, quickly dimmed, like a car door opening, and heard the distinctive crackle of a radio. The gate to Pierce's estate was over a quarter of a mile of gently curving road from where he stood, and the sound carried across the corrals and the fallow hay field to him.

Police. He must have missed some kind of alarm system. He wasted no time on agonizing over it, though he had a brief moment of surprise and chagrin. He hadn't expected Pierce to have a system that would summon police to his residence. Maybe neighbors had heard the shots. Irrelevant now. Jonny moved fast along the front of the house, skirting the light, and entered the bush line on the far side of the shooting range, opposite the side he'd come in on.

"Deano, he's out of the house and in the bushes on the side of the range farthest from the road." Mitch's voice was tense over the radio.

"Goddammit!" Hardaway tugged frantically at the gate.

One of the sheriff's deputies said, "Look over there, at that little box next to the gear box. Yeah. Open it up, there should be a manual override switch in there."

Hardaway fumbled with it, careless of the light from his Maglite, and got the gate motor activated. "Let's go," he said to the deputy. "He's out of the house and into the brush!"

Officer Rand shook his head as he spoke into his microphone. "We need some cars to block off both ends of County Road AA. Watch for a man on foot, probably making for a car he'll have parked out there. Armed with a long gun, use caution."

The deputy pulled his car through the open gate and Hardaway jumped into the backseat behind the two deputies. "Let's go," Hardaway said.

"There's only one?"

"Yeah. We saw him going in and coming out. There's two other people here, both in the main house, the owner and his handyman."

"Any guns?"

"Pierce has a bunch of them, but he's not stupid enough to shoot at us. The guy we saw coming out, he's got a rifle."

"Well, shit."

They drove cautiously, with running lights only, down the gravel road and rolled to a stop twenty yards from the house. All three officers got out. One deputy tugged the twelve-gauge Remington 870 out of the rack and worked the action. Hardaway led the way, his Sig P-228 locked out in a strong Isosceles, and approached the side door and peered in. He nodded to the officer with the shotgun and they entered, covering each other. The third deputy entered behind to watch their backs. It took only a moment to discover the bodies of Pierce's dog and Hardaway's snitch, both curled in the bonelessness of death.

"Harold's dead and I don't see Pierce," Hardaway shouted into

**NO OTHER OPTION**

his radio. "Get an ambulance and the other units in here. We're going after this guy."

"I can't make him out against the bushes, Deano." Mitch's voice was wheezy with excitement. "Be careful. The locals are putting blocking cars on either end of the county road. They figure if he's headed that way, he must have a car stashed back there."

"Okay. Watch us, brother." Hardaway led the two deputies straight out the back door and across the range into the dark. "Where did you see him last?" Hardaway said into the radio.

"Just ahead of you, about a hundred yards, near that big oak that's split at the top."

"Roger."

Hardaway stumbled along in the dark, his flashlight beam cutting a hole through the dark, probing at the waist high brush. The two deputies followed right behind him.

Jonny pressed up against a small oak tree twenty yards past the big oak with the split top. He knelt there and aimed his weapon at the figures stumbling toward him, silhouetted against the lights from the house. Their voices were clear and loud to him, as were the radio  transmissions. They were in a hurry, in pursuit, or so they thought, and came forward with no thought of noise or light discipline. Pity, Jonny thought, even as he was taking the slack out of his trigger, that more police hadn't spent time in the military. Even a grunt private would know better than to rush into the dark silhouetted like that. He peered through the larger aperture of his rear sight, thumbed off the safety, and set the front post center of mass on the man with the radio, the leader, and pressed the trigger.

"Fuck!" Mitch shouted as the flare of gunshots swelled in the night vision scope. "Deano, look out, he's right in front of you!"

Hardaway died first. The burst of 5.56 hit him in a tight cluster on his sternum and he was tossed up and back by the force of the shots, his handgun and his Maglite pinwheeling into the dark. His last thought, a brief one, was a sense of wonder at how bright the gun flashes were. The sheriff's deputy, a twelve-year veteran, jumped straight up at the sound of gunshots and accidentally discharged his shotgun. He managed to recover enough to work the action but the

**MARCUS WYNNE**

next burst of rifle fire stitched him from his shoulder to his opposite hip, splintering the shotgun's action and breaking his hands, dropping him. The third officer fared a little better. Crouched with both hands locked out on his Beretta 92FS, he emptied the magazine in the direction of the rifle's muzzle flash. Jonny ducked behind the tree, then rolled out and took the third officer with a short burst. Then Jonny was up and running, reloading on the run, heading fast for his car.

"Officers down! Shots fired!" the radios crackled loudly behind him.

"He's running along the tree line!" Mitch shouted into his radio, fumbling to keep the night scope one-handed on the figure running and ducking among the trees. "Shit! Where's the ambulance!" he screamed in frustration. "Officers down! Officers down!"

Officer Rand collared the officers who were rushing out of the house. "Hold on! He's got a rifle out there! Get the shotguns." Several officers ran out and unracked their shotguns.

"Okay, listen up," Rand said. "We've got people down out there and the shooter is making for the county road. We've got blockers out there. We're going to move carefully, cover each other every step of the way, until we get to our people that are down. Then we're going to set up a perimeter around them and then we'll send two guys to chase the shooter into the blockers on the other end, you got it?"

"Let's go," one of the older officers, Harris from Loretto, said.

It took them several minutes of cautious movement to find the downed cops. Hardaway and the sheriff's deputy were dead. The third officer was still breathing and semiconscious. The sirens of arriving police and ambulances grew in the distance.

"Okay," Rand said. "You all stay here. You and you, go with me, moving just like we did. This guy knows how to use that rifle. From cover to cover, people. Move out with me." The young policeman, who'd learned how to move in the dark while serving with the second Infantry, the famous Indian Head Division, on the Korean DMZ, led the two other officers out after their shooter.

Jonny moved fast. The brush whipped his face and his breath was loud in his ears as he moved surely through the woods back to his car. There would be blockers out there on the road and more coming. The police would be like bees from a beehive stirred by a child with a stick, furious at the death of three of their own, and eager to exact some revenge. But they don't know who they're dealing with yet, Jonny thought.

He jumped quickly across the small stream and scrambled up the low embankment. He turned and looked back over his trail and caught his breath, inhaling deeply, holding his breath for a count of two, exhaled to a count of two, inhaled for a count of two, held his breath for a count of two, and let the air out with a slight hiss. The M-4 shouldered, he watched over his sights and was rewarded with a hint of movement, then the sight of three men moving cautiously and almost tactically along the tree line.

Jonny studied them carefully. Despite the impact the gun flashes had on his night vision, there was sufficient ambient light for him to see that the man in front was directing the other two, literally pointing them into positions of cover to move their little fire team forward. He was the leader. Jonny nodded, then put his front sight post on the leader's chest, then dropped it down on his pelvis and legs and squeezed the trigger. He fired two short bursts and saw the man stumble and fall, screaming. The screaming went on and had plenty of volume, so he'd hit him in the pelvis and legs as he'd intended. That should keep them busy for a while, he thought, throwing a few rounds at the other two men, who'd thrown themselves flat. Gotta go, gotta go, gotta go.

"Jesus, Jesus, Jesus," Mitch prayed when he saw the exchange of gunfire. The screams of Officer Rand filled his handset.

"O God, O God, somebody help me, somebody help me, Oh, fuck it hurts, it hurts, somebody help me . . ."

"Jesus, God, somebody help him!" Mitch shouted into his handset.

"We can't get to him, that prick is up there and he's still shooting," one of the other cops broke in. "Get us a helicopter with a light on it! Get the State Patrol chopper out here!"

Jonny carefully put the rucksack full of money in back behind the driver's seat. He took a moment to examine the sights on the M-203 he'd taken from Pierce. The front sight post and the rear A-2 sight were set at a factory mechanical zero, which meant the rifle wouldn't do for any precision shooting. He flipped the quadrant sight for the M-203 up, and then down. He took a black and gold grenade from the bandoleer and locked it into the breech of the grenade launcher, and then locked one of his remaining magazines into the magazine well. Both rifles went on the front passenger seat, then, after a moment's thought, he took his M-4 and walked carefully down to the chain blocking the road. Listening and then watching carefully, he unlinked the broken chain and set it in the road before returning to his vehicle.

Now he was ready.

He started the 4Runner and drove out onto the road, not touching the brakes to avoid the brake flare, and then accelerated smoothly. The nearest intersection was a half mile down the road, where County 142 crossed County Road AA.

"What do they say? Anything?" Deputy Deb Morrow asked her field training officer, Deputy Duane Hawkins.

"They've got four officers down," Hawkins said, turning his radio down. "The shooter has got three officers pinned down. One of them is wounded and the other two can't help him because he's still shooting at them."

"I haven't heard any more shots since that last flurry."

"Me neither. He'll be coming out this way or the other. They figure he must have a car stashed around here someplace."

"We didn't see anything when we drove in."

"He must have something. The nearest house is over a mile that way, and those folks are getting woke up by the other deputies right about now."

"I'm a little nervous," Deb said.

"You'll be fine," Duane said. "There's something wrong with you if you don't get the jitters. No shame in that. Just got to control it. If he comes through here, he'll come through shooting. He's got nothing to lose. He's shot four cops tonight, and as far as I can tell, nobody's got a piece of him yet." He hefted the .30-.30 lever action carbine he'd taken out of the cruiser trunk to augment their shotgun. The battered deer rifle was useful for animal control, putting down wounded deer, dogs, or cattle that got hit by cars out here in the country. But it would do just fine on a dangerous human, especially

**NO OTHER OPTION**

in the hands of a Vietnam vet county cop and seasoned deer hunter. He was proud of this doughty little city gal who was turning out to be a fine police officer. She held the Remington 870 confidently at her hip and was doing a fine job of controlling her fear. She'd do just fine.

"What's that?" Deb said.

"What?"

"I thought I heard a car coming."

"Get back behind the cruiser," Duane said. The two of them took cover behind their cruiser, slanted at an angle across the middle of the narrow road. "Are you sure?" he said.

"I heard something," Deb said positively. "It sounded like a car coming, but it's stopped now." She reached through the car window and turned down the radio so she could hear better. "Nothing, now..."

It was Duane who heard the distinctive bloop of the M-203 and the old grunt knew it for what it was just a second or so before it hit the ground right in front of their cruiser.

"Deb! Get down..."

*Crack!* The grenade sent pieces of shrapnel and shattered pavement whistling. A stray bit shattered the passenger side window of the patrol car. Duane felt the overpressure on his ears and face. The old infantryman, who'd made his bones in the 173rd Airborne in Vietnam, looked around for cover and wasted no time wondering how the hell this shooter came to have a grenade launcher.

"Deb! C'mon with me, c'mon, we got to get the fuck out of here!" he shouted to his partner, who was shaking her head over and over, trying to clear her ears. "C'mon," he said, grabbing her arm and dragging her away from the cruiser, off the road and into the low ground and toward the trees. There was a fast series of bloops and he threw her to the ground behind a tree, down in the ditch, and threw himself on top of her as the ground shook. The grenades went off, on, in, and around their cruiser. One hit the fuel tank and the explosion set a flare of light and cloud of smoke billowing upward. Pieces of hot metal descended, clattering on the pavement, and Duane jerked as a hot piece of metal fell on the back of his thigh, burning him through his woolen trousers. He heard the vehicle coming now, accelerating, the hiss of tires and the muted roar of the engine as it came up fast. He sat up, ratcheting the lever of his rifle

**MARCUS WYNNE**

as he brought it to his shoulder, and saw a Toyota 4Runner neatly ram the burning cruiser precisely on line with its axle, knocking the police car out of the way. Duane just had a glimpse of the figure hunched over the steering wheel and snapped off a shot from the .30-.30, levering it and then fumbling to get a better position for his follow-up shot. With the sensory acuity that comes with being fired on, he heard at least one of his shots break glass as the Toyota sped down County 142 and away.

That was too close, Jonny thought as he sped away. Whoever was on that gun had his act together. Two for two, one in the rear driver's side window, the other in the back window as he drove away. Time to fly, he thought. Time to fly.

### 3.3

After the press conference they'd arranged, Dale, Herb, and Nina sat drinking stale coffee in the otherwise empty Major Crimes Unit squad room.

"That seemed like it went well," Dale said.

"They eat that stuff up," Herb said, grimacing at the taste of his coffee. "Nasty. Media loves to feel involved, like they're players. We'll get lots of calls. And maybe, just maybe, we'll hear from the boy."

Dale quietly noted how Jonny had become "the boy" instead of "Dale's boy." Nina noticed too, and gave Dale a quick smile.

"So what do we do now?" Dale asked.

"Go home and get some sleep," Nina said. "We'll be busy tomorrow."

Herb looked down into his coffee cup as though he'd found something interesting in the bottom of it.

"Yeah," Dale said. "Sleep would be good."

Herb's radio crackled softly. Then a steady tone, like a tornado warning siren, droned from the speaker. Nina and Herb jumped as though shot at. Herb twisted the volume up.

"What's wrong?" Dale said.

"That tone, it's the officer needs assistance call," Nina said. "Hold on."

"...Federal agents, Shakopee and Orono Police Departments request backup from the State Police and all available local units at the intersection of Minnesota 13 and County Road 154, heavily armed suspects are firing on officers, officers down..." the breathless dispatcher said.

"Let's go," Herb said, standing and scooping up his radio.

"Herb," Nina said. "They haven't released any Minneapolis units to go out there. Let the BCA get it organized and if they need more help they'll call us in. That's a thirty-minute or more drive from here."

"It's on my way home," Herb said. He lived in Edina, a southwestern suburb.

"Turn the radio up," Dale said. "Let's hear what's going on out there."

"It's a war zone out there," Nina said in shock. "Four cops down and the guy takes out a roadblock with a grenade launcher?"

"It is a war zone," Dale said, standing. "Where can we find out more about what's going on?"

"It was an ATF op...we can go over to the Federal Building, talk to the duty agent..." Herb said.

"I mean how can we keep track of where he's going? Do they have anybody on him at all?" Dale said.

"That's our boy? Is that what you're saying?" Herb said.

"Who else?" Dale said. "When was the last time your local bad guys racked up four cops in twenty minutes and took out a squad with a grenade launcher?"

"We need some armament if we're going out there," Herb said. "All we got down here is shotguns."

"We can't just run out there," Nina said. "State is putting an eye in the sky up and by now, hopefully, they'll have more roadblocks set up. We should sit tight till they have a fix on him."

Herb and Dale looked at each other.

"Is there anyplace closer to the action we could stage out of?" Dale said.

"She's right," Herb said. "We should sit tight till we know more about what's going on and where. Then we can head straight there for the party."

"Let's go, boys! Time for rock and roll!" Mad Dog called out cheerfully to his SOG assaulters. "Time to kill a cop killer!"

"Knock that off!" Jed said.

**NO OTHER OPTION**

Edgar and Tommy laughed.

"Yeah, Mad Dog, don't be talking like that. You'll get sent to cultural sensitivity training again," Edgar said. He grinned fiercely as he slid heavy assault armor on, then threaded fresh 00 buckshot into the side saddle ammo carrier on his short-barreled entry Benelli M-1 Super-90 shotgun. The shotgun went around his neck, the HK combat sling holding it horizontally across his chest, clear of his sidearm.

"I'm going to take great joy in lighting this Maxwell up," Edgar said. "And I don't care who knows. How many people has this piece of shit put down?"

"We don't know for certain that it's him," Jed said.

Edgar laughed a short, cruel laugh that caused Tommy to look up and stare at his long-time partner. "Jed, I don't know what has happened to us, dealing with this freak. It's always been just as clear as mud to me."

Jed had nothing to say at first, then he just shook his head in bafflement and said, "You best ease up on yourself, Eddie. This ain't no place to strain the game."

"No argument there, Jed. Let's go hunting." Edgar dropped  two extra boxes of shells into the leg pockets of his utility pants and followed the SOG team out the door and down the stairs. Tommy looked at Jed, then dropped his eyes and followed his partner out the door. After a moment, Jed followed, holding his CAR-15 in his hand.

Roger sat quietly in his hotel room, the lights turned down, the curtains thrown open so that he might look out at the city lights. From time to time he looked at the cell phone charging on the table. He smiled when the phone chirped, then picked it up and said, "Yes, Dale?"

"Go to 139.47 MHz. That's the State Patrol command and control frequency. I think Jonny's just made a hit, and he's taken out four cops and a roadblock. It's south of where we're at. On your map, it's the area around Orono and Loretto. County Road 142 was the last contact. He's driving a black Toyota 4Runner with two bullet holes in it."

"Who got the rounds into him?" Roger asked. He punched the

radio frequency into the small digital scanner he had set beside the cell phone.

"Local cop at the roadblock."

The scanner came to life with hurried voices snapping instructions, pleas for more ambulances, and the distinctive broken chatter of a transmission from a helicopter.

"Do you have a more positive ID?" Roger said, opening his local map book, and then spreading out a folding city area map.

"No," Dale said. "There is no positive target identification. They only got a glimpse of him. He's armed with a grenade launcher and grenades, probably a M-203 since the reports are that he used an automatic rifle in the shootings."

"What are you and police going to do?"

"Sit tight till we get a positive fix on location. They're up talking to the chief about it right now."

"Are they going public with his name and description?"

"Not unless we get a more positive ID. Then, probably yes."

"That would be unfortunate. Can you stop that?"

"Maybe," Dale said. "I'll talk to them."

"Right. Give me sitreps as appropriate. I'll follow on the radio. If I move I'll let you know via cell phone. Keep it close."

"Roger that. Out here."

"Out." Roger set the phone back into its charger, then turned the scanner volume down and began to note the location of the roadblocks on his map.

**NO OTHER OPTION**

Jonny drove fast and well. He cut off onto County Road 13 and made for the Interstate. He needed a new car and quickly. There was a shopping mall sprawling beside the Interstate. He pulled into the parking lot, which was already thinned out, and parked in the middle of a cluster of cars near the movie theater complex. After a moment, he decided to move on. He couldn't wait. Across the road was a twenty-four-hour Byerley's grocery store and its parking lot was still busy. Jonny pulled in, watching the Highway Patrol and State Police cars racing past on County Road 13. He cruised slowly, looking. A girl in her early twenties came out of the store, both hands occupied with the plastic bags she toted her groceries in. She had her head down and walked briskly to a battered old Honda Accord, its sides flecked with rust. Jonny waited till she set her bags down and began fumbling through her purse before he got out of the 4Runner and went to her.

Her name was Maria Clavell. She worked as a nurse's aide in the Golden Meadows Retirement Home while she went to school to get her nursing degree. She was smart and she knew she was in trouble. The hard case in her car had thrown his bags into the trunk, and she'd recognized the M-203 because her brother had been in the Air Force and had patiently explained to her what the ungainly looking weapon was he carried in the pictures he'd sent her. She loved her brother and she loved her family and she was going to get out of this okay because she was smart. Or so she told herself. She sat in the passenger seat and did as she was told because the vibe that came off this guy was stone-cold serious and the pistol he had tucked in the front of his pants was loaded. He'd asked her name, and had been really calm but firm in taking control of her and her car and keeping her quiet. And while she had little experience with violence and danger, her pragmatic nature recognized the threat in the cool, calm, and collected way this guy went about his business.

He was definitely in the business of hurting people.

Jonny drove the Accord, an old manual five-speed, slowly and carefully at the speed limit, north on I-35 into Minneapolis. He watched the police cars, lights flashing, racing south on the other side of the highway, pass by until they appeared in the rearview mirror.

"Are they looking for you?" Maria asked.

He saw no point in lying. "Yes."

"What did you do?"

He looked at her, amused. "Murder. Robbery. Rape. Destruction of public property. Escaped from prison. Pissed off the wrong people. Made friends with the wrong people. Should I go on?"

She was doing a good job of controlling her fear, he noticed.

"I have herpes," Maria said.

"Does that work?" Jonny asked. "Have you ever really heard of that working?"

"No, but it's worth a try," she said.

Jonny laughed. "What do you do?"

"I'm a nurse's aide at an old folks home."

"Do you like that?"

"Yes. I love old people. They're sweet. They're grateful for being looked after. I like my job a lot. I like to look after people." She paused. "Have you ever had someone look after you?"

Jonny was quiet for four off-ramps.

"Not when I was growing up," he said. "I always looked out for other people. Took care of my mother when my father . . . took care of my family. They're all gone now."

"I'm sorry. How did you lose them?"

"I didn't lose them. They lost me."

The light of passing headlights gleamed in the close interior of the car, casting washed-out reflections of the two of them on the inside of the windshield.

**NO OTHER OPTION**

"I had friends. A few," he said.

"Friends are the family that we choose."

"Why do you say that?"

"Because it's true," Maria said. "You choose your friends. You don't choose your family. We don't get any choice in that. But you do choose your friends, who you keep around you. And they choose you. I have a friend, Diane, we've known each other since grade school. I was the maid of honor at her wedding and she'll be the matron at mine someday. We're going to look after each other's kids. All because we chose each other a long time ago. How did you choose your friends?"

"They were good at what they did. They were the best at what they did, all of them. They stood by me . . . for a long time."

"Did you have a special friend? Someone you could always talk to, who was always there for you?"

"Yes," Jonny said. "I did."

"Who was it? What was his name?"

"Dale," Jonny said. "Dale."

244

"This is just peachy keen," Tommy said.

"Fuck you, La Roux," Edgar said, walking back to his squad car and throwing his shotgun into the trunk. The other police officers and the members of the Marshals' SOG hardly looked at him; all of them, a knot of black-clad tactical ninjas, were clustered around a dirty, battered Toyota 4Runner with bullet holes in the left and rear windows abandoned in the Byerley's grocery store parking lot.

"We're canvassing now," a senior sergeant from the State Patrol said to Jed. "So far nothing. He must have stashed a car here. No reports of any stolen vehicles, nobody saw him pull up or out. Nothing."

Jed nodded. "Thanks. We'll put those prints into our system and get back to you ASAP. Anything on the vehicle?"

"That's interesting," the state trooper said. "The plates don't match up the Vehicle Identification Number. Same year and make of vehicle, but come back with a different VIN. We sent a squad for a drive-by at the address listed on the plate, turns out there's a 4Runner there but with different plates. Your guy stole plates off another 4Runner and swapped them off. The other owner hadn't noticed, hell how many people would? Pretty smart. We got a name and address for the registration associated with the VIN, one Chad Bergh over in Dinkytown."

"Anything?"

"Nothing yet. The BCA went there, it's a college kid's apartment building. Landlord let them in. Nobody's been there for a while. The mail was stacked up and the answering machine was full. He had a couple of calls from family—they sounded pissed off that he hadn't gotten back to them. We've got people running that down and calling the family, see if they can locate this kid."

"You guys do good work," Jed said. "Let's see if we can keep up to your standard with the prints."

"You do that," the trooper said. He shifted his Smoky hat and went back to his squad to confer with his compatriots.

Mad Dog tugged on the ends of his handlebar mustache and nodded to Jed. "How you doing, partner?" he asked.

"How do you think?" Jed said.

"As slowly as possible," Mad Dog allowed. "It strains the brain."

"Yeah."

"We'll catch him, Jed. We ain't but forty minutes behind this boy, I figure. Let it work the way it's supposed to. It don't help none to push and beat up on yourself. Not to be helped, you understand?"

The light from the squad cars flashed blue, then red, then blue across Jed's face.

"Forty minutes," Jed said. "May as well be forty years."

"Came to shit but only farted," Mad Dog said, twirling his mustache ends. "Let's put it to bed, *compadre*. Tomorrow is another day. Our boy has gone to ground and grounded he will remain if he is smart, and this boy is nothing but smart. So let us adjourn cheerfully."

"Anybody for an early breakfast?" Tommy asked. "Eddie? Jed?"

Edgar shrugged. "May as well."

"Jed?" Tommy asked.

"Nah. I'm gonna stay up, talk with ATF, see what we can put together," Jed replied.

"You'd be better off getting on the outside of some greasy eggs and bacon and then getting some sleep. They know how to get you if something breaks. You ain't gonna be no good to anybody if you don't get some rest," Tommy said.

"You in Nursemaid's Anonymous now or what?" Jed said.

"Somebody's got to look out for your sorry ass, Peerless Leader. Jo Anne told me she'd kill me if I let you run yourself into the ground again, and I'm seriously afraid of that woman."

Jed laughed at that. "Well, you ain't alone in that. Let's eat."

**MARCUS WYNNE**

"Forty minutes. That's what they said. They figure it was forty minutes before they found the car." Nina shook her head in disgust. "I wish we could catch a break here."

"Did you talk to him?" Dale asked.

Nina said with faint derision, "I don't think rubbing Loveless's nose in this is a good idea, Dale. Everybody's working this now. There's an APB, BCA has people at the airports, bus and train stations; the Metro is getting a Xeroxed flyer, we've got the whole Cities covered. We're going back to the TV and newspapers and get Jonny's face out everywhere and fast. The national media is descending on us. Four cops killed in one night by one guy? This will be on *60 Minutes*. We'll have Morley Safer out here."

"All right," Dale said. "I got to call somebody. I'll be right back."

Dale went to the office adjoining the break room and used the phone to call Roger's cell phone.

"Yes?" Roger said.

"Are you up on the situation?"

"Pretty much. What have you got?"

Dale ran down the vehicle information and the dead end leads. "So what do you think?" he asked Roger.

"I think he's got a bolt-hole," Roger said. "A safe house of some kind. I think he's going to sit tight, shift cover, and probably just drive right out of here and across the border and fly out of Canada someplace. He probably scored a substantial amount of cash in this hit—only reason for taking such a risk on his own and taking down those cops . . . Jesus, what a mess. Any idea how much he got?"

"Only speculation from ATF and DEA. ATF had Pierce for guns, and they found a shit pot full, but apparently he was moving large quantities of marijuana as well. They found five hundred pounds of premium dope bagged up for a buyer; he was waiting for somebody, maybe Jonny."

"Jonny's no doper. How would he find a top-level dope dealer? They don't advertise."

"That's a good point," Dale said. "Let me run that down with the cops."

**NO OTHER OPTION**

"I'll sitrep the boss for both of us. He's got some contingencies for this going public thing."

"Nothing we can do about it."

"Right. Out here."

"Out here." Dale hung up the phone, turned, and almost ran into Nina.

"Who you talking to, Dale?" she asked.

She was a funny woman, he thought. Leaning against the doorway of the darkened office, she seemed boneless and relaxed, her normal athletic vigor and erect bearing gone, her voice soft. She had the knack of dropping and putting on her game face effortlessly, something he envied her for.

"My people."

"That was a local call."

"There's somebody local."

She came closer. "You didn't tell me that."

"No."

"Why?"

"How does it matter?"

"It matters if they're going to be a problem, if they're going to get in the way."

"They won't."

"Hmm." She touched his chest. "What was it he asked you to run down with us?"

"He had an idea. About Jonny," Dale said. "He wasn't a doper. Where did he find out about a major arms dealer and dope trafficker?"

"Probably in Leavenworth," she said. "There's probably a con down there who knew this guy Pierce and put Jonny on to it."

"He had to have some kind of intro up here," Dale said. "He wouldn't have run this thing just on a con's word in Leavenworth. The ATF agent on the surveillance, the one who saw the whole thing, he said he knew his way around. Knew just where to go and most important when to go. Some of that he might have gotten through reconnaissance, but I think there must be a local connect. What about through the victims? Any chance of something there?"

"That's possible," Nina said. "We could see where Pierce socialized, see if he had contact with any of them . . . the college girl, I don't think so, but that artist...maybe. Seems thin. Have you got anything on connects between Pierce and anybody in Leavenworth?"

"Loveless would have that."

"Gee, we'd have to ask him for something?"

"May as well."

"Maybe you should."

"I could do that."

"Hmm," she said. "There's a couple of things you could do. We could do them together."

"Where's Herb?"

"Went home. Nothing else is going to come up tonight. Our boy is going to ground, come down from the rush, collect himself. We should do the same."

"That makes uncommonly good sense."

"Doesn't it?"

Roger sat silent in the dark and sipped his green tea. The curtains were pulled back from the big double window in his room, giving him a fine view of the city and the airport lights gleaming blue like a field of sapphires spilled across a black velvet drop cloth. Steam from the tea warmed his nose and soothed his sinuses. He'd sworn off coffee when he found himself increasing his daily intake to the point of affecting his nerves and his shooting. An article in *Men's Health*, a magazine he read devoutly, had praised the physical and mental health benefits of green tea. Everywhere he went, he carried a box of the Chinese herb with him so he could brew up in whatever hotel room he found himself. It was a pleasing ritual to him, the brewing of the tea and drinking it from the porcelain mug he carried, a ritual he enjoyed as much as cleaning his pistol. It was a fine way to cultivate patience. Roger had lots of patience, but in his business there was no such thing as too much patience. When he was younger and less experienced, he might have argued that point, but with the vantage of years and seasoning, he saw that aggressiveness and boldness were good traits, but the master's attribute was patience.

And Roger was a master.

He sipped his tea and thought of Jonny out there in the sea of lights, somewhere. He would be holing up, with the police not far behind. That was their goal: to lessen the time they were behind him, till sooner or later they occupied the same space at the same time.

**NO OTHER OPTION**

And then some of them would die, because Jonny was, despite all the other things he'd been or become, a truly great and fiercesome warrior, a fighter without peer when pressed—and he was surely pressed right now. Roger had a history not too dissimilar to Jonny's, and he was, under the right circumstances, nearly as formidable a close combat fighter. But his real strength would come in outthinking Jonny, to catch him unaware and off guard, to come from the direction least expected. And that required him to stay close to Dale.

Roger sipped his tea and thought of how that might unfold, of what the ramifications might be. His sense of the situation told him that the window was closing quickly. If Jonny wasn't dealt with, now, there would be a long and perhaps never-ending wait for reckoning. That was unacceptable.

Outside, on the highway, police cars screamed by, blue and red lights flickering through Roger's darkened room.

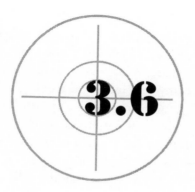

**3.6**

"What is your friend doing now?" Maria asked.

"Probably looking for me."

"He's going to help you?"

Jonny shrugged. "I don't think so."

"Why?"

"Because it's not his job to help me. He's supposed to find me."

Maria sat very still as Jonny took an off-ramp that brought them onto the North Side of Minneapolis. "Is he with the . . . police?" she asked hesitantly.

"No."

"I don't understand."

"Shut up, Maria," Jonny said, not unkindly. He approved of how she instantly complied. She was a smart kid. She knew what she was into but still kept thinking on her feet. He drove carefully through downtown Minneapolis, past the Marquette Building and City Center. He watched her carefully as he drove past two squad cars parked on the median strip on Hennepin, the officers talking to each other. The old Honda wound through the maze of streets where the neat and orderly progression of avenues and streets turned into a convoluted tracery around the Chain of Lakes. Maria stayed silent until he pulled in behind an old Catholic church, in a parking lot hidden from the road by the church building and a stand of trees.

"What are you going to do with me?" she asked.

He liked how she managed her fear. She didn't bluster, she didn't cry, even though he could tell she wanted to.

"That depends on you, Maria. We're going to get out of the car and I'm going to get my bags out of the trunk. You're going into the trunk. I'm not going to tie you up. You stay there, quietly, until I'm long gone. That might be ten minutes, it might be an hour. I have a car not far from here, but I might come back and check on you. Here's the deal—you stay there and be quiet. Come daylight, you can make all the noise you want. I'll call the police and tell them where you are after sunrise."

"Why would you do that?"

"Because I said I would. You won't give me a hard time now, will you?"

"No. I won't."

"That's why I'm going to do it."

They got out of the Honda. Jonny popped the trunk and put his bags on the ground. "Get in," he said.

Maria climbed in and curled herself up in the trunk. She looked up, then looked away from him.

"Remember, Maria. Be quiet," Jonny said.

"Yes."

Jonny shut the lid gently. Then he bent over his bag, stuffing the M-203 into the long duffel and hefting it. It wasn't too bad.

Father Henri Smeets stood in his bathrobe and slippers and watched the woman climb into the trunk of the car parked behind his rectory. A light sleeper since his youth, he'd been awake and walking to ease the pain in his side when he heard the car pull up. He waited until the rifle was put away before he stepped out onto the back porch and challenged the man he pinned in the beam of his flashlight.

"What are you doing there? Come here, now," the seventy-three-year-old priest called out. The voice was not loud, but strong and used to command. Father Smeets had known men with guns in his youth when he fought in the Dutch resistance during World War II, and his fear of them had fallen away with years and his love of God.

Jonny swore under his breath and walked into the light. "I need some help . . . ," he said.

"You stop right there," Father Smeets said. "I saw you put that girl in the trunk."

Jonny came forward with the smooth and deceptively fast glide of someone used to close quarters violence. He took the flashlight in one hand, turned the frail old man, and pushed him back against the door. He lobbed the heavy duffel through the open door, then shoved the old priest after it, shutting the door behind them.

"Who else is in the house, Father?" he said.

"You are in my house, young man," Father Smeets said. "You stay or leave as you wish, but you will not leave that young woman in the trunk of that car. Let her out now."

"She'll be fine, Father. Who else is in the house?"

"There is no else one in this house except the presence of the Lord; God is watching you now. Is this how you conduct yourself?"

Jonny left his duffel where it lay and drew his pistol. He tugged the old priest along, one big hand wrapped easily around Father Smeets's thin and bony upper arm. They went through the kitchen, past the small chipped table with a metal teapot and porcelain cup set out, into the front room. The walls were covered with photographs above the threadbare couch. There was a single armchair and ottoman in front of the small television set topped with picture frames.

"Sit down, Father," Jonny said, pushing him toward the couch. The priest turned and gazed at Jonny with dignity and no fear, then drew the robe around himself. "Sit down, Father," Jonny said again, roughly.

"I am an old man," the priest said. "And I have lived a good and a full life. You do not frighten me with your sad eyes and your bag full of guns and your pistol. I've known men like you before. I will not be bullied in my home."

Jonny raised his hand as though to strike the old man, then lowered it.

"Once more, Father. Please. Sit. I don't want to hurt you."

"I . . ."

Jonny struck the old man with the palm heel of his free hand, knocking him straight back till his calves hit the couch and dropped him into the faded cushions.

"Stay there." Jonny looked out through the curtains at the street,

**NO OTHER OPTION**

then turned to consider the priest. The old man's face was wide and wrinkled. Wattles of loose skin were gathered at his neck. The face was split by a broad nose, giving him the look of a withered Charles de Gaulle.

"The girl," the priest said, ignoring the pistol and looking intently into Jonny's face. "I want her out of there now."

"She's fine right where she is, Father. For now. She can breathe. She'll be okay. What is your morning schedule like? Do you have a morning service?"

"Are you curious as to how long it will be before anyone misses me? What kind of man are you to lock a young girl in a trunk and threaten a priest? You were some kind of soldier. You have that look. Is this how a soldier conducts himself? Terrorizing young girls? What's wrong with you?"

The old man was absolutely fearless. Two in one night, Jonny thought. I wonder if that's an omen.

"What do you know of soldiers, Father?" Jonny said. "Were you a chaplain?"

"I was a soldier and I was a chaplain. I have ministered to warriors and I have ministered to those laid waste in war. I have fought and I have killed and I have laid my life out before Jesus Christ and the Lord our God in penance. I have done terrible things in service, but I have always kept my honor and before God I never made war on women. Now let that girl out now or I will do it myself!" Father Smeets struggled to get to his feet.

"Back, Father!" Jonny pushed the old man back onto the couch. "We'll get to the girl in good time. Tell me . . . morning schedule?"

"You will have to kill me, because I will see that child freed," the old man said.

"We'll let her go, Father. Shortly." Jonny sat down in the armchair, his pistol resting on the arm. "What wars have you fought, Father?"

The old man stopped, visibly collecting himself, then leaned forward to study the man whose eyes alternated between deep sadness and a soulless coldness.

"You're fighting a war, aren't you?" the priest said. "Inside. I can see it. How long have you been a soldier?"

"All my life."

**MARCUS WYNNE**

"Yes. It shows. Once a soldier, always a soldier. Were you an officer?"

"No."

The old man breathed slowly, once, twice, his thin shoulders rising as he looked at Jonny's eyes. "Why are you doing these things?"

"What things are that, Father?"

"You have done evil things. It's on you. I don't think you have always been this way."

Jonny tapped his pistol on his thigh. "What does evil mean, Father?"

"It is when we corrupt the essence of good within us, the gift from God given us at birth. When we corrupt it willingly and with forethought. When we do evil to ourselves. We do evil first to ourselves and only then to others."

"Haven't you done evil, Father? Didn't you say that you did terrible things, things you had to do penance for? Isn't that what happens in war? Terrible things?"

"Yes. I have done terrible things. But God has forgiven me, as He can forgive you . . ."

"Terrible things sometimes need doing, Father. You say you were a soldier. It's the soldier's job to do the terrible things. To do what needs to be done, no matter the cost. That's the price we pay for the honor we carry. We do what needs to be done. No matter how distasteful, we do it."

"What war are you fighting now that you have to do these things? You lock a young girl in the trunk of a car, you stink of blood and fear and guns, you sit in my front room, before God, with a weapon in your hand. What war do you have with that girl and with me?"

"The war is everywhere, Father. It's inside, it's outside, it's everywhere. It's not nice and clean-cut, bad guys in black and jackboots anymore . . ."

The veins stood out on the old man's brow. "What do you know of men in black and jackboots! I fought Nazis, I killed Nazis, God forgive me, and they went the way of all souls in war. Who are we that you make war on us? I ask you! What have we done? What have you done that you bring this on your head?"

Jonny let the old man's words wash over him and he felt a

strange disconnection and peacefulness as he relaxed into the arm-chair.

"Have you killed many men, Father?" he asked. "In the war against the Nazis. You're not originally American, are you? You sound Germanic."

"I'm Dutch-Belgian. I fought in the resistance, first in Amsterdam, then when the Nazis broke my cell, I escaped into Belgium. It was a very long time ago. I don't think of how many men I have killed."

"Do you remember the first?"

"Yes."

"Do you remember how it became easier with time? After a while you grow accustomed to it. Never fully, but it becomes a part of you. Do you remember?"

"Yes, I remember."

"Is that what you mean by evil?"

"Do you enjoy the killing?"

"I enjoy living. I enjoy winning."

"Answer my question."

"Sometimes, yes, I enjoy it."

"Yes, that is evil."

Jonny nodded slowly in agreement. "Have you ever had a woman, Father? As a young man, did you have lovers? Was there someone for you, were you married?"

"Yes. I was in love. She died during the war. Afterward, there was no one for me, and Christ called me to His service."

"Didn't you ever feel lonely? Don't you have the same needs for women that any other man has?"

"I have needs and I have been lonely. I am an old man now, and I am past those things, but when I was younger, yes, I felt those urges. My faith in God sustained me during those times."

"I have never had faith in God, Father," Jonny said. He held up his pistol. "I have only had faith in this."

"You're in pain," Father Smeets said. Compassion deepened his voice. "You were hurt a long time ago, and it's left a scar, a seed of darkness in you that has grown and festered for so long you don't even know you carry it with you. Have you never had anyone you could tell? Anyone who would listen to you and take it all from your shoulders? There's someone now, someone who has always been there for you ... and that is Christ in all His forgiveness. Give up the gun and embrace the word of God and let your burden be lifted from you, son. There is no need to carry that weight alone."

The pain in Jonny's eyes was plain to see; the mask, for a moment, peeled away to show the wound in all its rawness.

"God will never forgive me, Father. I have done terrible things."

"I did terrible things and God forgave me."

"Ah, but how do you know that, Father? How do you know He's forgiven you?"

"I feel His Grace and His Presence with me."

"Is He with you now?"

"Yes."

"What does that feel like? To feel ... grace?"

"It's love. You feel love. Have you never been loved?"

"No one has ever loved me, Father. And no one ever will. That's the price I paid for doing what has always needed to be done. You took up the Bible. I took up the gun. We're both priests. I just don't think I need to convert everyone to my faith."

Jonny stood, certainty in him.

"Good-bye, Father," he said, leveling the pistol. "You were a soldier. You understand."

The priest looked back at him, nodded, and dropped his head. There was no fear in him. "You're a soldier of evil," Father Smeets said. "I will pray for you."

"Do that," Jonny said.

Still silent in the trunk of the car, Maria jumped at the muffled gunshot. Outside, the thin light of dawn began to creep through the trees.

**NO OTHER OPTION**

"No vehicles reported stolen anywhere in the area," Herb said briskly. "Closest one was over on Hennepin near Twenty-first Street. That's a long hike out of the way and nobody saw him. We're going to be doing a house to house starting at the church and spreading out from there. The television stations are all over this. They're going to break in with the pictures and we've got crews that will be going along with the door-to-door search. Every cop in this part of the state is here getting organized by Minneapolis. We'll be part of a command and control group colocated with the marshals. The SOG is working with our ERU. They'll do any entries that need to be done. He can't be too far. We've got roadblocks—it's raising hell with the commuters—and we've got the search going. We're going to find him. Once the medics get the girl calmed down, we'll talk to her . . . he may have told her something."

Dale looked at the photos of Jonny Maxwell they were putting on the air. There were two of them: one an older picture, with his longish hair combed straight back; the other a recent prison picture, his hair parted on the side, the face leaner and more wolfish. He'd already advised Roger and Ray Dalton. Roger was standing by his cell phone, waiting to hear from Dale. Any hopes for a discreet operation were completely blown. The killing of three police officers and one federal agent, two drug traffickers and a Catholic priest by an escaped felon still eluding capture had put the incident at the top of the national news, much to the chagrin and frustration of those responsible for DOMINANCE RAIN.

"How do you see your part, Dale?" Nina asked. The wanton abandon of her sex play was gone from her face as though it had never existed, even though four hours before she'd been pleading and moaning beneath him.

"Just front Loveless," Herb advised. "He can't do a fucking thing about it. And we're in the mix whether they like it or not."

"I'm going solo on this," Dale said.

"What?" Nina said, taken off guard.

"I'm going to do what I was sent out here to do. I'll do it on my own. There's too much involved, too many people, for me to work best," Dale said. "I can run him down and bring you in."

Herb shrugged and looked at Nina. "It's a little late for that, Dale. Like it or not, you're in our game now."

"What you going to do, Herb? Arrest me?"

Nina stepped between them. "You can't just go waltzing off on your own without some help, Dale. You need us to run liaison with the search. Quit talking this nonsense and let's go."

"I can do it like we've been doing," Dale said. "Listen to the radio, call you on the cell phone when I need something. You can still feed me information."

"He's got a point, Nina," Herb said. "We'll just be throwing it up in Loveless's face, and we'll waste time explaining hows and whys when we should be concentrating on getting Maxwell. If Dale's out of the way, he might be able to do something to help us, instead of being a nuisance."

"I don't like this," Nina said. "What aren't you telling us? You've got some of your people local, you said that. What's the deal?"

"I told you. I need to do this alone. The same way Jonny's doing it. It's the only way I can get into his head," Dale said.

"There's a feast of snakes," Nina said. She held out her cell phone. "Here, take this." She wrote down several radio frequencies on a piece of paper. "I assume you've got a scanner that will pick these up. That's the command and control net for the search. We'll be on it. You've got our pagers and our cell phone numbers and my spare phone." She reached up and turned Dale's face to hers. "Use them and stay in touch, Dale. Stay in touch."

**NO OTHER OPTION**

"Sure," Dale said. His eyes were impassive and cold. "I'll do just that."

Dale looked around Roger's neat and orderly hotel room, the bed made up before the maid had a chance to, the duffel bag placed precisely under the window, the radios lined up on the table near the window for best reception, the two pads of legal sized notepaper with extra pens set between them on the table. The odor of Break-Free was in the room and he knew that Roger had recently cleaned and wiped down his already immaculate weapons, checked each individual round, and touched up the edges of his fighting knives.

"You want some green tea?" Roger said. "I got some if you want. I can make hot water in the microwave."

"No, thanks, Roger."

Roger sat down in an armchair, his steaming mug of tea resting on his knee. He was boneless and relaxed and slightly smiling.

"So," he said. "Are we ready?"

"Yeah," Dale said. "I'm ready."

SWAT teams are like athletic teams. Any room where fit, aggressive, and determined men come together to do a job takes on a certain smell, a certain feel—and the roll call room co-opted for the tactical briefing of the Minneapolis Emergency Response Unit, augmented by the Marshals' SOG, was thick with the smell and feel of uncertainty. The too loud joking, the endless checking and handling of weapons, the creak of leather, the hiss of black Nomex overalls, the swish of camouflage BDUs, the restless shifting in the seats—the men were nervous and uneasy, racehorses trembling in the start gate.

There was fear, of course. It's not the being afraid, it's the not being able to control it that concerned them. And the truth be known, almost without exception, these highly trained men had never been up against an opponent like Jonny Maxwell. Criminals are dangerous human beings, yes. But what gets lost in the blur of crime statistics, and overlooked by the average citizen, is that most criminals are dangerously stupid, unskilled with the weapons they like to brandish, and cowards who will use violence only when they are completely assured of their success. There are exceptions, of course, and SWAT teams existed to deal with those criminals.

Theoretically, they existed to deal with men like Jonny Maxwell.

"We've never gone up against a guy like this," Lieutenant Kinder, the ERU commander, said. "He's smart. He's tough. He's as well trained as any man in this room. He's used to using his skills in the real world—and winning." He looked over the faces of his men. "And we're going to take him down. Sometime soon, we're going to flush this guy out. We're fairly well assured that he's still in the city, probably in the same area where he killed Father Henri Smeets last night. It's going to get violent. This guy will not be taken if he can prevent it. You all know how many officers he's killed already. He is completely without conscience and will kill you without compunction if you give him the chance. Our job is to stop him. We'll take him however we can get him, but we will not risk an officer's life unnecessarily. Am I understood on this?"

The men looked at one another in the silence.

"Sounds like 'shoot on sight,' Loot," said a voice from the rear.

"I didn't say that. I said that we will not risk any officer's life unnecessarily. This man will be treated like any other suspect, am I understood?" Lieutenant Kinder said again, meeting each man's eyes.

They got the message. Shoot on sight. A cop killer was going down.

Jed and his marshals sat against the wall, part of the team and yet not. Jed watched emotions ripple across the sea of faces: fear, anger, excitement. Drunk on adrenaline, some of them. Some of these boys weren't going to survive their contact with Jonny Maxwell. Some of his own troops might not, if he wasn't smarter and more cunning than he'd ever been. That thought straightened him in his seat. That's right. Smarter and more cunning than he'd ever been. But he felt so tired now. More than anything else, he felt tired and sad. This dirtbag Maxwell . . . he'd done something to the thinking and the functioning of his team. They'd all been so turned around with this case, from the very beginning. And where was Dale Miller in all of this? He was certain that there was a game being played parallel to their own, and that they were being manipulated like puppets by someone on the sidelines.

"Inspector Loveless? Do you have anything to add?" Lieutenant Kinder's voice shook him out of his reverie.

"No sir, I do not," Jed said. "This is your show, and we're just proud to be here and help you out."

His southern twang, and the folksy sound of competence that old pilots and old warriors carried around, brought a few glances from the other police officers. They seemed glad he was there. Jed nodded to the men who caught his eye, settled back, and while a part of him listened to the lieutenant outline tactical responsibilities for the group, another part of him turned a cold and dispassionate eye on his own fear and misgivings. People were going to die, soon, and a deep down part that Jed despised for its cowardice fervently prayed that he wouldn't be one of them.

Jonny slumped on his bedroom floor, his back against the wall, and stared at the still form huddled beneath blankets on his bed.

"So, Tony," Jonny said. "Anybody ever love you? Did that crazy bitch artist love you? Did she tell you that? Or was there somebody else? A special someone thinking about you right now? Wondering where you spent the night, wondering if you're going to show up for work?"

He hugged his knees to his chest.

"You don't say much, do you? You're a good listener, though. I'll give you that. That's a rare quality. Not many people in my line of work have that."

He laughed. "My line of work. I deal in lead, friend. You ever see that movie *Magnificent Seven*? Great movie. They copied it from a samurai movie. *Seven Samurai*. That was a great movie too. You ever get into samurai movies, Tony? Ever sneak into one, watch it, wonder what they were saying? You probably didn't get one thing from it if you did—even with subtitles. Maybe you had a glimmer, maybe, once, but no, you didn't understand. That's why you're dead. That's why you're there and I'm here, that's why I'm going to be walking in a man's country and breathing good air and you're going to lie here and stink till my neighbors work up the balls to knock on the door."

Jonny laughed, a hollow sound, even to him. He stood and stretched his back. He'd slept away the morning. According to the

TV news, the search was still ongoing. They were concentrating around Cedar Lake and despite their roadblocks they didn't seem to have a clue about how he'd gotten clear of them. It was a fatal weakness that police never learned to think like infantry. He'd just walked out, humped fast and hard with his duffel through the parks and along the trails that connected the Chain of Lakes. The only time he'd actually been on the street was when he crossed the old trolley tracks near Lake Harriet to enter the back alleys that took him to his apartment building. In running clothes and carrying the big duffel, he looked like he was going to the gym for a morning workout. No one paid him any attention and his neighbors were used to his odd hours.

He was safe, comfortable in his armchair, and he could follow every detail of the citywide search on television. He could have a beer or two, send out for pizza. The old photographs they showed on TV were of a Jonny Maxwell that didn't exist anymore. The eyes . . . those were the same, the hardest part of the face to change. He touched the Ray•Bans on the table beside him. With his shaven head, mustache and goatee, the different style of clothing and posture, only a skilled observer who'd known him well might recognize him.

A brief commercial broke in from *America's Most Wanted*, about the special they were running on Jonny Maxwell, the Green Beret Rapist. While *America's Most Wanted* had a high success rate, most of the people the show helped capture didn't have the discipline or the understanding of how to effectively change their appearance. But Jonny wasn't going to tempt fate. He'd be gone soon. Get another vehicle and make the long drive north. Hike across the Canadian border and head for a town and catch a bus to Montreal, get on a plane to London, then on to Johannesburg to disappear into the Mahpumalanga Province with enough money to live out his life in ease.

That's what he told himself. There was some part of him nagging for expression, repressed with long practice, something that wanted out and wanted to be done with it all. He grimaced and went back into the bedroom to check the weapons leaning against the wall. He took a punch and rotated the front rifle sight on the M-203 down two clicks, then twisted the rear sight knob until the indicator moved right two clicks. Close enough for government work. He picked up the Remington 11-87 Police Shotgun he'd taken from Snake's cabin and worked the well-oiled action several times.

**NO OTHER OPTION**

Why fight?

Why not?

It was as though there was a committee fighting in his head, factions shouting at one another, desks overthrown, chairs hurled, fists flying. He was on a long circular slide, narrowing as he descended ever faster, through a hell of fiendish laughter and grinning faces illuminated with brief flashes like gunfire, the faces of Annie Ma, the priest, that fucking priest, Tony, Ron Pierce, the young cop—the sharp one who took charge as best he could when he came after him—his face when he'd gone down, disbelief and fear.

Fear.

He knew about fear. He'd lived with it all his life, this one and all the others before it. Fear was his ally. That which does not kill us makes us stronger. He'd written that on his troop room wall at Delta, on his locker in the Virginia suburbs where DOMINANCE RAIN quartered.

Dale.

That's what he kept shoving away. Dale was out there, somewhere. He remembered the first time he'd seen him, the new kid at the ranch, another young tough face with absolutely innocent eyes. Dale had a purity about him, not the Christian thing so many troopers espoused, but a willing naivete, a willingness to continue believing in the good and the positive long past when anyone else would have said to hell with it. He wondered what Dale was doing now. They'd be picking Dale's brain for how he would move, what he would do next, how he'd react, how he'd think. Dale would know. Dale understood the way he thought. Dale was one of the few who did.

Jonny's unpredictability was one of his strengths . . . no one really knew what he was going to do next. He himself often didn't know, not consciously anyway, but that's what they strove for in their training, to automate and fine tune the part of the brain that took over in action. You automated it so you could forget about it, let the automation get on with things, get the job done while the rest of the brain looked for and created options . . .

Like what to do about Dale. He'd show up. He'd never quit. Jonny had taught him how to stick to the trail, how to do the hard thing. They'd killed together, and that is a deep and complex bond those who have not experienced will never understand. Like love, or marriage, or sex, it fosters an unprecedented intimacy. For Jonny it was the closest thing to real family he'd ever known.

"He's my brother," Jonny said out loud.

Then he shrugged, picked up his rifle and went into the front room, then went back into the bedroom and replaced the rifle against the wall. He went back to the front room and watched the police on television. He muted the sound and looked at the footage of the tactical unit in their military garb, the off-duty officers with their badges on their belts and their big bellies (why were so many cops fat?), their holstered handguns flopping as they postured importantly beside the roadblock barricades.

Jonny reached behind his hip and took his High-Power out of the holster and press-checked it to make sure it was loaded. Then he dropped the magazine into his lap, pulled the slide back, and caught the Cor-bon round in his hand. The copper-jacketed hollow point and the brass case gleamed. He pressed the tip of the bullet against his forehead so hard it left a red dent above his right eye.

He wondered what it would be like. He wondered if he would do it.

**NO OTHER OPTION**

# 3.10

Roger and Dale bent over a city map Roger had spread out on the bed supplemented with several pasted together Geographic Survey topographic maps.

"The police are all clustered here, as though he went to ground. He walked out, man. He followed this," Roger said. He traced with the tip of a ballpoint pen a creek that connected Cedar Lake and ran parallel to the roadway. "He followed that or else just went along the parkway. There are runners out that early. He could have had workout gear with him, stashed in his rucksack. This parkway goes all the way across town to the airport. Did they have something in place out there?"

"Such as it is," Dale said. "I wonder what the girl had to say?"

Maria Clavell had been found midmorning by the same parishioner who'd discovered Father Smeets.

"I'd love to ask her about his state of mind," Roger said. "What about those detectives you've been working with?"

"They're talking with her now. I'll call Nina and find out." Dale pointed at the map. "You think he's along this axis?"

"Wouldn't you be?" Roger said. "You can be right in the middle of the city and disappear. I'd have a hide or a safe house somewhere along there. You could get out via car, public transport, on foot, even into the bush if you had to snoop and poop. What do you think?"

Dale nodded. "He'd see it like that. We should pass that on to the cops, have them throw the net out farther. I'll see if they have an updated description from the girl he let go and when they're going to get that out. It's afternoon and they have nothing out yet."

"Call your cops," Roger said. He stretched and cracked his back pleasurably. "Let's get their update."

"Done."

"He seemed so . . . sad," Maria Clavell told Nina. "Sad, more than anything else."

"Sad? Sad about what, Maria?" Nina said softly.

"I'm not sure. He was so cold, like a machine, or like a shark, if a shark could walk and carry a gun, you know? At first, I mean. When he took me. Then after I made him laugh, he was different."

"What did he laugh about?"

"Well, I asked him what he'd done. He told me he'd raped and murdered and other things. Right away I thought, Oh, my God, he's going to rape me. I remembered what one of the safety counselors at school had told me, so I said I had herpes."

"He laughed at that?"

"Not at first. He asked me, 'Have you ever heard of that working?' And I told him the truth, I said no. And then he laughed."

Nina looked at Herb and raised an eyebrow.

"Then what did he do, Maria?" Nina urged gently.

"He started asking me things about myself, like where I worked and how I liked it."

"How was he asking you? Like he wanted to know where he could find you, or he was making conversation, or he wanted to know how you thought, what do you think?"

"It was . . . it was like he was really seeing *me* for the first time, you know what I mean? Like, before, I was just somebody with a car. It was like he woke up or something and saw that I was really there. I didn't want to look at his face too much, you know, but I could get glimpses of it when we passed the lights . . . When he first came up, I was so afraid, I couldn't tell you what his face was like . . . While we were driving, it was strange, like in the flashes of light, you know, one minute he'd be this hard-faced guy, so scary, and then in the next flash it was like a little boy's face, like my little nephew's when his dog died . . . so sad," Maria's voice slowed and dropped a tone. "He didn't really hurt me, you know. He could've. I asked him what he was going to do to me and he

**NO OTHER OPTION**

told me the truth. It's terrible that he killed that priest, but he could have killed me too and he didn't."

Herb took over from Nina.

"Maria," he said. "This guy Maxwell, he's raped maybe hundreds of women, killed eight police officers, wounded four more, and killed probably at least four other people whose bodies we've not all accounted for. He's one of the most dangerous criminals that has ever walked in this country. You are the only person we know of that has ever encountered this guy and walked away unharmed. We need you to help us find this guy and bring him in before he hurts anybody else. The next person whose car he steals might not be so lucky as you. This guy, don't let the fact that he didn't hurt you cloud your judgment. For whatever reason, he probably decided it wasn't worth his time. That you weren't worth his time. He had no compunction about killing that old priest, now did he? An old man, a war hero, a priest! You need to get your mind here with us now, help us out, huh?"

Maria blinked, surprised by the heat in Herb's voice, and looked to Nina for support. Nina nodded and leaned forward, resting her hand on Maria's shoulder and looking at Herb in disapproval.

"It's all right, Maria," Nina said. "I know you've been through a lot. And you're grateful now for being alive and for him letting you live. That's perfectly natural. Remember now, remember what he said to you. Why did he let you go?"

"He said it was because I wasn't going to give him a hard time," Maria said. "I think he liked me. I think he liked me because I was straight with him, and I asked him about his friend."

"Friend? What friend?" Nina said.

"He said he had a friend once. He was thinking about him."

"What was the friend's name?" Herb and Nina said simultaneously.

"Dale," Maria said. She was confused by the look the two cops gave each other. "Why, do you know him?"

"There's something wrong with this picture, Nina. The whole thing stinks," Herb said in the hall outside the interview room. "These spooks, these military guys working for them . . . this is a bad thing. Why is Maxwell describing Dale as a friend when he's here supposedly helping us to take him down? I sure as hell wouldn't be describing you as a friend if you were here to take me down."

"I don't believe that, Herb," Nina said. She studied her friend and partner. "You know I'd always be your friend."

Herb looked down, embarrassed. "Okay, whatever. I see what you mean." He looked up again, his face furrowed in angry confusion. "But I don't believe it of this guy! I think there's something else going on. Why Dale all of a sudden taking off on his own once we get close to this guy? Who are these 'other people' he's supposedly got around here helping him? Why is Maxwell acting this way? It makes no sense. Leave the girl, kill the priest? What is that? He could've took that priest and tied him up, hell, locked him in the trunk too. It's like he wants to be caught, like he wants a fight. This is just getting wackier and wackier and we ain't no closer to this guy. Look," he said, pointing out the window. "It's starting to get dark. We've been on this guy since last night, ran down Maria and the priest this morning, the search got the whole city in an uproar, we got everybody from CNN on down out here and nothing! The guy disappears into thin air? I don't buy it."

"So what do you think is going on?" Nina said.

"I think your part-time squeeze is here to spirit his buddy out  of here for reasons known only to the high gods of spookdom. I think he may already be gone. If he's not, I think we need to get right up Dale Miller's asshole and follow him, because I think of everything going on in this city, he's got the best chance of finding Maxwell—and we want to be there when he does. Because I don't believe Dale is bringing Maxwell in. And if we want him, we're going to have to take him away."

Herb's face was bright red. "Look, Nina," he said, "I know you got feelings for this guy. I know you got a feeling about him. But so do I."

Nina's face was drawn in the intensity Herb knew so well. Her eyes searched his face, back and forth in quick short snaps.

"Maybe you're right, Herbie," she said. "I don't think Dale's doing what you think he might be doing, but I think you're right about one thing—he's got an idea about how to get Maxwell and he's not telling us."

"What do you think he's doing?"

**NO OTHER OPTION**

Nina touched the tip of her tongue to her upper lip. "I think he wants Maxwell all to himself. I think he wants to kill him."

"I can see that," Herb said. "I want to kill the son of a bitch."

"He wants to be there first—for whatever reason. And you're right. We'll go to him."

"That's my girl," Herb said with satisfaction. "Let's get Maxwell and bag his sorry ass."

Nina nodded, then grinned. "C'mon, old man. You got the talking part done."

"I'll follow you. I like to watch."

"Tell me about it."

The two partners laughed.

Herb sat in the driver's seat, his hand on the keys in the ignition, and listened to Nina talk on the cell phone.

"Look, we're on the way out," Nina said. "Tell us where you're at, we'll meet you and fill you in. We spent some time talking to the girl, got some good take. I don't want to go into it on the phone. Where are you at?" Nina paused and listened. "No, we should talk face-to-face. I don't want to get into it over the phone. Okay, I know where that is. What room are you in? Okay. See you in about ... thirty minutes. Wait, you guys eat? Want me to pick something up? Okay. Sandwiches for how many? Just two? All right. I'll stop at Champs, get a couple of those good roast beef sandwiches with the curly fries. Sound good? It'll be closer to an hour, then. See ya." She pushed the END button and set the phone back in her pocket.

"Only him and one other guy?" Herb asked.

"Yeah. They're in the Suites down in Bloomington, this side of the airport by 494."

"I know where it is. Call ahead to the Champs in Richfield. We can swing by there. Get me a roasted eggplant on sourdough."

Nina nodded. Herb noticed but didn't comment on the sadness that came, then went, across her face.

"So what are these two like?" Roger asked.

Dale was silent for a moment.

"Both real sharp operators," he said. "The woman, she's tough. Tough as in for real. I watched her interview a rape victim. She could teach our interrogators some stuff. She killed a guy, just a few weeks ago, that went for her and her partner. Knows her stuff. The guy? I think he's more than half in love with her. Real protective. Tough guy, old style cop, looks like Colombo with a bigger gut. Sharper than he looks. Don't like soldiers, don't like operators, don't like anything or anybody except cops. Fucked me around some, here."

Roger watched Dale's face. "What, he think you were coming on to the broad, or what?"

"She's not a broad," Dale said. "I like her."

"Yeah," Roger said dryly. "I get that. Is this going to be a problem?"

"No."

"See that it doesn't become one. We're way off the reservation with this and I don't like the idea of a couple of civilians, cops or not, getting in this close to our play. Can you handle them?"

"Yes. Don't worry about it. They've got info we can't get any other way, unless you want to go hanging your face out there in front of CNN, ABC, and every other alphabet soup combo that can field a camera."

"Yeah, there's that," Roger said. "Jonny's probably following the whole thing in prime time."

"How's your sandwich?" Nina asked Roger.

"Very good, thank you," the neat man said, taking small, precise bites out of the focaccia bun sandwich overflowing with strips of lean beef.

Herb sat in the other armchair, away from the other three, and said nothing. Dale and Nina sat across from each other at the worktable, radios and maps pushed aside to make room for their meals. They were both careful not to make too much eye contact, to both Herb's and Roger's open amusement.

"So you think, based on what the woman said, that Jonny is fixating in some way on Dale?" Roger said, setting his sandwich down and picking up a single curly fry. "How do you think we could use that?"

Nina shrugged. "That's why we're here. We're fresh out of ideas. We kicked around the idea of having Dale go on the air, call Jonny out on the TV, but one, we don't think that will work, and two, we didn't think you guys would go for it."

**NO OTHER OPTION**

Dale looked at Roger, who said, "I appreciate your thinking of us, Nina. We'd like to preserve whatever low profile we still can."

"Fat chance of that," Herb observed. "People are more likely to be surprised that you're not out in front."

"Well, this is a law enforcement function," Roger said. "We're only supposed to be here in an advisory capacity. Since we can't do more than that, it doesn't make much sense for us to be out in front."

"Yeah, whatever," Herb said truculently, taking a huge bite of his sandwich. "How about you advise us some, then? We told you what we got. What have you guys got? Any ideas?"

"We've got a couple of ideas," Dale said. He looked to Roger for concurrence and then explained, using the maps, their theory about how Jonny would have left the area around the church.

Herb and Nina looked at each other and nodded.

"That's a good idea. Solid," Herb said. "We should pass that on to the command and control guys. What else?"

"Do you think he would have gone directly to the airport?" Nina asked.

"Doubtful," Dale said. "We think he may have a safe house somewhere along the axis of this green belt. You see, he can get in and out of most anyplace along this line by public transportation, bicycle, walking, running, or obviously by car. Not even mentioning cabs and so on. He has the maximum options here."

"So he's been set up for a while then," Nina said. "What we should do is have them shift the search down here."

"No way," Herb countered. "Look at that. You can't shut the whole damned city down. The public is screaming bloody murder about the traffic backups just around Cedar. You're talking about putting a cordon across the entire metro area. Won't work. What we need to do is get the updated face info out, along with an appeal to people to take a look at any neighbors they've seen coming and going at odd hours, carrying a bag and meeting the description. It would be somebody who's only been here for a while, what, a month, six weeks max?"

Roger nodded. "That's a good idea. What happens then?"

"ERU and the marshals," Nina said, looking at Dale. "They have teams broken down, six-man entry teams deployed along with the search units. If they get a positive ID, they're supposed to isolate and contain, set up the perimeter, then the ERU will take him down."

"They're going to go dynamic right off the bat?" Dale said in surprise.

"What?" Nina said.

"Are they going to do a dynamic entry, kick the door, right away once they ID him?" Roger clarified.

"Heh, yeah," Herb said. "If they get the drop on him, they're going to take him out hard and fast. They don't want to take the chance of any more civilians getting hurt. If they don't have everything lined up, then they'll evacuate the neighborhood and contain him, talk him out, or gas him out. Minneapolis is famous for that."

"I've heard," Roger said politely. "There may be a way to use this and come to a peaceful resolution with no unnecessary risk of bloodshed."

Dale looked surprised, but covered it well, Nina noticed.

"This I got to hear," Herb said.

"Jonny is sitting tight right now," Roger said. "And wherever he's holed up, you can bet he's hardened the place and has got weapons close at hand and ready to go. He'll have a way out, probably several, and some means of maintaining an awareness of what is happening around his neighborhood. Maybe he's made friends, maybe he's staying with people he co-opted, like in Milwaukee. If we put this information out, we can let him know that the net is tightening. He won't sit and wait for us to come to him. He'll move. Once he's mobile, he'll be easier to spot, especially if we look at containing the major egress routes. If he doesn't think that we're directly on him, he'll look for a low-profile way out. We can put a National Guard helicopter up with FLIR to patrol the parkway, put two up on synchronous orbit. Random stops at the roadblocks on the main avenues out—there's plenty of choke points. We flush him out. Get him moving. Then we'll be able to take him in the open, away from his barricade."

"Not bad," Herb said. "But I'll tell you now what the white shirts are going to say. They're going to say it's safer to take him in isolation someplace instead of risking him mobile out in the community."

"But that's missing the point," Roger said patiently. "He will have thought this through. Wherever he's at along this line," he said, slapping the map. "He's sitting tight and waiting to see what happens, to see where the weakness in the net is. He knows how to be low-profile and low-key, he probably fits in just fine in his place. He's not going to move until things blow over or he has to. Your search operation is so ponderous that you can't swing it to cover these areas without every news crew jumping all over it and having it on the air in real time. We have to set up in advance, shake the bush and get him to move, and take him when he comes out."

"You're right," Nina said. "We just don't know if the bosses are going to buy this. And it's not something we can approve on our own."

"There's the phone," Roger said. "Give it a shot. In my opinion, it's the best one you've got."

**MARCUS WYNNE**

There was a loud knocking on the apartment door. Jonny looked up, stood up, and held his pistol behind his leg as he went to the door and said, "Who is it?"

"Pizza delivery," said the man on the other side of the door. He stood far enough back for Jonny to see through the peephole the Domino's Pizza uniform and the pizza box he held.

"Yeah, hang on," Jonny called. "How much do I owe you?"

"Eight dollars fifty."

Jonny tucked his pistol back into the inside-the-waistband holster and went to the bedroom, pulled a twenty out of his bag of cash, and came back to the door. He opened it up and handed the Middle-Eastern-looking man the twenty and took the pizza.

"Thanks," Jonny said. "I was so hungry I forgot I ordered it."

"I get like that when I don't eat," the pizza man said, making change. "Here you go." His eyes widened when Jonny reached for his change and he glimpsed the pistol holstered at his waist. "Is that a High-Power?" said the pizza man, whose name was Asiz Ibraham, a Lebanese immigrant attending the university and working his way through delivering pizzas.

Jonny froze for a moment, then relaxed and said, "Yeah. You know pistols?"

"Oh, yes," Asiz said. "I enjoy shooting. When I was a boy, my father had a High-Power. He taught me to shoot with it. Are you a policeman?"

"No, I work security downtown."

"Oh, I thought that you might be a policeman."

"Is it pretty bad out there? Traffic and all? It was when I came home."

"Oh, yeah. I came down France Avenue, so it was pretty easy."

"All right. Well, take it easy. I got to eat."

"Good night, Mr. Martin."

"Yeah. Take it easy."

Asiz Ibraham got back into his car and drove onto his next delivery, thoughts of his father and his old pistol on his mind.

"These are the latest artist likenesses of escaped convict and cop-killer Jonny Maxwell," the blond news anchorwoman said in her most serious tones.

The early evening crew at the France Avenue Domino's Pizza watched the TV set up above the ovens while they threw and pounded pizza dough.

"I seen her once, down on Nicollet Mall," said Cokie Mattell, a short and pudgy twenty-something with a straggly goatee. "She don't look so hot in person."

"What do you know about it?" the manager said, lobbing a ball of dough at Cokie.

"Knock it off, Jerry," Cokie said. "I got to make a run."

Jerry Cretone, a struggling novelist on the management track with Domino's, laughed. "So run already. Asiz is pulling up, you can go."

"Oh, I can go? Fuck you, Jerry," Cokie said. "Really, man. Fuck you."

Jerry laughed and lobbed another ball of dough at the irate Cokie, who grabbed his pizzas and headed out the door, brushing Asiz aside.

"Fuck you, Jerry!" Cokie shouted.

"We will read about him in the paper someday," Asiz said, setting his pizza warming box down on the counter and grabbing a soft drink.

"You think?" Jerry said.

"Yes. He will either kill you or climb a tower with a rifle someday."

Jerry laughed. "Cokie, come down from the tower! Cokie, come

**MARCUS WYNNE**

down from the tower! Your mama is here, she wants to talk to you, Cokie!"

Asiz shook his head. He tipped his soda up and drank greedily, then looked up at the television, where the blond TV anchor cut away to a close up of an artist's sketch of Jonny Maxwell with a beard and shorter hair. "Police have drawn several possible variations, using a sophisticated computer-aided design program," the anchorwoman droned on.

"That's weird," Asiz said.

"What, that computer program?" Jerry looked up.

"No, the picture. Looks just like the guy I delivered a pizza to just now."

"Get out. That could be any guy with short hair and a goatee."

"No, really. It looks just like him. That guy Martin, over on Forty-fourth Street."

"Pepperoni and light cheese."

"Yeah, that's the one."

Jerry looked back up at the TV, which cut away to the blond anchor again. The insert at the bottom of the screen showed a toll free number and a local phone number.

"No way, man," he said doubtfully.

"This guy had a pistol," Asiz said.

"What? Did he threaten you or what?" Jerry said.

"No, no, he was wearing a pistol. Browning High-Power. In a holster. I saw it when he came to the door."

"What's he wearing a pistol for?"

"He said he was security downtown."

Jerry looked up at the TV again. "They say this guy has killed a lot of people," he said. "You really think it was him?"

Asiz nodded. "I'm not saying it's him, I'm saying that picture looks just like him."

"Shit, let's call it in," Jerry said. "See what happens."

Jonny sat in his armchair and watched his face appear on the television screen. He slowly and thoughtfully chewed his pizza. He finished the piece, picked up another and ate it slowly, and sipped from a glass of milk. When he was through, he picked up the glass and the half-full pizza box and set it on the kitchen counter. He rummaged under the kitchen sink and brought out several flat cookie sheets and a can of Coleman white gas. From the closet he pulled out a small toolbox and set it on the counter.

In the bedroom he didn't look at Tony's body tucked under the covers. Despite the scented candle and air freshener, the air was thickening now with a sick-sweet odor. Jonny checked his weapons again, then pulled stripper clips with gleaming bullets from a can and loaded all his M-16 magazines. He put the magazines into his chest pouch harness and tucked a few extra pistol magazines into the small pockets on the side of the harness. He checked the edge on his Emerson knife, and then went back into the kitchen to cook something up for the visitors he felt coming.

**3.12**

It was the thirty-seventh reported Jonny Maxwell spotting and Edgar Harris's tenth time to get into the white Minneapolis ERU van and ride with an assault squad to check it out. For initial checks, the SOG put one marshal with an ERU assault team. Their methods were simple: any reasonably solid spotting was checked out by an assault squad, who did an area survey and evaluation, talked to witnesses, and checked the suspect out. If suspicion was high, a full-size containment and assault element would scramble to the location. Since the TV broadcast, there had been hundreds of calls, but only thirty-seven of those precise enough to act on immediately, and of those only two had warranted a full-scale Operation 100 deployment. Both had been dry and scared the shit out of the suspects: one a graphic designer living off Hennepin, the other a bike messenger who had gone to jail anyway for taking a swing at the cops who had busted in on his heated home moviemaking with his girlfriend. The tape had been seized and was playing to the raucous amusement of the SWAT cops sitting in the ready room.

"What have we got?" Edgar asked the sergeant in charge, a short stocky Norwegian named Nordstrom.

"Pizza man says he delivered a pizza to a guy that looked like Maxwell. The guy was wearing a gun," Nordstrom said laconically. He didn't care for Feds.

"Wearing one?"

"Browning High-Power in a holster."

Harris scrambled from the bench seats lining the two sides of the van, bumping his seatmate, who cursed him. He gripped the screen that separated the rear crew compartment from the front seats.

"The guy was wearing a High-Power?" Edgar asked.

"Yeah," Nordstrom said. "According to the pizza guy. Says he knows pistols and recognized it, asked the guy about it. The guy said he was a security guard downtown."

"Who carries a High-Power?"

"I work the downtown beat and I never seen or heard of any of the security guards carrying a single action auto," Nordstrom said. "Course, he might be with one of the private security companies or a PI."

"This Maxwell, he favors a High-Power."

"Well, before we get all wet and excited, let's talk to the pizza man first," Nordstrom said. "Then we'll go down and check it out. The address for the suspect is over by Lake Harriet in Linden Hills. Nice little yuppie part of town. Right around the corner from the Sebastian Joe's Ice Cream Café."

"How are we going to handle it?"

"Let's worry about that after we talk to the pizza man."

"This is it," Edgar said. "I know it. I can feel it."

"Let's not get all excited, Harris," Nordstrom said. "We'll do a drive by and recon it. Then we'll go knock and enter, check him out."

"I think we ought to call an Operation 100 on this."

"I appreciate your opinion, Harris," Nordstrom said. "This is a Minneapolis operation and we'll run it the way I say. We'll check it out. If it looks the least bit hinky, we'll back off and call in the rest of the boys."

Asiz, the pizza delivery man, was unsettled by the intensity of Harris's questioning. After debriefing Asiz, Nordstrom ran a check on the telephone number through the phone company.

"Billy Martin, works for Northwest Airlines, new listing, no previous service," Nordstrom said.

"How new?" Edgar said.

"A month," Nordstrom said, nodding.

Tension ran through the back of the white ERU van. The other officers settled into themselves and put on their game faces.

**MARCUS WYNNE**

"We're just going to take a look, do a recon," Nordstrom said in the silence. "We'll call it from there."

The van rolled on. It was quiet inside.

Jonny watched television. His chair faced the TV at a ninety-degree angle to one of his windows. There was another window behind the TV, directly across from him. The one lamp in the front room was beside him and threw full light on his face. The television set was turned down to a murmur.

"Is that the building?" Harris asked. His voice had dropped to a whisper.

The driver slowed the van and stopped in the middle of the street in front of the converted brownstone.

"Yeah," Nordstrom said. "See, it's got two addresses on it: 2712 and 2714. Apartment five is around the back. We can go that way." He pointed at the driveway that separated the brownstone from the larger apartment building next door. "I've been out here before."

"Here?" Harris said.

"No, this apartment building, the big one. There's a parking lot in back."

The driver turned the big Econoline van into the narrow driveway marked NO TRUCKS and inched slowly down the driveway, his window down. The big engine throbbed and echoed between the two buildings. There was a door on the alley side of the brownstone, then a dark window, then a lit window with a curtain, then another lit window, the venetian blinds open to the street. The officers could see a man sitting in a chair watching television. The man was wearing a rolled up watch cap on his head, but they could see his face clearly. The man tipped up a bottle of spring water and took a long sip as they watched him watch the television. He didn't seem to notice them. They drove farther down into the parking lot that opened up behind the larger apartment building. Behind the brownstone next door was a small yard with a flower garden, three enclosed garage stalls, a dirt driveway, and a small parking area. The back of the brownstone had another window in it. They could see the profile of the man inside. There was a security door at the back of the building.

**NO OTHER OPTION**

"Pizza man says you go through the security door—there's a buzzer there—and then Apartment Five is the door on the left. One other apartment across the hall," Nordstrom said.

"What about the other door, on the side of the building?" Harris asked.

"Probably a fire escape door, or maybe storage."

"Shit, he's just sitting there. Let's go check him out," Harris said. He'd seen the man's face. He did look like the photos, but so had the other men he'd seen tonight. This guy was way too relaxed for the guy Edgar was expecting. Watching TV?

"Let's check on the Operation 100 status," Nordstrom said. He got on the radio and spoke for a few minutes, the responses crackling loudly in the enclosed van. There were two Operation 100s running simultaneously, which left only one in reserve. Per their plan, one 100 team—the full containment and assault package—was to be kept in reserve pending an absolutely positive ID. That meant they could wait for one of the other teams to stand down, or they could go ahead and take Billy Martin, question and ID him and be done with it.

Nordstrom stared into space for a moment, then looked at the

lit up windows of the apartment. "All right," he said. "Let's do a knock and enter, take a look at this boy close up. We know he's got a gun—and Billy Martin doesn't come back with a valid carry permit. We'll stack tactical, enter by ringing first and kicking only if it looks like he's attempting to flee. We'll leave Mosely with the vehicle, Todd on the corner of the building, this side, so you can cover the windows and that side door, Harris bring up the rear behind my stack. Bulldog goes first with the bunker, me second with the MP-5, Franks with the shotgun, Pee Wee rear security. SOP all around. Any questions?"

The men shook their heads no.

"Where you want to park the van, Sarge?" Mosely asked.

"Leave it right here," Nordstrom said.

The men opened up the back doors of the van and exited quickly, jogging the short distance to the building and avoiding the open windows. As they moved into position, the man inside the apartment stood and stretched lazily, then switched off the lamp. The apartment living room was illuminated in only brief flashes from the television screen.

**MARCUS WYNNE**

"Did he hear us?" Nordstrom said.

"He's going to bed," Edgar said.

The men stacked quickly and one of them quick peeked into the window. "He just shut out the light in the kitchen and went into the back, Sarge. Looks like a bedroom. That light's out now, too," the stocky Pee Wee Moran said.

"I don't like this. Let's go," Nordstrom said. He reached over Bulldog's shoulder, who crouched holding the bulletproof shield they called the bunker, and leaned on the buzzer for Apartment Six. After a moment, a tall college-aged kid in baggy pants and no shirt opened the back security door.

"What's going on? What do you want?" the kid asked as the stack of police officers brushed him out of the way and poised outside Apartment Five.

"Who's in that apartment?" Nordstrom said, pointing at Five.

"Billy. Why? What did he do?"

"Do you know him?" Nordstrom demanded.

"Yeah, I know him. He's a flight attendant, he's gone all the time. Why?"

"Get back in your apartment. We'll be over to talk to you in a minute," Nordstrom ordered. Bulldog was crouched before the door,  the heavy bunker on his left arm, his Beretta 92F with an extended twenty-round magazine in his right hand. Nordstrom crouched behind him, a silenced MP-5SD tucked into his right shoulder. Behind him was Franks with a short-barreled Remington 870 and Pee Wee in the rear, his assault vest strung with preclipped plastic wrist restraints and his Beretta in his hands. Edgar stood halfway in the open security door, where he could see the outside security man and the men stacked in the hallway. He was armed with his trusty Benelli short-barreled entry shotgun, and tapped his foot nervously.

"Let's go, knock on the door already," he muttered under his breath.

Nordstrom reached over Bulldog and knocked loudly on the door.

"Minneapolis Police! Open up!"

There was silence.

Nordstrom knocked again loudly. "Minneapolis Police! Open up!"

More silence.

"Kick the fucking door," Edgar said.

"Avon," Nordstrom said.

Franks moved forward and threaded an Avon ceramic lock-buster round into his Remington. He placed the muzzle close to the lock plate and said, "Avon calling!"

The shot was loud. The ceramic shell struck the lock and then disintegrated into a fine powder, transmitting all of its shock to the lock and bolt system, blowing it out of the door and sending it flying into the apartment. The door swung open into the darkened apartment, the only illumination the flicker from the TV screen. Bulldog banged the door hard with his bunker and the men entered behind him, each pressed up against the other and urging them forward with the sudden and welcome release of adrenaline into action, one hard unit crashing in. Bulldog turned sharp right, facing down the hallway in the direction the suspect had last been seen. He stumbled, his legs caught on something he couldn't see, and began to fall forward. Directly behind him Nordstrom cursed as something very sharp and unseen snagged the flesh of his face, and other sharp points caught at his uniform shirt, pulling him upright as the others pressed against him from behind.

Laid out prone on the bedroom floor, his chest pouches in place, and holding his Remington 11-87 Police Shotgun aimed down the hallway, Jonny Maxwell watched over the tritium front sight of his weapon. The men entering his apartment were silhouetted against the backlight from the television and perfectly illuminated for his glowing green front sight. The first man, the bunker man, hit the metal trip wire strung at ankle and shin height across the hallway and stumbled forward; the fishhooks suspended from the ceiling tiles by monofilament line caught at the faces and clothing of the men behind him.

It was an easy layup.

The first round of 00 buck came over the top of the lowered bunker into Bulldog's face. At fifteen feet, the shot had barely begun to separate and struck his head like the Hammer of Thor, lifting everything off above the mandible to continue to strike Nordstrom in his midsection. The second round came low, below Nordstrom's vest, into his groin and pelvis, blowing away his testicles and penis, shattering his pelvis and fracturing his lower spine, dropping him;

the remaining six rounds of 00 Buck went into the mass of men stumbling forward and tripping over each other in the fatal funnel of the first few feet between the door and the hallway, all the rounds emptying into the men in less than two seconds. Jonny threw aside the empty shotgun and picked up the M-4 and emptied it on full-auto into the pile of men, the door, and the sheetrock wall. When the first thirty-round magazine locked back he dropped it, threw in another, and continued to fire into the heaped men and through the door.

Edgar had leaped straight up at the gunshots; he ran forward the last few steps even as pellets and bullets bit through the sheetrock around the door and struck his legs. He fell, painfully, onto his shotgun. Directly in front of his nose, Pee Wee Moran's Rocky boots twitched frantically in convulsions. And just as suddenly the shots stopped.

Jonny dropped his second empty magazine and threw home a third, rolled to his side and picked up a M-26 fragmentation grenade, courtesy of Ron Pierce, pulled the already straightened pin and lobbed it underhand, gently, into the pile of men in his door and hallway. He rolled up and back around the wall of his bedroom, one of the few concrete load-bearing walls in his apartment, scooped up his empty magazines, and dropped them down his shirtfront.

The grenade landed on Franks's back and rolled off, almost into Pee Wee Moran's face. Moran lifted his head and said, "Oh, fuck."

Edgar looked up just as the grenade went off.

The detonation sent a shock wave of overpressure through the apartment, but Jonny was ready, his hands pressed against his ears, his mouth wide open. Immediately he got up and threw his rucksack on his back, peeked quickly around the corner and fired a few short bursts as he went into the kitchen, a wire and detonator switch dangling from his left hand. He crouched down beside the wall in the kitchen and pressed the detonator switch.

In the bedroom, where Tony's body was propped in a sitting position beside the window frame, the shaped charge of explosives on his back blew out the supporting exterior wall and window in the bedroom. The dead body provided good tamping and helped shape the charge properly, which blew a huge hole out into the alley.

Jonny ducked back into the bedroom and went hastily, but at the ready, through the hole and into the alley, out into the dark night. All in all, a little over a minute had elapsed since the police had come knocking on Jonny's door.

# 3.13

"They're getting hundreds of calls," Nina said, setting down her cell phone. "And they're doing entries all over the place."

"Hundreds?" Roger said in surprise.

"Calls, yeah," Nina said.

"Oh, yeah, you betcha," Herb said. "Every time you go public with one of these things you get hundreds of calls. Lots of concerned citizens and every nutcase in town. It's a full moon tonight, too, which don't help matters any. Girlfriends pissed off at their boyfriends call in on them, kids call their buddies in for a joke, lonely women call in so they can meet a nice cop. It's just a great time, working the phones on some shit like this."

Dale stood by the window and looked out at the car lights whipping by on the freeway, long lines of red in one direction, white in the other. The moon was low in the sky, but climbing. "I bet it's pretty down at the lake tonight."

"What are you talking about?" Herb said.

"Down at the lake. Lake Harriet," Dale said. "Moon on the water, I bet it would be pretty tonight."

Herb snorted disdainfully and shook his head. He threw a meaningful look at Roger and Nina. "Yeah, your head's in the game."

"How's your bad feeling meter, Herb?" Dale said. He stared out the window.

"Why do you say that, Dale?" Nina said.

He turned and looked at the others. "Somebody's seen him tonight. Somebody has called it in. We're going to go for it. Tonight."

In silence, Roger studied Dale. Then he nodded. He took a small folded daypack from his duffel bag and began transferring gear from his duffel: a medical kit, a flashlight, several spare magazines for his pistol. He took out one of his MP-5Ks and handed it to Dale. Herb watched with interest as both men took bungee cords and attached them to the stockless machine pistols, then hung the bungees around their necks and over one shoulder, slinging the machine pistols beneath their leather jackets.

"You guys psychic or what?" Herb said with disbelief. "How do you know?"

"I just know," Dale said. "You got any long guns in your car?"

"Two shotguns," Nina said.

"I think we'll need them."

"I think you guys are crazy," Herb said. The radio on the table squawked and sputtered with traffic. Then the tone for officer needs assistance came clear and high over the background chatter.

Less than fifty yards from the front steps of his apartment building, between the church on the corner and the converted garage of the house beside it, Jonny lay prone behind his M-203, the rear sight flipped to its largest aperture. The first emergency vehicles had rolled through his sight picture and he'd watched the entire response scene take shape before his eyes. He chided himself for not taking out the ERU van and its driver, but the two ERU officers outside had been too focused on the downed men, their friends, to look through the blast of flame and rubble in the alley. If they had, they might have seen Jonny move quickly across the street and up the hill, into this little alcove he'd noticed the day he moved in: a natural hunting blind, with good cover and concealment, two escape routes, and a clear field of fire down into the alley, the street in front of his apartment, and a good slice of the parking lot behind the neighboring apartment building.

Jonny watched and waited for the responding units to sort out their picture of what happened. He listened to the frantic calls over the loud radios that carried clearly to his hiding place; he heard the panicked voices and saw the urgent rushing around to make sense of the scene. A sergeant took control and blocked off the street and directed the ambulances in behind the fire trucks dealing with the small blaze. The entire building hadn't gone up, as he'd planned, but it seemed to be working well enough. He'd covered his tracks and he'd watch his back trail long enough to be sure. Then it would be a quick hard hump along Minnehaha Creek to the wetlands below the airport, to retrieve one of his caches of civilian clothing, identification, and still more money. Then a day's drive to the Canadian border and then gone. Gone.

A part of him urged him to go now, told him that he'd seen enough to know that his back was covered and that he was needlessly risking himself here. Another part urged him to stay and be sure—or maybe it was really the voice urging him to fight, the part that wished for and wanted a stand-up fight, to show these men, like he'd shown those in his hallway, who the better man was, who the real hunter was, and who had fooled themselves into thinking that wearing the garb and carrying the arms of the hunter imbued them with the same attributes. He felt a growing sense of dislocation, like the spray of cracks radiating from a blow against a mirror, all the lines of fracture running through him, all discrete yet part of the whole, the shattered reflection of himself, a holographic entity encapsulating the whole, yet separate, each with its own peculiar voice, each urging him to go one way or the other, and some central part, the chairman of the board, banging the gavel for order, order, order to get him gone and get him out of here.

And then the unmarked police car arrived, and he saw the woman detective get out with her partner, and behind them were Roger and Dale, his brothers in arms from DOMINANCE RAIN. Jonny's brain stuttered, literally; for a moment he saw double, then his vision united behind the rear sight of his weapon. Dale and Roger. He'd known Dale would come; he'd hoped that he would. Not to kill, not unless he had to, but just to see him once more. But Roger, here ... that meant the hunting license had passed from Dale ... Roger would not be here to assist in his capture, no, Roger would be here to ensure that he never survived capture. He knew how Roger worked, and why. He'd admired his skill while keeping himself away from him, maintaining the competitive edge and the distance both men needed to do their work. Roger was a solo operator, rare in their rarefied world—just like Jonny.

So unlike Dale, who was best when working with someone, a

partner or a team. A people person, as Jonny had mocked him a time or two.

Roger had to go. Now. And he'd have to slow down the others. He knew how to do that.

"Oh, Jesus," Herb said as he pulled their squad car up to the wooden barricade blocking West Forty-fourth Street. There were four ambulances, three fire engines, at least ten Minneapolis police cars and several unmarked cars, all with their lights flashing blue and red over the scene.

Dale was struck with the same dread he'd felt in Milwaukee, which seemed a lifetime ago. It was the same scene all over again: the paramedics rolling their gurneys loaded with limp bandaged forms, the background crackle of radios and the falling whir of arriving sirens, all lit with the inconstant flicker of emergency lights. "Christ, how many this time?" he said softly.

"We can't drive down there," Herb said. "Get out here. We'll walk down."

Nina opened her door and got out and opened the rear doors for Dale and Roger. The four of them went past the barricades, unchallenged by the pack of stunned and angry policemen milling in the street.

Herb recognized the senior officer, an inspector. "Nicky, what the fuck?" he said.

"Herb," Inspector Nick Gardner said. "You just get the call?"

"We're working this case," Nina said. "Working this guy Maxwell. What happened?"

"I'll tell you what happened," Gardner said in fury. "This son of a bitch had the goddam apartment booby-trapped. The team got hung up on the entry and the shitbag shot them all to hell and blew the apartment all to shit and burned my boys, that's what the cocksucker did!"

"He burned them?" Herb said in disbelief.

"Burned them. I got two men alive of the eight that went down there. The Fire Department just got the fire out. It was a miracle they got here as fast as they did; the van driver, as soon as he heard the shooting, called for backup, paramedics, and fire. The Fire Department got here just a minute or two after the bomb went off."

"Bomb?" Dale said.

"Yeah, bomb. That's what I said. Go look for yourself," Gardner said, barely containing himself. "Who the fuck are you?"

"He's a Fed, helping us out," Nina said.

"He can help you pick up the pieces then," Gardner said. "There's pieces of that cocksucker all over the alley."

"He's dead?" Nina said.

"I wish I could have killed him myself," Gardner said.

"He's not dead," Roger said.

"What?" Gardner turned and looked at the small operator. "What are you talking about?"

"He's not dead," Roger said. "He's either right here, watching and waiting, or else he's long gone, but he's not dead. I'll guarantee you that. If you don't have your people searching for him, you'd better get them on it. Because he's out there. Right now."

"Bullshit," Gardner said. "I had a man sitting in a van watching the whole thing. He didn't see anybody come out."

"No bullshit, Inspector," Roger said firmly. "I know this man, personally and professionally. I can guarantee you that if there was a body in there, it wasn't his. And he's very likely . . ."

Dale was watching Roger's face when the bullet struck it. The bullet entered the left side of his skull and punched a huge exit wound, sending a piece of skull flying to strike Herb above the eye. In the slowdown of his senses that came with the sudden jolt of adrenaline, Dale saw the flesh open above Herb's eye, saw the pale yellow-white of exposed bone and the raw flesh bead instantly with red and begin to spray.

"Get down!" Dale shouted. "Get down!" He grabbed Nina and half threw, half spun her behind the inspector's unmarked squad car. He scrambled to join her, crouching behind the wheel well as shot after shot broke into the milling mass of police and rescue personnel.

"Herb!" Nina shouted, pushing Dale's hands away. She scurried out and grabbed the heavy man and began to tug him toward the cover of the car. Dale grabbed Herb's collar and pulled him halfway out of his shirt dragging him behind the car.

"Fucking bastard!" Nina screamed. She pulled her pistol out and began firing wildly. Dale grabbed her hand and pulled the gun down.

"Don't! You'll draw his fire and we don't know where he is," he said. "You don't know where you're shooting."

**NO OTHER OPTION**

"I'm going to kill him!" Nina screamed.

"Listen to Dale," Herb gasped. "Listen to him, Nina."

"Oh, God," Nina said. "We need a paramedic, hold this against your head, Herb," she said, ripping her pocket lining from her blazer.

"Go get this son of a bitch, Miller," Herb said. "Go get him now, you hear me? GO!"

And Dale was already gone.

A paramedic jogged toward her and suddenly stumbled, his white pants spotting with blood as he clutched at his leg and fell, surprise on his face; a Minneapolis sergeant—what was his name?—crouched behind his car, racking the slide of his shotgun and shouldering the weapon only to have his hands and face suddenly bloody, the shotgun stock splintering, as a burst of rifle fire caught him; three men down in the open, screaming for help, wounds in their legs; two brave men running out to help them only to be cut down too, shot in their legs and pelvis, adding to the screams; maniac shouting as police officers opened up wildly with shotguns, MP-5 submachine guns, and handguns, in some instances firing on each other from across the street; strange lulls of silence, when no shot rang out, and the groans and screams of the wounded seemed to hang in the air.

Then a distinctive bloop.

Nina stumbled as Herb pulled her down. "Get down," he choked out. "Stay down!"

Six men huddled behind a squad car. The first grenade set off the gas tank and flaming men fled screaming. Nina lost track of the number of grenades landing systematically near any cluster of men, taking out fire trucks, shattering and collapsing ambulances.

"Oh, Christ. Oh, Christ," Nina heard herself saying, as though from far away. She held Herb's hand.

"Don't go out there," Herb said. "Please don't go out there."

Nina hugged her wounded partner with one arm. Her other hand held her pistol, which twitched impotently at each shot and each explosion.

"I'm here, Herbie," she said. "I'm not going anyplace."

If he could see them, he could hit them. They weren't expecting the attack, and under fire they bunched like sheep with the mindless reaction of the untrained. A few, he'd seen them, combat experience or just plain guts and common sense guiding them, had rolled out, deployed, and began to return fire. Those were the first to go. He hit them hard and fast and long. In the open leave some wounded, count on the instincts of men who work together to bring more running out into the open and drop the would-be heroes, add bodies to the stack, get them behind cover where he could drop grenades into their midst and break their will on the anvil of superior fire-power and send them fleeing as though the devil were on their heels. Tonight, he was.

He'd done enough damage. Time to run. He sent a rapid flurry of grenades, loading and firing the M-203 as quickly as he could, then emptying a full magazine across the front of broken and fleeing men. He threw in a fresh magazine and ran away, up the hill, into the dark. The streetlights posed a problem, but that was something he'd planned for.

Jonny jogged away from the church along the back alley that led toward the lake. He cautiously crossed an intersecting alley that led out to Forty-fourth Street. Next to a garage there was an electrical utilities pole with an oversized junction box. Jonny took out the last of the explosives he'd taken from Snake Pissolt. One block here, another on the opposite side but higher, wrapped and linked with the last of the det cord. It was a moment's work to set the chemical  delay fuse, twist the spring-loaded timer, and duck behind the protection of the garage. The minute seemed to take forever. Dogs barked in the alley. Then the tree-cutting charge cracked and the lights went out all around Lake Harriet.

Dale had fallen back alongside the brownstone, and followed the bushes back behind the building. From there he'd moved from cover to cover out to Upton Street, where panicked onlookers fled down the hill, away from the ice cream café. It was a long route to flank Jonny, but the best bet he had with only a pistol. He'd have to take Jonny by surprise and up close. Dale cursed himself for not grabbing a shotgun, but there had been none handy. He had two thirty-round magazines for the MP-5K slung under his jacket and three magazines for his High-Power, which gave him one hundred rounds of pistol ammunition. It wasn't much to go with against one of the best CQB men in the world, armed with an automatic rifle and grenade launcher.

He reached the crest of the hill and was girding himself for the quick rush across the open area when the lights went out. Businesses, streetlights, homes, the stoplight down the hill—all went black. He heard the crack of explosive not far off and put it together. He ran through the side yard of the church, his MP-5K extended at full arm's reach, the tension from the stretched bungee cord around his neck and shoulders holding the weapon almost as steady as a conventionally stocked weapon. He rolled out around the wall. Nothing. He inched forward and saw the bright brass casings of the rifle rounds and the larger 40mm casings from the grenade projectiles. Dale put his nose to the ground and saw how the field of fire had been perfect. There were two routes out. The explosion had come from the direction of the lake, so he would be going that way—down to the water, down to the wooded area. So it would be the parkway. No time to set up a blocking operation or set an ambush. And besides, he didn't want it like that anymore. As it had always been, as he had always refused to admit to himself, it was personal.

Dale set off at a slow trot, weapon at the ready, on the heels of his old friend.

"Where's Dale?" Herb said. "Did he get him?"

"I don't know," Nina said. "The shooting stopped, and then the lights went out. There's a power line down someplace. Hang in there, there's more EMS coming in now."

"I'll be okay, it's just a bad cut, made me shaky it hit me so hard. Did Dale take a gun?"

"He had his pistol, I think."

"He needs a long gun, get him a long gun," Herb said.

"I'm staying right here with you, partner. We'll get you fixed up."

"Have there been any more shots or grenades? Since the lights went out?" Herb said.

"I didn't hear any."

"He's still out there, then. Who else is going after him?"

"I can't tell, Herbie. Just lay still."

"Dammit," Herb cursed softly.

Nina saw Jed Loveless and one of his marshals rushing from vehicle to vehicle, covering a nervous pair of paramedics who moved from body to body.

"Over here!" she shouted.

**MARCUS WYNNE**

Jed looked up, spoke to the medics, and led them to the bullet riddled squad car. The medics paused for a moment over the body of the dead inspector, then came to Herb.

"What we got here?" the paramedic asked.

"He got hit in the head," Nina said.

"We've got it," the paramedic said. "Glad there's one here we can fix."

Nina watched anxiously as the paramedics busied themselves with Herb.

"He'll be okay," Jed said. "Just a bad head cut. Piece of metal?"

"Piece of skull," Nina said. She pointed at the shattered body of Roger Magritte sprawled in front of the car. "His."

"Cop?"

"No," Nina said. "He worked with Dale Miller."

The other marshal, whose name tape on his black coveralls read LA ROUX, said, "Where's Dale at now?"

"He's chasing his buddy."

"Which way did they go?" Jed said.

"You got another one of those?" Nina asked, pointing at Jed's carbine. "Or a shotgun?"

"No," Jed said.

"There's probably one in the trunk," Nina said, standing and reaching through the shattered window for the trunk release. The trunk popped open and she took out a short-barreled Remington 870 and two boxes of shells.

"Herbie, you going to be okay, baby?" she said to her partner. The two paramedics looked up as two more wheeled a gurney over, each man still crouched as though expecting the shooting to begin again any moment.

"Go, Nina. Be careful. Loveless!" Herb shouted. When Jed faced him, Herb said, "You watch over my partner, Loveless."

"Let's go, boys," Nina said. "I'll show you where he went."

Jonny moved fast through the back alleys, across unlit yards, quickly rushing across streets between cars, a shadowy figure that was there, and then gone, barely glimpsed by people looking out from their candle- or flashlight-illuminated homes. The power outage had cut off the TV coverage of the shooting, but most of those living in the neighborhood had heard the gunfire and explosions, and in the way of mindless spectators everywhere had gone outside to see what they could see. The people channeled Jonny into yards, behind bushes, and through the alleys, ducking from cover to cover to make his way along the lake.

He had to reexamine his exit route. To get to the cache he had along the Minnehaha Creek running paths, he'd have to go through several blocks of blacked-out homes, with more people out in their yards to see what was going on, talk with their neighbors, and report the heavily armed man fleeing in their direction. Time for Plan B. He'd head in the opposite direction around the lake, along the more heavily wooded area around the trolley car station and the Lake Harriet band shell, cut through the nature preserve into the huge and sprawling cemetery behind it, cut through there and come out on the Uptown side, jack a car on a side street and drive to his cache, pick it up and get gone. Things were falling apart too fast and Dale was out there somewhere—maybe even close behind.

Jonny jogged down an alley that came out on Forty-fourth Street at the bottom of the hill, directly on the lake. He crouched at a low retaining wall and looked up the street where the emergency lights flickered in front of his old apartment building. He waited till a police car turned off the Harriet Parkway and went up the hill, its headlights temporarily blinding anyone looking in his direction, and then dashed across the street and through a side yard of a house overlooking the lake.

Dale ran down the alley where the shattered remains of the downed power line sputtered and sparked. This alley led down to the water. The moonlight dimly illuminated the alley. There were people in the yards but he didn't speak to them; he just looked them over quickly and was gone. Once a little boy looked up and saw Dale flitting past the back fence.

"Mama, a ghost!" he shouted, clinging to his mother.

"Shhh," his mother said as Dale disappeared into the dark.

He paused at the intersection of another alley. Nina's apartment was to his left, on the corner of Harriet Parkway and Forty-fourth Street. It was surreal to Dale, to stand here in the dark and look up at the back of her condo, the memory of her naked and pleading with him fresh in his mind, to stand here with his submachine gun in his hand and his game face on and his friend out there somewhere and to feel, truly for the first time, the real need to kill him. All that passed through his mind in the place with no time that a fighter and a hunter carries with him, that place of instantaneous processing of vision, hearing, feeling, tasting, and smelling, the part that sorts out all the overwhelming rush of data into something coherent, a picture of the threat, of the intention, of the direction of the prey. In that place a clear picture came, preceded by a sense of foreboding, and Dale turned to his left and ran down the alley back toward Forty-fourth Street, just in time to catch a glimpse of his friend and mentor rushing across the street and up through the yard of a house on the corner.

"He'll be heading for the Minnehaha Parkway," Nina said. "Probably right along the lake down to where the bike paths connect up to the Minnehaha paths, over by Fiftieth Street."

The two marshals looked at her in puzzlement.

"How do you figure?" Jed asked.

"Believe me, he's going to. Probably has a car stashed along there somewhere. Dale and his dead partner back there called it down to a T on this guy. That's where he'll be heading. Where that blast came from, shit, it's not a block from where I live, right down there on the corner."

Jed lifted the radio handset from his tactical vest and gave quick, concise orders to his units to establish blocking positions along the Minnehaha Parkway.

"What else?" he said.

"Let's get going and see if we can run him down," Nina said. "I'll drive. Let's go."

They got into the shot-up inspector's car and drove across Upton into the church parking lot and examined the shell casings and flattened grass where Maxwell had lain and fired on the police below.

"See, he went down that way, through the alley, and then over to where the pole came down," Nina said. "We can't drive there from here, we'll have to go around." She looked down the darkened alley. "Maybe somebody saw him."

It took several minutes for them to drive around, and for Jed to rally the arriving police cars into a grid search pattern. Every street and every alley between Forty-fourth and Minnehaha Creek was patrolled by a car with at least two men in each, one with a shotgun or rifle at the ready.

"This place is crawling with citizens and cops," Nina said. "Somebody must have seen him."

"We've got people all over Minnehaha Creek now," Jed said.

Nina stopped the car on Harriet Parkway, blocked off now at several points by squad cars. "Too many cars, too many people out, too many houses," she mused. She looked out over the moonlit lake, the light of the moon falling across the water and onto the tall glass set in the back arch of the band shell on the lakeshore. "There's more dark, more trees over there," she said, pointing. "By the bird preserve, over that way."

"That's going the wrong way," Jed said.

"She's got a point," Tommy La Roux said. "If he's seen all this going on over here, he might try to go around the long way. Where could he go from there?"

"Lakeview Cemetery is on the other side of the nature preserve," Nina said. "From there it opens into the Uptown area by Lyndale. It's residential. He could cut down from there to pick up the Minnehaha Parkway, it's not far down to Fiftieth Street. Be a big loop, but he could do it pretty easily on foot and run less of a chance of being seen. We better get some squads over that way. We can drive over there and have a look."

She nosed the squad out and rolled slowly along the edge of the lake. There were a few citizens out walking, most of them hurrying now that the lights along the parkway were out. She shone the spotlight on several of them, who scurried away like cockroaches in a suddenly lit room.

"Get off the street, fools," she muttered.

"Up there!" Tommy shouted. "Somebody on foot just ran across the roadway over there!" he said, pointing.

Nina gassed the car forward and turned off the lights. She rolled the car to a stop well clear of where Tommy was pointing. "Where?"

"In that little depression," Tommy said. "Other side of those shacks. Came up from over there." He pointed to where the trolley car track went over a small tunnel.

"Let's have a look," Nina said, getting out. Jed and Tommy looked at each other and got out too.

"I'll go first," Jed said.

"I got your back," Tommy said.

Nina hung back and to the side, her shotgun at the ready. The three of them inched quietly toward the wooden shacks, which were the old public toilets. On the other side of the shacks were a picnic ground and a children's playground sheltered from the road in a low declivity.

Dale followed as quickly as he dared along the old trolley car track. It would be the fastest and most logical pathway for Jonny; level and smooth with some cover and shielded from view from the streets, the trolley car track ran through the greenery around Lake Harriet and continued on to pass by the Lakeview Cemetery. He jogged along and stopped every ten to fifteen paces to look and listen, then jogged on again, weapon at the ready, eyes probing each corner and each piece of cover. When he came to where the tracks crossed Forty-third Street in the open, he knelt down, paused, and carefully scanned near and far, low and high.

He saw Jonny about fifty yards in front of him, crouched down,

**NO OTHER OPTION**

and then disappearing into the brush beside the track. Dale felt the surge of adrenaline peak in him and forced himself to take a deep breath, hold it for two seconds, then let it out for two seconds. He heard first, and then saw the unmarked squad with its lights out roll to a stop in the intersection just below him. For the first time, a different sort of fear injected itself into the heady mix of emotions he felt when he saw Nina get out of the squad car.

Jonny had gambled on dashing across this relatively open area to cut over to the nature preserve. The one car coming in the total blackout had to be a police car, and now three cops were on foot coming toward where he crouched behind a wooden shack. There was no real cover between here and the nature preserve on the far side of the little hollow, probably a hundred yards away. He'd have to drop down into the grassy depression, which wouldn't work with the cops above him able to shoot down, or run in the open, or take down the cops. But they did have a car and that was a tactical opportunity.

Jonny took a quick stock of his ammunition by feel. He still had six full magazines, two bandoleers of 140 extra rounds each, his pistol with two spare magazines, one more bandoleer of eight grenades for the M-203, and three fragmentation grenades. Plenty for a little fight. Okay, police, he thought, easing himself into the prone beside the shed, c'mon in.

Dale eased himself slowly around the corner of the rough concrete tunnel that crossed beneath the trolley car tracks, his weapon at the ready, slowly pieing out from behind the cover. He saw Jonny easing down into the prone behind the two sheds not twenty-five yards from him, and saw the three police officers, two in front and Nina in the rear. He put it all together and punched his MP-5K out at full arm's length against the bungee and fired a long burst at Jonny.

"Nina! Break left!" he shouted.

Bullets tore into the old and peeling woodwork above Jonny's back. He turned on his side, almost in a fetal position, the rifle still tucked into his shoulder but laid out sideways, and let a long burst of automatic fire in the direction of the warning voice and shots. The muzzle flash lit up around him and hot brass rained down on his cheek and neck. Still firing, he hunched himself forward like a

wounded caterpillar till his whole body was behind the wooden structure, providing some cover from the unexpected fire on his flank.
Once behind the cover, he immediately switched his fire to the front
for a short burst, then back around the side of the building, back
and forth till he'd emptied a magazine. He dropped it and threw in
a fresh one. He pulled a hand grenade out, tugged the pin, and
lobbed it underhand in the direction of the three police officers, then
buttonhooked backward, firing at the tunnel across the street, then
back behind the second building as the flat crack of the grenade and
the white flash of its explosion cut the night air. He fired the grenade
he had ready in the M-203 at the tunnel, then sprayed the tunnel
with rifle fire. Then he turned and sprinted for the tree line across
the street and the nature preserve.

Nina cut left. Angling to the left put the wooden shacks between
her and Jonny, and she saw Dale, his arms extended and the flash
and clatter of his machine pistol.

"Look out!" she shouted to the two marshals.

Jed had his rifle shouldered and the slack out of his trigger, his
eyes assembling the shadows drawing together and the sudden stab
of fear in his stomach and the sudden thought, unwelcome right now,
of his wife, Jo Anne, as all of those things told him that the man he
hunted was right there and the rifle flashed and it wasn't his. It was
Maxwell firing back at Dale on his flank and then suddenly at him,
no noise in the face of fire, only the flash and everything slowing
down, the sudden stumbling as the huge surge of chemicals flooded
him inside, and Tommy La Roux was shouting and firing his rifle,
the brass hanging in the air, and Jed was shouting, something hitting
him a fierce hard punch and so bright he was falling back and look
at the sky see how pretty the stars are and I'm too old for this shit,
and I shouldn't've come on this and oh, Jo Anne, what was Tommy
doing standing over me, hunched over his rifle and screaming and
now he's dragging me, leave me alone, I'm tired and I'm old, and I
need to sleep right now just leave me be, will you, for Christ's sake,
Jo Anne where are you?

Nina racked the action of the shotgun again and again and magnum
loads of buckshot tore into the wooden shack, blowing basketball-
sized holes in both sides as buckshot tore crazily through the old

**NO OTHER OPTION**

fixtures, and Jed was down and Tommy was dragging him with one hand, firing his rifle crazily half into the sky and half in the dark, shouting obscenities and the grenade flash in the tunnel where Dale had been standing only a moment before and the flat crack and concussion she felt on her face to the front and then suddenly from the side something biting into her face, her ribs, across her right breast, her hips and falling, the slide locked back on the shotgun and on the ground, rolling, rolling, down off the curb, hug the sidewalk for cover in the gutter, lay on her back and thread fat shotgun shells into the magazine, box of five but more where that came from, then rack the slide and roll up, leg and hip suddenly flaring with pain, something running down her face, but goddammit she was Nina Capushek and she was her father's daughter and she had a shotgun and she was going to do this motherfucker up right and again she fired and again she fired at the figure she could dimly see running away and again and again and again till the slide ratcheted and the weapon clicked and then she reached again for another box of shells from her pants pocket and they were all wet, did she piss her pants or what, and while she was fumbling shells into the magazine she looked up and there was Dale.

Nina was hit bad. Fragmentation from the grenade had shredded her right side. She was bleeding from the face, chest, ribs, and hips, but her eyes blazed up at Dale.

"Yeah, I got into him, I saw him jump, me and Mr. Gauge lit his dog ass up, sorry motherfucker..." she hissed. "Let's go get that son of a bitch, he's my meat..."

"Oh, Christ, Jed," Tommy said hopelessly. "Christ, we got to get some medical out here."

"Take care of it, Tommy," Dale said. "I'm after him."

"You do that, you son of a bitch," Tommy said. "Take care of it like you should have a long time ago. If you'd been doing your job..." Tommy ran to the squad car and began shouting into the microphone. In the near distance, sirens began.

"Don't leave me here, Dale," Nina said. "I gotta go, gonna bag him..."

Dale touched Nina's shoulder and her whole body convulsed.

"Oh, that hurts," she said in a childlike tone of surprise. "I'm hurt, Dale." She wavered.

**MARCUS WYNNE**

"Nina, stay here with Jed," Dale said. "I'll be right back for you. Just stay here for a minute with Jed."

"Okay, Dale," Nina said dreamily. Dale eased her back down to the pavement, hesitated when he saw her blood running into the gutter.

"I'll be right here, Dale. You come right back, you and me and Herbie, we'll get him now. You hear me? Come right back," Nina insisted.

"I'll be right back, Nina. You just stay here and keep Jed company, he needs company right now. I'll go see where Jonny went." Dale stood and looked at the dark nature preserve and the tree line across the street. "I'll be right back, Nina," he said. "I'm just going to go see where he went."

**3.15**

Jonny ran through the parking lot to the Cyclone fence on the nature preserve's perimeter. He threw himself up, onto, and over the fence, snagging and ripping his trousers but falling and rolling clear. He ran into the brush, feeling pain in his left side and buttock where something, probably buckshot, had bitten into him. Jonny pushed the pain away with a strange mix of gladness and recognition: someone had finally drawn blood on him. A fighter. Maybe it had been Dale. Somebody who could keep their shit together. No time for thinking of that now. He moved fast, heedless of the noise he made busting through the brush and then onto the wooden planked walkway that ran through the preserved marshland, his boots thumping hollowly and the whole elevated walkway trembling beneath his feet. Birds squawked. A huddle of ducks lifted off, their wings exploding like gunshots past his face. The water beneath him splashed against the wooden pilings.

Time to flee. He remembered that only a few hundred yards away was a service road that led into the back of the sprawling Lakeview Cemetery. Between the gravestones and the gravel walkways and the winding, smoothly paved roadway he could run until he came out on the other side. Then he could find a car and make a frantic dash northward. They knew where he was heading now, but it would take them time to get organized, and he still held all the advantages.

———

Dale scaled the fence, rolled into the brush, and listened. He saw the flushed birds and heard the thump thump thump of Jonny's feet heavy on the wooden plankway. Dale moved quickly, his weapon at the ready, and saw the elevated pathway trembling on its pilings just in front of him. He saw Jonny at the end of the pathway turning round a bend and out of sight. Nothing to do but follow; Dale didn't know this area and had only a rough idea where the cemetery was. He visualized the map in his mind, the map that he and Roger had pored over, and oriented it to the ground he raced over. That way was the Lake Harriet Parkway, that way Calhoun, that way the cemetery, that way Lyndale. Okay.

His only chance was to get up close behind Jonny while he was focused on fleeing. So let's go. Let's go.

Jonny fled. It was as though he were running through the halls of one of those big Cineplex theaters, the ones with twelve different movies playing, and each door was open and he was getting little bits and pieces of the stories as he ran. On one screen, Jonny running through the broken buildings in Beirut, the Hezbollah security force after him, their rifle shots spanging loud off the concrete walls that gaped like shattered teeth around him; on another, with Dale in Bosnia on a close target recon outside of an "ethnic cleansing camp" and how it felt to swallow the vomit that rose in him, even him, at the sight of it; over there, fighting through the jungle in Indonesia, up and down the endless hills, soaked in sweat till his skin felt as though it were sloughing off, a snake's skin melting away beneath his clothes; here, on night patrol in the Korean DMZ, outside of the truce village of Panmunjom, where the North Korean Kim Il Sung Brigade practiced their infiltration techniques in the deadly and secret game of hide-and-seek. He'd been the star of all those movies, the main player even though he hadn't known it at the time and wouldn't have believed it if he had. Now that he looked back he could see that. Always running, always someone gaining on him, but time and time again he'd beaten them, run farther, hit back harder, jumped higher in his magical Keds like the Keds he'd worn as a child, trying to play and slapped down for it, each day a day in the kill zone and not understanding why, but in the resigned acceptance of a child of rage taking what he had to and learning to avoid it, to see it coming long before anybody else picked up on the cues, learn-

**NO OTHER OPTION**

ing to hide away his wants and desires, to make a secret of what was really in him, all that hidden away in the dark and festering there. And it had come out, and he hadn't been able to control it, hadn't wanted to, and the shame of that, and he'd been running since, as he always had, because it was what he knew best and what he was best at. What everyone else thought was courage, he knew was just that he was more afraid than anyone else, and had to fight harder than anyone else, just to deal with his own demons each and every day.

Each day a little harder.

Each step now a little harder; the shotgun pellets had dug deeper than he thought, and the weight of all that money on his back seemed heavier, or maybe it was all his ordnance. It was E and E now, escape and evade, and while he didn't think anyone survived his little contact, there might just be hunters on his trail now.

Hurry up, an inner voice urged, and he didn't know if it was to him or to the hunters that he spoke.

Dale followed as fast as he dared. He had one magazine of ammo left for the machine pistol, and with a six-inch barrel and no stock, he had no intention of trading shots with Jonny at anything other than very close range. As he closed the distance, he caught a glimpse of Jonny limping less than a hundred yards ahead. He felt as though there were another Dale, one hovering just off his shoulder, watching the other Dale moving quickly from cover to cover in the steps of his friend and mentor, and that this Dale was a silent witness, cut off from the voice in his head urging him forward, fixing Jonny in his sights, calling the shot as a no-go and moving forward for a better angle. He both felt and didn't feel, and it wasn't important anymore, what was important was the job at hand and that was dealing with the target (Jonny, man . . . ) and for that he needed to be closer (Jonny, just stop, man . . . ).

Dirt road now, and down past the maintenance garages where the City of Minneapolis parked its trucks and to the Cyclone fence that separated the city property from the Lakeview Cemetery. No gate, no time, throw the rucksack over (bullet holes in it?), then quickly up and over, snagging a pants leg again, tearing the meat of his leg this time, then down on the ground, disoriented for a second, then

**MARCUS WYNNE**

finding his rucksack and swinging it back into place, then across the grass with its low inset plates of brass, over the graves, across the smooth paved road, then into a little hollow, pause to get his bearings, the little lake, the crematorium, and the service chapel to his left, bear right and head out for the far side toward Lake Street and Lyndale.

Jonny heard the sirens rising and falling as he crested the hill. He saw more police cars and ambulances racing down the Calhoun Parkway toward Harriet. He settled down into the tireless lope he had and raced in the opposite direction and heard, sharply and clearly, the sprang of a Cyclone fence flexed and the clang of metal against metal, not far behind him.

Dale cursed as the MP-5K bounced off the support pole as he scaled the fence. The loud sound carried farther at night. He dropped to the ground and rolled to one side, extending the weapon out in the direction he'd last seen Jonny. The grass was low here; in the moon-light, inset brass plates gleamed with names and dates. The simplicity of the humble brass plates were in stark contrast to the gleaming white monuments of marble, stone, and granite that sprouted like a forest of misshapen mushrooms from the gently sloping hill across  the road. Here a cross, there a raw hump of veined marble, flattened on one side, gleaming in the moonlight with an eerie, internal light; old and rough formed marble, carved by hand in the 1800s. Dale moved from stone to stone, his weapon extended, his heart pounding. He'd lost sight of Jonny somewhere on the military crest of the hill; no matter his hurry, Jonny would never skyline himself with hunters behind him. He'd quarter off to round the hill and stay off the ridgeline.

Did he know someone was right behind him? He'd be thinking of that, even though the bloodying they'd taken back on Harriet would have caused any sane man to hesitate before racing out into the night after him. Jonny had been moving so fast, despite his injury, he would probably lay up someplace in here to check his backtrail, and then get out the other side . . . unless he knew or believed himself to be compromised, which was possible, in which case he'd just beat feet as fast as he could to get out and hijack a car.

But he'd still watch his backtrail from somewhere up ahead. Especially so if he'd heard the noise Dale made back at the fence.

**NO OTHER OPTION**

Dale slowed even more, and sent his senses forward like a scout to look at each gathering of shadow, to hear the slow breeze moving through the tombstones, the distant wail of sirens, the sound of water just over the hill; to smell the night air with the keenness of a hunter, tasting for the scent of sweat and blood and fear and fighting anger. It was as though there was some ectoplasmic entity he could project forward to sense around each corner, each potential hiding place gleaming on one side with the cold light of the moon and dark on the other with the shadows it cast.

Just round where the hill curved and began to slope down to the waters of a small pond, where the moon's reflection gleamed like a lunatic face, Dale saw an unnatural shadow beside a tall tombstone. Along the axis of the shadow he saw the muzzle of an M-203, aimed to the right of where he approached. He froze, lowered himself slowly, forced himself to use his peripheral vision and made out a long shape, the silhouette of a rucksack, the length of the rifle.

Jonny was laid out in the shadow, covering his backtrail.

Dale lowered himself to the ground, crawled slowly and silently and cautiously, inching himself along on one hand and two knees, one hand holding his machine pistol out in front against the bungee cord. Sweat trickled down his face, and he forced himself to slow his breathing down and to breathe through his mouth, opened wide to cut the sound. He fought down the urge to urinate. Every movement he made seemed to be so loud; the breathing he fought to control, the creak of his boots, the swish of his Levi's against the dry grass, the faint clicking of the metal bungee attachments on the sling guides of his MP-5K. It took long, agonizing minutes to move slowly from shadow to shadow to get uphill from where Jonny was laid out, almost but not quite on line with the tombstone where he would have a clear shot down the hill into Jonny from behind his own cover.

He was almost there.

From behind him, Jonny Maxwell said, "Hey, Dale."

## 3.16

"Nina, you're in no shape to go anywhere," the paramedic said. "You've lost a lot of blood and you're all tore up. We need to get you to the hospital right now."

"Just wrap it up," Nina said through gritted teeth.

"Lieutenant, talk to her, will ya?" the paramedic pleaded with the ranking officer in the crowd that surrounded Nina.

"Loo, listen to me," Nina said. "You guys got to get the cemetery blocked off, that's where this guy is going, out that way, we got to bottle him up . . ."

"Nina," Lieutenant Torelli said firmly. "We got it. You need to go to the hospital."

"What about Loveless?" she said.

Torelli shook his head. "He didn't make it, Nina. The other guy, he didn't take a scratch. You got most of the shrapnel. I can't believe you can stand up."

"The cemetery . . ."

"Nina, I got squads moving into position as soon as you told me. It's done. Your partner, Miller . . . does he have a radio?"

"No."

"Great. We'll probably hear the shooting first. Look, you're out of here. Now. That's an order. In the ambulance. Go."

"I want . . ." Nina said.

"Now!" Torelli turned away and shouted at the paramedics, "Let's go! Get her out of here!" He went back to his squad, leaving

Nina standing there with the pudgy paramedic tugging gently at her elbow.

"C'mon, Nina," the paramedic said.

"I got to get my purse out of the car, it's got all my shit in it," Nina said. "I'll be right back."

She went to the inspector's car, the engine still idling, and stood there looking in at her purse on the seat, the duffel bag that belonged to Jed, the broken side window glass on the floor. Nina felt faint and woozy; for a moment the world spun, and she gripped the door tightly.

"Oh, Nina," she said to herself.

Then she got into the squad, turned on the lights, and pulled slowly away.

"Nina! Stop!" the paramedic shouted, chasing a few futile steps after her.

Nina drove slowly and very cautiously as waves of nausea and dizziness came over her. She steered through the crowd of police cars and ambulances and drove past the trolley tracks to the road connecting Harriet and Calhoun. At the roadblock there the cops and the State Police pulled aside the barricades to let her pass. It was a short drive, a quarter mile or so, to where Hennepin met Thirty-sixth Street at the entrance to Lakeview Cemetery. There were two Minneapolis squads there, the officers out on foot speaking to each other.

"Jesus Christ, Nina!" one of the officers, a woman named Patrice Harding, said when she saw Nina pull up. "You're hurt!"

"I know. Why aren't you guys inside?"

"The gate's locked. We got a call in to have the night maintenance come and open it up."

"Who's got bolt cutters?" Nina said.

"Is that an inspector's car?"

"Yeah."

"There should be a break-in kit in the trunk."

Nina popped the trunk release. "Do me a favor, Patty. Dig those cutters out and pop that gate lock, now."

"Nina, you need EMS," Patty Harding said.

"The lock, Patty! Now!"

"I got it," Harding's partner, a young rookie, said. He cut the chain looped around the gate, pulled it free, and pushed hard against the motor-driven gate. It opened only a foot or so.

"Go inside and hit the switch on the motorbox next to the wall," Harding said.

The young cop did so, and the gate opened wide.

"Cut your lights, break out your gauge, and follow me," Nina said. "Other squad stays here."

Nina cut her own lights and pulled slowly into the blacked-out graveyard.

**3.17**

"Stretch your right hand forward, all the way, and get down flat," Jonny said. "That's right. Now duck your head down and let the bungee cord go over it. Toss the weapon to your right."

Dale did as he was told, conscious of the High-Power tucked behind his right hip, hidden beneath his jacket, and the Emerson folding fighting knife clipped in his right front pants pocket.

"So here we are, bro," Jonny said. "Nice stalk. If it'd been me down there instead of my rifle and ruck, I'd be in the shit right about now."

Dale craned his neck and looked back at Jonny. "Seems like I'm the one in the shit."

Jonny laughed. "It looks that way. I thought it was you, back when you crossed the roadway. Thought I'd be sure instead of just sorry. It *was* a nice stalk. If you'd had another body or three, might have worked out." He sniffed. "How you been?"

"How I been?" Dale turned his face away. "I been a lot better."

"Ain't it the truth," Jonny said. "Ain't it just the truth? You, me, the whole fucking world, we've all been better. How long you been on this project?"

"What project?"

"Me."

"Since you got out."

"Ray put you on to it, or did you volunteer?"

"Ray put me on to it."

"Why'd you take the job?" Jonny said. "It don't suit you. No offense, brother, but you don't have it in you for this."

"I don't have what in me? Raping, murdering, killing cops, is that what I don't have in me? Damn right. I'm a soldier, you son of a bitch." Dale pushed himself to his feet and turned to face Jonny.

"Easy, Dale." Jonny stepped back a few paces.

"You think I'm gonna plead with you? Like that girl? You gonna kill me, kill me. Look me in the face, right in the eyes, when you do it."

Dale calculated the distance between them—just five yards, but Jonny had his pistol aimed at him, both his arms locked in a combat isosceles, his right thumb resting on the safety of the High-Power, twin to the one concealed beneath Dale's jacket.

"I'm only going to say this once. Stop where you are or I'll cripple you. I'm not going to kill you," Jonny said. "But I need you to stop and listen. I'll put one in your pelvis and when you're down I'll put one in your spine. Think before you move. Get down on your stomach."

"You're going to kill me anyway. I'll take it on my feet."

The subdued click of the tuned combat safety seemed loud when Jonny brushed it off with his thumb. He studied Dale over the sights, his index finger taking the slack out of the trigger. "You've changed, Dale."

"I'm not the one who changed."

"Why'd you do it?" Jonny said. "The whole thing."

"You were never going to stop. Then or now. You can't."

"I can. You can help me," Jonny said. A faint note of pleading entered his voice. "Tell them they'll never hear anything about me. I've got what I need, I'll disappear, I won't be in the country, I'll be someplace else. They don't need to look for me. I won't give up anything about us, I won't play against the team. I've got enough money. Dale, it's enough. I can get out of here, these Keystone Cops will never get close to me. It was only you that got them this far."

"What happened to you?"

Jonny skinned his lips back. The muscles in his face were taut, his eyes shadowed, something flickering there.

"I happened to me," he said. "You don't get that, do you? Not yet. Easy for you to stand there and judge me. Here and back then. You're almost there, where you need to be. This is your first time.

**NO OTHER OPTION**

To go right up to the edge and look down and see all that blackness there . . . You know what I'm talking about now, don't you? That's why you're here. That's why you took this project. You needed to be sure you learned how to go all the way and then some. You know how to kill. That's not so hard, is it? You've been there, done that. But you never crossed the line, not till now, and that's what it takes. That's what old Ray doesn't want to tell you, that it's our job to cross the line, come what may. It's part of the job and he needs to know you can do it. He needs to know if you're ordered to hunt and kill a friend you will. And now you know you can. Don't you?"

Dale shifted his weight forward to the balls of his feet.

"I didn't come to kill you. I came to bring you back. That's what Ray wants, that's what we all wanted."

"You were always naive. It's your weakness. You never want to believe how fucked up things are. That nice neat midwestern upbringing made you weak. Roger never brought anybody in. He liked killing and made no bones about it. That's why Ray made him his number one boy after he lost me to my 'weaknesses,' as he called them."

Jonny laughed bitterly. "Dale, Dale, Dale. When are you going to grow up?"

"I grew up, Jonny. Just not like you."

Jonny nodded. "That's true. Not like me." There was a metallic sound in the distance. Jonny cocked his head as though listening, then smiled.

"What's so funny?" Dale said.

"The end of things." Jonny flicked the safety back on, but kept his thumb resting on it and his finger indexed alongside the trigger, the muzzle pointed at Dale's chest. "Remember that time in Marana, when we climbed Picacho Peak?"

"I remember."

"That was a fine time. Blue sky, the clouds, the desert below . . . we were on top of the world."

"Yeah."

"I never wanted to come down that day."

"It was a fine time."

Jonny's eyes were like dark pits drawing Dale in. "You . . ."

Bright light from headlamps and a spotlight mounted on a squad car lit up the hillside, throwing sharp silhouettes of the two

**MARCUS WYNNE**

men against the ground. Over the squad car loudspeaker, Nina's voice was loud and clear.

"Hey motherfucker! Remember me?"

Jonny hunched, turning toward the new targets, his pistol pointing at the lights. Dale threw himself to the side, shielding his face and rolling behind a granite tombstone. He drew his pistol as the heavy boom of shotguns and the flat crack of shotgun pellets hitting the stone monuments hammered his ears. He rolled out and came up shooting, marking Nina's position and angling across it, the High-Power bucking in his fist. He saw Jonny pinned in the light as the third or fourth shotgun shell hit his hands, splintering his fists in a wet snap and throwing his arms out to the side as though crucified. Dale fired into Jonny's shoulder, chest, neck, and face and saw him turn his head even as he fell and Jonny was nodding, not in surprise, just nodding, and for an instant as Dale advanced firing, there was a glimmer of recognition, of satisfaction, of pride, of happiness and release on his face as Dale's slide locked back and he speed-loaded the pistol and Nina was there, fumbling with her shotgun, blood running down her side and face and then Dale knelt beside Jonny, pushed Nina's shotgun away, and looked at the ruined face and neck, the cruel mouth bubbling blood around his last words, "Thanks, bro . . ."

**NO OTHER OPTION**

**3.18**

In a nondescript office on the general aviation side of the Minneapolis International Airport, Ray Dalton sat behind an unused desk and steepled his fingers and looked at one of his shooters, a hulking man in a leather jacket and jeans.

"We're not sure where he's at, boss," the big man said. "He may be with the woman, but we haven't seen any movement at her condo. He's destroyed the finder in his pager. All we got is this."

He held up a videocassette still in the paper sleeve.

"Get me a VCR player," Ray said.

The soldier left the room and returned a few minutes later, wheeling a cart with a TV and VCR hookup. He plugged it in, powered it up, then held his hand out for the tape.

"I'll watch this alone," Ray said.

"Roger that. I'll be down the hall."

"Thanks, Jim."

Ray put the tape in and pushed PLAY and watched and listened while Dale Miller gave a succinct rendition of the entire sequence of events leading to the death of Jonny Maxwell—including a précis of the operations Jonny had been involved with prior to his conviction. Everything on the tape was classified higher than Top Secret—Special Compartmented Information. And it was recorded on a common variety videotape that had been delivered by messenger to the CIA's cover office here at the airport.

There was a message in that.

"...You can make it happen, Ray. Honorable discharge. Retirement pay. Health benefits. I deserve that," Dale said. On the monitor, he was relaxed, in a big green armchair, a blank wall behind him. He stared out of the screen as though he were looking Ray in the face across his desk. "The rest? You know there's more than one tape. It's an easy deal. Do the paperwork. I go away. You leave me alone. Somebody shows up, I either bag 'em and tag 'em, or they tag me. Then the video goes to the press. All the majors and most of the minors.

"You can't kill everybody, and you can't get all the tapes. And you know me well enough now to know this is all I want.

"Leave it alone, Ray. Leave me alone."

Ray Dalton rubbed his steepled fingers beneath his nose. The tape ended and blurred into blue static. He stared at the ceiling.

"Let him go," he said out loud to the empty room. "He'll be back."

**NO OTHER OPTION**

**3.19**

Dale sat in Nina's big green armchair pulled up before the windows looking out on Lake Harriet. Darkness was falling. Fireflies lifted like sparks from the dark summer grass. His hearing seemed somehow more acute; he heard the voices of people walking outside on the lakeside trail, the clink of anchor chains from the sailboat slips, the hissing of car tires as they passed, Nina's breathing from the bedroom behind him. A stillness filled him as he watched the light fall across the water and he thought of nothing at all.

Outside, two boys were playing guns on the lawn next door.

"Bang! Bang! You're dead!"

"No, I'm not!"

"Yes you are!"

"No, I'm not!"

"You boys come inside now," their mother called. "It's getting dark out there."

| OCT 2 5 2002 | DATE DUE | |
|---|---|---|
| OCT 2 8 2002 | | |
| NOV 2 6 2002 | | |
| OCT 2 7 2003 | | |
| NOV 1 2 2003 | | |
| | | |
| | | |
| | | |
| | | |
| | | |
| | | |